The Ever Queen

Book Two of the Arw'an Chronicles

Gavan Connell

Book Layout © 2014 BookDesignTemplates.com

The Ever Queen/Gavan Connell -- 1st ed.

ISBN: 978-0-9945743-3-6

For my Ever Queen

Lorena

and

My Ever Princesses

Cy, Alexandra and Maisie

"If you build an army of 100 lions and their leader is a dog, the lions will die like a dog. But if you build an army of 100 dogs and their leader is a lion, all dogs will fight like a lion."

Napoleon

Foreword:

This book, "The Ever Queen", is the second in the series, "The Arw'an Chronicles", Ch0n's meticulously kept record of his days on Arw'an, as given to the high Priest Verge of the Eñame and Chief Archaeologist of Arw'an by Ch0n, himself. It is best read after the first book, "Ch0n", which takes us from the days before and after the clone, Ch0n, became marooned on an earth-like planet, to the bloody battle against the Matáng that led to the uniting of three former warring tribes.

"The Ever Queen" follows the personal development of Ch0n and leads us to the stronghold of the Eñame, a fierce seafaring race once ruled by aliens whom Ch0n's queen, the beautiful and ruthless Karín of the Matáng, is destined to rule in accordance with an ancient prophecy.

After the chance arrival of another space exploration ship, Ch0n is joined by four reluctant colleagues from his home planet, Earth. Together they expand the technology, knowledge, influence and capacity of the three kingdoms ruled by Ch0n.

Prologue:

These many years have passed now since the Great War that protected our place from the would-be exploiters and the Lord Ch0n is long buried beneath the cold earth next to his much loved Buyo and his queen, Karín of the Matáng. To his devoted servant, the archaeologist Verge of the Eñame, he entrusted the shining tablet with all his deeds and all his life's work chronicled. This work Ch0n carried out faithfully, tho' in a sense he was betray'd by those who promised him a rescue he sought not. Verge in turn passed it to me and I took the same vow he took as its first guardian. It was then and still remains an object of magic and wonder to me, this thing he called a tablet and so I have spent my years following faithfully in the steps of Verge. Verge too has long passed and is buried deep in the chambers where the Eani of ages past once lived and then died. Now the chronicles of Ch0n are almost transcribed into the same books we former priests of the Eñame studied so as to follow the true path of the Eani, the Sky People who came long before Ch0n and whose legacy he and the Ever Queen, Karín destroyed, then nurtured and rebuilt in turn.

The reign of Karín, the Ever Queen was born out of the ancient Eani prophecy. I saw it all, first as a priest and then as an archaeologist to the court of the Lord Ch0n and the Ever Queen herself. There was never a more loving queen, nor a more cold-blooded one as you will see.

I am tired now. I have but one more volume, the last of eight to transcribe until I release the project unto the care of my trusted apprentice, the scholar, Ribau. It was the will of the Lord Ch0n that the chronicles be passed one day to a peaceful mission from his native Earth for the good of all. If you are reading them, his wish has come to fruition.

Temen

Royal Archaeologist and Second Guardian of the Arw'an
Chronicles

Chapters

Chapter One: Aliens

It was done. The battle was over if Jez's appearance at the castle with the defeated King Sith's head would sway his troops. On the knoll overlooking the approach to the castle, Ch0n stood over his dead enemy, Mastel, with the same cold nothingness in his heart he almost always felt when he saw or caused the death of anything. It was life or death for one combatant or the other and so far he had managed to prevail. He had felt differently having killed Alangadale and when the Lancers had ridden into a hail of arrows and been cut to pieces. But not this time. He looked down the path to the gates over what seemed to be thousands of corpses and reminded himself there was some unpleasant work yet to be done.

"When can I just rest for a while and enjoy what I have?" He almost shouted it.

Karín had watched the proceedings at the knoll from the tower. She saw the oruk-mounted pair and the Lancers defeat the security guard on the rise. She saw Ch0n kill the king and she watched as Jez left him alone apart from one other. She knew the dialogue. She had heard it with Izaki, with Alangadale and with Mikares. She knew it would end one of two ways and when she saw Ch0n go into the horse stance she knew the enemy commander had given the wrong answer. Ch0n had been swift to end it. The Matáng had barely moved and Karín had not even seen the sword stroke but the unmistakable follow through told her the story. What surprised her was that Ch0n took up the head, placed it on the body and bowed before he hauled himself wearily on to the oruk and started the slow walk back to the remains of the guardhouse

Ch0n was deep in thought when the two squelch noises broke his concentration. He switched frequencies.

"Yes?"

"You know we have to land. You pick the place. It will be in another five days or so to give you time to mop up. We have one serviceable landing module available so in a sense we face the risk of being marooned on the same planet together."

"I have a place less than a two-day ride from here. It has water and shelter. I lived there for three months trying to get my head around this. I'll go there in five days and wait for you and guide you in. I was told it would be seven years before anybody came for me. I'm not leaving by the way. Living the way I used to live, the way you live now isn't for me. I will give you the information you need. I know it will be twenty years before anybody can process it and then send a colonizing ship here. By then I won't care. Don't break radio silence on the other frequency again. Monitor this frequency. If I want to talk to you I will do it here."

He switched back to the main frequency and pointed the young oruk at the burnt out gate. It ambled forward, glad of the chance to recover from the headlong uphill charge.

"Mastelik! Where are you? Come forward. I have witnesses that saw me slay the king in single combat. Do you accept my right to be king of the Matáng? Before you answer, your father told me I should choose you to lead the Matáng under my rule. Do you accept my right?

"I do but do you accept the right of any Matáng to dispute that right and challenge you?"

"I do. Let them come forward and we will allow them to challenge. Are you one of them?"

"Not if my father accepted your right."

"He did. Now are there any among you Matáng who dispute this man, your commander, Mastelik's right to speak on your behalf? Come forward and speak for yourself. Good. Mastelik of the Matáng, will you swear fealty to me and swear to serve me all your days as you did your previous king, Sith? Kneel before me if you do or draw your sword if you do not."

Mastelik knelt.

"I do swear it for myself and for all here present."

"Good. I appoint you commander of the Matáng Battalions of the Arw'an Army. I hope you do as good a job as your father and that I do a better job than your previous king. Know that to break this oath is treason and is a capital offence. Know it all of you. Now. You will be fed and housed here for two days during which time I will tell you about our rules of law and your men will help repair the damage they caused to the camp. After that time you will march back to the Matáng lands with those who were of your army until they came here. They have served me well even in the face of their own kin and now they have earned the right to return to their people and their families if they so wish. You will do well to heed them for they are well schooled in our ways."

"Thank you My Lord."

"Thank your father. He raised you to be honest. He would not accept the position you now hold out of some misguided loyalty to the dead king or for another reason I do not understand."

"He was not a man to accept failure and he failed here."

"His life. His choice to make."

Later in their quarters, Karín was on the offensive.

"I heard someone on the radio talking to you. Who was it?"

"Another ship has arrived. Their computer found us and now they are waiting to land. It will be five days. I don't want them to take me back but I know they will try. Take half the Lancers to where the herds are near my landing place. You know it. Take Jez but go both of you in the guise of herders on the backs of the tlaque. Wear your turban to hide your hair. I will give you some things to take and to hide in the fort until I arrive. Once you get there and the herds are on their way back, do not under any circumstances leave the cave, even at night. Stay under the overhang and inside the gates. Do not use the helms except for personal protection against the dragon. When I arrive I will be talking to them on the ship. Do not listen to what I say to them even should you understand some of the words. Listen only to me now and what I say to you. Once we are separated there will be no contact between us by radio for they will hear it and know my plan. Now. Get Jez and bring him here so I can tell you everything you need to know and do. If I miss something, you will have to fill in the missing pieces yourselves."

Ten miles high G2 was arguing with the commander.

"We don't need him. He will give us his tablet with everything he has on it."

"Listen to me G2. He has first-hand experience living on a planet other than earth with breathable air and humanoid sapients. He knows. He can tell of it face to face."

"Tell whom? Another recording device? If the landing module keeps going it could be years before we even think of going back to earth and then it will take another three years or more to get there. If we download all the information off his laptop and burst transmit it back to earth it will be there in three months. He is of no use to us at all. Why don't you go to the planet with the landing module? That way you can spend days talking to him if you want to. You get everything on disk and come back here and flash the entire thing off. I will stay aboard the ship and send you with H4 to the surface. If he wants to come back we leave a space available so we send you, four others and one spare seat. If he doesn't want to come back we leave him weapons and ammunition. He could use more .177

and .22 and all sorts of grenades and crossbow bolts. We could send two hundred pounds of cargo down there every time we send the module with crew. If he does come back, the locals can use it. They'll probably be at war again as soon as he leaves anyway."

"You go. You leave the spare seat and he comes back in chains if necessary. That is an order. I will log it so there is no doubt. After he is back on board we will send the module back as if for a normal mission until all the scientists are done. Do you understand me?"

"Yes I do commander but what happens if he decides to sabotage the ship when he gets here? You can't chain him up in here. There is nowhere safe enough. He'd have to be kept permanently in a capsule and that would serve neither you nor the mission. I accept your order but I request that you consider the options."

It took both armies and all the civilians two days to collect the bodies and burn them. There were almost two thousand of them, including more than a hundred of Ch0n's troops. The Lancers' remains were burnt separately. The smoke and stench from the fires made everybody gag and vomit but finally the piles of bones was cleared up and crushed into fertilizer.

When Mastelik left with the fully-armed eight hundred and seventy remaining Matáng soldiers, he was dressed in the uniform of a space commando, carrying one of the precious katana with the handle sticking up over his right shoulder in the manner of Ch0n. He was astride a tlaque. Ch0n warned him he would suffer for not having ridden much before, but the beast and uniform were gifts of good faith. He also had with him a small cage of dáguia and a message guide. At the same time Mastelik left, Karin and Jez rode with a troop of Lancers and herders for Ch0n's original landing site with several travois and Ch0n took the remainder of the Lancers, Alik, Beny and Buyo to their beloved overhang to bury their sisters' remains under the trees full of birds and monkeys, the very spot where they had seen Ch0n kill the charging oruk bull with nothing but cold steel.

Ten miles high, G2 was watching everything. He identified Ch0n and watched his group. He paid less attention to the group Karín was with and even less to the Matáng soldiers who were on foot. This was part of Ch0n's plan. He wanted to draw the attention of the watchers on high to him and away from Karín and Jez. When Ch0n and the Lancers arrived at the overhang, they buried their dead under the trees amid tears and angry recollections until Ch0n reined them in.

"These Lancers died because you were too close to that part of the battle. The role of Lancers is to disrupt the battle without ever getting caught up in it. Cavalry are best used against small groups, groups already engaged in another activity and fleeing troops. There are other roles when both sides have cavalry but so far we have enjoyed the advantage of fighting men on foot and without bows. We should not need to go to war again if Mastelik is true to his word but it is up to all of us to maintain the peace and ensure that he also plays his part. If not, we have to act so that he never gets the chance to raise an army against us again. Mourn your sisters here lying below the cold earth but learn from their deaths. This place is now sacred ground. We will not set up a village here but will take the clay and process it elsewhere. These sisters deserve to rest in peace. So shall it be."

They swam and stayed the night under the overhang. Alik and Beny, the heroes of the Lancer resupply of arrows, were the recipients of their just rewards, thanks to Marelik and one of the newly promoted Lancer trainees. Buyo made the most of her time with ChOn and in the morning they left early to return to the castle. ChOn had to leave for his fort the following morning and so they pushed the tlaque harder than normal to make time. Meanwhile, Karín and Jez had slipped un-noticed into ChOn's old fort. Jez found the rock pile ChOn had told him about with the covered track from the sally port of the cave and in the heat of the day under their shelter, he rearranged them so he could sit under a slab of stone with the breeze flowing through. Karín stayed in the cave as instructed, played with her tablet and did the reading exercises ChOn had designed for her.

ChOn turned to the frequency he had arranged with G2.

"I am leaving the castle in the morning and will arrive at the place the following day. If you follow me you can program in the co-ordinates when I get there and come straight down. I have the master tablet. I will need another. It is a detailed log of everything I have seen and done and a map of everywhere I have walked or ridden in the past year."

"Is there anything we need to know before we land?"

"You may feel dizzy because the air mix is a little different. More oxygen and the gravity is less. If you land, take the tablet and leave, you will not notice anything."

"Are you coming back with us?"

"Why would I do that? I have discovered how to live. I am a king of three kingdoms. I have everything I could possibly want in the form of companionship and I have fulfilled my duty to earth a dozen times over. I was ordered by my commander to stay here and gather information until someone came for me in seven years. That isn't you."

"OK. This commander has finally agreed to go down in my place. He will take four scouts with him and the fifth space will be taken up by a bin of stores you might need."

"OK. I will leave tomorrow morning. That's all. I will call you when I leave so you can watch me."

"Where is the woman? The red headed one who was with you on the tower?"

"She is bleeding. Look it up on the minitron. When they bleed they isolate themselves from the group because they are unclean. When she bleeds I take another."

"We noted that at the river. Nice spot, that."

"We like it. It is where we get the oruk. The buffalo I was riding at the end. And the white goats. The Lancers have a soft spot for it and so we decided to bury their sisters there."

"And where is the other Knight?"

"You mean Jez? He is here at the castle. When he isn't being a Knight he is my garrison commander and he dresses in the uniform of the day. It's more comfortable. I am the only one who wears this all the time."

"Have you found anything of value there?"

"I have found tar for my arrows. I have found gold and silver and diamonds but of course they are of no value here. I will give samples to the commander tomorrow. I have a diamond as big as a woman's fist. I cut it myself with a grinding wheel. It's all detailed on the tablet. Listen, it's been just great talking to you but I have to sleep. Well I have to go to my quarters anyway. If Buyo is up to her tricks I won't be sleeping for some time but I won't complain. If there is one single reason I would never return to the ship it is that I have discovered that I have a sex drive. It took almost the entire year for me to find it but now? Well let's just say I'm not going to lose it now I have found it."

The following morning, Ch0n rode through the gates alone and made for the fort. He pushed the tlaque past the fruit trees, the bamboo copse and the other now-familiar waypoints and finally set himself up for the night in the small cave he always used. It was big enough for the tlaque and himself with the wolf guarding the entrance. He set off again at first light and arrived at the fort at mid-morning. He looked up at the sky at four o'clock high.

"This is it. That area over there is flat and clear of the trees and the hill. I'll just get out of the way. How long?"

"They've been standing by for take off for an hour already. Separation will be in eight minutes and the descent will take another ten to twelve."

"I'll be right here."

Exactly eighteen minutes later the module hovered into view. The mass driver hummed silently for the last half a minute as the loadmaster dropped it the last few feet and it settled gently on its three hydraulic legs. Ch0n dismounted from the tlaque and let it loose. He stood unarmed facing where the ladder would be deployed, his two arms in the air. The loadmaster fired the earth pin into the ground and jumped down. He nodded to Ch0n and went around to assist with the door and the ladder. Moments later, three scouts jumped down and took up defensive positions facing away from the module. Finally a man in civilian dress came down the ladder and approached Ch0n.

"Commander Guerra."

"Clone H Zero N. But they called me Ch0n. My Commander was called Guerra."

"All commanders are called Guerra."

Ch0n reached into his thigh pocket. Here is the tablet. It has everything on it. A year's work. This is a gold nugget and this is a silver one. This beauty is a diamond. I don't know the quality of it but it's pretty darn big. The only other thing of interest I have found is a tar pit but that is about four days ride from here."

Gavan Connell

"Soldier, I need you to come back and give a first-hand account of all this."

"There is a first-hand account of it all on the tablet. It's better intel than anybody has ever had. Ever. My going back won't make it any better."

"That's your opinion. I am ordering you as commander of the ship to go back."

"Well, Commander, I'm the king here and I think I outrank you. Now get yourself back on that module and leave me in peace. You don't need me and I don't want to go. One thing is for sure. I won't go peacefully anyway so you can save yourself the trouble."

The commander signaled to the scouts. One of them raised his stun gun and pointed it at Ch0n

"I don't want to have to use that," said the commander.

Ch0n sighed.

"I gave you the chance but you want to make it hard for us all. OK. I can live with that." He looked at the hilltop and nodded. The rest of them followed his gaze only to hear an explosion and see a ribbon of smoke trail across the grass to the module. The projectile hit the vehicle in the widest point and punched a hole from one side of it to the other.

Ch0n dived at the Commander and rolled over so he was underneath him. The first scout raised his pistol to shoot but dropped dead where he stood when a bolt appeared out of nowhere and lodged in his ear. The others had no idea where it had come from and backed away warily. Ch0n stood up and dusted himself off.

"Welcome to Arw'an, gentlemen," he said.

The commander just stared open mouthed before shouting at Ch0n.

"You idiot! You've destroyed the landing module and we don't have a spare. We're stuck here just like you. You've destroyed the mission. You've destroyed my life's work."

"Don't shout at me. I'm the king here and unless you want to find yourself as a slave, you had better calm down. You three. Drop your weapons and lie face down on the ground. Spread your arms and legs."

"Nice work, Ch0n. I was wondering if you had a plan. I'm guessing the redhead isn't bleeding as much as H4 there and the Knight, Jez is somewhere on the hill. I can't see him, even with the thermal imager. Or the woman for that matter."

"OK. You can either help me or just leave. The ship has no other landing module, I heard you say. I have just given you a ticket back to earth. You have two non-returnable capsules you can send me. I am about to send you a list of things I need. Stack the capsules well; full by weight and volume. I will look after the commander and the others until someone else comes." He took his tablet from the commander and booted it. Seconds later a message flashed through space. Ten miles up, a list flashed on to the screen on the bridge.

1.   All the helms of all the scouts
2.   All the katanas
3.   All the weapons belts
4.   All the electronic weapons
5.   All the clasp knives
6.   All the 177 and 22 ammo
7.   Rail gun
8.   Anti armour tube and twenty mixed rounds
9.   Drone
10. All the crossbows and bolts
11. All the mirrors, soap, combs and brushes
15. All the sprayform cans
16. All the sewing kits and first aid kits
17. All the cordage, spring clips and carabineers
19. Boots and slippers, including small sizes
20. Firelighters
21. Axes
22. Explosives and detonators
23. Flares
24. Cable ties
25. All the whiteboard markers
26. Led lighting strips all you can spare
27. One tablet with images of the inside of the ship.
28. Pack the spaces with pyjamas and beanies
29. Anything else useful

"That's quite a list.   You might ask my boys if there's anything they would like. Anything personal."

"Like a photo of the wife?   Come on.   You know we had nothing personal.   Now get to it.   It's hot here in the sun.   You! Commander!   I want you to imagine you are going to live here the rest of your life.   You will be in a position of power or if you choose not to comply with my rules, you will be a slave or you will be executed.   It's entirely your choice.   Is there anything on that ship that you would have your man send here?"

"No, but there is on the ship a communications micro-satellite that can be launched from the ship itself into a stationary orbit.   Your previous commander didn't tell you because he didn't know you would need it.   If it is launched where our ship currently is, it will provide you with voice communications and even video from one side of the planet to the other.   It comes with a code that would enable every helm and tablet on the planet to be connected to it for telephonic and video comms.   There are also something like ten hand held radios in the emergency stores which would be able to communicate with the satellite.   And a colour printer that plugs into the power source of any tablet and uses refracted light to select the colours so it never needs maintenance."

"Is there a way to project images from a minitron or a tablet on to a wall or screen?"

"Of course.   How do you think we teach the children?   It's another function of the printer.   It uses the power of whatever device it is plugged into and projects whatever image is on the device."

"G2. Send all that. If you need to make space, get rid of the pyjamas. And get that satellite into space ASP so we can test it. Set it to retransmit this frequency and frequency eight. I also want frequency eleven for my own personal use and Karín's helm. Can that be programmed?"

"How the hell would I know? Wait." He looked across the bridge at a technical clone who nodded. "Yes it can." He signalled to the tech to get on with it. "It's under way."

"Ch0n. I have a flute in my locker. It was given to me by another clone several missions ago. I would like it," said one of the scouts.

"OK. G2?"

"Done."

Ch0n took the four in to the cave.

"This is the situation. You three can thank your commander for your comrade's death and your position. All I wanted was to stay here and after a while you will understand why. I am offering you the rank of Knights in my army. Basically that means you will ride round on an elk all day or a buffalo when we have them trained and do what I ask. You will be revered and feared by all here. All I ask in return is that you publicly declare your acceptance of me as your king. That way the people will know that if you betray me they can kill you on sight. I will take your energy weapons from you until I am happy you are going about life here the way I want. You may assume you will be watched day and night. I will assign you each a squire to see to your needs. You will find the females here very willing, especially as you will have a position of power and direct access to me. I don't know why but it took me almost a year before I reacted to their attention. The penalty for breaking your oath to me is death by the way and your would-be executioner is standing over there." He pointed to Karín, who, not having the slightest idea what ChOn was talking about, smiled sweetly.

"Now you, commander. You are not used to taking orders although you are a stickler for the rules so in a way it is the same thing. I am happy to find you a position of power in the kingdoms under my nose of course. I need someone to draft laws and judge them. The minister for justice if you will or a chief of staff. But you would need to be more like Solomon and less like Cromwell if you get my gist." He paused and wondered where he had plucked those names from. "We have no jails here. The penalty for any crime against the state or the crown is usually death. If not, it is something social like temporary slavery or permanent I suppose if we wanted it. What do you say? Are you interested? The options aren't as pleasant. I could make you the personal assistant to my mayor. She is a hard woman but fair and a good thinker and planner. Yes! Maybe that's the position for you."

"I need to be busy. Find me something meaningful to do and I can put up with anything. Including taking orders. Believe me, being one of only a couple of humans conscious for years when all the rest were in a coma wasn't a fun life. And it was because of the chemicals. The reason you weren't interested in the females, that is. We injected everybody with a compound to stop production of testosterone and to make sure that all the natural urges are under control. We administer it every ten earth months. It lasts for a year. The next dose is due in three weeks. The effects of the previous dose will start to wear off in a month or so. Just so you know."

Ch0n's squire, Alik left the castle with the Royal Beastmaster, Doni and all the female tlaque pulling travois. Half the Household Cavalry went ahead at a fast trot. They had been told to ride all day and night until they arrived at the fort and not to be surprised at what they found. What they did find was a stripped space craft in the middle of the clearing, two large metal tubes, two large parachutes a variety of stores and four aliens along with Ch0n, Karín and Jez. They were leading three tlaque.

"Lancers! These are from the same place from whence I came. This one is a scholar and the others are soldiers like me. I have plans for them all if they will swear fealty and if not? Well Karín has plans for them." The Lancers laughed and the four looked around uneasily. Ch0n continued,

"Yonder is the flying vessel in which they came. Jez has rendered it useless with one blow and so they will be staying with us. Now I need you to help me take it apart, unload these tubes and distribute the stores so Doni can have them taken back to the castle. Hurry now because I want to return home. Now. You four. Mount up and spend half an hour riding. Take an hour off and try it again. There is no easy way to tell you this but you are going to suffer a lot of pain for a few days because you have never ridden. I had to learn it the hard way. Stretch your groins and hamstrings and it will be a little easier but by the time we get to the castle you are going to wish the commander had accepted the tablet and you had returned to the ship. In a month or so you will be glad you stayed. This is a great life. I hope nobody from earth ever arrives to spoil it but if they do, we will be waiting for them."

Later that morning Doni arrived and the stores were stacked and tied down. Ch0n gave Doni's people time off during the process but then asked them to turn around and go back. The Lancers left before them, four of them with passengers behind.

They arrived back at the castle and Ch0n allocated each of the three soldiers a plot of land next to the main castle alongside Jez. He put the 'architect' Boro to work to construct three dwellings equal to Jez's.

"This street will be reserved for Knights of the realm, of which you will be the next three. When Doni gets back we will have a council meeting and you will be appointed. Think of names for yourselves if you like. I want no more stock numbers for names. Look up the minitron for ideas if you like or I will name you something anyway."

The commander he housed on the second floor of the castle in the guest quarters adjoining Ch0n's own quarters. The door faced the door to Ch0n's quarters and every time Commander Guerra approached his door, the wolf growled.

"You will find this pretty comfortable when you get used to it, Guerra. In time you will find an aget to share it with and maybe you will have offspring. Meanwhile, I need you to get to work looking for the comms satellite and setting it up. You can start by taking this helm for yourself and pairing it up with mine as a test net. I'll be listening. I want only mine and Karín's on frequency eleven and I want only the Knights, Karín and myself on frequency five. Tell me when it's done. You will not have access to a helm but a hand-held to begin with. The radio from your module will be set up here permanently. I want you to set up a comms section here in the castle and I will get people sent here from every village to train up."

"OK."

"On the ship, we had ranks and protocols. Here we do too. I will call you 'Guerra' and you will call me, 'My Lord' like everybody else. The villagers will call you 'Commander' because I'll tell them to. You'll be the commander of the comms section. The scouts are going to pick themselves some names so they can feel like people and not droids. We'll all get used to it. One other thing. From next week, we will speak only the local Arw'an dialect so you had better get the dictionary downloaded from my minitron and start learning it in your sleep like I did."

"Yes My Lord."

Ch0n smiled. Guerra did not.

At the council meeting, Ch0n called in the four.

"This is the go. You will swear fealty to me as your king in the Arw'an dialect. I have written it down for you phonetically. I will then appoint you to your posts and tomorrow in the square you will be recognized by the people. Now, what names have you chosen for yourselves?"

H3 had selected 'Harry' because it was as close as he could get to his usual title. I2 had selected 'Arturo' and I4 had selected 'Ivor."

They stood in a line in front of the council with Ch0n standing apart. One by one they approached him and knelt before him.

"I, Guerra, promise that I will in the future be faithful to thee lord Ch0n, never to cause you harm and will observe my homage to you completely against all persons in good faith and without deceit."

"Guerra. You are appointed Commander of the Communications Section of the kingdom and will be known henceforth as Commander Guerra."

"I, Harry, promise that I will in the future be faithful to thee lord Ch0n, never to cause thee harm and will observe my homage to thee completely against all persons in good faith and without deceit."

Ch0n unsheathed his green katana, Shiew and all present heard the hum as it cleared the koiguchi at the mouth of the scabbard. He placed it on Harry's shoulder, the keen edge touching his neck.

"I dub thee Harry, Knight of the Realm of the three kingdoms to serve me and the people with self-discipline and honour. Arise Sir Harry."

The others followed in turn.

"Doni. These three Knights will be needing tlaque to learn to ride and oruk when they are available. Jez. I need three families to send me their sons to serve as squires for these Knights and to help them with the language and the culture. You will select them for their intelligence and willingness to learn and to serve. One day they will stand here before the council as Knights in their turn, like yourself before them. Doni. I need to see the keeper of the birds, Mori. I have some urgent messages to send to the Buq'ue and Matáng regarding Commander Guerra's communications section. Commander Guerra will need to be there of course. Tomorrow is the first day of peace and quiet I have known in the castle. For the first time there is no threat of war with the Buq'ue or the Matáng or the aliens from Earth. Tomorrow is a holiday. Kelda has been pre-warned. There will be feasting from midday and each year from now, this day will be celebrated. It will be called, 'Ituba Aran.' 'Independence Day.'"

Chapter Two: Insurance

Guerra spent the next day working with the comms technician on the ship until the satellite was working as Ch0n had ordered. They had tested it by talking directly to the helms of Izaki and Mastelik who had been previously out of range. Thanks to Mori, they had been pre-warned to turn on their helms and wait for the contact.

Mastelik was amazed to be spoken to by Ch0n after eight days of silence. He had had plenty of time to review his situation and to decide whether or not to be true to his word or to use his new-found knowledge to raise a mobile army and attack the Buq'ue and Arw'an anew with superior numbers of both ground troops and cavalry. He also knew how to make the stronger bows and arrows, how the dáguia communications system worked and where the former Buq'ue fort was located. He had contemplated attacking it out of spite on the way past. He certainly had enough troops at his disposal and they were angry and frustrated at having lost so many of their comrades at arms in what had been such a one-sided fight. He did not know that Ch0n had told Izaki to prepare the fort for such a contingency and that he had stood by the King's Own to mount a counter attack should Mastelik betray his word. In the end, Mastelik knew that he would never survive such a treasonous act even if he were successful in taking the Buq'ue fort. Ch0n had the upper hand in every way and besides, he had shown himself to be a just ruler to the Buq'ue and Arw'an and there was no reason to believe he would be anything else to the Matáng. He, Mastelik, would have all the trappings of a prince in his own country once he arrived. The army was loyal to him. They all owed him their lives for they knew had he not accepted Ch0n's offer, they would have been massacred to a man. Mastelik decided to arrive at the Matáng capital at the head of a conquered but not disgraced army and implement Ch0n's rule of law using the army to enforce it if necessary until things settled down. All the Matáng villages and towns would have to be visited in turn and councils established. He would be busy for a long time and there was no need for war under a single and just ruler.

Izaki had sent scouts with dáguia to the route Mastelik would have to take and they monitored his progress until it was obvious he was not going to attack the fort. He stood the fort down and told Ch0n he was about to start the normal routine again, building up the logistics and the herds so that Ch0n's plan of mounted Infantry would come to fruition in due course. Ch0n's reply had surprised him a little when he was told that the villagers should take a whole week off to relax and contemplate what changes had happened as a result of the war. After the week they could resume their progress towards building the defences and logistics of managing a large town.

"We need to go as soon as possible to the Matáng lands to show them we are serious about uniting the three tribes. We need to establish a Matáng troop of Lancers and station it here in Arw'an Castle. The Buq'ue troop will relocate to the Matáng capital and the Arw'an troop to the Buq'ue fort. If we do that we will be expanding the concept of unity and interaction between the tribes you suggested before we did it with the other two troops rotating."

"Yes, we do need to go. I would like to make sure Mastelik is not betraying you before he gets too strong. I think we should take the entire Household Cavalry on an extended patrol with a company of mounted Infantry for good measure. Between the castle and the fort we must have enough tlaque by now to form the mounted Infantry. The spare mounts we have here for the King's Own and those at the Buq'ue fort number forty. I know the herders have twenty they are using as mounts so if we were to start the company with two platoons of thirty and a commander, we could let the two beastmasters train more for the herders. The logisticians have enough females for us to sustain a force if we forage as well. Water, there is aplenty between us and the Matáng border. Once we get to the border we can have Mastelik meet us and take us to the capital. Or we can use the aerial images to find our own way. What say you to all that?"

"I say we will leave in thirty days. That should be long enough for us to set it all up. Meanwhile we have earned a break. I want everybody to take the week off except for Guerra, who is enjoying his work with Carmodi, and the three new Knights who will continue with their squires. Kelda's crew can work half this week and half the next to make up for it and of course the guard will be maintained."

"My Lord," said Karín when he signed out of the transmission. *"Will you take me somewhere? Just the two of us on one tlaque as we once travelled? Now we have radio*

comms with the entire kingdom we can go where we like and not be out of range."

"Yes. We will do that. I need to slow down somewhat. There is no threat as far as we know. How about we travel south? I have not explored to the south." He changed frequency on the helm.

"G2. What is there south of here we might like to explore? Within a couple of days' easy ride."

"Wait out. I'll get G2. He's not on the bridge."

"OK."

"I hope the end of this war means we can all settle down and live normal lives, whatever that means. I have spent all of mine in a state of war in one form or another and you have lived most of yours in a ship. What do you think 'normal' will be for us, my Ch0n?"

"I think we will not be truly settled for a long time yet. Once the Matáng are integrated, we should have sustained peace. I think we could have offspring and enjoy living in the castle with occasional forays to our outposts but letting Izaki and Mastelik run things independently. We know that in seven years a ship will be back to get my report. They don't care about me personally but this planet is immeasurably important to Earth for what it is and what it has. Once that ship has all the information it needs it will return to Earth or at least send back images and maybe samples and perhaps leave a team of scientists and logisticians here to prepare for the arrival of large scale mining and population of the planet. That will take at least another ten years so we might have fourteen to twenty years of relative peace and quiet before they come. Or we can stop them one ship at a time so they can never come in force. We have enough weapons and soldiers here to defeat a reasonably large force if they send one. It would have to arrive in small groups and we know they are vulnerable when the landing craft is on the ground or still landing. So we have time to live peacefully and we have time to prepare. We have time to have offspring and watch them grow up. I would like to see that."

"Ch0n. This is G2. South of you and east there is a large lake with what looks like a sandy beach on the north side. You will have to cross the rocky hills to get to it from your side. It looks as though there are caves and even a ruined structure of some sort. No signs of occupation. The comms tech tells me there is nothing more to do here for us. I have started the process of shutting the ship down for the return trip. I have assumed command until Guerra junior is ready. Looks like I'll be travelling first class instead of in the tube. Watch Guerra. I am not sure he can be trusted. He was born to command and has been trained all his life to give orders and to have them followed. He was not an easy man to work for on those occasions I had to do it. I'll talk to you before we leave orbit."

"Thanks for the warning but I have contingencies in place for any treason. Just the same, I'll certainly watch him closely. Ch0n out." He changed back to frequency one before returning to his talk with Karín.

"There is a place on the other side of those rocky hills we can explore just the two of us and the wolf. I'll tell Jez we are leaving for a few days. As soon as we are ready, we'll go."

"ChOn. Are you really ready to have offspring? It is a big decision to make because it will take me away from you for twelve moon cycles and afterwards things will never be the same for us. We are two and all my feelings are for you. When we have offspring that will change. I will have to divide my feelings between you and it. I don't know how I will cope with that or you will either. I have thought a lot about it and I am not sure it will be a good thing. Even though I desire it, I fear it."

"I have you and I have Buyo. When I am with you do I think of her? No. I think only of you. Yet I am sharing my feelings. I feel the ebon for you and not so much for her yet I desire her company and her presence when you are away. It will be no different when we have offspring. We will have enough feelings to go around."

"Then we will see what happens," she thought to herself, "This very day I will stop giving him the milkyweed tea and we will see if his seed will sprout inside me. If it is meant to be it will happen but first I will talk to Kelda about something else."

That night ChOn called a meeting of the new, enlarged council.

"Karín and I are going to explore to the south for two or three days. Meanwhile the castle is on holiday for a week. Commander Guerra and the three new Knights will continue their language training and the guard will remain alert. You have all earned a break. Life will get quieter for a short while and then we will build up for a state visit to the Matáng capital in thirty days. Doni, I need thirty tlaque kitted out for the mounted infantry. Jez, select the thirty from those with experience with the Lancers. In time the numbers will be greater but in thirty days we will take them and a platoon like them from the Buq'ue fort to Matáng. You three should plan to go with us. By then it will be time for you to get to know your new home. Jez, Boro, I need to speak with you after this. Thank you for coming. The meeting is closed."

"My Lord, Ch0n," interrupted Kelda, "before we leave, I would speak about something that many have mentioned to me since the battle. It seems we are about to enter a time of peace and prosperity and many wish to partake in the pairing ceremony as our grandfathers did. It is a time for males and females to be recognized before the people as a partnership, agen and aget mutually committed in the eyes of the Gods. Usually the shaman carried out the ceremony but we can find an alternative easily enough."

Karín smiled behind her turban at Kelda's suggestion, the seeds of which she herself had planted not more than a few hours before.

"Ahem," coughed Ch0n. "Well err, I suppose it would be all right if the other members of the council so think." He looked around to see all except the new arrivals nodding wisely. He did not see the mirth in their eyes nor did he realize they had all been briefed by Karín and then sworn to secrecy under pain of death. "Hrrumph! Then it looks as though we should plan it. Tell me, Kelda, what form does this errr ceremony take?"

"Well My Lord, it is a dance of two lines and was once performed each spring when the ground was most fertile. It was thought that the time of year would also help the maids get with child. The men seeking agets line up on one side of the ceremonial square and the women seeking agen on the other. The drums and whistles play and the two lines move closer together, both males and females changing their position in their line until they are facing the one of their desire. The women carry a small circle, usually of flowers but it may be of something special to her or her proposed agen. It represents that part of a woman that makes her a woman. The men carry a small carved wooden spear that represents that part of a man that makes him a man. When the two lines are almost touching, the men make as if to stab the woman opposite and the woman presents her circle of flowers to him as a sign she will take him as her agen. The man places the spear in the circle and they are paired for life. Sometimes, if the man or woman has not been able to manoeuvre to a position opposite the one of their desire, the woman will refuse to present the flowers tho' the man opposite plays his part."

"And that is it? They are then formally paired?"

"Ummm. Yes and no. The party usually lasts all night and sometimes things happen that would not usually happen in a public place."

"Yes. Well we shall have to watch out for that. Who decides how many are in each line?"

"Well, My Lord, if a woman wished to pair with a man, she just places herself in the line of women. If the one she desires is paying attention, he will do the same and opposite her. If a man wishes to pair with a woman he just puts himself in the men's line and the woman of his desire or a woman who desires him will enter the women's line. Sometimes a man will have to choose between women or a woman between men and sometimes there are men and women left over because their desired one has not entered the line or has gone with another. It is no small thing to enter the line. It is much loss of face to be left standing alone."

"How long will it take to organize this thing?"

"My Lord. It is a dance. All we need is music and a place. If I were to say we should do it right now, it would happen before the village sleeps. But I am thinking tomorrow would be better if only to allow those who would be paired to carve what they need."

Ch0n looked around at his council. Then he looked at Karín who nodded.

"So be it, then. Tomorrow we will have the pairing ceremony."

Jez, Boro and Karín stayed behind when the others left.

"I imagine we will get little work out of the villagers on the morrow," Ch0n opined. "But we here have work to do even though those around us are readying themselves for the pairing. Now. Back to the business a hand. There will be a period of time during which we will have to watch the new arrivals and see if they can be trusted. They will take some time to settle in and after that they will naturally question their place in the scheme of things. We all know they will have the right to challenge for the throne and I am content for that to happen for I have their measure with the sword. But I am not able to cope with treachery unless I plan ahead and that is where you three come in. First you, Jez. While the rest of the castle is on holiday, I want you to make three saddles for the new Knights, up to the point where they sit on them to create the final shape. In the pommel between the horn and the actual seat, I want you to place a fragmentation grenade armed and encoded for the remotes. Three separate numbers 12, 13 and 14. I don't think we will ever need them but I would like to know I can defend against treason and how you might defend yourself against the three if I am gone. Do you understand what I want?"

"Yes, My Lord. I had wondered how we might insure ourselves against so much new power should it be turned against us when we are not ready for it. I have instructed their squires to report anything unusual to me as well but in the past few days they have done nothing. They have not even spoken to each other in your tongue so the squires could not understand. That pleases me. I will make the saddles as you instructed."

"Boro. You have used the explosives to make the stones for the walls and the castle. As you are building the three dwellings for them, I want you to place one device under the sleeping platform of each. Each detonator is to have a separate number not the same as the saddle numbers. 16, 17 and 18. I will place a grenade in Commander Guerra's quarters with the number 15. Do you understand what your task is?"

"I do, My Lord and I too had wondered how we might prevent treason. This way we have the means to punish it even if we cannot prevent it."

"Karín. You are present because you need to know what is happening. I know you will protect me as you always have but now the threat is different. You would not be able to better any of the three for they are trained to the same level as am I. My advantage comes from the one I call Shiew, which they have seen but they know not that she can destroy a normal sword with a single stroke in combat. It is why I used to train with a standard katana on my ship. You have to watch your own back as I will watch it. They see you as my protector and executioner and if there is treason happening, you will be at risk. As will you, Jez for they know you to be true to me."

"Who will know of this, Lord?"

"We four will have remotes programmed to the grenades and explosives. Nobody else must know of them. Nobody. Jez, not Malek. Not Buyo. Not your woman, Boro. Not Izaki. Not the squires. Nobody. I give each of you leave to use them if you see the need but it has to be real. It will have to be in the defence of one of us present, Izaki or Mastelik. I don't think anybody else will be in danger. If one of them wishes my throne, he will need Sonja and the others to run things. Are you all clear on this?"

Gavan Connell

 Ch0n looked at each of the three and they nodded to him in turn. Jez and Boro left the room.

"I too wondered, My Lord Ch0n. You give much on the word of a person and twice you have been betrayed. You are too trusting. Well I thought you to be but this plan will help should we suffer treachery. Once they feel the need arising in them as you did and they covet the things you have, they will have to decide their place. One thing you have in your favour is the loyalty of your people. You have given them things they have never had. Peace. Respect. Power to change their lives. Look at Jez. Alik. Sonja. Mori. None would allow harm to come to you. And then there is me. You have taken me from the position of village freak, bodyguard and sometime lover of a despotic king and made me the commander of a force none has ever commanded before. And you have given me something I have never known, the ebon we share. There may be one among the alien four who would betray you and try to take your throne but they will do it over my dead body. And Jez's. And Alik's. And Beny's. And Reny's and her Lancers. Just so, this thing you have planned with the…. grenades will make me sleep a little easier."

Karín left the room and Jez, who had been waiting outside, slipped in unseen.

"My Lord. Forgive me for what I am about to say but I think I need to say it in case you do not think of it yourself. You should be the first in the village to take his place in the men's line tomorrow night. I will be beside you to show you what to do. It is very simple. We just move slowly forward to the sound of the drums and place the spear through the circles of Malek and

Karín. Kelda told me this ceremony was Karín's idea and she will be well pleased to see you eager to formally claim her as your aget. If she joins the women's line before you join the men's, she will still pair with you for you would then join me at my side but it will give her much face if you are first among the men."

"Jez, it is this sort of advice you give me that sets you apart from all the others. They revere me and obey me but you are the truest of all my friends. When Kelda mentioned the ceremony I wondered how I should involve myself in it if at all. I had not had much chance to think of it and I did not want to talk to Karín about it just now. You have told me that which I needed to know. When you give me the signal, I will indeed be the first in the men's line. I hope Karín joins the women's line or I shall have to choose another and Karín would surely kill her. Even if it is Buyo."

"My Lord, you may choose only one woman at any ceremony. If you wish at some point to take a second wife, it may happen at any time but the formal pairing ceremony involves just one aget at a time. Buyo knows this. She will not join the women's line because she knows Karín would be your chosen one and she would lose much face because no other man would select the concubine of the king even if she were to place her circle over his spear ten times. Now. I will carve your spear. It is a simple task and I will use the tool you gave me the day I became your squire."

Gavan Connell

Chapter Three: The Pairing

The following day, the keep was full of giggling women and makeshift stalls buying and bartering for carved spears and circles of flowers. Ch0n smiled to himself at the thought that the invention of 'money' had created a cottage industry overnight. He waved and chatted to as many of his people as time would allow, calling many by name or position. It was now customary for the Lancers and soldiers to wear their uniforms in the street. Many bore the aluminium star of service proudly on their breasts and people nudged each other as they passed. Ch0n was on his way to the baths and he sought out Marel whom he hadn't spoken to since well before the Matáng siege. When he entered her stall, she stood and bowed to him before drawing the woollen curtain.

"My Lord, Ch0n. It is an honour to serve you after so long. I assume you are here so I can prepare you for the pairing ceremony tonight. You are going to choose Karín of course and we are all so excited at the prospect of seeing it."

"Aah, Marel! The capacity of the ijbar to spread gossip is legendary in the castle. I will not give you news to spread tho' you threaten to cut my neck."

Gavan Connell

He sat on the stool and lay back into Marel's lap. She placed a pungent-smelling, steaming towel over his head and started to massage his face.

"My Lord. Your squire is forbidden to take an aget is he not?"

"Yes."

"But he is not forbidden to take a woman is he?"

No. He is only forbidden to have an aget or a woman living in his loft.

"My Lord, when you sentenced Marelik to death I thought my own life would be worth nothing and then when you changed it to a life of isolation and slavery for her I wished you had not done so for death would have been sweeter. But the Gods have been kind to her and to me and now she is one of those who wears the star with pride and she has Alik tho' he may not take her as his aget. I am grateful to you and to the Lady Karín for not killing her."

"She provided the means of her own salvation. The time will come when she will be the aget of a Knight of the Arw'an but not just yet. They are both young. Alik has just started to grow hair on his face. He is only seventeen. Marelik is what? Nineteen?"

"Nineteen My Lord and soon she will be old for a woman with no aget."

Ch0n smiled under the towel.

"Karín is more than twenty and she has only just become the aget of a king. There is time for Marelik if she desires Alik. If not, she can place herself in the women's line tonight and take her chances."

Marel removed the towel and expertly shaved Ch0n's scalp and face. She put some astringent liquid on him that almost took his breath away but he refused to flinch. He stood up and dropped an experimental gold peso into her bowl. She looked at it, knowing it was important, bowed to him again and drew back the curtain for him to leave.

"Who's next?" she shouted. *"Who would pay to have the king's favourite ibar shave his face?"*

As usual before a feast, the square was busy all afternoon but this day there were no long tables being set up inside the space. This time they were being set up around the outside of it. The space in front of the dais was being swept of all sand and stones, ready for the many bare feet that would tread it later in the day. Off to one side, men were setting up their log drums with hide skins. There seemed to be a pattern to their placement. In front was a line of smaller drums with the skins on the top. Behind them were three long horizontal ones with the skins at the ends and at the back was one huge square one formed from bamboo trunks glued together with sap and tlaque skins stretched fast across it, back and front. It was four feet off the ground with the skin vertical. Ch0n stood watching an old man he recognized by sight standing in front of the huge drum with two long sticks, tapping it gently in practice. At the sound of Jez's voice, he turned to greet the Knight.

"Well come, Jez. It seems we have a band for tonight."

"Greetings My Lord. I know not what a ...band is but I am guessing is has to do with the drums."

"A band is a group that plays music. I have many examples in the minitron. I will show you some next time we are together. Who is the old man with the biggest drum?"

"He is called Taiko. He is Alik's father's father. He and all the drummers are old for it is a skill almost lost to us. He told us that in the olden days there would be a pairing ceremony every spring and that the drums were used more often than that. The largest drum is the one that controls the rhythm and the smaller ones follow him. Only the old men remember the rhythms but I think that is about to change after tonight. I brought you something."

He handed Ch0n the small, ornately carved spear.

"It is a poor exchange for the gift you have given me but I made it with affection, knowing its purpose."

"It is a gift like no other I have ever received. Thank you, Jez. Now we had better get ready for the ceremony if we are to be the first in the men's line."

Later, Ch0n took his place on the throne as the sun was dropping towards the horizon. The light from several fires gradually took over as the red orb disappeared. The merriment swarmed below them in the square for some time until a single drumbeat rent the air and the crowd melted to the edges of the space, leaving it vacant. Ch0n looked for Karín to take her place beside him but saw only Jez and the new arrivals on the dais. The single drum beat sounded again followed by another and then another. Then in unison, the mid-range drums filled in the gaps between the long beats, followed by the faster, well-synchronized smaller drums with their fancy paradiddles and backbeats. Suddenly, the whistles started. Ch0n could see several men and women playing what looked like bamboo shoots. They repeated four musical notes over and over, holding each note in such a fashion so as to create a variety of melodies.

"My Lord," said Jez, *"They are calling the people to form the lines."*

Ch0n looked around for Karín.

"What if she doesn't come, Jez? I will look foolish to be left alone in the line with no woman to claim me."

"Fear not My Lord. Every woman here is hoping you will join the line and Karín will not show. Buyo is not here either as far as I can see, although she is so small she would be invisible in this crowd."

Ch0n smiled at the irony of Jez's remark.

"Come on then, Sir Knight. Let us be first among the men."

They descended the steps to the roar of the crowd. All present had been waiting for ChOn. Marel had been telling her customers ChOn had hinted he would take part and the word had buzzed around that nobody was to enter the square until the king had taken his place. No sooner had ChOn and Jez arrived than the flood of men and women started. There were several score of men and a similar number of women.

But no Karín.

The drums maintained their beat and the whistles their four-note melody. ChOn found himself moving his feet to the rhythm and he looked at Jez's to see what they were doing. All the men and now ChOn were pivoting on their right feet, their left feet stepping forward and then back. The line swayed as one. Fifty feet away, the women were doing the same. Guerra and the others watched from atop the dais as he two lines went back and forth. Suddenly there was a murmur from behind the crowd and a gap opened in the throng. Karín stepped on to the square and joined the women's line diagonally opposite ChOn. She was wearing an olive-green, parachute silk dress that touched her body from shoulder to hip and then dropped gracefully to her left thigh and her right ankle. Around her neck she wore a necklace fashioned from the teeth of the dagononum ChOn had given her. Her red hair was highlighted by a band wrapped around her forehead and tied off behind her head. In her right hand she held a ring carved from the thighbone of the oruk bull ChOn had slain with the green katana. She looked at ChOn and took up the movement of the women's line.

"My Lord, you will have to make your way to the other end of this line if you are to place the spear in that ring. The men will not make it easy for you for it is part of the fun. They will not prevent you either so be gentle with them. It is not usual for a man to kill those between him and his desired position in the line. Watch Karín. She may move towards this end of her line but I doubt it. She arrived last to make a grand entrance for sure but also to make you go to her. She might just as easily have put herself next to Malek at this end to make it easy for both of us. I suspect it is a plot. I can not go with you to the other end for Malek is here. For once, My King, I am unable to fight at your side. In a moment the music will change and the lines will move together. We move two steps forward and one step back. The women will do the same. There is no hurry to get to the other end but no time to waste either. Listen. The beat has changed. It is time for you to claim your queen and for me to claim mine."

The whistles took up a constant four-note rhythm and the men started to chant,

"Nu..aw Ek..we! Nu..aw Ek..we! I'm going hunting! I'm going hunting!"

And when they paused, the women took up their own chant,

"E..bu I..ne! E..bu I..ne! Stab here! Stab here!"

Ch0n took up the men's chant as he bustled his way against the tide to his right. Every now and then his way was blocked by someone who wouldn't let him past but Ch0n just shouldered them aside in turn and the laughter of those around him followed him as he went. Every few steps he looked towards Karín who was chanting along with the other women but maintaining her place at the far end of their line. She was looking at him every time he glanced up at her, the same smile on her face, every curve in her body calling him as she danced closer and closer. ChOn finally arrived at the end of his line and took up the chant with ever increasing enthusiasm as the two lines approached each other. Karín's eyes never left ChOn's nor his, hers. Atop the dais, Guerra and the others watched the scene playing out below them. ChOn was a giant among the men. He was dressed in the only thing he thought suitable, boots, black trousers and a tee shirt that showed every muscle in his upper body. Karín was a full head taller than the next tallest woman. She was long and lean and the silk she wore highlighted every detail of her curved body whereas the other women mostly wore special outfits made from fine white mohair.

"She may be every bit the savage but she is every bit the queen tonight," thought Guerra. "To look at her now, one would never guess she is a ruthless killer. No wonder he didn't want to go back. Neither would I. He has done us all a favour." He looked across at the other three. They were all absorbed in what was happening below them.

"That'll be us next time," he shouted to them. *"Once the chemicals wear off, we'll know why they are all so keen to get together."*

The two lines were now only a few feet apart and the men started to make stabbing motions towards the women who were taking two steps towards them and then one away. Their floral circles were ever nearer, only to be snatched away again until at last they were within reach. Ch0n's ears could hear the music but his senses were filled with the closeness of Karín. His hand was moving the little spear towards her and then away and her hand was moving the bone circle towards him and then away. Finally she stopped moving her feet and stood swaying her hips, rocking on the balls of her feet. Ch0n held the spear towards the circle and moved to take it on the point but Karín took it away. She moved it down the front of her body until it was resting just below the mound between her thighs. She moved her hips as if they were making ijon and Ch0n put the spear through the bone circle. She caught it with her thigh muscles and held it there, still rocking her hips. Ch0n put his hands on her and she pressed full length against him. Reaching down between them, she removed the spear and the circle. Then she knelt down before him and placed her forehead on his feet. Ch0n looked to his left. All the women were in a similar position. Suddenly, the music stopped and Boro's voice rang out.

"It is done! I, Boro, Royal Architect of the kingdom of Arw'an, Buq'ue and Matáng announce you all to be agen and aget before the Gods. I further announce that the king, Ch0n and the Lady Karín, Brigadier General and Commander of the Household Cavalry are joined before the Gods as …. husband and wyf according to the language and customs of the place from whence he came." He nodded at Taiko who started a new rhythm and the rest of the village joined in the dancing.

Karín was breathless with joy and lust. She was still kneeling at Ch0n's feet, her chest heaving, her arms around Ch0n's thighs.

"Husband," she hissed up at him. *"Take me to our quarters with haste or I will do something with your dewen that will give the Arw'an cause to talk about this night for generations."*

Chapter Four: The Cavern

The next morning after breakfast, Ch0n and Karín left the castle with the wolf trotting behind. Karín was in the front position and the tlaque knew that it would have to stride out harder than usual or suffer the consequences. They turned east and crossed the river at the first ford they came to before turning south and into the foothills of the rocky ridge that ran East-West behind the castle. They climbed steadily towards a pass in the range and when the sun reached its zenith they were staring across to where the lake spread out before them. They arrived at the shore just before last light and Ch0n was keen to look for a place to spend the night. The stone ruins were close enough to provide a possible shelter so they pushed hard towards them, checking for dragons as they rode. They reached them in time to clean a space under a solid roof and with four walls to protect them from the elements and any predators. Karín spread out the bedding and they stabled the tlaque in the next 'room' before settling down for the night with the wolf lying by the entrance.

"What was this place?"

"I don't know. In the morning we will explore it and see what secrets it may reveal. It is interesting because it is of stone and obviously meant to last."

Gavan Connell

"We have not had much time alone of late. Things have been moving so fast that we have always been running around organizing, planning or fighting. This new peace will take a lot of getting used to."

"I thought after I killed Mastel, the Matáng Commander, that we would have no peace until I had visited the Matáng Lands. I still think that. After that we can just settle down and hopefully there will be many times like this."

"ChOn, the words you spoke to me before we climbed to the battlements to begin the defence of the castle… They touched me greatly. Had I died that day I would have died knowing that you feel for me as I do for you. I know it is not easy for you to speak of these things but when you did, it made my heart soar like a hawk to hear you. Now I have something to say to you. I wish you to know before we sleep this night that I deem myself whole for being your official aget before the Gods. I hope we get to live the peace as we have lived the war. And now I want you to plant your seed in me so I can grow it into a fine young boy who will be king in his turn."

They woke as the sun's rays touched their faces through the open 'window'. The wolf was nowhere to be seen. They rose and let the tlaque free on its hobbles and then ran to the lake and swam and coupled and returned to the ruins for a breakfast of porridge and goat milk. Then they started to explore the ruins. The 'building' had been constructed from the local stones that littered the foreshore of the lake behind the sandy beach. It consisted of two small rooms with their stone roofs quite intact and one large room where the roof had collapsed some long time before. ChOn searched for evidence in all three rooms but could not fathom why the building had existed. From the doorway of the large room he could see what seemed to be two 'lines' in the water. Straight lines. He knew that they had to be man-made so he waded into the lake and found them to be the edges of a channel. A man-made channel.

"That is a channel made so a boat could come to the shore. That building must have been some sort of permanent storage or dwelling or both for the people who used to come here by boat. That means there is another race of people here on the planet. Or that there used to be because for whatever reason they no longer use this building. It is hard to guess how long it is since it was last used. Maybe they stopped coming and so the roof fell in through lack of use or the roof fell in and they stopped coming here. But why would they come here in the first place? There must have been a reason. It may have been a mine or a fishing port or a place where they traded with the Arw'an years ago but nobody has ever mentioned that. And where did they come from and where did they go? This lake must be enormous or it must have a river leading from it to the sea." He changed frequencies again and called the ship.

"G2 this is Ch0n."

"Good morning, Ch0n. I see you are enjoying the lake. I am sorry I didn't go down with the others and get marooned along with them. That thing you do with the woman looks like fun."

"You have no idea. Listen. I need close up images of the lake shore and any river that flows from it. This ruin is some sort of warehouse or was and there is a canal or wharf in front of it that probably won't show up on the images you have. Can you send them to Guerra for analysis? I think there is a

Gavan Connell

seafaring people here and if there isn't, there certainly once was. In fact, if you could have your analyst scan the shores of the ocean nearest us for some sort of town or port and send back what he finds that would be good. I don't know how much space these images need but the more you can send Guerra the more work I can give him. How much longer will you be around?"

"We have started the process of shutting down the humans. The soldiers are already in bed. No need for them up here. The comms tech is still awake and the photo techs. The ground crews are the next to go to sleep and then the photo techs will send their results off and the comms tech and I will stay awake to look after the bridge and of course the nursery will stay functioning. Those kids will probably have some sort of normal life on Earth and I am planning on something similar if I can."

"Thanks for your help. Send that stuff to Guerra and get back to me before you leave station. Ch0n out."

"Ch0n, there is a path at the back of the building. I just found it. It is hard to see up close but if you look in the distance you can see it winding up to those caves on the slopes."

"Karín, grab your helm and we will look where it leads. Perhaps there is some sort of mine in the caves."

They wended their way along the path to the first of the caves. Ch0n checked for predators with the helm and then they made their way inside with the light intensifier activated. Once inside they were greeted with the sight of a huge cavern decorated with ancient art. Ch0n activated his flashlight to see better. There were images of men and tlaque, goats and oruk. Birds flew in painted lines and then what seemed to be men and women. Ch0n recalled the images in his own cave where he had seen this same being. He took images of them and they moved further into the cavern. The images continued until Ch0n stopped in his tracks. There in front of him was the unmistakable image of an enormous flying craft, next to it a much smaller, egg-shaped one, then these same beings.

"Look at this! This planet was visited or even colonized by aliens centuries ago. Hundreds of years ago. Maybe thousands. There is speculation that my own planet was colonized or at least visited by aliens and I have seen this type of art before somewhere. I will look it up on the minitron when we get back. If that is the case, it will explain how you and I are so similar. They left some of their number here to colonize this planet or to mix with whatever race was here before. Come on, Ch0n. Where have you seen this stuff? Planet of the Gods? No. Chariots of the Gods. A book written hundreds of years ago. It must have been part of our training for me to know that. It was written by a man who believed that Earth was visited or colonized by aliens who came and went. I will have to look it up. I can't remember more. He was laughed at by the scientists I remember. Well perhaps he was more accurate than they thought."

"To me it is a real thing. It happened with you. If I were to come to this place with a blank wall and draw in my way what has happened, it would include images of you with the flying craft, the landing of the others, you on a tlaque, the castle and so on. In ten thousand years someone would chance upon my work and laugh at the possibility that you came here from

another world. This fills me with the hope that we are alike enough to share offspring. To you it is fantastic even though you are living it. To me it is realistic because I am living it from another perspective. This should make your life's sacrifice worthwhile. All those years spent asleep. The lack of a real life in the service of what? Exploration of what you call space. Now you can stop and enjoy your life knowing you are not the first and not the last. You are just another among us. Now you know."

They went further into the darkness until they came to a smaller cavern with a throne at one end and six stone sarcophagi along the wall in niches. Ch0n opened them all in turn. Each bore the mummified remains of a tall creature that bore no resemblance to the tribes he had seen. He checked each stone casket and found what he guessed were five females and one even taller male. Each wore a bracelet and a ring and the male had a short rod under his body. All the items were of a lightweight shiny black stainless metal that told the two explorers they were certainly not of the planet.

"It is proof you are not the first from another world to set foot here, My Lord. These have been here for many generations. The ruins may have been of their making but I have one question. Who buried the last of them?"

Ch0n was playing with the bracelets. He opened one and gave it to Karín. She put it on her wrist and closed it. There was a faint vibration as she locked it and then she couldn't unlock it. The join had disappeared.

"This one is different from the others. They have their arms by their sides and this one has his arms across his chest. Perhaps he closed the roof of his own tomb and just waited for death."

"ChOn! I can't undo it. It won't fit over my hand. What does it mean?"

In response, ChOn selected the one from the tallest of the alien corpses and placed it on his own wrist, feeling the same vibration.

"Now we are wed. They can do no harm if they were worn by those who came before me. Perhaps one day we will see what they can do. Put the ring on your finger." They both did. Nothing happened and they were able to remove them and replace them at will.

"Now for the wand." ChOn picked it up and examined it. It was about fifteen inches long and there was a faint groove running around the circumference of the base of what seemed to be the handle. The shaft itself was about an inch wide at the handle and three-quarters of an inch at the tip. The tip was solid but had what seemed to be a camera shutter on the end. It seemed to him to be a weapon but he had no idea what it might do. In the process of examining it he found that the shaped knob, or handle at the thick end was not fixed solid and when he rotated it, he felt the rod come to life in his hand. He disarmed it again.

"I don't want it to go off in my hand inside in case it brings the roof in," he said looking a little sheepishly at Karín."

"How can it be that they and you had so much knowledge and we have so little?"

"Time. Your people are young in the history of humanoids. So are the peoples of the planet from whence my people come. Less than two thousand generations for us, of which only the last fifty have had the knowledge to do what they have done. These beings went to earth two thousand generations ago. They came here maybe fifty generations ago. Their descendants will probably be further developed than the Arw'an or the Buq'ue or the Matáng because those peoples didn't have access to them when they came. But you have access to me, which is the same. Our offspring will have my genes and yours and that will be a powerful mix. Come outside. I want to play with this."

They went outside and took images of the cavern entry for the map and returned to the ruins.

"I am guessing that people came here to meet with them or maybe even worship them. We will send Guerra here. He will love having this to play with. We will find someone in the village who likes to tell the old stories. They will come with him and together they will write the history of these people and we will find their descendants." His helm came to life.

"Ch0n, this is G2. I have sent those images to Guerra's tablet. We have identified a river leading to the sea and along the northern shore we found another river with a possible town."

"Thanks. That fits my theory. I'll bet Guerra has fun looking at them and trying to sort it all out. Now! I have some images to send to you. You will want to be sitting down when you see them. I am not the first alien to visit this planet. The aliens who supposedly visited Earth were here. Here they come. ChOn out." He pressed, 'Enter' and the tablet sent a compressed file into space to the satellite which relayed it to the ship.

He took up the rod and examined it. He twisted the handle through three positions and saw different light patterns appear with each one. On the third, he was able to move the knob at right angles to the shaft. It sat easily in his hand like a pistol. There were three green lights near where his thumb sat. He pressed one, aiming the rod towards the lake. Nothing happened. He pressed the second. Nothing. He pressed the third. Still nothing. He smiled. A weapon he knew nothing about. A challenge. Karín was watching him, feeling his brain working.

"This handle has a false-fusion power source like the ones we have. Otherwise it could not maintain a charge for hundreds of years. My pulse gun is something like this and it needs my thumbprint to program it to me. This will need something similar. He studied the rod closely and then laughed. He took the ring from his finger and slid it on to the rod, pushing it up until it would go no further. He had thought the tiny marks in the rod were ornamental but looking at the ring, he had realized they were a match. He rotated the ring so the marks aligned. The three lights changed colour. One blue, one orange and one red. He pointed the rod towards the lake again, pressed the blue light and released it. A bolt of blue shot from the lens across the lake and dissipated several hundred feet away.

ChOn looked for a target close by and fired the blue bolt at a tree. The bolt hit the tree and shook it.

"A pulse gun," said ChOn. He pressed the button again and held it. The tree took the full force of a continuous blue beam and a hole appeared in the trunk and continued to grow. ChOn shattered a rock with it. "And better than mine."

The orange pulse sent a beam slightly narrower and further across the lake before fading to nothing. He fired it at the tree but nothing seemed to be happening until it suddenly burst into flames where the beam was touching it.

"Flame thrower," said ChOn. "Now for the big finale."

He fired a single red pulse at the burning tree and it exploded.

"Hmmm. High explosive laser of some sort." ChOn tried the pulse out to a hundred yards and the targets exploded, albeit with less violence. He put the handle into the normal position and rotated it one click. Five glyphs appeared. The ring went out so ChOn removed it and put it on his finger.

"Numbers?" thought ChOn.

He pressed them in turn until Karín started. Her bracelet lit up, a series of lights flashed and a small screen appeared. She could make out ChOn's foot.

"Point it at that burning tree. I can see it here. It's small but clear. It's a communications device. Talk to it."

"Ch0n started the alphabet. In the distance, Karín's face changed.

"I can hear you. Not through my ears. In my head. The bracelet must have a way to send the sounds to my ears."

Ch0n already knew that because when she spoke, his own bracelet booted and he could hear her as clearly as if she were standing beside him.

"None must know of this. The bracelets we will have to wear. The rings, we will have to see about. The rod will stay with me always but disarmed. Its existence should remain a secret for now. The other four bracelets we will put aside. Perhaps for our offspring. I will have to study this thing at length and find out its functions. There is still one position to explore. He turned the handle to the first position and his bracelet started to warm almost imperceptibly. A mechanical voice 'spoke' to him. Just a few words in a strange tongue. Then it spoke again in another less guttural tone and paused. Then it spoke in Arw'an. Just one sentence.

"If you understand this language, respond only 'yes' or 'no'."

"Yes," said Ch0n.

"You have found the staff I left for your people. It appears a symbol of power but it has many other functions. You should locate the other five bracelets and rings. Each of the females has one of each. Find them and you will be able to communicate with them. The wearer of the bracelets will have the power of the bracelet for life. Before you allow another to wear a bracelet, know that once worn, they cannot be removed. Only in death will the signals from the living brain cease and thus allow the clasp to be released. Do you understand?"

"Yes."

"Only the wearer of a bracelet may use the staff but any who wears one may use it. There is a function which requires a secondary security measure to access it. Only one who has the intelligence to work out what it is will be able to access that function. You will have to find that for yourself. Do you understand?"

"Yes."

"On the handle there are several lights. Follow the steps we tell you and you will receive instructions on how to access all the functions of the staff but the one already mentioned. When you are ready, press the first button. That is all."

"What was that, Ch0n? Was it talking to you?"

"It was and I will show you how to enter it. Even more now do I understand the importance of keeping the function of the bracelets and rings a secret. I will tell any who may ask that it is something from my ship given to me by a metallurgist. Like the Katana, Shiew. No. I will tell them I made it myself and polished it and the bracelets as symbols of our ebon. I can easily explain the lights inside them. I have a box of them and people have seen them. Guerra might guess otherwise but we can tell him they were lying around in the cavern and we just took them. The two of them.

I am sorry to ruin or little holiday with work but now we can go for a swim and enjoy what we have left of the day."

"Ch0n, if they came here deliberately, will they not have a ship somewhere that might be useful? The drawings show a large craft and a smaller one."

Ch0n's heart thumped involuntarily.

"They might. If they do, it will be nearby. Perhaps we can send the Lancers to look for it. Perhaps we can set up a base here by the lake, a scientific base where Guerra can live and work with a team of the most intelligent among us. He will know how to select them. Look at Boro and what he has achieved with no learning. He just did it. This building can be rebuilt. It is small enough to put permanent lighting in. We can set up a school for the brightest children. He will have a project to last him his life and one that will give him space from the castle. I think Carmodi is already attracted to him. You will need another adjutant before long. She will teach him the ways of the ijon and will want to be with him as his woman. And he will be like me. Once he discovers the delights of ijon, he will want her around him all the time. Now. Stop thinking about work and start relaxing. You might start by showing me that thing you did with your tongue last night."

"Even better, My Lord. I will show you how to do the thing Eloik used to do to me with hers when we were girls growing

up. But first we should swim. We are hot and dusty and I prefer to be squeaky clean for what comes afterwards."

Chapter Five: The Matáng Expedition

They arrived back at the castle the following night. The guard was alert when they approached but inside the walls, the holiday was still in full cry. The central square was full of revelers. Ivor was playing his flute to an appreciative audience of dancers and wide-eyed children. The other two Knights were sharing the leg of a goat and Guerra was sitting to one side with Carmodi, Jez and Malek. The new squires were nearby looking at their masters, waiting for a signal to jump into action. The others of the council were sitting at the same long table with their families. Buyo was alone as usual but ran to them when they appeared. She bowed to ChOn and kissed Karín and put her arm through Karín's as they went to sit with the rest. They took time to greet each in turn before Alik and Buyo went to get food and the local brewed beer.

Guerra was the first to notice the bracelets.

"Pretty trinkets. Where did you got them?"

"'Get', not 'got'. I made them from a metal given to me by a person on my ship." He glared Guerra into not asking more questions. "I see you are practising your Arw'an. Good for you. Carmodi must be a good teacher. You have a lot to learn and not just about the language." Only Karín, Buyo and Carmodi understood the meaning behind this last comment. The first two smiled and Carmodi looked at the ground. Karín noted her reaction.

"Our Lord ChOn says we are to mount an expedition to the Matáng Lands." Said Karín. *"I know we are on holidays and I shouldn't talk about work but I think it will be a great chance for our newest citizens to see the land and what it has to offer. It will be wonderful to ride to the outposts without having to worry about being ambushed. I can hardly wait."*

"We will be away for a month at least. We will take the entire Household Cavalry, thirty of the Infantry, who will by then have their own tlaque and the three new Knights will accompany us. Commander Guerra will have the option of going or staying but I would like him to know the countryside. Commander, should you choose to stay, I will have Sir Jez show you around. It will take some time to recover from the damage caused by the advancing Matáng Army but its beauty will still be there to see. Karín and I have just found a lake on the other side of the mountain. By now you may have seen the images sent to you by your former ship." Guerra nodded. "There is an exciting project to be managed from the ruins by the lake. It will need a team of people to manage it and I would suggest that, Commander Guerra be the one to do it. His background and capacity for detail are unmatched among us and I can think of none other who might do the project justice. What say you, Commander? Would you like to have your own outpost with an important project as its reason for existence?"

Guerra looked back at him, puzzled. In his native tongue he said,

"I am sorry My Lord but I was able to decipher less than half of that."

Ch0n spoke to him in English.

"I will tell you later what I said. You have done well to understand as much as you did. Well done."

The others smiled and murmured in agreement. Guerra nodded to Ch0n. "This won't be as hard as I imagined," he thought. "This man is a far better king than I was a ship's commander. I might have done better to have been less aloof."

Ch0n allowed the holiday to run its full seven days, even though he was champing at the bit to get back to work. The only person to seem as eager to work was Guerra.

"Talk me about the strangers. I have to knowledge more," he had said to Ch0n within minutes of arriving back at the castle.

Ch0n corrected him and told him everything he knew, leaving out the part about the power of the bracelets. He showed Guerra the rod and he could see that Guerra knew it was the key to something and not just a trinket. He did not push the issue when Ch0n insisted it was just a toy. Guerra instinctively knew it was linked to the bracelets in some way but decided to leave well enough alone. Ch0n's project was so enormous and detailed he would have enough to worry about for the rest of his life. He saw himself as living as some sort of university professor and research fellow here on a backward planet and knew history would treat him kindly. There was just one thing he could not come to grips with. The woman, Carmodi, was suffocating him. He liked her well enough but wanted space from her. He thought his reaction might have something to do with his suppressed hormones. He hoped it did. He saw what Ch0n had with Karín and thought it might be nice to have the same. Carmodi obviously wanted to be close to him. If only she would back away until he could react positively towards her.

While Ch0n was briefing Guerra, Karín and Buyo were with Carmodi.

"I have tried to get close to him but he rejects me. He is a man so full of intelligence and is pleasing to my eye but when I am close to him and I feel the need to touch him, he recoils from me. I am ashamed. You two between you can barely keep the Lord Ch0n satisfied. I have heard you across the passage at all times of the day and night engaging in the ijon, yet my Guerra is as passive as one of the Lancers' castrated tlaque."

Karín spoke first after putting her hand on Buyo's arm to silence her.

"Carmodi. You are a beautiful woman in the eyes of all. And you are loyal and hard working. You have managed the logistics and personal aspects of the Household Cavalry as well as I could have wanted. You will make a wonderful wyf for Guerra if he should choose you. But you need to know. The Lord Ch0n had no desire to touch me for more than ten moon cycles, even though I was as eager you. Maybe more so. I

slept at the foot of his bed next to the wolf. Every day I went to him and showed myself to him in subtle and obvious ways. It was not until I spoke to him about the ebon and the ijon that he even knew a man and woman would lie down together for pleasure. Guerra told the Ch0n that they give those on the ship some sort of potion to stop their urges. Just like the root we give our men to calm them down and the male tlaque we now give the same root when the wild bull is close to him. You need to be patient with him. Give him some space. Talk to him about what a man and woman can do and then when you think the time is right, lie with him in the darkness and tell him you are going to test his dewen to see if it will harden. Tell him you will be patient with him and when his dewen grows hard, use your hands on him to make him discharge. After that he will do anything for you. But a word of caution. He will not know the ways of ijon and will want more and more but he will need to be taught to slow down. They are grown men but have the skills of boys just growing their hair below. You might start by asking him if he would like you to massage his body. He won't need to know anything at all and you can find out easily enough that way if he is ready."

"Oh! I did not know any of that about the Ch0n. Not that I would need to know. Nor about their suppressed desires. The other three will be the same. They have not even looked at the Lancers they work with, even though Beny has been showing that Harry her iduw across the eating area at every opportunity. She is persistent if nothing else."

"I would add to your words, Karín," said Buyo. *"I know I am but the second of My Lord's women but I have noted that I have to take the initiative with him. Yes, he is willing enough but he*

still knows little about the actual ijon. You will need to show Guerra the thirteen ways because he knows none of them."

"Thirteen, Buyo? I know of eleven. You will have to tell me of the others."

"Aah, my lady. And take away that which allows me to offer him something new? He would have no need of me then. Perhaps he will show you himself." They all laughed and Carmodi added,

"I thought there were only eight of the ways. Perhaps I need to get some extra tuition from you two. My mother was obviously not well taught by her mother. I will have to learn from Guerra as well as teach him. That could be fun. At least now I know why he spurns me. But I will try the massage."

When the holidays ended, Ch0n called the council and set them the task of preparing for peace. He also set them the task of reorganizing the makeup of the Lancers and Infantry and told Doni he would need thirty more tlaque from the wild herd to make up the numbers the Infantry were going to take from other areas. He set the deadline of twenty three days for things to be ready for a month-long absence to the Matáng Lands. He gave Izaki similar instructions and told him he would be arriving at the Buq'ue fort in twenty five days to pick up the remainder of the group to go to Matáng.

Things moved quickly from the outset. After the first week, the thirty tlaque were assembled from among those belonging to the herders, Kelda's group and the spares. Doni had in the meantime gone to the grazing grounds of the wild herd and brought back thirty reLeif mounts from those earlier gelded and released. It had been a masterstroke of time-saving on his part, saving all the need to house and domesticate the beasts. They were allowed to remain in the herd because the new dominant bull instinctively knew they were no threat to his dominion. In fact he was the only bull in the herd. Even the calves had been gelded when the herd had been corralled back at the castle.

The thirty Infantry went straight to their mounts and trained under the watchful eye of Jez and Karín. The Lancers helped them manage their beasts in the new stables Boro had had built months before when the idea of mounted Infantry had been first mentioned. All the saddles had been completed, the armour had been made to fit each individual and five of their number had been placed in a special section and allocated a pulse gun or a metal storm kinetic pistol. Their commander, Marik was dressed in the boots and trousers of a galactic scout, helm, and a modified tunic and the armour of the mounted infantry. He also carried a pulse gun. The remainder would fight with their traditional short swords and a stabbing spear ChOn had designed after the assegai used centuries before by the Zulus. Each of the soldiers had a designated rider, who was armed with a longbow. The tactics were designed in such a way that the fighting force would be deployed and dropped in their forming up area, and the riders would provide the fire-support force with bows. At the end of the skirmish, the riders would rendezvous with the soldiers as the Lancers had previously done and transport them to their next position. The entire force was independent of the Lancers who would be able to assist them from the flanks or rear. ChOn at last had his anvil and his pincers. Or as Shaka the Zulu King had called them, the horns of the buffalo. All they had to do was train and train.

Gavan Connell

The King's Own rebuilt their troop from reinforcements. They had been lucky not to have been in the front of the assault that had killed so many of their sisters from the Buq'ue Troop. They had lost just two of their number in the battle and had promoted two of the trainees immediately. For the Buq'ue Troop, however, it was a case of starting almost from the beginning. They had lost twenty-five, including Eloik, their Troop Leader and almost as many tlaque. Izaki was busy under Karín's orders selecting those to replace the dead. Ten he had promoted from the ranks of the reserves Eloik had had but the remaining fifteen were new girls. He used the same selection method Karín had used with a point to point race and the fifteen plus the ten reserves selected themselves. He put them onto tlaque from the herders and those from the wild herd. Each new girl was paired with an experienced 'sister' to learn the ropes. He had to rely on extra tlaque from Doni's eastern herd because they had lost so many. By the end of the first week there were enough for the Lancers as well as the Mounted Infantry. He put them all to training straight away.

Ch0n was in constant touch with Mastelik. He was getting daily reports on how things were progressing in the Matáng capital and was heartened by the responses. The former Matáng platoon had immediately had an impact on their former comrades and before long all were sporting short hair and the new, clipped beard that Mastelik had deemed suitable to appease their God and Ch0n alike.

"If I can take hold of it, it is too long!" he had roared from the front of his army the day they arrived back to a sorry welcome. He had immediately exiled Sith's band of soothsayers and

advisers and identified two men and two women in the style of ChOn's two councils. The Matáng capital was a sizeable town and so each of the four was allowed a small committee to help them realize Mastelik's orders. But not all were happy. One day, one of the former council members openly challenged Mastelik's right to command the garrison and the town.

"You return from the worst defeat in the history of the Matáng and tell us what we may and may not do. This ChOn, whom you say killed our king and so has the right to the throne, has never been here. I do not accept his rule. Nor yours, even though you are Sith's nephew and the last of his family."

"So be it, Tomás, brother of Palik, who swore allegiance to two kings and betrayed them both. You would not have me as the commander of this garrison and city. I accept your challenge but know that even tho' you may prevail, you will have to deal with him for it was he who appointed me and only he may replace me."

Mastelik walked to the front of the troops where he could be seen. He was dressed in the black uniform he had brought from the castle. Off to the left of the square, Tomás walked towards him, sword in hand. Mastelik drew his katana and adopted what Jez had called, 'position one.' It was the side on stance with the sword pointed at forty five degrees towards the sky outside Mastelik's right shoulder. He looked more confident than he felt. He was not wholly comfortable with the long blade and hoped Tomás couldn't see his nerves. As Tomás drew closer, Mastelik drew a long slow breath and let it go. He concentrated on Tomás's eyes. Tomás adopted the front-on crouch of the Infantry soldier, his right hand holding the blade towards Mastelik and his left hand in a matching position for balance. He was inside the arc of the katana but too far to strike with the shorter weapon. He looked at Mastelik's face and then at the sword. As soon as he took his eyes from Mastelik's, the katana swept easily and smoothly across and down, taking Tomas's head and right shoulder. Mastelik stood, wiped the blade on the still twitching body and sheathed it.

"Now hear this! I swore to serve the ChOn who killed Sith as I have killed Tomás. My father led the Matáng Army to a defeat so comprehensive that had he chosen to do so, the ChOn could have killed every man who opposed him. But he did not. I and each of them owes his life to the new king, ChOn. Each women and child here owes the life of her agen and father and brother to the new king. He is a soldier. He could have ruined the Matáng forever but he chose to give me and those behind me the option for an honourable life in his service. My father had that option given to him but his shame was so great he challenged the ChOn and died for it. I chose life over death because had I chosen death, it would have been death for all and none would have returned to this place. None! He allowed us our weapons. He gifted me a talake to mount, this uniform which he, himself wears and the blade you have just seen at work. They are symbols of trust in me and those behind me. If any still wish to challenge, let him or them step forward now or forever be silent. I will have all challengers but no cowards. Kneel now before me and swear fealty to the new King ChOn as I have done. Or leave. But if you choose to leave, do not return under pain of death."

They knelt as one and repeated the words he shouted at them.

"It is done, My Lord. The Matáng Capital is now under your rule. The outposts we will have to convince one by one."

"Send runners to each outpost and tell the village elders I will be in the capital in thirty days. Perhaps thirty one. I would have them present to greet me and hear my plan. By then, please have some baths ready. I know not your town but it is near a river, I assume. I will be arriving with about three hundred and fifty in the group." They will need a space on the outskirts of the town and a place to cook and food to eat. I suggest you get to work rounding up the nearest tlaque herd. If you can at least identify where it is, we will be able to take the entire herd to you. Do you have the bamboo forests where you are?"

"No. We do not. They would be a handy thing to have, though. I saw what you have done with them. I will send patrols out to find the talake herd."

"Send people to the river to dig away at the banks. And make it into a river-flat one hundred paces long and one hundred wide where we can plant the bamboo. I will take a travois loaded with poles to plant. They will take root and grow quickly and you can just keep expanding the forest as you harvest the trunks. Within a few moon cycles you will have useable trunks. You will need something to make a space to hold the tlaque. They are docile and it need not be too complex but it will need to last at least those few months while the bamboo grows. I will ask Doni if we can take some spare females for you to use as beasts of burden. Thank you for your loyalty. I will admit to being a little nervous about letting so many of you go fully armed. I know this is a big thing for you to do."

"My father was a soldier as are you and as am I. Before the battle ever reached the stage it did, he was imploring Sith to call it off for the sake of the troops and their families back home. Had he not been so loyal to his word, I think he may well have killed his own brother to save those lives. I see his honour in you. I hope you see it in me. There has been enough killing."

"That there has. Ch0n out."

The weeks passed. Karín sent Buyo to Ch0n during her time of bleeding. Usually she was content to do it but this time she felt a little sad. She had taken Ch0n off the milkyweed tea after the battle and had hoped his seed might have germinated in her this first cycle but it had not. Buyo as usual made the most of her short time with Ch0n and he with her. As always she lay spent on his chest whispering to him that she wanted his child to grow in her.

Across the hall, Carmodi had finally convinced Guerra that he should let her ease his tension with a body massage. She had some difficulty at first because he would not relax and finally she just told him that if he didn't let her do it properly, she would go back to being Karín's adjutant and he could work alone on the comms project and get another language teacher. Perhaps Sonja. He allowed her to strip him naked and lie him on the bed. An hour later, she discovered that he was in full working order and he was left looking wide eyed at the ceiling.

"Guerra. My body is burning. I am going to sit astride you. You will feel a similar sensation to that my fingers gave you but much more intense. This is the ijon. I am going to teach you the ways of it and you are going to teach me for I have never taken a lover. Just lie back now while we get you ready again. Once you are in me, recite in your mind the list of the parts the radio has. Think of anything but what you feel. I need you to last a little if you can."

ChOn went to visit Doni and see how the oruk were coming along.

"Do you think he will be able to trot to Matáng with me astride him? I know he can bear the weight but it is the distance I am concerned about. It is fourteen days walk from here. Five days trotting. Maybe six."

"I would think so. Your weight is nothing to him. His horns already weigh half as much as a man. These beasts pass all their lives walking and running by day and sleeping by night. This one has you and Alik walking him daily with the saddle and riding him most days. If you go to the Buq'ue fort and rest him, you will know how his stamina is for the trot. If he blows up before you get to the fort, just leave him there or send him back with Alik. Alik can ride your tlaque in case you have to do it and if you don't, you will have your choice of mount at Matáng while Alik is looking after the other. Jez can do the same. The two we were going to use as beasts of burden can also go with two of the other Knights and their squires. They are accustomed to people handling and riding them. Making a grand entry into Matáng with four Knights astride oruk will turn

heads. The only problem is, which among the Knights will miss out?"

"Jez is not going. I need him to stay behind and command the garrison. If he is willing, I will allow one of the three to ride his oruk and the other two you will have ready. If Jez is unhappy, I alone will ride one."

He walked to Jez's quarters, where he found the Knight making saddles.

"Well come, My Lord. What brings you to my stable looking so thoughtful?"

"Well met, Sir Jez. Are these the saddles we spoke about with Karín and Boro?"

"They are, My Lord. This is the third one. The others are over there waiting for the Knights to come and sit on the sprayform. The modifications you requested are installed here. I have placed a metal sheet from your vessel under each grenade in an attempt to protect the tlaque but I hope we never find out if it works."

"Good work, Jez. I can't feel it at all. When are they coming to sit on them?"

"They are with the mounted Infantry all day today explaining the concept of holding ground after it has been seized. I am glad I am not an Infantry soldier."

"Hah! And so say all Knights and Lancers. Especially during a long march. I have a question to ask you. A favour if you like. Know that the answer should come from your heart and not out of any sense of obligation. It will not vex me if you say 'no'. I am going to ride the oruk to Matáng. There are two more that Doni will allow me to use and yours, which would normally remain with you unless you will allow one of the new Knights to ride it. Give me your answer tomorrow. You do not need to justify it either way. It is your beast. I gave it to you and you have husbanded it since it was a week old."

"My Lord. I can give you the answer right now or rather you can answer it yourself. You tasked me to make you three saddles, each with a grenade armed and in place in case of treachery. You tasked Boro to do the same under their beds. You did that because you do not as yet trust the three. Yet one day later you ask me if I will allow one of them to ride my oruk alongside the two others, also mounted on oruk, none of which have grenades in their saddles. My question is this. If you were I, would you lend your oruk to a Knight when your king had tasked you to protect him by placing an explosive in that same Knight's tlaque saddle and his bed? The answer you give me is the answer I will give you."

Ch0n looked at Jez and for the first time, Jez heard him laugh out loud. It was more of a chuckle than anything but a laugh it certainly was.

"None but you or Karín would have answered me thus, first among my Knights and staunch friend. Boro chose you well and you have learned much but your honesty comes from your father and mother who brought you up to be forthright and loyal.

Gavan Connell

If I were you I would not allow my king to lend my oruk to a Knight who had still to prove his loyalty."

Jez grinned from ear to ear and went back to his saddle making. Without looking back at ChOn, he said,

"Then that is my answer to you, My Lord."

"So be it," said ChOn, walking through the door.

Kelda allocated her best cooks to the expedition because it was going to be a hard task, feeding so many. She decided to send ten cooks and ten stores personnel, who would double as kitchen hands. She suggested to ChOn that he have saddlebags made so each rider could carry additional supplies to relieve the logistic burden and ChOn set Karín and Izaki to the task of organizing it. The plan was to march on porridge and dried meat to the Buq'ue fort and eat there, march to the Western outpost and eat there and then march to Matáng and eat there. That way the cooking would be restricted to porridge and the provision of hot water for making tea and washing. They knew where the water points were located as far as the outpost and they knew there was water en route to Matáng from there.

In the Buq'ue fort, a similar scene was being played out. Maken, the Buq'ue beastmaster and Izaki had managed to provide all the troops with mounts with Doni's assistance. Froncy had spoken directly to Kelda by radio to make a joint logistic plan and Jez was in constant touch with Izaki to make sure the Infantry training was as ChOn desired. They had yet to design a uniform for the mounted Infantry but decided to leave the foot-soldiers in their traditional tunic and skirt but with sprayform armour. Jez had discovered through experimentation that if the last coat of sprayform were sprayed directly onto a dye, it would incorporate that colour into the expanded finish. Karín had had armour made for all the Lancers in the red and indigo. It was just a matter of deciding what colour the Mounted Infantry would choose. They asked Marik to choose in concert with his Buq'ue platoon opposite number and Mastelik of the Matáng. It was a three-way radio conversation that resulted in red above and indigo below with the colours separated diagonally. Ch0n drew a design and sent it to Izaki and Mastelik. Marik got to work immediately on making the Arw'an platoon's.

A week out from the departure, Ch0n called the council to a meeting. He outlined the plans for the month or more he would be absent, allocating to Guerra the resources of Boro to rebuild the ruins by the lake and to have it ready to be occupied by the time Ch0n returned. Ch0n showed both Guerra and Boro the state of the ruin and told Guerra he would occupy one room as his personal quarters and office, He and Carmodi would have the other as a command centre and the main room would be used for eating, training, storage and accommodation for the team Guerra would need. Ch0n gave him the same instructions he had given Sonja a year before.

"Commander. Take as few workers as you need and as many. Jez will give you a squad of soldiers. Boro will provide the manpower for the rebuild. Doni will build corrals so they can run a few goats for milk and meat. Plant a bamboo forest close to the water. Sonja will locate the baths and the latrines. Kelda will see to the logistic needs. You will obviously need to take equipment for your work. The building is small enough to have artificial lighting installed. Take a false-fusion pack from the stores and rig it to a few strings of LED. One string for each room. I leave you to plan the details. You will answer to Sir Jez in my absence. Do you understand your task?"

"I am to rebuild the ruins, occupy them, set up a comms station and explore the caves and caverns behind the ruins. The rebuild is to be completed by Boro within the month. I answer to Sir Jez."

"Good. Any artefacts you find in the caves, and I mean any are to be logged and given to me after you analyze them. Failure to comply with this specific requirement will be punishable by death. Do you understand that part of your orders?"

Guerra looked at Ch0n, somewhat puzzled by this last direction.

"I do. I am puzzled by the need for it but yes, I understand."

"Good. Perhaps if you find something important, the reason will be clearer to you. In due course, a village will be established by the lake. It is a beautiful place with fresh water, shelter and fertile ground. Boro. There is a channel from the ruins that was once used by people from a tribe I will call the Vikings. They are sailors and navigators and may be warlike. Their boats are probably made from hardwood and will not easily be sunk. Because they are heavy, they will need access to the channel. Fill in the entrance to it. It will not be easy because the water is deep there. You will need to move stones from the shore and drop them in until it is less than waist deep at the entrance. Sir Jez, allocate one of the anti-armour tubes to the squad of soldiers. And take one of your giant crossbows and install it at the entrance to the ruins where it can be fired but not easily fired at. Boro, I will leave it to you to design a firing bay for it and the tube. We are going to build a miniature castle on the site of the ruins. Look at the place and plan it. Just a square tower six paces square at the base and five men high with the door two men's height from the ground, slit windows, a roof to fight from and a mount for the crossbow. You may use the retractable ladder from one of the landing craft to enter and leave. Store water and porridge inside. Commander Guerra, make sure there is a plan to hide all our Earth equipment in the base of the tower. I am not expecting any problems from the Vikings but they once used that place regularly and we do not know if they return from time to time. Sir Jez, maintain radio contact at all times between the ruins and the castle guardroom. Commander Guerra, if you see a boat approaching, get everybody out, guard the equipment you cannot take and leave the immediate defence of the tower to the soldiers, who will hold it until Jez can send re-enforcements. Do you all understand what I want?" He looked around. Everybody nodded. Nobody spoke.

"If you have any questions, we have the advantage of voice and image communications, thanks to Commander Guerra's foresight when he arrived and his work since. We still have a week to sort out the details but Commander Guerra can leave any time he is ready with Boro to review the site and make their plans."

Gavan Connell

They stood to leave. Ch0n motioned to Boro and Jez to remain behind.

"Boro. When you and Commander go to the ruins, I want you to commit him to the design of the building and make sure you know which room he will occupy. Put an explosive device in the wall or the ceiling with his number programmed to it. 15. Jez, stay close to him in the early days. Keep him focused on the rebuild and not the caves. The building is the priority. I want some trustworthy person on his excavation team to make sure he doesn't find and hide anything."

They both nodded.

Ch0n passed the week doing his rounds of the castle. The three new Knights were now to be seen riding their new mounts in and around the site. They spent a good portion of the day with the mounted Infantry, now resplendent in their dyed armour and leather helms. The night before they left, Ch0n called the three and Guerra to his quarters.

"I don't know how to put this so I will be blunt. By now you may be feeling certain umm changes taking place in your bodies. Commander Guerra said that the effects of the drugs to suppress your urges would be wearing off about now. I am telling you this because Karín has told me that some of the Lancers and village girls have taken a fancy to one or more of you. Commander Guerra has formed an alliance with Carmodi, which, judging from the noise coming from his quarters, has led to a successful joining of the two cultures. I will leave it up to you to decide if you like any of the women who may be approaching you with offers of err friendship or anything else. If

88

you do like one of them, let her lead you as she pleases through the err physical side of any liaison. You will know nothing about having sexual contact with a female but many of them are well experienced and know how to err get us started. There are no rules here about taking just one woman but I am about to make a rule regarding promiscuity. You may take a woman to be your wife and you may take a concubine or more than one if your wife agrees and only if she agrees but you must be able to provide for them all. I will not, however allow casual physical relationships between us and them, even though they may desire it. It lacks the dignity I want us to have in their eyes and it will separate us from them. No other reason. A thousand years ago, the Knights swore an oath of chivalry. It was a moral system which went beyond rules of combat and introduced the concept of Chivalrous conduct; qualities idealized by Knighthood, such as bravery, courtesy, honour, and gallantry toward women. I would have us all abide by this code, tho' it not be the norm amongst our folk. Do you all agree?" He looked at them in turn and they nodded their response.

The day before they left, the castle was humming with anticipation. There was to be a parade in the main square which would end with the column departing via the main gates for Matáng. For the first time on a ceremonial occasion, ChOn would be mounted on the oruk steer for all to see and the mounted Infantry would be paraded as a separate entity. Jez took the dais and made an appropriate speech to farewell the force and wish them well. ChOn waved to the crowd, turned the giant oruk to the gate and led his force down the path. He was followed by the three new Knights, line abreast in their full battle order with their katanas over their shoulders in the manner of

ChOn and Jez. Karín, Reny and the King's Own Cavalry followed in column of twos in their black turbans, red tunics and matching armour, then the Arw'an Company of mounted Infantry in their two-tone armour and black leather helms. Alik and Buyo mounted on ChOn's tlaque and then the twenty logisticians riding tlaques or seated on the travois behind the females, leading three spare mounts brought up the rear. ChOn had arranged for the guard commander to take images of the parade as it came towards the gates and he reached up and took his tablet as he passed below the tower. The expedition to Matáng had begun.

Two days later they arrived at the Buq'ue fort, ate and slept and then paraded the following day in the main square with the entire Household Cavalry and the First Battalion of the Royal Mounted Infantry as ChOn named them that day. They left the same day for the outposts. ChOn remained mounted on the oruk, which had made short work of the first two days. The entire fort lined the path to the gates to send them off and ChOn had the guard commander take an image like the previous one at the castle. Karín stood in her stirrups to look behind her. She caught ChOn's eye and he could see her smile even though she had her face covered by the helm.

A day and a half later they arrived at the new Western outpost, where they were received with great enthusiasm by the small village. Their new location was being developed in the manner of the castle and the fort with corrals, water conduits, a small communal bath and fertile soil being made from the mixture of goat manure and the sandy soil. The goat herd was now a communal one with just the one breeding male and the remainder of the males had been slaughtered for food or neutered. Ch0n was pleased with the progress and left the excited elder with a hand-held radio and a beanie.

They passed the grave of Alangadale and his Lancer companion-in-death. Some hours later they surveyed the scene of the massacre of the Matáng Battalion where the bones were still piled high and the smell of death still on the breeze, and by nightfall on the third day they were inside uncharted Matáng Lands. Ch0n ordered a change of formation with a few scouts leading and flank guards on both sides of the main body. The Knights formed the vanguard and then the Buq'ue troop of cavalry and infantry with the remainder of the King's Own Troop behind the logistic group as rear guard.

"We still have to prove to ourselves that this Mastelik is true to his word. Until I see him and his village I will remain cautious," he said to Karín. "We still have two days' march in front of us. Keep them vigilant."

"This is a lot different from the first day we met and we had to share the only domesticated tlaque between us, my agen. In a few short ...months we have become a formidable army. Even with our small numbers."

"It is the mobility as I have said all along. If Mastelik wants to betray me he will have only to form his own cavalry and we will be defeated easily on the field by sheer numbers of Infantry. It is important to maintain two advantages if you have the smaller force. One is mobility so you can fight on ground of your own choosing and the other is superior firepower. We had both with the cavalry and the hardwood bows but now we have lost the element of surprise. I have been reading about the laminating of wood on the minitron when I was looking for ways to strengthen and lengthen wood for roof supports so we could use lighter materials. I discovered that by sticking several thin sheets of wood together, you can create something very light but much stronger than something fashioned out of a single piece of wood. I think we should try laminating strips of the bamboo together to make a longer, stronger bow that will give us extra range. It might be that only the men can draw it and that would mean longer, slightly heavier arrows that should fly much further. Imagine hundreds of bowmen all lined up with a bow that could fire into the enemy's depth forces. Like a hundred of Jez's crossbows. All I have to do is work out how to stick them together and clamp them.

"Clamp?"

"Hold them with a machine that can be tightened by hand and hold the pressure so the glue sticks evenly."

"Glue?"

Ch0n sighed.

"A wet substance that when it is applied to one or both faces of two things, will stick them together when it dries."

"You mean like the liquid we used to make the big drum and we use to put the edges of the hide dwellings together so they don't tear in the breeze? It comes from the sap of a certain tree that grows everywhere. It is very sticky to the touch and we put it on two sides of the hides and when it is half dry we put them carefully together and put flat stones along the edge to hold

them in place for a day. When we take the stones away, it is impossible to separate the two hides."

"Exactly like that. Show me the tree when we pass one. I would know it and the sap. How do you harvest it?"

"We just cut the skin of the tree and it runs out. It is the colour of milk and runs slowly like porridge. We catch it in woven baskets that have been sealed using the same liquid."

"If it sticks leather hides, it should stick wood, sprayform, fletches and maybe arrow heads. Maybe stones or pottery. And it is a waterproofing substance? Now I am excited. Show me a tree."

"What is it like to ride the oruk? You have never told me or invited me to try it."

"I want it to be just for Knights. Like a symbol of their power and importance. In ancient history, soldiers rode in steel boxes with kinetic guns that my fist would enter. They were called, 'tanks' and struck fear into all who went against them because at first there was no weapon that could defeat their skins. Long before that, the king and his Knights were the only ones who rode. The Knights wore suits of metal and were so heavy that if they fell from their mounts, they had to be helped to their feet. From those Knights I have modelled ours but our armour is light. Their mounts, however and their appearance are designed as before to strike fear into all who oppose us. The cavalry are different. You have your tlaque for mobility and speed. In another year or so, the mounted Infantry will have the heavy tlaque to more easily bear the weight of two men. Three beasts with three different roles. One day when there are just the two of us I will let you ride the oruk."

"What are we going to do when we get to Matáng?"

"I don't know. We will move into the king's quarters. Mastelik will show us his village and we will take things from there. I am hoping you won't need to be executing any of their citizens, though. Better we leave that to Mastelik if it needs to be done. I have told him I want to meet the elders of all the outposts. If we have any rebels I suppose they will come from those. People who have lived far from their rulers sometimes get too independent and don't like being pulled back into line. Anyway, I don't need to stay long. If Mastelik is loyal and survives any challenge to his position, we will have no more problems with the Matáng. We can let them basically get on with their lives, make sure they are able to survive without needing to raid the Buq'ue again and we will visit from time to time. We will rotate the three cavalry troops, because they will have one but it will be based first at the castle for training and then at the Buq'ue fort for consolidation and then they will go home to Matáng where we will have had two troops already from the Arw'an and Buq'ue to make sure the villagers are loyal. I am thinking I might dispatch one of the Knights as well on a rotating basis to keep Mastelik honest for a while and to make sure that things are done my way. It is for their own good and all that will provide us with the social interchange you talked about long ago. Three tribes all taking husbands and wives from other tribes. Just one happy family."

"You make it sound so easy. I wish I were as confident."

"At the moment they have no means of defeating us in a battle. That is one way of making sure they serve us. When they are powerful enough to come back to the castle, we will have more warning, more weapons and a few surprises that they haven't seen yet. They will take a generation to recover from the loss of a thousand or more of their men. The single women will have to depend on other men or the welfare of the other villagers and the children will grow up accustomed to peace. Mastelik has seen what we have. He is his father's son and both he and his father told me he would have pulled back long before the end that I forced upon his king. No, I think we will have lasting peace as far as the Matáng are concerned. It is the Vikings I am curious about now. They obviously used to come to our side of the ocean a lot in days gone by. I am thinking they still do but not frequently and one day they may choose to look on the other side of the mountains to see who has set up a base at the end of their channel. There may be no issue but I plan never to be caught unawares."

"I too am curious but to see my people for I am one of them by blood if not by circumstances."

The next night they camped by the same waterhole the Matáng forces had used on the first night of their march to war. There was a guide waiting for them. He was dressed as an officer of the Matáng Army even though he seemed barely old enough.

"Well come My Lord! Commander Mastelik commanded me to proceed with you to the capital to show you the way. I am his cousin, Darel. He said you would know the significance of sending me alone."

"Well met, Darel. Yes. It is a sign of trust on his part and the offer of a hostage. You can mount a tlaque and take us to your cousin."

"I have ridden the talaque of Mastelik, My Lord. One day I will have my own."

"Darel, would you like to become the squire of the king of the Matáng?"

"What is a squire, My Lord?"

"A squire is like a personal assistant who learns by helping a Knight. We have four squires here." He turned on his microphone. "Alik. Bring the tlaque here next to me and take Darel with you. Tell him what a squire is."

Alik trotted up to Ch0n.

"Karin, take Buyo and then return to your place in the order of march. Alik. I am thinking that Darel might make a good squire for me. I want you to see if I am right. Tell me when we arrive. Darel. You tell Alik the way and he can pass it to me if I wander from the path." He gave Karín the hand signal to switch to eleven.

"That was a smart move, my Ch0n. If he accepts, we will have a hostage at the castle and you will have a future Camp Commandant for Matáng."

"I have a Camp Commandant in Mastelik. I want a Matáng Knight. The Knights answer to me alone and they have licence to roam the kingdom if they choose. I want much more than a Camp Commandant. I want a faithful Knight to watch over the entire Matáng and in a year I will have one unless I am mistaken."

Finally they crested a rise and saw the Matáng capital in the distance. Ch0n was surprised at its size. It was far bigger than the Buq'ue fort. The land around it was starting to show green tips from Mastelik's irrigation system but the barren plains told Ch0n much about why the Matáng had had to raid the Buq'ue. They could not sustain their town on the available grass. The women were additional prizes for the king and the raiders. The herds were the real target.

A lone rider left the town and approached them. Ch0n knew it was Mastelik as he was the only Matáng with a tlaque. He resisted the temptation to talk to him on the radio and instead held up his hand and halted the column.

"We will make him come to us. It's not much but it is a show of power on my part. Posture, we might call it. He has to come to me. I won't meet him half way. He will understand and it is why he didn't let us just ride to the gates unescorted."

"I knew you would do it. I would have done the same. As would any Commander or King."

Mastelik slowed his beast to a walk and halted in front of Ch0n's massive oruk. He dismounted and unsheathed his katana, holding it with both hands flat in front of his face.

"Well come, My Lord. I offer you my sword as a sign of faith and fealty."

"Well met, Mastelik. Sheath your sword. Your faith and fealty I doubt not." He watched Mastelik look around the lead group. "These Knights have recently come to us from the same place as I did. You will meet them shortly. Your cousin is at the rear talking to my squire. I think he would make me an excellent squire if he would choose it."

"He would My Lord, and for reasons not only relating to his ability. For he is my cousin, it is true but he is the bastard son of the former king, Sith, born to a woman who was not one of his concubines, but a Buq'ue slave and as such has no rank or entitlements before the Arw'an. He is not exactly shunned but he has had a hard life. Only I have been his ally. He lives in my household. His mother was… well she is no longer with us."

"Then it is settled," broke in Karín. *"He will be the king's squire. Or mine for he is my bastard cousin."*

Only Mastelik saw Ch0n's smile.

"Then it is indeed settled," he said. "He will be my squire. Now, Mastelik, mount up and lead us into my Matáng capital."

The column wended its way down the track and into the gates of Matáng. People lined the streets and watched in silent awe as the oruk followed Mastelik's tlaque deeper into the town. They were moved to whispers and murmurs of wonder at the female Lancers and then they became silent again as the mounted Infantry passed them by. Each one among them knew at that moment why the Buq'ue and Arw'an had been able to defeat their army so comprehensively. They had known it when Mastelik returned and gave them the news of the disaster but this coordinated display of might was living proof.

"Look at my subjects," Ch0n said to Karín. "This is why I wanted to come so soon. I wanted them to be awestruck and fearful so as to prevent any minor uprisings. Somewhere in the town are the elders of all the Matáng outposts and I want them to see this as well. Now. For the past while I have been thinking of a plan. It involves Alik. I had been thinking of sending him here as Mastelik's squire to show Mastelik the things he needs to know to become a Knight of the Matáng. But that plan involved selecting a squire from the Arw'an to replace him. He is not really old enough to become a Knight yet but I have to be flexible with the rules to suit my plan. And he did acquit himself well and bravely in the battle. What think you of making a special rank and position for him so he can stay here and assist Mastelik?"

"I think it is a sound idea. You are right. He is not yet ready to become a Knight. Jez was a lot older to begin with. More mature. Alik is younger. I will also need someone here to supervise the raising of the Matáng Lancers. I think Marelik would be suitable. I will select the sixty and she can supervise the building of the stables and the basic training of the Lancers while we are getting their tlaque. That alone will take several weeks to drive them here from their grazing grounds unless we find some herds nearby."

"Or we could leave thirty tlaque here and train new ones ourselves back at the castle. That would save months."

"Would you leave your tlaque here for Alik and train yourself another?"

"No. He is mine and I have had him since the beginning. He knows me and I, him." He laughed then and the sound of it washed over Karín like music as it always did. "But what if we take half the Matáng Lancers back with us while Alik and Marelik are training those who remain behind. The thirty we take back can return with thirty tlaque and lead the other thirty. Look. We are almost in the main square. Meet me on one."

Mastelik led the procession into the main square. Ch0n ordered them to form up by unit in line abreast to the dais. Mastelik dismounted and invited Ch0n to do the same. Alik appeared from nowhere to take control of the oruk. Ch0n looked around. Darel was towards the rear of the parade, mounted on Ch0n's tlaque. People in the crowd nearest him were nudging each other and pointing. Ch0n dismounted and was about to help Karín down when she threw her leg across the beast's back and landed lightly on her feet beside him. Before they had a chance to move, Alik spoke.

"Darel would be your squire, My Lord. I will train him well."

"No, Alik. I will train him. You will have other things to do."

Mastelik ushered Ch0n and Karín up the steps to the throne. He stood beside it and Ch0n seated himself. Karín took up a position beside him. Ch0n removed his helm. Karín removed hers and there was an audible reaction from the crowd. This was the warrior woman whose reputation was already well known to the Matáng. She had reportedly been born to one of Sith's slave girls who had been dragged from the far reaches of the country and who had then escaped to the Buq'ue, only to be returned years later manacled, whereby she had borne another daughter, the wife of Alangadale. This one before them was totally ruthless to those who opposed her aget, the king, in any way. She had formed the troops of female cavalry which had decimated their army from the day it set foot on Buq'ue soil and then had cut it to shreds in front of the Arw'an stronghold. Karín relished the reaction and looked at every face in the crowd in turn. Finally, Mastelik hushed them with a wave of his hand.

"People of the Matáng. Look upon your king and mine, the Lord Ch0n. I have told you how my father accepted his right to be king after the Ch0n defeated Sith in single combat and so saved our army from total annihilation. In battle he gave no quarter but in victory he gave us honour, which is more than Sith ever did for us. The Ch0n rode from his stronghold where his army, the likes of which we had never seen and part of which you now see before you, would have killed every last man among us. He rode through the midst of the battle on an orok, this very beast with another similarly mounted. Behind them rode their female warriors, those you see here. They rode to where Sith and my father were directing the battle, where the Ch0n slew Sith and my father in turn but not before my father had conceded defeat and ordered the surrender. The Ch0n had the head of Sith taken to the gates of the Arw'an stronghold where we saw it and knew the day was done, tho' we had known it long before. And so from a force of more than two thousand, we eight hundred survivors expected to be enslaved.

Gavan Connell

But instead, we were offered the choice of swearing fealty to the ChOn in return for safe passage back to this place where our families would receive us. We came fully armed. We came with honour for there is no dishonour in defeat by a superior force. And now the ChOn, your king and mine has come to show you there will be no more war between us and the Buq'ue or the Arw'an. Step forward the elders of each village and swear your fealty to the king or challenge him in combat. There is no other choice. Step forward now."

Mastelik went before ChOn and knelt before him.

"My Lord, this I have done before but now I would do it before my people so there can be no misunderstanding. I swear fealty to you as my king and I offer my sword in your protection and the protection of all in your kingdom."

ChOn waited patiently as a dozen groups of tribal elders came before him. Karín had moved a pace forward while this was taking place and her katana was naked, the point resting easily on the ground beside her. It was a move not un-noticed by those mounting the stairs. When they were all standing on the dais, ChOn stood.

"People of the Matáng, Buq'ue and Arw'an, hear me. There has been enough war. I will have no more of it and let any who provokes it know he will suffer greatly for his actions. Mastelik has told you of my origins and as unlikely as they seem to you, they are true. I came alone but now there are three more like me who have since come. He beckoned to them and the three mounted the dais and stood near him, giants all. These are my Knights. They answer to none but me. They will spend their lives in the service of the three kingdoms doing as they see fit or doing my bidding when I desire it. There are two more Knights, one from the Arw'an and one from the Buq'ue and soon we will have one from the Matáng but he needs to be trained first in the ways of Knights. And so I am going to leave among you, one who is not a Knight but who is a trainer of Knights. He is Alik. He holds the rank of Colonel in the Arw'an Army and answers only to me and the Knight, Sir Jez of the Arw'an. He will train the Camp Commandant, Mastelik until he and I are satisfied that Mastelik is ready to become the first Knight of the Matáng. It should not take long. Come forward, Alik so they may know you."

Alik handed the reins of the oruk to the nearest Lancer and slowly mounted the stairs. He badly wanted to run but managed to resist the temptation. He had no idea what a 'kernal' was nor did anybody else but he didn't care. He stood tall before Ch0n, who told him to face the crowd.

"This is he. Colonel Alik of the Arw'an. Heed his words for they come from my own mouth. I am taking as my squire, the Matáng Officer, Darel." He silenced the crowd reaction with the palm of his hand. "Darel may one day return to this place as the second Knight of the Matáng. Next, Brigadier General Karín, Commander of the Household Cavalry will select sixty women from among you who would be the first of the Matáng Lancers and ride into battle and to ceremonial occasions such as this, mounted as are these before you. Of the sixty, thirty will accompany us back to Arw'an Castle where they will enter the school of cavalry. The remaining will remain here and be schooled by one of the existing Lancers, who will be selected from those who would offer to stay with Alik. All those details will be decided by her. Now I wish to recognize the Commander of the Matáng Army, Brigadier General Mastelik of the Matáng. Step forward, Mastelik." Mastelik stepped forward and Ch0n took a medal from is pocket.

"To you, Brigadier General Mastelik of the Matáng, I award the medal of service in recognition of your loyalty and work here at Matáng. Wear this with pride as you are the first among your people to be awarded it."

He nodded to Karín who took up the thread.

"Those among you who are female, single, have no children and wish to be among the first of the Matáng Lancers, come forward to the foot of the stairs."

Ch0n donned his helm and spoke to the commanders. "I will instruct Mastelik to show you to your quarters. When I stop talking to him, leave the square in the same order you entered." He looked at Alik.

"Congratulations, Alik. But before you take up your position, I need you to show Darel how to get the beast off the square. Report back to me when all are settled."

"My Lord, you honour me with this thing, tho' I know not exactly what I need to do."

"I will tell you the what of it and you will have to work out most of the how of it for it is an idea recently hatched and I have no idea how we are going to see it through. I trust you and Mastelik to do it together. Go now."

Then,

"Mastelik, you may leave the square."

The troops paraded from the square with Alik leading the oruk and Ch0n's tlaque following with Darel in the saddle. Karín was at the foot of the steps talking to a crowd of women.

"The role you will play is somewhat complex and exciting as well as essential to the defence of all our people and the prestige of women in the village for we are an elite force in the king's army. Your army. The selection process is simple. I need sixty women. You are perhaps three times that. On the king's throne I am going to place sixty stones. Each of you may take one. But in order to do so, you first have to run to the gatehouse, run around the flag I have left planted in the ground outside, return and mount the steps. The first sixty will get a stone. No more. There are no other rules. Now GO!"

The crowd dispersed in a wild rush of pushing and shoving and women sprinted towards the gatehouse. Karín knew it would be several frantic minutes before the first of them would reappear. The flag was far enough outside the stockade for those who had been closest to lose the advantage and close enough so that it would be a reasonably quick process. She reached inside her tunic and brought forward the pouch, removing sixty small, smooth river stones, usually reserved as ammunition for her sling. She climbed the steps and placed them on the throne. Ch0n was waiting there for her.

"I love this process. The fastest will be here first and the most desperate last but we will get a good mix as usual."

"I will have to separate them into two groups of thirty. How will I do that? They will all want to go to Arw'an."

"Select any who were recently widowed and the remainder by lots. I want all the widows away from here where they won't be caught up in any talk of treason. In the Lancers they will be provided for. Here? They will need a man until we sort out the herds and the crops."

The first to arrive was a long striding, athletically built woman not unlike Karín herself but not quite as tall and her hair was fiery auburn, much different from the rest. She picked up her stone before the next woman had even arrived at the foot of the stairs. Karín told her to go to the far end of the dais. She looked at Karin and grinned and then looked quickly at Ch0n before she blushed deeply and turned away. Karín had not seen the interaction but Ch0n felt something stir deep inside him and his eyes followed her. When she turned around at last, she caught him staring. She looked away quickly and Ch0n saw the colour rise again in her cheeks before she took a long cloth from around her waist and made it into a turban that covered all but her eyes.

The women started to arrive in a trickle and then a rush and as for the previous test at the Buq'ue fort, the last group contained several bloodied faces, dirty tunics and scratched limbs. Finally there were no more stones to be collected. It was then Karín revealed she had one in her hand. She held it up.

"This is available for the asking. You five were the next. Decide among yourselves who deserves it and I will accept your decision."

Four of the women looked back at her and then at each other. The fifth ran up the stairs and took the stone from Karín's hand.

"We have decided," she said.

Karín looked at Ch0n. Ch0n looked at the woman and back at Karín.

"Welcome to the Matáng Lancers," he said. And then, "to you others, there will be a need for willing men and women here in the town. The work to be done to change the way of things will be just as important, tho' not so glamorous. Be disappointed but stay willing. Know that under my rule, men and women are equal. There will be no men's work nor women's."

They stayed only for a few days because the town could not sustain the herd of tlaque without degrading the capacity of the fields to sustain their goats. Ch0n spent those days organizing the council along the lines of the Arw'an council. He placed the priority on herd management and pasture improvement so the need to roam and raid the Buq'ue outposts would not remain. He told them to establish a ranch a day's walk away near the stream. He oversaw the planting of the thousands of bamboo cuttings on the river flats and showed them an image of the trees needed for their bows and their manner of drying and shaping. By the time he left, Mastelik had a list of projects to complete and the means of at least planning them. There was a known herd of tlaque within three days march but they were man-shy from having been hunted. Ch0n told Mastelik to get the projects completed and maintain constant progress reports so that when the infrastructure was in place, the Lancers would round up the tlaque herd and the new Matáng Lancers could be deployed to look for oruk and the silken goats in areas that Guerra would try and identify from images.

Karín, meanwhile, had separated her new recruits into the two groups she needed. She and the other commanders set them a punishing training schedule with the other Lancers. As Karín had imagined, Marelik had wanted to stay with Alik and she was selected. The story of her dalliances with two Matáng officers that had resulted in both their deaths was suppressed under pain of death. Almost all of the thirty recruits were newly widowed or had lost fathers or brothers in the recent battles. This group was shown how to stretch their thighs and buttocks by Karín and they also spent a time each day mounted behind their sisters.

Ch0n and Karín barely saw each other for those days so at night they lay discussing their work and planning for the next day. Buyo lay beside them listening and enjoying not having to be alone. She left only when the time for sleeping arrived and then she retired to her room behind the curtain and listened to the sounds of Ch0n and Karín coupling until finally she could stand it no more and went and lay with them while they were joined. Afterwards, she kissed Karín on the cheek and clambered over her body to where Ch0n lay. Karín said nothing, even though she knew Buyo wanted ChOn's dewen inside her. Later, only Buyo saw her smiling in the blackness.

They marched in splendour out through the gates of Matáng to a wild reception. ChOn had won them over in his short time, especially the women who saw him as their saviour from a life of being subservient to their men. They now had a voice on the council and meaningful work in the community. Their men were forced to clean and bathe themselves every few days and go to work somewhere. Their daughters and sisters were riding out to an exciting future as Matáng Lancers and finally they had a king who gave back at least as much as he demanded of them.

As they rode through the gates, ChOn stood in his stirrups. He had a final wave for Alik and Marelik as they started the slow climb to the rise. Behind him, Karín was also looking at the parade. Her Lancers now numbered two hundred in all, even though sixty of them were still without mounts. Darel rode behind Buyo and somewhere in the group, riding behind one of her new Lancer-sisters, rode Maní, the widow of Alangadale, her auburn hair hidden beneath a turban."

Gavan Connell

Chapter Six: Revelations

They pushed past the stream where the ranch was to be built and before nightfall they had reached the spring which was the last water before the Buq'ue border. They camped there for the night before Ch0n changed the order of march and the next day they passed the pile of stinking bones and turned towards the Buq'ue fort, or Buq'ue as Ch0n had taken to calling it. Around mid-afternoon, Karín rode up to him and asked him if they could stop for a short while as one of the new recruits was the widow of Alangadale and wanted to see where he was buried.

"His widow? Why didn't someone tell me? I would meet her and give her my condolences."

"Perhaps you might like to show her the grave, Lord Ch0n. Then you might confirm to her what she has been hearing from the sisters, that you slew him reluctantly after offering him what you offered Mastelik. I have seen her. She is very quiet, despite her obvious beauty and her athletic prowess. It was she who finished the selection race first. She is different from the rest as you will see. I feel a bond with her for she looks a lot like me."

Ch0n felt his heart skip. He told Karín to order the halt when they were closer and said he would take the woman himself to show her the place. Some time later, they halted and Ch0n waited while one of the Lancers rode to him and halted at his side.

"My Lord, this is the woman, Maní. Brigadier General Karín told me to bring her to you."

Ch0n nodded to the honey eyes and held out his hand. Maní took it and the tlaque fell in behind Ch0n. He wheeled the beast around to the right and walked it slowly to a copse of trees where a red ribbon still fluttered above a pile of flat stones. He drew the oruk to a halt and Maní dropped lightly to the ground. Ch0n followed her and they stood side by side looking at the grave until Maní broke the silence.

"I am told you slew him mercifully and buried only him, leaving the rest of your enemies to the sun and carrion eaters."

"I would have slain all of his men gladly to have saved him alone had it been possible but his honour would have none of my offers and his bravery in the face of certain death knew no bounds. I knew not that he had an aget, not that it would have changed things but perhaps it were better that I knew not. And now you have the Household Cavalry instead of a fireplace. I am truly sorry for I have no love of killing, tho' I am a soldier. Or perhaps because I am one"

"Be not sorry, My Lord. The manner of his death and the honour you bestowed upon him is far more than he would have received from his stepfather, Sith who was a cruel king and mourned little the loss of his three sons, all of whom you slew, directly or indirectly. And yes, now I have the sisterhood that

you offered me through the Lady Karín and I will be as good a soldier as was my agen. And I would serve you as I did him for just as he is entombed here with one of the sisters without me, so am I living here without him but among them."

"Woman, I would look upon your face."

"Your every and any wish is my command, My Lord, but first tell me why for you have already seen it."

"Because it pleased me beyond words and I would see more of it. I can give you no better reason than that."

"And you gazed at my back as I walked from you. I felt your eyes burning me and when I turned, they were upon me still but only briefly."

"Yes."

"My Lord, to be a king is to have whatever one would choose to have. Do I see it in your gaze that you would have me?"

Ch0n laughed.

"Just show me your face. I saw something in it that filled me with wondering."

Maní unwound the turban from her neck and then from her face. Ch0n looked closely at it. Maní lowered her eyes and blushed but Ch0n lifted her chin.

Gavan Connell

"You are a true beauty cast in the same furnace as Karín for if I were to be sure of nothing else, you have the Viking blood as does she. Your hair is darker but different from the rest of the tribes I have seen. Your nose is finer and your eyes are not black. And you are taller than everybody except for myself, Karín and the three Knights. We will have to talk about your family background when we arrive at Arw'an."

"As you wish, My Lord."

"Mání. I am not sorry I stared at you but I hope it did you no offence."

"To be hungered after by a king offers no offence, My Lord, tho' it did surprise me."

She rewound the turban and went to the grave.

"Goodbye my love. Lie well in the earth beside your new lover."

They reached Buq'ue two days later. The new recruits were the scene of much curiosity, given that their mothers may well have been abducted from within the Buq'ue. For two days, they stayed and rearranged the allocation of tlaque and other resources before Ch0n set off again with the new King's Own Troop, the Arw'an Mounted Infantry and thirty new Lancers. Two days later they were within sight of the castle. Ch0n waited on the rise while Karín led the Lancers past him. He watched them all in turn as their eyes widened when they saw the castle. He picked out Mání as she passed him. She sat well on the tlaque and Ch0n knew she would command the troop before long.

They had been away a month. In that time, the post-battle cleaning up had been completed and with the new grass showing lush green through the blackened plain, all signs of it would soon disappear. Ch0n called a council meeting and was briefed by all in turn.

Boro had completed all of the Knights' quarters. Jez had moved from his quarters into what had been Ch0n's before the castle was completed. Ch0n asked Guerra if he would like to move into Jez's old quarters to which he agreed. Boro nodded knowingly when Ch0n told him to make any changes necessary if Guerra required them.

Sonja had been in maintenance mode cleaning up after the battle. The town was tidy and humming.

Kelda's crew was expanding to fulfil the needs of an ever-growing population and she asked Ch0n if he might investigate the construction of the brick ovens he had mentioned when they found the clay. Ch0n suggested that as well as that, it was time to re-enforce the concept of money and expand the system of barter in the kingdom so people who knew how to cook, wash clothes or cut hair could sell their services and take pressure off the public system. He promised to show them his plan the following day when they had found someone who could be trusted to control the mass-production of the silver and gold pieces. Guerra suggested aluminium and copper pieces as well, forged from the salvage from the two landing craft, which seemed so obvious to Ch0n that he chided himself for not having thought of it before.

"Are you in a position to oversee the introduction of a monetary system?" he asked Guerra afterwards. "It would need a system of weights and measures so we would know that only the official gold and silver entering the 'mint' would be weighed and no extra or shortfall would occur. I have the templates for the pieces already ground into the moulds and the Fresnel lenses will melt the metals easily."

"I could oversee it but I could not actually do it because it is work anybody can do under supervision and I will be needed more for the checks and balances of the day's production. We would need enough for everybody to have something to start with. Then we could pay the public servants a salary and that would inject cash into the economy. From there it would be just an experiment. You could buy raw gold and silver for say, thirty-five percent of its weight in pesos. That would encourage a mining boom and treasury could control all the known resources."

"Will it lead to crime and corruption? We have no crime at the moment because everybody has something and nobody has anything that is worth stealing. Except the Knights. Once we go down this path will we need to start a bank? Oh Dear! I hope I haven't bitten off more than I can chew."

"The option is to just divide Kelda's resources and separate them. Two cooking areas, two hospitals. It could easily be done. We have the space. Have you noticed that most families

have only one child, by the way? There are exceptions but the majority are one-child couples."

"I think it is typical of a nomadic race where food is always in short supply. In Buq'ue they have more and in Matáng too. I think we will see a population explosion in a year or so. Let's try the money and see how it works. Let it be known that any crimes of theft will be punished by expulsion from the castle and the forfeit of all goods and property of the guilty party. Grand theft will be punishable by the forfeiture of all property followed by death by the sword. That way we won't need to build a jail."

"I'll get on to it. On another subject, I have taken Carmodi as my aget. I suspect the Knights are already feeling their hormones racing and will soon be finding the joys of ijon and taking women of their own. Being smaller, I wasn't dosed up as much. The scouts had enough to drug two of me. You might tell Karín to keep an eye on her Lancers. You were right, by the way. I could never go back now either. Not after living free like this. Your preparedness back there in disabling the module did us all a big favour."

"This is just the beginning of it all. You can still carry out your mission from here, far better than you could have with a month on the ground and a stream of information heading back to Earth. This way you can live it and breathe it and then send it back. One day you will be a household name on earth. We all will. I just hope that when they come we are ready for them. I would rather try to trade than be colonized. But that is a long way off yet. Maybe twenty years. Now. Enough of money and love. Tell me about the alien site and the ruins."

"I have mapped the cavern and its contents as far as I can tell. The sarcophagi where you found the two bracelets revealed nothing else of interest. There is a flat table in front of the throne which seems to be a map of the universe showing four planets and if I am not mistaken, the worm highways. One of the planets is a long way away and the other three relatively close. I am going to hazard a guess based on what I have seen and what we know exists on Earth, that this planet and Earth are two of the three, that there is a third and the fourth is the aliens' home planet. In the middle of the table is a pattern of circular depressions the size of the two rings you found and in the centre of them, a circular hole some fifteen inches deep. I am assuming that at some point, there were other rings and some sort of joystick." He looked knowingly at ChOn. "Maybe it's a communications device. Maybe it's a flying table. Maybe they had teleportation back then but I doubt it or the entire planet-load of them would be here. The ruins have been cleaned out of debris but nothing more there because we concentrated first on blocking the entry to the channel as you ordered. My theory on it all is that the aliens lived in that cavern system for years and the locals used to come here for religious education or dancing. There is no evidence inside the main cavern of trade. It is as clean as if it has been swept of everything except the aliens. We have found more tunnels but I told my team not to venture down any of them because you would want to be first. That's it. No. I was able to monitor all your radio communications back here so we know we have constant comms from Arw'an to Buq'ue and Matáng, which we knew anyway but there are no dead spots in between. I didn't monitor any traffic on a frequency other than Freq One."

"Good. Well done on all that. You're especially right about one thing. I'd like to take Karín and explore the tunnels. We will need cordage and LEDs. Next time you go, we will go along for the ride."

Guerra nodded and left ChOn's rooms and went across the corridor. Carmodi was waiting for him there in the office. Guerra took her by the hand and led her to their cottage.

"It's past our bed time, Carmodi. Now. Show me that thing you did last night."

"My Lord, Guerra, it is just twilight!"

Though it was getting dark, ChOn went to the corrals where Doni was waiting. On the way, he chatted briefly with Mori and his parrot. Mori was now living in a stone and bamboo dwelling behind the main cage. It was a small but neat dwelling with a cage of small whistlers hanging from the rafters. The parrot had a perch on a stand with a stone water bowl. It lived on Mori's shoulder and slept on the perch. Occasionally it would stretch its four-foot wings and soar skywards, round the tower atop the castle and return to Mori's shoulder. When ChOn passed, it was on its perch and Mori was sitting in his doorway. He didn't stand for ChOn but merely waved to him as he passed.

"Good evening, King. What do ye think of me new 'ouse, then?"

"Greetings, Mori. It is a house indeed fit for the Royal Bird keeper of the Arw'an and his prized kwidada."

119

Gavan Connell

"Ye know, King, people walk up this path and stop to look at me dáguia and me tweeters and me kwidada. They used tae stop outside me old shelter and laugh at me for a silly old fool. Now they nod their 'eads to me and say nuthin'. Ye couldn't know 'ow that feels, ye that is a mighty soldier and a king, tae have people respect ye where they once ridiculed ye. One day I'll be on me death bed and I 'ope y'ur there so I can thank ye one last time for it. That's all now, son. Be off wi' ye."

So, dismissed by his bird keeper, ChOn left him to his new house and continued up the path. The words from old Mori had touched him deeply. He had heard similar from Karín praising his ability to give humble people a role in his scheme of things but to hear it from the man's own mouth was a different thing altogether. He arrived at Doni's corral with a spring in his step.

Together, ChOn and Doni inspected every corral and stall, every beast and newborn. Doni, once the herder, was now managing many hundreds of head of stock that crossed four breeds. He was revelling in his work, the results of which were easily seen in the clean paddocks and corrals with their healthy-looking beasts.

"I have heard that the oruk went easily over the ground and did not tire, My Lord. I am pleased for you. It is still only half grown but they are almost as strong as fully grown creatures so it was but a walk in the sunshine. They have been known to cover great distances, the oruk herds and your weight was as nothing to him. He would have walked that distance easily only a few days after he was born had the herd been migrating. It was a good test of him. How are your thighs?"

"I have been astride the tlaque every day for a full year, Doni. My thighs are fine. I raised the stirrup cup so I didn't have to spread my legs as wide. Having a custom-made saddle helps as well. The oruk program will be a success. I am impatient to see how the half-oruk, half tlaques turn out. They should be wonderful creatures, taller or as tall as and heavier than a standard tlaque. If it weren't interfering too much with the natural way, I would kill all the oruk bulls and put a tlaque buck to run with them. There is nothing to do but wait."

"That is so, My Lord. Have you given more thought to the people being allowed to own a house goat? I feel that when the next drop occurs, we will be able to neuter all the males and allow people to keep one female for milk with her castrated male kid at foot. We could allocate females already pregnant and let them live in the villages eating the grass and weeds and eventually providing milk. The kids would be weaned and sent back here. It would reduce pressure on the pastures."

"How about each house where there is a person too old to work but willing to tend a goat? It will be some time before Boro has nothing to build and we don't want people becoming nomadic herders again. It is too inefficient. I will ask Sonja because she will know if there is enough green space to do it. Maybe just a select few will have the space and the means."

"My Lord, when are we going to need the extra sixty tlaque? I fear we may not have enough neutered males left in the wild herd. Already we have taken more than a hundred. The herd is now almost all females with the one bull and what remains of

Gavan Connell

those we cut. We need to enlarge the herd quickly and find more males to cut or we will not be able to supply our needs."

"Good point, Doni and one well-made and timely. Tell your herdsmen that in three days we will leave for the overhang and we will bring back the entire herd as we did with the others. Then we will drive those we don't need immediately to where the other herd is grazing and the bull there can look after the females, even tho' he is young. I will kill the dominant bull as I did with the domestic herd and my tlaque will lead them back as before. Make sure you have everything ready in six days. We will drive them here and separate them straight away and operate. We know that if we cut them and sew them they will recover so after we do it, we can just let those we don't keep to run loose the next day. I have told the Matáng to build a ranch, which is a place dedicated solely to the raising of goats and tlaque, half a day's forced ride from their village. If we go downriver from here, we could do the same and release this space for expansion or just for goats. The tlaque, breeding goats and the males could stay there with just those waiting to be slaughtered actually within the walls. It need to be just far enough away so the water is clean enough for the animals to drink. I would like to talk to Sonja also about allowing selected families to live outside the walls to husband the stock in smaller holdings, called farms. They would build a permanent shelter away from here, no closer than the ranch, where they could keep one or two female tlaque for breeding, or twenty goats with one central male at the ranch. They could then sell or trade them to us. Having a central ranch is a good way to manage stock but it is a lot of work to feed so many. I do not want outposts as such although we could probably have them now if we control where they are. It is all part of yours and

Sonja's city and animal management as well as Jez's defence of the villagers."

"I think the idea has merit, Lord. We are many concentrated here in such a small space. If we allow those who wish to move out and yet still be close enough for us to control, it would take a lot of strain off the 'logistics' as you call them. And it will also stop people who are used to moving getting bored with being always in the one place."

"Then we will come up with a plan that sees people leave or stay and the castle becoming a place to where they can come to trade as well as for shelter in times of need. The space inside the walls will be more dedicated to things military, such as the barracks and the Lancer school."

Ch0n went back to his stables where Buyo and Darel were still cleaning their tack. Buyo was a thorough teacher and the oruk's saddle was shining like new on its rest. Darel was a strapping young man with the stubble of his beard well formed.

"How old are you, Darel?"

"Almost twenty summers, My Lord. I am older than Alik by several summers so I suppose it is usual for a squire to be a lot younger."

"There are no rules for the selection of a squire, Darel. They are selected for their qualities, not their age. But you are indeed older than the other squires. Because of that, I need to tell you that you may not take an aget while you are a squire. You may take a lover or more than one but no woman may share your quarters as your aget. I need your undivided service until you resign or become a Knight in your own right. Do you understand that condition? If you are not happy with it, I free you now from your service. I see you have met Friday, my wolf."

"I do understand it. And I am happy to abide by it for the rewards are great for so little an inconvenience. And yes, I have, My Lord but he likes me not. He would allow me to scratch his ears as Buyo does but would not allow me through the entrance to your rooms."

"He will get used to you. Do not push too fast with him, let him decide when. Once he knows your position in the household he will let you come and go. Just click your fingers and call him. It will help if you have a morsel for him in the beginning. Buyo and Beny will continue to show you the things you need to do here. Beny will show you where to get your uniform and boots. Tomorrow we will start your daily weapon training with Brigadier General Karín, the four Knights and their squires and myself. Beny will show you what you will need. In due course you will become the second Knight of the Matáng but first you must learn the ways of Knighthood. Buyo, I think Karín has need of you inside. Darel, I would speak with Sir Jez. You may retire now but listen for my call."

Harry, Arturo and Ivor were deep in discussion.

"Now we are back here and have our own quarters I am going to take Ch0n's advice and let that Reny try my dick," said Harry in English. "She has been pestering me since we arrived and I had no idea why until Ch0n's talk before we left. If

Guerra's experience is anything to go by, I won't regret it. None of us will."

"Might I remind you we are forbidden to speak anything but Arw'an, Harry. I know it was easier for us when we were alone before but now we are able, it is to disobey Ch0n and that is not something I wish to do," cut in Arturo.

"I will never get used to this language if I live to be a hundred. But my point remains. You two should do the same if you have the opportunity with your admirers. Or maybe an alliance with the Matáng would be better. Ch0n wants to unite the tribes so to have one of their women living here with the privileges of the wyf of a Knight would help the national interest."

"The woman, Salina has been the foremost of the Lancers in wanting my time," cut in Arturo. *"I find her pleasing to the eye more so than the rest. Perhaps she has seen me looking at her and so knows she is more favoured. If she wishes it, I will invite her to my dwelling."*

"Before we start looking for a permanent woman, we should first see how long it will be before we are in working order and then we need to choose carefully because of the limitations put upon us. Your Reny is willing enough, Harry. You have been telling us for weeks. As for Salina, Arturo, I know her not. I, too have had my share of sidelong stares from the Lancers but I have seen one of Kelda's girls making eyes at me and of all I have seen, she is the one that pleases me the most, tho' I still do not know her name. It is time to see if we are real men. I

propose we all invite someone to share our beds and then we can compare notes on how we fare."

They separated and went to check that their squires had cleaned their tack and that their tlaques were properly housed. A short time later they regrouped and headed for the central eating area in the hope they would come across their prospective lovers.

"Jez, I think you need to find another squire because Beny is going to have a big task in front of him teaching four new squires. It will take him away from you to the point where you will find yourself lacking in assistance. I propose that he be promoted to Senior Squire and appointed Chief Instructor of Squires. He would remain in your service so you may continue his training but you would have a second squire whose training you would share with Beny and he would in turn share his time with the other Knights and their squires. What say you?"

"In truth, My Lord, he heard of the honour you bestowed upon Alik and has been loitering around me ever since you returned hoping something might happen. Had you not proposed this, he might well have suggested it himself. He is ready for such a position. Will I send for him? I suspect he is probably waiting at the door in hope."

'Call him and we will see."

After Beny had come and gone, Ch0n called to Karín and she and Jez discussed the plan Ch0n had made to go to the overhang and move the entire tlaque herd to be united with the free ranging domestic herd.

"Things are moving quickly with the expansion of the Lancers and the mounted Infantry. I want everything in place as soon as possible so we can concentrate on the exploration of the caverns and the establishment of the Lakeside Communications Centre and a separate tlaque and goat breeding ranch downriver. I had hoped that we might have time to settle down after the war but it seems we have more to do before then."

"My Lord, before we talk more about the tlaque herd, I have selected another Adjutant for the Lancers. Or rather, Carmodi has selected one for me and I have appointed her. She is similar to Carmodi in every way. In fact it is Carmodi's sister, Freda. Carmodi told me she and Freda have always had similar likes and dislikes and their mother was very strict with them so they have the honesty we want. I would not have known how to select another so I am happy for her to be on trial for a while under Carmodi's instruction. She has already asked me if I will approve the enlargement of the new barracks for the school on the third side of the square you call the parade ground. If Sonja agrees and you do, I will ask her to oversee it with Boro as her first role. She wishes to ask the sisters how they would change their quarters to make it easier for them. I like that idea."

"I am happy to let Sonja decide the location. It seems sensible to have the new barracks there but it is for her to decide. Once she is happy, we will discuss the when and the how of it with Boro."

"And the trip to the overhang. Will it be for all the Lancers? They have not had a trip to the overhang since the battle. I think they deserve one and the Matáng Troop will see what being part of the group means to us and will want to share that with us."

Ch0n grinned.

"How could we go to the overhang without all of them? It is part of their training to have a holiday in that paradise. And it will give them all a chance to see where their sisters are buried. Jez, organize a council meeting for the morrow after breakfast and we will discuss the plan in detail. Good night."

"Good night, My Lord. Good night, Karín."

"Will the Knights accompany us to the overhang?"

"What do you think?"

"I think there are things that only the king should see and I am one of them."

"Then they will not go. I will send them separately with an escort when we return. I want them to know the area and I want them to enjoy what they have. They will have agets from the Lancers and they will not want me to be seeing them naked. Find out from Freda if there are any we should leave behind on this trip. They would be those interested in the Knights. We will manage with the rest of them. If necessary, you and I can take two of the Matáng sisters behind us. Buyo can take Darel. The herders can come one day later and we will travel light so Kelda's crew is not robbed of too many back here."

"I had Froncy send your bath from Buq'ue to the castle. Would you like me to shave you before we retire? If you are to practice that which I showed you last night, you should be smooth-chinned or it will cause a painful rash to my inner thighs."

The three Knights approached the eating area which also doubled as the community gathering and games area. People were scattered around in groups playing the local table game with numbers generated by hand movements and moving small tokens on a painted hide. They looked for and found Reny and Salina in a knot of their sisters. Ivor looked for Kelda's girl but could not find her.

They went to the group of Lancers and asked permission to be seated. Most of the group melted away but Reny and Salinas were among the few who remained. Harry sat next to Reny and Arturo went to Salina. Ivor remained standing, still looking around for Kelda's assistant. When it became obvious he wasn't interested in any of them, the rest of the Lancers left, leaving just Reny and Salina.

"Whom do you seek, Sir Ivor?" asked Salina.

"There is a girl who works with Kelda here in the kitchens. I wish to meet her but I know not her name."

"Is it the fat one with crossed eyes?" asked Reny. *"Or could it be Roda's grandmother, the grey-haired beauty?"*

"It is one even more beautiful than either of those, tho' both would make a fine aget for a Knight."

"Ooooh! So the three Knights are here in search of their agets, Salina! And we two are the only sisters left to choose from! I thought they were here perchance to learn to play 'uckers' but I did not bring a board or any tokens. Did you, Salina?"

"I brought nothing, Reny. We may have to teach them something else but there are three of them and only two of us. Is it possible?"

"I might be able to teach all three, Salina but not all at once. Go and fetch someone to help us. While you are gone I will ask these three how they enjoyed the trip to Matáng astride a tlaque."

Salina jumped up and with a sideways glance at Arturo, disappeared into the shadows.

"Fear not, Sir Ivor. She will find you someone to your liking. Now, Sir Harry. How did you enjoy the trip to Matáng astride your tlaque?"

"I enjoyed it well enough. It is a lot more enjoyable than being asleep inside a metal container with tubes inserted into every orifice of your body."

"I have slept with something inserted into my body and I found it most satisfying. Salina told me she enjoys insertions *into her body. Could it be that there is something wrong with us? Sir Harry, do you think there is something wrong with me?"*

"I think not, Reny but I would know if there is something wrong with me."

"Carmodi told me of the potion they gave to you. I told Salina and she told some of the others. Carmodi told me it would take time before you would feel the urges felt by other men but in time they would come. She didn't say so but we think the Lord Ch0n was the same because Karín was with us for many moon cycles before she bore the look of a woman satisfied. Fear not, Harry. When you think you are ready, I will show you if you are able. And Salina will show you, Sir Arturo. And we will find someone to show you, Sir Ivor, if she pleases you. We have been here night after night, waiting. The others were waiting for you, Sir Ivor but now they know you have eyes for another they have left. We knew this day would come. You will know soon enough if your parts are in working order."

"I will choose my own woman, Reny. I don't need Salina to choose one for me."

"Before you deny her, know whom she has chosen, Sir Ivor. Here they come now."

Salina returned with Kelda's assistant in tow.

"She was at the baths preparing herself for you, Sir Ivor. She has done this every night and waited here with us for you to come. Because she works late she has to go and bathe and dress. Had you arrived a little later, she would have been here

waiting. Her name is Vana, which is also the name of the rare orange flower that grows from the crevices in the walls."

Ivor bowed to the girl.

"Thank you for coming. I would have chosen none other but you."

"You flatter me, My Lord for my position is not as exotic as the Lancer sisters. Nor am I as bold."

"I would have no other that I have seen. And it is for you to decide our immediate fate and not I."

The six left as if by agreement and went in pairs to the Knights' quarters. Reny and Salina wasted no time in leading their Knights to bed but another scene altogether was being played out elsewhere.

"My Lord, I know this is a new thing for you. Reny and Salina know the way of the ijon but I know nothing of it in practice, only what my mother has told me and of late what Reny and Selina have told me for they knew I had cast my eyes at you and that you had eyes for me. It is not fitting that you should learn from one who knows nothing."

"Guerra told me that this thing is truly wondrous. He told me that Carmodi has shown him everything though she was not experienced. I would have it no other way, knowing that we are to learn together. If you know the basics, I am sure we will find the way. First, we have to know if my dewen is functioning at all and for that, you will need to explore it. Come now for

though I want to be patient with you, I am impatient to know if I am whole."

ChOn rose early and did his rounds, his substitute for checking his perimeter. Usually he found the Knights doing the same but this morning they were nowhere to be seen. It struck him as strange but when he went to waken them, he was stopped by an unlikely person in Mori.

"Let them be, King. Last night all three of them entered their quarters in the company of women for the first time. If I'm not mistaken, none of them will surface until they are needed. The women have already left. Last I saw them they were walking down there together agigglin' like three children."

"I hope my sentries are as alert as you, Mori."

"You work with birds, you keep bird hours, King."

Harry was the first of the three to present himself to ChOn.

"Mori tells me you weren't alone last night. Did everything work properly?"

"Yes, My Lord. I am happy to report that it does."

"Good. Now bring me the others. I have orders for you."

The three Knights were all present within minutes, dressed in their tunics.

"Firstly, the informalities. Are the three of you all in good working order?"

They nodded in turn.

"I am pleased for you all because now you will see what it is like to live as a normal man with or without a wife. I repeat what I said previously. The women have no qualms about taking various lovers until they find their mate. After that they don't mind if you take a concubine or even two for those times when a woman is indisposed according to their culture. And nor do I, provided it is with the wife's consent. But taking advantage of various women because of your position is forbidden. I hope you find someone to settle down with if that is your desire. Now. To business.

"In three days I am taking the Lancers minus a section to a place we call the Overhang. It is a trip we have made three times so far and one we all enjoy but now that you have arrived, I am going to divide the trips into two. I will go with some and you will go with the rest. By the rest, I mean your agets and the rest of a section. I am doing that out of a sense of privacy towards Karín and your agets, whoever they be. I am sorry but I need you to tell Karín who they are so we can make arrangements accordingly. Harry, I am assuming yours is Reny because you and she have been making eyes at each other for some time. Arturo and Ivor, I have no idea who you have selected from those that selected you. Just let Karín know. Reny will lead the next expedition and you three will go along so you know where the Overhang is. It is an important source of clay for the castle and we will soon be setting up the means to extract and use it. It is also the place we get the oruk and the silky goats, although we have found a second herd of the goats a little closer. This time we are going to bring back the entire herd of tlaque minus their dominant buck and integrate it with the domestic herd which is roaming the plains east of here near where you landed. While I am away, which will be no more than three days, I want you to head east along the river looking for a place where we can set up a village. It will be at least a half day's ride from here and we need it to be not too vulnerable to attack. I prefer it to be beside a bamboo forest because that material provides most of what we need. It should have an easy route from here to there in case we need to deploy to protect it. Travel alone. Enjoy the solitude of the place and enjoy your own company. When you return, it will be time for you to go to the Overhang and you will enjoy it all the more for the company that will be with you."

The three left and went as one to Ivor's dwelling where they discussed excitedly and in detail the revelations of the previous night.

Gavan Connell

Chapter Seven: Vikings

The Lancers left for the overhang in a blaze of colour and discipline with straight files and lances all at the same vertical angle.

The Matáng had selected orange as the colour for their tunics. It was an easy colour to produce because the roots of one of Kelda's medicinal shrubs, which had to be boiled before they could be used, produced a deep orange residue after boiling and the tunics went straight in to the mixture when the mashed roots had been sieved off. They wore the same black turbans as their sisters. They were mounted behind the king's Own, which was being led by Karín in Reny's absence. Reny had stayed behind with ten of their number including Salina. Maní was mounted behind Ch0n, who had signaled for her to come to him when they were being allocated mounts. Karín had been too busy to notice but not Buyo, who was never far from Ch0n and always had him in view. She did not know which of the sisters he had called but knew she would find out as soon as they stopped. She knew Ch0n had his favourites among them and was not concerned in any way. She, after all had played him for all she could in order to get her position in his household and could imagine any of the new sisters would do the same. She had Darel behind her. He sat well on the beast and didn't need to wrap his arms around her, unlike Ch0n's passenger, who looked as though she were petrified of falling.   Karín also had a passenger and the others were straddling the female tlaque pulling the travois.

Karín led the column with ChOn behind her and off to a flank so the King's Own could maintain their formation.   ChOn maintained a watch on his flank more out of habit than anything and it was his alertness that led him to see the dagononum waiting on the edge of the copse close to where he would pass. He drew the stun pistol from its holster and just as his tlaque started to get skittish, shot the dragon from forty feet away. He called Karín to halt the column and called her to one side.

"How can it be that I was the only one to see this?" he chided her quietly but firmly. "You were leading the column and rode past it.   Had I been on the other side, this beast would have probably killed one of our number or a tlaque. We all have to stay alert and for you and me, that includes looking for dragons. It is easy to ride along in the sun with the sisters behind, thinking about what is to come at the overhang but we have to maintain our vigilance.   There are lessons to be learned at every turn and one of them is constant vigilance."

Karín flushed at his admonition of her. Nobody else could hear but she was not used to ChOn being angry with her.

"You are right as usual My Lord. I was dreaming of the cool water after this hot sun. You told me once before when I told you I was bored, that constant vigilance was needed and I have let you down. And myself. I might easily have lost one of us except for you. I know that you will not always be with us and it is my responsibility."

Ch0n dismounted and went to where the dragon was lying. By now, all could see its dull orange colour.

"Some of you have never seen a dagononum. Look upon this one and know they are all around us. This is why we need our commanders to have helms and why the helms are so important to protect. Without them, we are vulnerable as are our tlaque. I find no joy in killing these creatures but sometimes I have no choice."

He unsheathed Shiew and those close enough could hear the humming of the blade as it cleared the locket. He went to the dead beast and cut the bottom jaw from its head. Then with his hunting knife, he skinned the jaw and cut away the flesh, leaving only the jawbone and bottom teeth. He called forward one of Kelda's women and stowed the grisly trophy on a travois.

"When we get there, put that thing on an ants' nest for cleaning and we will take it back."

He washed his hands with a canteen of water, replaced his gloves and mounted the tlaque. Maní settled herself against his back and Ch0n gave the signal for Karín to move off. A few hours later, they were dismounted at the Overhang. The Matáng sisters were told to help with the tethering of the mounts and Kelda's team set up the few kettles they had brought to boil water. Ch0n showed Darel where the buck would be tethered and told him to keep an eye on him in case the tlaque herd arrived early. When the work was done, Karín made the announcement they were all waiting for.

"Lancer day at the Overhang!"

Gavan Connell

The Matáng sisters watched the others strip naked and rush into the water and then they joined them. A usual, Ch0n and Karín were off to one side.

"You are angry with me."

"I am but it will not last. I am angry because you were lax for a time but I can not remain angry with you because you are so diligent in every way. As long as you learn from this. Sometimes we are given a second chance and sometimes we are not. The jaw is for you. I am going to take the teeth one by one and fashion them into a jewel for you to remind you to be watchful and to remind you that I feel the ebon for you even when I am angry."

"I will wear it to remind me of both. Now. I was dreaming about this water. Are you going to let me get into it?"

They both stripped off and went to the edge of the water. As usual, all eyes were on Ch0n as he waded in. Most of the Matáng sisters had seen a naked man before but like their Arw'an and Buq'ue sisters-in-arms, they were surprised at the size of Ch0n's manhood and like their Arw'an and Buq'ue sisters they wondered what it would like to be Karín or Buyo. Buyo watched them with delight, knowing that any of them would trade places with her. Ch0n lowered himself into the water only to see the face of Maní in front of him. When he looked at her she lowered her eyes but this time instead of blushing, she smiled. Buyo was watching her and noted the reaction. Then she watched Karín slide beneath the surface.

"We will have to watch the Matáng widow," She thought to herself. "She is too much like me to be trusted."

The tlaque herd arrived on schedule as the sun was about to drop below the horizon. ChOn was mounted on the buck waiting for the wild herd leader and when the two set up a trumpeting challenge to each other, ChOn was ready. He let his buck get close to the herd leader and slid free of the saddle. As the two charged at each other, he shot the herd leader with both his and Karín's pulse guns at the same time. ChOn's buck piled into the still-standing but dead male. He lifted the body off the ground with the impact and then when it landed, he gored it to pulp. Then he raised his nose to the sky and trumpeted his victory. The dominant herd females went to him and he rubbed his scent on their rumps with his chin. There were no further challenges from the lesser males, which was something ChOn had worried about but they stayed where they lived, on the edge of the herd waiting for the chance to surprise a doe in heat. ChOn took some of Karín's root from a bag and went to the buck. Despite the wild look in its eye, it allowed ChOn to walk up to him. He took the sweet morsel and moments later, ChOn led him back to where he had been tethered and left him with Darel.

That night, ChOn lay between Karín and Buyo. During the night, a spent Karín made no protest when she felt Buyo's hands on ChOn. In the darkness, from her position astride ChOn, Buyo turned her gaze to Maní, just a few short feet away. Maní's eyes were wide open, staring towards them, seeing nothing but hearing and imagining all.

The tlaque herd with its third dominant bull in half a year, was quiet when ChOn woke. It was dawning pale orange in the East. He stepped over the sleeping Buyo and picked his way across the sisters to where the tlaque was tethered. Darel was asleep sitting up with his back to a tree close to the tlaque lines. The wild herd was lying down to a beast, patiently waiting for the new herd buck to stand up and lead them to their grazing grounds. A few of the dominant females had wandered to the tlaque lines and were lying, mingled with the domestic animals. Kelda's crew had the fires already lit and the water heating in the iron pots. ChOn wandered over to where they were working and sat down. Moments later, Maní came over and sat opposite him.

"Good morrow, My Lord. I trust you slept well."

"I did. There is nothing like a day's riding to put one to sleep."

"Or listening to a king night-riding two women less than an arms distance away to keep one awake."

"It is part of the reason we all come to the Overhang, to let go of the formality of the castle. This is the special place of the Lancers and we come here when we can. I know the women lie with each other as well. Some of them have men but they like the change. Some do nothing. Some, I have seen playing what Karín calls the slippery finger. Nobody cares. When we leave here we become the Lancers again and I am King. I like being just ChOn from time to time with people I can trust. Perhaps one day I will know you well enough to trust you."

"When that day comes, My Lord, beckon me and I will do your will. Now I will go. It is almost light. I would take another swim before breakfast. Please watch out for me in case I drown."

ChOn turned to face the pool. The Lancers were stirring and some were moving to the sloping stone that led down to the water's edge. Maní stood up and lifted the orange tunic over her head, folded it and put it down in front of ChOn. A minute later she was waist-deep and then she slid from view.

"If there is any porridge ready, I'll have a bowl', he said.

Buyo lay watching ChOn and Maní at the cooking area. She could tell ChOn was flirting by his facial expressions. Then she watched Maní leave him and go for a swim with ChOn watching her every move.

The tlaque herd was milling around restlessly by the time ChOn's tlaque moved. They were confused by the delayed start to their day. When he did move, they were further confused because they were going in the wrong direction but they followed anyway. They didn't realize that they were surrounded by domestic tlaque that were walking with them and steering them after ChOn. They had to take it slowly at first because the herd needed to graze after chewing cud all night and ChOn was glad Doni had warned him to allow two days for the return. The problem was the lack of water on the way. After a few hours, ChOn allowed his tlaque to trot gently. The matriarchs picked up the pace and then the whole herd was trotting in a long, controlled mass towards the castle. Darel was riding with ChOn because Buyo had said he needed to be able to chat to ChOn as they went. Maní was with Buyo and from what ChOn could see, seemed to be managing quite well without holding on to Buyo as tightly as she had done with him.

That night the herd had to go without water. They didn't settle well and ChOn stayed awake all night riding his tlaque among them so they would feel his presence. The Lancers were on fifty percent stand to, riding the edges of the herd to keep them still. The herders who had joined them during the day were riding the flanks with them. By morning, they were glad to get back on the trail and as mid-day approached, the leading beasts smelt the water in the river and there was no turning them away from it. Eventually, though, when they had slaked their thirst, Karín had the Lancers push them towards the castle gates where Doni was waiting to separate the herd into males, females and calves. All in all there were more than two hundred beasts in the herd including seventy almost mature males and another ten mature but non-dominant males. The remainder was made up of eighty mature females, sixty juveniles and seventy calves. Doni would have to geld a hundred and forty males before the herd could be released to graze with the main domestic herd near ChOn's fort.

"We have eighty mounts here, My Lord,"

"I was hoping for more but so be it. At least we can mount the new Matáng Troop and one Infantry company. The others will have to wait unless we find another big herd. Have Kelda bring the hot water and sewing kits. We might as well get started right away. Karín. Dismiss the King's Own and bring the Matáng Lancers. Have them draw lots for their turn to select their tlaque after you have separated the sixty you want for them. Darel. Take mine to his stable, clean him up and then clean the tack. Take my weapons with you and clean them all. Afterwards, go to the baths. I may need you later so stay close to your quarters."

The gelding process was by now a fluent operation. Ch0n, Doni and Karín stunned the beasts as they approached the cutting area and three teams had the bags washed and cut open, the testicles removed and stored for the cook pots while a third group sewed the cuts and put ashes on the wounds. Most of the beasts recovered consciousness within a few minutes and wandered unsteadily away to join their fellow steers in the corral. As the beasts grew smaller and younger, the three with the stun pistols dropped the charges accordingly. The entire hundred and forty six beasts were gelded in five hours. Sixty-six of them had marks on their rumps denoting them as Matáng Lancer mounts and each of those had been further marked by the Lancers themselves in the order of the lots they had drawn.

"I need a shave and a bath," declared Ch0n when it was over. "Well done Doni to you and your team. Well done to Kelda's people. Now it's time to clean up before we feast on meat balls and peppers."

Ch0n and Karín went to their quarters where Darel and Buyo were ready with clean tunics.

"I will shave our Lord if you like, Karín so you can go and relax in the warm water. You are filthy beyond description, as are you, My Lord."

"So be it, Buyo for I am too disgusting to be doing anything but cleaning myself up."

Ch0n stripped down to his undergarment and sat on the stool. Buyo put the hot towel on his face and went to work cleaning the grime and blood away.

"My Lord, I note you have eyes for the Matáng woman, Maní and she for you. I do not trust her at all because she shows no respect for Karín or me. She blatantly seeks you out and though Karín did not notice it at the overhang, I certainly did and Karín will notice it now we are back. Heed me in this thing. A time is near when you may take her as your lover because both Karín and I will be with child. While we are carrying, it is forbidden for us to lie with any man. It will fall to Karín to select one suitable for you from among those available and if you wish it to be Maní, you must show no interest in her until the time is right or Karín will kill her. It is not for me to say these things but I see Karín in her. They are of the same blood line, the blood of the Vikings as you call them. They are probably sisters or cousins. She would be the second concubine. I will watch her for you and for Karín and when the time comes, I will tell Karín whom to pick and she will listen to me for we are now as close as two sisters. Meanwhile, leave her be. Until I know her, please heed me. Now. You are shaved. I would lie with you both tonight but Karín would not have it again in the castle now things have settled, even tho' you can mount us both with ease. I will instead go to the Matáng Lines and become invisible for a while."

"Buyo. There is wisdom in your words and I will do as you say. Yes, she has sought me out but she has never done more than swear to serve me."

"My Lord. A king you may be and a soldier such as none of us has ever seen but you have no idea how to read the signs a woman sends you unless it is Reny showing you her iduw like a tlaque doe in season. Now go and bathe yourself and then go and make Karín with child so I may have you to myself until I too have a full belly."

When Ch0n and Karín returned to their quarters, Guerra was waiting for them.

"My Lord! I have found them! I have been searching the image strips for days and yesterday I found something! I used G2's images to narrow down the area. Come and see! Karín. You too!"

He dragged Ch0n by the arm to his desk where he had set up the projector to magnify the images from the cameras of the two motherships. He pointed to an image and told Ch0n to identify what he could see.

"This is from your ship. It was in orbit a little towards the other side of the planet from ours and so our camera didn't pick this up. But it is as clear as day. At the base of those cliffs is a cave. Look closely at the entrance to the cave and tell me what you see."

"There is a dagononum swimming out of it."

"No, no, no. It isn't a dagononum. It's the front of a boat with the head of a dagononum carved into the prow. It's a large boat sailing from a hidden port and somewhere in that port there are sapients. Vikings! I've found our Vikings!"

Chapter Eight: Plans and more Plans

Ch0n looked closer at the image.

"Can you enlarge it?"

"No. This is as big as I can make it without distorting it. As you can see, it is on the edge of the image. If it were central, I could make it big enough to see how the eyes on the figurehead are painted but the edges of each pass are not so clear. The previous pass shows just the cave entrance and the next one runs the other line and the cave is not showing. Centuries ago there was a saying about the information you needed always being on the join of four maps. Something to do with a scholar called Murphy, it seems. This is proof that his law holds true although I have never been able to find the equation that defines it. Anyway, we will not gain any more from these. If you wish to know more you will have to send a patrol. Or an Army."

"How far away are these Vikings in earth miles?"

"Two hundred and sixty seven in a straight line."

"So it would take twenty days or so to get there by tlaque or twice that for a large force."

"No. It will take about a hundred days to get there and twice that for an army because there is a strait between us and them and you would have to go around the land form. Or build an ocean-going boat. And we have the drone."

"It can be done in any of those ways but I prefer feet on the ground where possible. We know nothing about them apart from the fact they have been here before and maybe they will one day return. Good work, Commander Guerra. To find this is of great significance to us."

Guerra bowed at the head and Ch0n left for his quarters with Karín.

"We know now for certain that there is another tribe living here on this place. We know that some hundreds of years ago at least they had access to the aliens who found or even seeded this planet. We also know that they have the technology to build an ocean-going boat and have had that technology for perhaps hundreds of years while the Arw'an, Buq'ue and Matáng have not developed to the same extent, even though they were closer to the alien base. I am going to assume that one day they will return to their port on the lake and when they do they will find us. It is even more important now that we develop a defensive position there because we have no idea what secrets lie in those caverns and we have no idea what weapons the Vikings may have available to them. If we have one of those rods, they may have one. Or five if each of the female aliens had one. I am going to send the three Knights on a mission to map the route to the Viking harbour and to log any villages or defendable places along the way. It will take them away for months."

"My Lord. You should seek the council of Jez before you decide this. If you send away the three together with all their arms and tablets, their helms and their knowledge of your kingdom, they may form an alliance against us and bring the Vikings here to conquer what we have."

"I doubt they would do that. It is unlikely all three would be traitors but you are right that I should seek Jez out. I can't send them away unarmed, though and it is a long way to send a troop of Lancers unless they can forage along the way. This is the same problem the Matáng had when they were coming to us but the distances are ten times longer and the logistics to maintain them in the field would be enormous. The Knights will also have an idea of what they can and can not do. You and I will discuss this further with Jez and when the council next meets we will talk of it to all of them. Now. I am ready for sleep. We achieved much in the past few days"

"Before you sleep, you have one more task to perform. It is not a difficult one and afterwards you will sleep even more soundly."

Guerra and Carmodi looked up from the desk where they were both poring over the strips of images around the Viking harbor.

"What was that, Carmodi? It sounded like a muffled scream from across the way. Do you think there is treachery afoot?"

"No, my innocent one. It is a sound you have yet to hear from me but in time you will. It is the sound a woman makes

151

when the pleasure from the ijon is so intense, it can not be kept within and manifests itself in involuntary spasms and shouting to the Gods. You will learn how to give me such pleasure. It takes time for a man to learn the special places of a woman but you are a good student. Hearing that sound makes me want to stop this work as important as it is and see if you can remember that thing I showed you last night. It took me to the place of pleasure and from there it is but a short journey to where the Ch0n is taking Karín."

Buyo watched Karín as she buried her face in Ch0n's chest and screamed. The sound was still echoing in her soul as Karín collapsed onto their master and whispered,

"At last the Gods have seen fit for me to see the blinding light and hear the drums that beat in the place where they reside. The seed you spilled this night will grow in me and fill my belly and I will bear you a prince blessed by the same Gods who sent you to me."

"If that is their will, so be it."

"Indeed," thought Buyo. "If you are with child then I will have him to myself for a while. And when I have him, he will fill me as he has filled you and I, too will bear him a prince."

"So, Jez. That is the situation," Ch0n said the next day. "Tell me what you think."

"Well, to begin with My Lord, as senior Knight, I would like to go. I think two of us or perhaps three would be enough. We could just live off the land like the Knights errant you told me

about when I first joined your service. You could send me the most trustworthy or the least if there is such a one. Either way your personal interests would be served as well as those of the kingdom. Perhaps we could take a tlaque with one of the new cargo saddles bearing basic provisions such as a…. tent, porridge and water with a few cooking utensils and no more. That way we could make good time, travel where we can easily hide and not have to worry too much about logistics. Of the three, I most enjoy the company of Arturo. He seems honest and loyal and has learned the most of our tongue. I tell you that, My Lord in case you decide to use my plan and select a companion for me."

"Jez, I am not sure I can manage here without you. You are the rock upon which this castle has been built and I can not imagine not having you to fix everything I need fixed."

"My King," interrupted Karín, *"you have me and you have Guerra, whom Carmodi tells me loves his new life as your right-hand planner. She told me that the moment she took hold of his dewen, he became another person and has said to her that he is grateful to Jez for causing him to be stranded here where his life's work can be fulfilled in a far more meaningful way. I tell you, My Lord that Guerra has no heart for the throne. He knows he can not fight for it and if he were to gain it by whatever subterfuge, he would have to fight to keep it. He is an intelligent man and now a happy one with a purpose. Let him fix the things that need fixing. Let Harry and Ivor fix those other things that Jez does for you and then let me fix those things that they are unable to fix. Keep your enemies or potential enemies in sight. Jez has earned his reward. Let him be the first to go to the Vikings and see if they are peaceful or warlike and from*

Gavan Connell

there you can plan your next move." She looked across at Jez who nodded to her in agreement and thanks at the same time.

"Aaah! Those I trust above all others are conspiring against me in front of my very face," laughed Ch0n and the sound washed over Karín like rain as it always did. So be it. Jez, take Arturo to one side and tell him of our plan. Instruct him to tell no-one where you are going, only that I have a special mission for you both that will see you absent from the castle for some time. Take a spare tlaque each. You may need to rotate the four. Better. Ask Doni if one among the first oruk calves we brought can be trained to the saddle and you can take two oruk with two tlaque. This would have been the perfect task for one of the half tlaque-half oruk. You will need to make a special oruk saddle if Doni says the oruk can go. One with Arturo's code signal."

"If he is not loyal, My Lord, I will have plenty of opportunities to find out on the journey. Salina will not be pleased to lose him so soon, though and he will hate to lose that which he has recently discovered."

"And you, Jez? What of you and Malek?"

"She thinks she might be with child. She will know in the next moon cycle. If she is, it will be a good time for me to be away. The Arw'an women, I am told by my father, are not to be trifled with when they are waiting for their offspring. Better for me to be on the other side of the kingdom."

"Why congratulations, Jez. I hope it is true. I wish to be the first to know when the news is confirmed and of course we will help her parents look after Malek while you are away. At tomorrow's council meeting I will ask Guerra to tell the assembled that he has found the Viking harbour. I will announce that you and Arturo are leaving on a special mission. They can work out what it is without our having to tell them. Go now and talk to Doni about the oruk and then tell Arturo of your mission and ask him to come to me so I may task him personally."

The following day at the council meeting, Guerra made his announcement and ChOn made his regarding the Knights. He also made another about gathering the three tribes together for a special occasion.

"I wish to expand the concept of the village games. I wish them to be contested by teams from all the three tribes. The same games but with twenty from each tribe competing against each other in teams and individually and the Lancers competing against each other as well. We will have the usual sports which Karín won last time they were held here but I am going to introduce more, based on some things I have learned since I have been here. I have seen them on the minitron and they are based on teamwork as well as speed. The games will be called 'The Gathering' and I will award prizes to the winning individuals and the winning team. I have drawn up a list of events and the rules on my tablet. I will send them with images downloaded from the minitron to the Buq'ue and Matáng. We will meet in exactly 100 days on the plain between here and Buq'ue, where the ground slopes down from the hill to the lake. We will have to rid ourselves of the dagononum for a time. I think with so many around it will probably stay away anyway. Karín, the Matáng Lancers will be at some disadvantage because they have yet to accustom themselves to riding as a troop and they have no troop leader. You might select one and then spend some time training them for the event. I will be happy to assist if you need me."

"I have already selected the Troop Leader, My Lord. It is Robia from the King's Own. She is the most able. I was going to select one from among the Matáng but there is none even close to ready and Robia has earned a promotion from second in command. She is ready and able."

"So be it. Commander Guerra, please remain behind. These games are going to need quite some planning. I think you are just the person."

The others left, leaving Guerra and Ch0n alone.

"I am told you have quite settled in to your new role, Guerra."

"I have My Lord and I would have it no other way now I am free to pursue my work almost unencumbered. These games will slow me down, somewhat. How am I to organize them?"

"I will have Izaki and Mastelik appoint someone from their villages to organize each village committee and I will appoint one from here. You will then simply plan the sequence of the events and appoint the judges from those provided by each village. I will be the chief judge and any appeals will come to me and my decision will be final. You won't have a lot to do. I suggest you put Sonja and her counterparts to organize the games village as there will be hundreds present, including spectators, should they wish to attend. This should be fun. I will strike medals cut from the landing craft for the winners of events. I have to find a trophy for the winning village to hold until the next games. If you have any ideas, please let me know."

"I take it, Jez and Arturo are going to the Viking harbor?"

"They are. Only you and Karín and Doni will know apart from the two. And myself of course. The others may guess all they like but we will not tell any other unless I deem it necessary. I was going to ask you if we could assign a secret frequency to the mission. If it can be done, I would like those two, myself and Karín and your comms centre to be the only stations programmed to it. I want you to log every call and image on the main tablet and have them downloaded to my own as backup. By the time they get there we should have a way to plan an advance to contact with a force large enough to conquer them if they present a threat to us in any way. They have the technology of boat building and sailing. I have been studying it off and on since we surmised there were Vikings but now I am going to concentrate on it and see if it is possible to build a war boat or boats. For the moment there is no threat but I have been one to counter any possibility well in advance and I see no reason to change that now. I am happy to live here in the peace we enjoy but I also wish to know what we need to do should that be interrupted. I leave you to your work as well as to the planning of the games and I will get back to being king."

"My Lord. Your ship found this place and mine did. There are scores of ships roaming this sector of space. It is only a matter of time before another arrives. We landed where you

told us to and as a result we find ourselves here but what happens if another arrives and lands elsewhere?"

"I have thought about that. You landed where I told you because you wanted me to talk to you and to take me back. Any ship that comes here will monitor our frequencies as you did, will work out quickly we are marooned here and will contact us. Or they will contact you first because you are the comms man. We have a force big enough to fight off any landing, even if they deploy all their commandos. With three Knights and the infantry kitted out with energy weapons, we can fight it out with three sections of space commandos. We will do exactly what we did last time and disable their shuttle. That will stop them in their tracks. Why do you ask?"

"Because I am not a soldier but I am a planner and I need to know there is a plan. As commander of the ship, I had to make sure there was a plan for you soldiers and whilst I am not commander here, I like to know that we will not be winging it when the time comes."

"There is no plan other than what I just said. We will use that as the basis and when they contact us we will have five or six days to form a plan and execute it before they have boots on the ground. When it happens, and I agree that one day it must, I will plan the military side of it and you will plan the comms. If nothing else, it will give us a steady supply of Knights and weapons if ships keep coming."

"Or the Vikings if they don't like the look of us and go to them instead."

"By then, Guerra, I will have a plan for the Vikings as well. I am not out for conquest. I am king of three kingdoms and just want peace in the region so we can get about our lives. If any should come, whether they be from Earth, the other side of the planet or aliens from the other side of the universe and try to disrupt that, we will be ready to defend our people."

Ch0n wandered to the Lancer lines to check the progress of the Matáng Troop tlaques and the other recently-gelded beasts. As usual, he was bored unless he had something specific to do and he wished he could go with Jez to the Viking harbour instead of Arturo. The three Knights were scheduled to go to the overhang the following day and then it would be a matter of a few weeks until the second oruk was ready to mount and Jez and Arturo would be leaving. He went to Freda's office to see how she had settled in. He knew her quite well by now. She was Carmodi's sister in every way. They even looked alike. She looked up when his bulk blocked out the light in the doorway and jumped to her feet.

"Well come, My Lord. It is some time since we have seen you here at the lines. These times of peace must find you wondering how to fill your days. I wish I could say the same."

"Well met, Freda. So how are the new Lancers coming along with their tlaque?"

"The tlaque are doing fine and the sisters are doing fine. But this administration is growing all the time. I would like to have a record of each Lancer, those here in the troop and those in the other troop. And those in the school. And those at Buq'ue. I know about every tlaque assigned to the Lancers and when it

passes wind. Did you know that your Lancers now number one hundred and ninety eight plus one Commander plus eighteen in the reinforcement platoon? In all, My Lord, they number two hundred and seventeen, of which sixty six are at Buq'ue and the remainder here in these very lines?" We have two hundred and twenty mounts, of which there are seventy nine on line and usually enough for each trooper to have a mount in case she needs it. But today we have three tlaque not feeling well so they have been taken off line and put in with the trainees. And now we have another seventy-two tlaque, all newly neutered and all waiting patiently to be brushed and fed and watered and healed so their new owners can sit on their backs. I have to keep all those numbers in my head because we have no means of keeping records. I know not the scratches you use. Neither did Carmodi but she only had half the numbers to worry about. In short, My Lord, I need something or someone to help me before I revert to being everybody's mother and the tlaque can please themselves."

"I will bring you a tablet and you can use it to monitor everything. I should have thought of this sooner. Find another who can assist you and you can train her to take over from you when the time comes. The tablet has a feature where you can talk to it and save what you say in a special place. When you need it, you look for it and open that place and it will talk back to you. It is easy to use and you do not need to know the scratches. But it tells me also that the time has come for us to start to teach the children to read them. We have so much to do and so few who can do it. Find your assistant and then go to Karín so we can program the tablet to you both."

"What means 'program' My Lord?"

Ch0n sighed.

"It is the way we make the tablet respond to you and no other so it remains safe even if it falls into the wrong hands. The information you put on this tablet will be sensitive and of tactical importance so it has to be safe from prying eyes. That is what 'program' means."

"Oh.."

"I am going to wander through the lines and see how the new tlaque are faring."

"As you wish, My Lord but be aware the Matáng sisters are in their barracks and many are returning from the baths at this time."

"I will be careful not to disturb them. I wish only to see the tlaque."

He wandered across the parade ground where the Lancers practised their formations to the new barracks and looked into the first stall. The tlaque was calmly eating forage, its coat recently brushed and the stall was clean and tidy with the new saddle in place and the tack hanging from pegs. Ch0n was pleased that their new Commander had moved already. Her red ribbon was hanging from the ladder that led to her loft above the stall and her newly acquired orange one was attached to the lance. He continued down the long line that housed the sixty six beasts and their riders. The same story was repeated stall after stall. The Matáng sisters were taking their new roles very seriously. He had the chance to chat with one or two of the sisters who were downstairs at the time. They were excited at the prospect of being soon able to work with their mounts instead of practising on those of the King's Own Troop. Towards the end of the line of stalls he was surprised by Maní who called to him from her loft.

"I am up here, My Lord and will come down as soon as I am dressed. I have just returned from the baths."

ChOn looked up to see Maní's face looking down from where the ladder disappeared through a square in the roof. Her bald head reminded him that all the newcomers had had their locks shaved just a few days ago. He had only seen the sisters with their turbans and their new beanies. He looked around the stall, which was exactly as all the others had been and then Maní started down the ladder. ChOn instinctively looked up. The girl was wearing her tunic and nothing else. ChOn's heart missed a beat and he felt his manhood stir at the sight of the shaved iduw only a few feet from his face. He could have reached out and touched it. Maní paused in her descent and then went back up to her loft. She stood at the top of the ladder almost astride the opening and looked down at ChOn.

"I forgot my beanie. I feel so naked with no hair."

She disappeared for a short while and once again started her way down. This time, ChOn noted, she was wearing her undergarments and he felt a mixture of disappointment and reLeif.

"*So what brings the king of three kingdoms to the Matáng quarters, My Lord? Does he wish to run his eye over his livestock? We have not had the pleasure of your company these past few days. Some of us have missed it since the trip to the overhang. I had hoped for it. Look. My stall is well prepared for inspection by a king as are my sleeping quarters. The beast is well brushed and I have selected well for even after a few days he enjoys my ministrations. He knows me already and trusts me, even when I am inspecting the place where his balls once were. We will make a good team. I am already learning the ways of riding from Salina, whose tlaque I mount and who is herself mounted by the Knight, Sir Arturo. I envy her but soon I will have my own mount will I not?*"

"He seems to be a fine beast but they are all much the same as they were all sired by the one bull and their mothers were all sired by one bull. Their genes are the same so they are the same. Now I must continue my inspection."

"*My Lord, I am sure you have seen that which you came to see. All is in order here. Your Matáng Lancers are ready to serve you. None more than I. You only have to wish it of us and we will ride into battle for the good of all.*"

She bowed to Ch0n and he left her for the next stall.

"She is playing a dangerous game and I must not succumb," he thought. "Buyo is right. One day she will become the second concubine if Karín selects her. Meanwhile, I will do nothing to encourage her flirtations."

He finished his inspection of the lines and went back to the castle where he had Darel fetch one of the spare tablets and then a thought struck him.

"Fetch me a minitron as well if you would, Darel. Karín! I have an idea!"

"It would be a strange day that you did not have a new idea, My Lord," said Karín when she had rushed in from their rooms. *"Now tell me of this one which is so exciting you have disturbed me from my sword practice."*

"I am going to use the minitron to teach a teacher how to read and write. I need the smartest women or men in the castle to be found. I will do some tests to find out who it is and then we will make him or her a teacher of the children. I have programmed three of the minitrons that came with me on the shuttle using the dead soldiers' eyes to boot them. They are now all programmed to my eye. I should have thought of this ages ago for you. I will give you one too. You can learn to write the scratches that your language makes on paper. While you sleep, the minitron puts images into your brain using some form of subconscious retention. I don't know the mechanics of it but it is how we learned most of what we know. Now... I need to see the elders of all the original villagers so as to have them pick candidates for my intelligence test. There is one on the minitron especially for sapients and I have never even thought of it until now. I can't believe I have been so thoughtless."

Karín laughed.

"*You have not had a moment to yourself to think of these things my ChOn. You have built a castle, a fort, a kingdom and fought and won a war since you have been here. I think you should forgive yourself this one thing at least. Now, it is past time for the mid-day meal by a long way. This morning you have had a council meeting and had a trip to the Lancer lines to occupy you. Let's go and eat and we can find the elders from there.*"

The candidates from the thirteen villagers were all invited that night to sit the sapient intelligence test. It involved a series of basic visual learning experiences followed by tests to see what had been absorbed and how much the subjects could extrapolate the basic knowledge into the tests, such as short-term memory capacity, visual pattern processing, spatial processing and speed of processing. It was a basic test, designed only to try and establish the subject's capacity for learning. ChOn was going to use it for that and then try and adjust it to identify the capacity to teach. He already knew Boro was as intelligent as any human he had met on the ship, based solely on his capacity to resolve problems he had never previously encountered. The castle and the outer walls were testament to his spatial awareness to begin with. He, Karín, Jez, Doni, Kelda and Sonja had all been plucked from the group and had each been able to adapt with no outwards signs of stress, apart from Sonja's missing tooth of course but that was someone else's reaction, not hers. ChOn had twenty volunteers from among those thought by the elders to be the most likely candidates plus those who wanted to try their luck working for the ChOn in a position of trust. Those who had served him well had all been well rewarded.

The minitron did not have any baseline data to use so ChOn assumed that this was the first time the test had ever been used. He put the master tablet, now in the care of Guerra to record the process and by the next night he had his two prospects selected and ready to be briefed. They were both women. One, Valda was quite young and had outperformed the rest on the test. The other, Rai was closer to what ChOn assumed was middle age. Even though she had not achieved the best results, ChOn selected her as the first teacher based on her experience in the village as a midwife and healer. The younger girl was still in her teens and ChOn decided to make her Rai's understudy.

"Valda and Rai, you will be the first among us to try this process. You know what it is from the initial talks and you have both proved to me you are capable. I will have Boro and Sonja select a place and build a building next to the Lancer training rooms. We will call it a 'school'. 'School' is a word in my tongue that means a place where children and adults may go to learn. You will be teachers, just like the teachers you now have in your clans but you will not be teaching just the history of the Arw'an and the way of nature that you live with but the things we talked about yesterday before the test. Among us there are five who can read the scratchings, which we will call, 'writing' and we will help you with the learning. The minitron will fill your brain with all you need to know in a few months but you will need to practice and so Commander Guerra, Sir Harry and Ivor and I will help you with that. Your first students will be Carmodi, Darel, Karín and Buyo, Freda and her new assistant. That class will give you students to teach and learn from. Afterwards, we will select the most intelligent of the children in the village and finally we will try and have all the children pass through the school so as to be able to read, write and calculate the basics. You will teach in the school but you will sleep in the loft where Darel sleeps but on the other side. When the minitron has performed its task, you may return home to sleep but will return to the school to work and prepare your plans. Do you understand me Rai? Valda?"

"I do, My Lord," replied Rai. *"I also understand that this is a task of great importance. The children of the village will be the next Boros, Donis, Sonjas and Keldas. They will be the next Jezes."*

"And they will be the next Rais and Valdas. Valda?"

"I understand, My Lord. I see how this all fits into the plan you have for us, each to his or her own skill-based task. It will also let the children grow up like children and not have to go so young to the fields or the kitchens to work. I heard one of the Knights playing his…. flute, I think he called it and I would like the children to learn music and all sorts of things that we have never had the time to learn before now."

"And that's why you did so well on the test," thought Ch0n.

"To you I will entrust such things when your time comes. But first the basics. Now Rai. This is called a minitron. It possesses all the knowledge of my world up until the time my ship left my planet. Guard it with your life for that is the price I put upon it. It will only work for me. It needs to scan my eye before it can be re-programmed. I will re-program two to teach you both the reading and writing letters used to speak Arw'an and Buq'ue as well as the Matáng dialect. Each night you will

Gavan Connell

simply press the 'on' button, here after you are in your cots and these buds are in your ears and this thing touching this part of your head behind the ear. At first you will hear only music. That music will put you to sleep and then the minitron will start teaching you everything I have told it to teach. In the mornings you will know more than the night before and in a few moon cycles, you will know everything you need to know to start teaching the basics. The minitron will tell me when you can stop the cycle. Then, Valda, you will stay here in the loft and I will program it to teach you about music and dancing and games children play while they are learning. It will teach you how to make drums and other basic instruments that need no special materials. Do you understand?"

"My Lord," said Rai, *"what means 'program'?"*

ChOn sighed.

"Better I show you than try to explain it. Now you first, Rai. Valda, you watch and learn."

"Where will Buyo sleep?" asked Karín when ChOn told her about the teachers moving in to the loft.

"She will sleep in one of the spare rooms we have now Guerra and Carmodi are in Jez's place. It is fitting for her to move in with us. We have several rooms not in use until we have offspring to occupy them so let her use one, the one that is next to our sleeping quarters. That way she won't have so far to walk after she watches us making the ijon."

"She watches us? Every night?"

"You will have to ask her that but I have heard her often as she enters and leaves. It is hard for her to know you are enjoying that which she desires. Watching makes it easier for her."

"And she told you that?"

"Yes. Has she never talked to you about it?"

"Not yet but that is about to change. I will forbid her to watch us. It is not right."

"We have lain together the three of us and you caressed her iduw even as she was in her ecstasy at the overhang. It is nothing. I would have her share our bed all the time if it were proper. As much as I feel the ebon for you, there are times when I would have her afterwards when the heat is on me. She likes to watch and I suppose she plays the game of slippery finger afterwards for her need is as strong as yours. We should both be thankful she has not sought her reLeif elsewhere."

"For the concubine of a king to lie with another is treason and death, Ch0n. She knows that."

"And for the concubine of a king to watch her lady make ijon when she has the gift of night-vision is normal and you will not forbid it. She is loyal and we both need her in our own way."

"Ch0n. When I am with child she will be with you all the time for it is forbidden for a woman carrying to lie with her man. What am I to do then? I do not feel any resentment to her while

Gavan Connell

I am bleeding or while we are separated but for ten moon cycles it is a long time. What if you feel the ebon for her during that time? I will have to kill her for I could not suffer it."

"What I have for Buyo is not what I have for you and can never be. Fear not. You and I will still be together but I will use Buyo for my physical needs and you will be beside us. We have done it before, the three of us and it will be no different. Is it forbidden for a man to pleasure a woman in other ways during that time? Or for a woman to please her? I think not. Besides, she will be there to support you. Now. It is decided. Put your fears to one side."

"It is not so easy but I will say no more of it."

Buyo was of course ecstatic to be moving in to the royal apartments. For her it was the final acceptance. She had now been promoted from first concubine to second aget of the king. If she were to bear him a male child it would be a prince and not a halfling to be denied. That night she slipped silently from her bed in the new quarters and stood at the entrance to Ch0n's seeping room. He was locked together with Karín, who was strangely distracted. When Ch0n paused, Karín called out to her.

"Buyo. Are you watching?"

"I am here, Karín."

"My Lord has forbidden me to tell you not to watch so if you must watch, come with us and I will not feel your eyes on me, but your hands."

170

Buyo padded across to where Ch0n was still kneeling over Karín's form. She lay down beside them and trailed her finger under Karín's belly to where she and Ch0n were joined.

Jez and Arturo left the following week. Guerra had finally worked out how to isolate a frequency for them via the microsatellite. Doni was satisfied the second oruk was ready for the saddle and so Jez made one to fit it and Arturo's backside, making sure the fragmentation grenade was well hidden in the sprayform just where Arturo's legs joined. The two tlaque were tethered to the saddles of the oruk. One of them was saddled with Arturo's usual saddle, the other bore a cargo frame with cooking pots, water and porridge as well as a crossbow and bolts, a synthetic tarpaulin, general supplies and a polished-aluminium, concave mirror for solar-heating the cooking pots. Ch0n checked their kit before they mounted. He knew it wasn't necessary but custom demanded that a commander do some ritualistic pulling and pushing before dispatching his troops.

"Go well, Jez and Arturo. You know what you are to do. Make sure you report in to Guerra each morning and night. I will repeat this, though. The energy weapons, tablets and the helms must not fall into strange hands. That is paramount. Any ground force you encounter must be avoided at all costs or if battle is joined, there must be NO survivors to tell of the tlaque and the oruk."

"Jez, if I had a brother, I would want him to be like you. I entrust to you the life of Sir Arturo. Go well."

"Arturo, you have not been with us for long but I entrust to you the secrets of the kingdom and the life of Jez. Go well."

They both bowed to Ch0n.

"Stay well My Lord," said Jez as he hauled himself onto the giant oruk.

"Stay well, My Lord," repeated Arturo and he too pulled himself up into the new saddle. Together they turned their little caravan towards the gate where Malek and Salina, arm in arm cut a lonely pair together.

"They will be gone a long time, My Lord."

"They will, Karín and I wish there were another way to find out about the Vikings but the drone can not feel that which we need to feel nor get as close as we need to get. I will miss Jez around the place. If you are my left hand, he is my right." Ch0n wandered back into the castle and mounted the steps to the turret. From the roof he watched his two Knights trotting gently up the rise to the knoll that overlooked the castle and then they were gone from view. To his right he could see the Matáng Lancers on the parade ground astride their mounts for the first time. He looked for and found Maní. She was easy to find, being a head taller than the rest and he already knew she was in the third pair, front rank. As he watched her, she looked up at him on the tower and even at that distance, her eyes met his and held them.

He needed something to do. His days were filled with touring the castle, the pens, the new school, which was starting to grow and then talking to Guerra about the Lake Settlement and the Gathering. Word from the outposts was that they had already selected teams for the games and he knew the Arw'an team was training under the Infantry Commander, Marik. He had seen the men's tug-o-war team pulling against the remaining oruk and the women's against a tlaque. The drill and formation teams were on the parade ground for hours a day and the Lancers were furiously practising their tent pegging and target practice with the longbows.

He decided to go to the place the Knights had found downstream to build the ranch. It was less than a day's ride east of the castle and they had marked the spot using their tablets and the magnetic field positioning system. Ch0n downloaded the map and went to the castle where he found Karín just returning from the parade ground.

"I want to take you for a ride to where the ranch will be built. We'll just go on my tlaque like we used to. We will stay there overnight. It will be the first time I will have left the castle without having Jez back here to look after things. I feel a little strange about it. I will have to nominate someone as being in charge. Should it be Boro, Malek, Guerra or one of the Knights?"

"Boro is the only one who knows about the explosives in the saddles and beds. If you leave him in charge, he will be the first one killed. Malek would be all right but she isn't really experienced enough. I am thinking Guerra would be best. He has commanded before and the Knights should obey him. If one or both of them decides to take command in your absence, they will have to kill both him and Carmodi for she will defend

him like a she-wolf in a fight. It is only overnight and I don't think there will be any problems."

"I am glad you nominated Guerra. I had thought the same. But we should wait until the morrow before we leave. I want to call the council to tell them so there can be no misunderstanding."

They sent Darel to inform the council that there was to be a meeting and then to prepare ChOn's tlaque for a two day trip. ChOn used the time to talk to Guerra about the command arrangements. Guerra was genuinely surprised and pleased.

"My Lord. I would have thought that one of your trusted Arw'an Lieutenants might well have been given that honour," he said.

"None is as prepared as you with the possible exception of the Knights, who were under your command on the ship. I am assuming that you and they will just carry on as if I were here. The council is here and my Arw'an Lieutenants as you called them will all be here going about their business. In future, I will leave Karín here but on this occasion I want to take her with me. Her female insight into my plans has never left me wanting."

The meeting went without incident. Boro was invited to remain behind and ChOn gave him a separate briefing regarding security and the use of the grenades.

The next morning, they set out with Karín up front as usual and the tlaque reluctantly stretching his gait an extra foot to accommodate her. The wolf trotted along behind and beside them and occasionally in front but always in sight. They reached the site after the sun reached its zenith and Ch0n explained what he wanted to do.

"There will be a big structure here to accommodate the herders and the admin people under one roof. The overseer will live in a separate wing. Over here we will build corrals and stables. The flats will be planted out with additional bamboo trees as soon as it can be done so they are already well established by the time building commences. We will build a long wall from that side to that side using the bend in the river like we did with the castle. It will be of living bamboo to keep the stock in and to slow down an enemy long enough for the Lancers to get here and sweep them from one side to the other. The land slopes down to the river so if we can draw water from the river and pipe it using the bamboo to the highest point and let it run back down the hill under control, we will have permanent grass and that will take the strain off the fields in front of the castle. This is where we will breed tlaque and goats. They will be neutered here and grow here until they are ready to be moved and fattened near the castle. I am going to encourage people who wish it, to move here and set up their small farms in the surrounding fields so that they can raise their own goats again but not to breed them. Breeding will only take place here using the breeding bucks. That way we will maintain the quality of the herd."

"Would Doni move here?"

"Not yet but much later when he has someone trained to do his job at the castle. He would stay where he is to manage the herd. The majority of the beasts will pass through the castle for mounts, beasts of burden or as killing stock. This will be a breeding area and as such one of his men could manage it."

"So it would be a breeding master here with enough herders and their families to manage the herds and the gelding during the season. The gelded ones would then be driven to the castle for fattening and killing?"

"No. Only the goats and special breeding programs like the oruk females to be crossed with a tlaque male will remain here and then go to the castle. The tlaques would be different. They would be brought here from the wild herd, sorted and gelded, those needed would be taken away and the herd would be sent back to its grazing grounds. The dominant herd buck would be selected by us and would never have to fight because all the other males in the herd would be gelded. When we want another buck we just do what we already do and keep one whole male at the castle."

"So what would happen if we go to war again? What would happen to this?"

"We would move the killers back to the castle, filter off any that may be needed for remounts and drive the rest away to the main herd. The buildings we would leave here. It can't be defended against a reasonable force but against a raiding party it could. If it were to be seized by an enemy force we would just let them have it. It is of no strategic importance."

"Then I can see why we would do it. But is that the only reason you brought me here? To give my woman's opinion about your future plans?"

"No. I wanted to be alone with you. We have so little time alone these days. And I wanted to give you something to tell you that I feel the ebon strongly for you and to stay your fears for when you are with child and I am with Buyo. It says on the minitron that on earth when a man feels the ebon for a woman and she for him, that they marry in a formal ceremony and he gives her the gift of a precious stone."

"My Lord, you know I need no gift from you to show me that you feel strongly for me. I know that the ceremony we have just had was more for the village, than for me. I already knew how you feel."

"No. It may have been for the village but it was more for you. I wanted to show you in front of them that you are my aget, not to show them in front of you. I will give you this for that reason, here where none can see. I found it at the overhang the day I fell over in the mud and we took the image of us together. It is a diamond from the cave of the dragon I slew that day. I have cut it with my grinding tool into a thing of beauty such as this world has never seen. On earth, it would be a thing men would kill for so great is its value, tho' here it is worth nothing. I give it to you as a symbol of the ebon I feel for you and as a symbol of my commitment to you."

Ch0n took the pale-orange diamond from his pocket and held it between his finger and thumb. It was as big as a dáguia egg with dozens of flat facets catching the orange sunset. He had set it in melted gold and silver and attached it to a necklace woven from copper thread and her own titian hair, salvaged the day he had ordered it cut. Karín looked at it with wonder in her eyes. The flashes of light touched her face through the orange prism. Her teeth flashed white against her cinnamon skin and she took it from him and placed it around her neck. It hung to a place just above the neck of her tunic.

"My Lord. Tho' you say this thing has no value here, you are wrong. This...diamond.. will cost the life of any who would take it for you see, a thing of beauty may be coveted by many but possessed by just one. I accept it as a symbol of your ebon and commitment and I will wear it when the occasion demands, with one of my garments made from the cloth of silk. I would wear it always but I am sworn to wear the necklace of dagononum teeth you are fashioning for me to show me you...luv... me even when you are angry with me. Now I have to give you something in return and I will tell you later what it is. It will be of far more worth than this diamond and will forever remind you of the ebon I feel for you. Now. We need to set up this tent and go for a swim or it will be dark before we are ready."

They swam in the cool river and then in the darkness of the tent, after they had coupled, Karín told ChOn she had not bled and that she thought she might be with child but that she would not know until another cycle had been missed.

"That is my gift to you, ChOn. A prince of the Arw'an, Buq'ue and your Earth. Perhaps of the Vikings and the Aliens as well. Or a princess. But I will not be sure for another moon cycle. In

the meantime, we have to make up for the time I am forbidden to lie with you."

Ch0n lay awake in the tent with the woman asleep beside him. He was busily thinking. He would have to make all sorts of plans for his child. It would be a natural child, not a clone. It would be a child of three races, perhaps four, two of them alien to the planet. What would he want for it? A soldier's life? A teacher's? A leader, surely and that meant both a soldier's and a teacher's. He finally slept. He dreamed a dream. He was lying in the lap of the woman and she was crying.

Gavan Connell

Chapter Nine: The man who would be King

They returned to the castle the following day. All was well. There had been no coup attempt.

For the next few weeks, Ch0n continued to plan for the ranch, the Lake village, the Gathering and the possibility he might soon be a father. He spent more and more time with Rai and Valda in their training room next to the almost completed school. The minitron was proving a great success with them both, whether it was because of their aptitude or because it was such a great manner to teach. Regardless, after three weeks of subliminal training in the alphabet and phonetics, they were able to read anything Ch0n wrote on the whiteboard, provided it didn't contain too many diphthongs, which still confused them. He surmised that within the two months allocated they would be able to write the sounds as well as recognize them and from then on it would be plain sailing. He had suggested to Karín that she use his minitron at night for the same purpose but she was not keen, saying that she could not perform either her wifely duties or those of his bodyguard. Ch0n suspected it was because she wanted to spend all her energy, conscious and unconscious, on being with him. She had been ill for a month with vomiting in the mornings and she said it was a sure sign she was with child. In a week she was due to bleed but she was now in no doubt. Buyo was fussing about her like a mother hen, half concerned and half delighted she would have ChOn to herself for almost a full year or until he filled her. ChOn, on the other hand was thinking more of ways to circumvent the no-ijon ban.

ChOn's daily routine started at first light when he left his quarters and wandered through the outer castle with the wolf. It was as near as he ever got these days to checking his perimeter but he enjoyed the walk through the near-deserted village within the walls. Usually the herders were wandering to the corrals, the kitchens were preparing for the first flush of diners and of course, Mori was awake outside his house with the kwidada on his shoulder or perched on the rail at his head. The dáguias were now rendered obsolete by the communications satellite and were used only to maintain the skills. ChOn opined that the satellite would possibly be the first thing to be disabled in a battle with any earth ship, though Guerra maintained that it would be invisible to any ship that did not launch it and besides, the ships had no space for missile capacity, although they did have a basic laser weapon that could destroy the satellite if they found it and were close enough to it. Mori was usually on for a chat with ChOn about the goings on in the castle and ChOn never failed to stop and pass the time with the old man and his talkative pet. Then he would go to breakfast in the central eating area where he made a point of sitting at a different table every morning so as to have the chance to talk with the various groups of Lancers, soldiers, stonemasons and herders who might be present. They were never backwards in telling him what they thought if they were unhappy, knowing that if their complaint had merit, ChOn would find a way to make their situation more tolerable. Maní never missed the chance to make eyes at him across the tables, a point not lost on Buyo or Ch0n, though Karín seemed oblivious to it.

Immediately after breakfast, Ch0n, the Knights, and Karín spent an hour practising with the katanas. The squires joined in where they could as part of their training. Ch0n never used Shiew at these practices.

"One day I might have to use her against one of these Knights and I don't want them to know she can chop their katanas apart edge to edge," he had explained to Jez and Karín. When the katana drills, katas and sparring sessions had been completed, Ch0n and the Knights would spend another half an hour or more training with the sai and the short sword. He and the other Knights had learned the routines from their minitrons and so to watch them sparring was something many of the villagers enjoyed. They didn't realize that the sparring was a highly choreographed routine or that the Knights were so skilled at the sequence, that it was highly unlikely one of them would ever be touched by a point or an edge. Meanwhile, Karín would spend the time with her sling or slingshot off to one side, although for the past few weeks she had not been able to attend due to her nausea and vomiting when she woke and ate anything. After the training, Ch0n would bathe in his rooms with Karín shaving him or Buyo, depending on circumstances. Then it was off to the corrals and then the classroom with Rai and Valda and finally a trip to the turret of the castle to watch the Lancers wheeling on the parade ground.

These days, his afternoons would be divided between his time planning the Lake Settlement with Guerra and watching the Arw'an team training for the Gathering. The days of twenty

Gavan Connell

volunteers competing for the glory of victory were gone forever. These were for individual and tribal pride. Individuals were throwing spears and shooting arrows, running back and forth to the top of the knoll overlooking the castle, wrestling with each other on the sandy parade ground when nobody else was using it, sparring with their wooden swords and shields and climbing ladders. ChOn had deleted the standing jump from the schedule because it could be won by a tall person with no other real ability. The skills were more militarily directed than before.

The team events were no less keenly being practised. The Matáng Lancers were now into their third week of riding and they were being given extra time to practice their tent pegging and stabbing with the lance at the gallop. They would also be firing their bows at the gallop in the manner of the ancient Samurai ChOn had learned about.

In the evenings, he could often be found in Guerra's office talking to Izaki and Mastelik on the video link. He was well pleased with them both and made them aware of it at every opportunity. But he did like to needle them about the Gathering and the fact he thought the Arw'an would win the overall trophy. It was his way of making sure the other two tribes took the competition seriously. Not that there was any need for his goading because they were as keen as ChOn for the victory.

Jez and Arturo had long ridden beyond the capital of Matáng. They had spent a short time there with Mastelik, taking the opportunity to look around and report to ChOn after they had left. In the weeks they had been together, they had formed a strong relationship, with Arturo telling Jez everything he could think about of his life aboard the exploration ship and

Jez telling Arturo everything about his life before ChOn, the reaction of the villagers to his first appearances and the lead up to the battle at the castle. Arturo already knew most of the story of the war but he had never heard it from Jez. Their route had taken them past the hill above the lake where Palik had fled, to Buq'ue where they spent time with Izaki, past all the main sites of the battle with the Matáng and they discussed the tactics ChOn had deployed. Arturo was fascinated by the battles. He was a soldier like ChOn but unlike ChOn had not had the need to study battles involving large forces. Nor was he aware of the existence of the great Zulu King Shaka or Chaka, whose tactics ChOn had used along with the concept of the assegai. He had never heard of the wonderful Sikh Cavalry or the British Hussars at the charge of Balaclava led by none other than the British cad, Sir Harry Flashman, whose extraordinary military career had been chronicled by the man himself in a series of papers. Before the war, ChOn had studied Flashman's fascinating life, published by the famous Scottish author, George McDonald Fraser, and he had wondered how a single individual could have had such an improbable life but it was there in print for all to read. It became clearer and clearer to Arturo why and how ChOn had manipulated the battle with the Matáng to suit his own ends and he realized that any alien force from Earth to land here on Arw'an would not stand a chance against such tactics. The space commandos were adept at individual fighting and skirmishing but that was all. Any battles involving more than a few armed sapients was destined to be lost and one against a well-trained army with modern weapons was doomed from the beginning. He thought back to how ChOn had tricked them when they landed. Guerra had ordered G2 to keep an eye out for ChOn, Jez and Karín but a simple trick to defeat the thermal imaging and infra-red systems had allowed

Jez to hide under a hot, flat rock in the cool of the shade and fire a single anti-armour projectile from close range at their shuttle. Meanwhile, Karín had just stayed in the cave where she was out of sight of everything. Perhaps for days. He admired and envied Ch0n more and more for what he had managed to achieve with the sapients in such a short time and the castle was the crowning glory of it all. The four newcomers had gathered together that first night, partly out of fear and partly to discuss the unlikely possibility that an iron-age sapient could have built the castle from nothing, using only a picture of Eilean Castle in Scotland. He wondered briefly if the success of Ch0n might not be repeated elsewhere.

The two rode easily on the giant oruk, which trotted at their own mile-eating pace all day with no problems. The tlaque, although lighter, were almost as tall and so had no problems matching their gait. They took images of every copse of bamboo, every water source, defensible hill, cave, fruit grove, herd of tlaque and oruk they saw. There was no sign of sapient occupation of the Matáng territories until they came to the place three week's ride west of the capital where a sizeable river crossed their front. There was a Matáng outpost of about two-hundred folk where the river went into a split in the mountain and disappeared from view.

"Well come, Knights. We have been expecting you. The dáguia arrived here several days ago with your drawings. This is the frontier of the Matáng Territories. It is just a village with not much of a military force, just a few soldiers in case we get invaded." The village headman laughed at his own joke.

Jez and Arturo both took images and registered the waypoints on the tablets. They also took images of the river and how it seemed to have split the mountain into two with a steep-sided gorge the only place the water could run.

"How can we cross the mountains, old man?"

He pointed to a place well to the north.

"You can cross the river with your beasts two days walk from here. Once you cross, if you go towards the sun after the middle of the day, you will see the way across. It is loose and stony but not too difficult. In the pass there is a small lake fed from a spring that issues forth from the ground. On the other side there is a vast plain of green where there is water to be found at every turn. It comes bubbling from the ground in places and in others it comes from fissures in the rocks. It is said that the lake empties from underground and spills out of the rocks where it can for no stream runs from it. On the plain there are orok and talake like those you are mounted upon and others smaller and one called a bauda that has an orange hide thicker than a man's arm with two curved horns that point forwards and grow longer as the beast gets older. They attack almost anything on sight for they are very territorial. We have heard also of a great predator that can not be seen. That it attacks silently and kills. It is told that my father's father once slew one because it attacked through a fire and became visible where it displaced the smoke."

"We will rest up here for the night and then be on our way" announced Jez. *"But first we will bathe and then eat. Where is your village bath?"*

Gavan Connell

"Bath, My Lord Knight? What is that?"

"It is where you clean yourselves so you don't stink."

"Aahh. The women bathe once a moon cycle but we men have no need of it."

"It is the king's wish that every village have a bath and a latrine sited where it will not foul the water supply."

"A latrine we have, My Lord but a bath? When the king, himself comes to tell us, then we will build a bath."

"Listen to me, old man. I speak for the king. I am going to leave tomorrow morning and cross the river. Then I will cross the mountains and the valley and go where the path takes me. In four moon cycles I will return to this village. If there is no bath by then, I will stay here as your village head until you personally have built the baths with rocks you will carry from the river's edge. Come with me and I will show you where it is to be built. One big area. Women one day, men the next. Shave your heads and wash your clothes and all your belongings in the river. I need a bath. Send me a woman to shave me and one for my fellow Knight for we have travelled a long way to sample the hospitality of your filthy village. And make sure they are comely or you will feel the flat of my sword."

They went to the river and Jez told the head man where to build the baths. They were fortunate that the river was not fast flowing on the inside of the bend and there were many flat rocks and pools formed by them. He looked at Arturo. *"I am going to swim in that pool right there after I am shaved. You can pick one of your own."*

They un-saddled from the beasts and brushed them down before tethering them in a grassy clearing. They took their weapons with them to the edge of the river and waited for the Matáng women to arrive. They came down to the rocks giggling together but stopped when they saw the Knights. As always, the sight of them struck fear and awe into all who saw them for the first time.

"Come down here you two. We won't bite you. We need your help to shave and bathe us but first you will have to wash yourselves and your clothes because I can smell you from here."

The girls walked down the bank and on to the rocks where Ch0n and Arturo were waiting.

"Come, on, then, take your clothes off and wash yourselves with this while we wash our uniforms." Jez gave the closest of the girls a bar of soap and mimed the action of washing himself with it. The girl smelt it and showed it to her friend. They watched the two Knights strip naked and start to wash their uniforms in the clear pools. They needed no further invitation and did the same with their tunics and then used the soap to wash their bodies. They were still washing themselves when Jez beckoned one of them to go to him. She looked at her sister and obeyed his signal. He led her to the pool he had selected and took out the multi tool Ch0n had given him. He rubbed his arm with soap and showed the girl how to use the blade to take the hair away from a section.

"I want you to shave my head and my face like that. Slowly and carefully. If you cut me I will not be happy."

He positioned himself sitting between her legs, leaning against her. When he had soaped his face and head, he threw the slippery bar to Arturo, who managed to catch it in his tunic. The girl was fascinated by the tool.

"What manner of thing is this, My Lord? I have never seen its like."

"It was given to me by the king as a reward for serving him and I continue to serve him and speak with his voice. It is a gift to treasure is it not?"

"It is, My Lord," she answered as she scraped the blade carefully over his scalp. *"But why do you shave the hair from your head and your face. Does not your God demand that you have hair on your face as does ours?"*

"The king demands that all people must cut off their hair and beards and wash their clothes and burn anything they do not need so as to rid his people of the animals that live on their bodies. That is why I asked you to wash yourselves. If you like I will cut off your hair when you finish so that when you lie with me tonight you will not infest my bedding."

"My Lord! The head man said nothing to my father about lying with you. Only that you wanted a girl to shave and wash your clothing."

"What is your name, girl?"

"Caron, My Lord."

"The king's aget is called Karín. It is a good name. I am Jez of the Arw'an. Well, Caron, would you not like to lie with me this night? I have been a moon cycle on the trail without the sweet touch of a girl and I feel the need strongly."

"I can see that, Jez. Let me think about it while you cut my hair."

Jez laughed.

"Be careful with that blade on my neck, girl. It is not a fitting way for a Knight to die, bleeding to death while shaving."

"How short will my hair be afterwards?"

"Karín shaved her head in the manner of her Lord, Ch0n. but if I cut it with the cutting blades I can leave this much." He held his finger and thumb to show her.

"Did this Karín look beautiful with her head shaved, My Lord?"

"Aye, she did."

"Then I would be shaved but be careful you do not cut me for a woman may not lie with a man if she is bleeding."

The next morning the two Knights set off for the ford after reporting in to Guerra and downloading images of the outpost and the surrounds. The two girls bade them farewell until their return. Caron was sporting a silk beanie and her sister a silk turban around her head. Jez was humming the alphabet song to himself and Arturo was just grinning under his visor.

"If the crossing is two days walk from here we should reach it shortly after the middle of the day" said Jez. "And I hope we can make good time over the mountain. I am just a little concerned for the beasts, which are accustomed to walking on flat ground. If the slopes are stony and slippery, they may get frightened. I think we may have to lead them. Maybe give them a little of Karín's root to calm them. I hope not."

"Jez, is it always so much fun? Being with a woman, I mean."

"I know not the answer to that. I have only ever been with three, Sonja, Malek, my aget who is with child and so forbidden to me, and now this one. I have never found it not to be enjoyable. But after what you have told me of your previous life, anything would have to be better."

"How will they be viewed in their village after lying with us?"

"They will be seen as favoured by us. They will show the head man their shaved heads and he will know that what I said to him is true. He will now build the baths and they will all shave their heads. I told Caron that Ch0n has allowed a short beard to appease the Matáng God but nothing that can be grasped. When we return, all the men will be clean and all their

women will be grateful to us for making them bathe. Caron and the other one will come straight to our beds and will probably beg us to take them away, which we will do. They will have the choice of remaining at Matáng or returning to the castle with us as new recruits for the Lancers. They won't care if they share our beds along the way. It will be part of their adventure. They will just want to escape from here after all. That's why they were the first two to volunteer to shave us. They knew we would desire them after a long journey and they were prepared to lie with us from the beginning."

"So we will be back in four moon cycles?"

"I hope so. I want to be back at Arw'an as soon as possible to see my new son."

They crossed the river where it was wide and shallow. The beasts were sure-footed in the water, which made Jez more confident about the climb through the mountain pass. Once on the other side, they made good time across the sweeping plain to the foot of the mountain.

"We are now outside Ch0n's kingdom from what the elder said. We will camp here by this spring and start early on the morrow," decided Jez. *"I want to be up and over the pass and down the other side in one day. We leave at first light."*

"You assume command easily for one so young," said Arturo testily. *"I don't recall Ch0n placing you in command of the mission."*

"Someone has to decide. Your turn will come when it comes. If you have a better plan, let me hear it. If not, dismount and ready your beasts for the night. I do not seek an argument."

"Then do not assume I am at your command. We are all equal as Knights. I would not assume to command you."

"If it is an issue between us, I will have the ChOn decide it when we speak. Then there will be no doubt."

"We both know he will appoint you. You are favoured by him."

"Yes. I have served him since the first day he arrived in our village. I have fought by his side and at his back. I am the commander of the Castle Garrison. He took a village boy and turned him into the first Knight of the Arw'an with all that goes with it, good and bad. He sent me on this mission and asked me to select the one I would have at my side. I selected you for your good sense and good humour. Don't prove me wrong for we will be together a long time."

"You know me not, Jez. I was born anew not three months ago and I have changed much since then. I thank you for giving me this opportunity to grow more but do not assume I am at your command. We are two out here and the king is a long way away."

Suddenly Jez felt uneasy about the situation. The argument had come from nowhere, after they had so recently been laughing and joking about the night before. He knew at that point that his back wasn't safe.

"Would you defy the king tho' you have sworn an oath to him?"

"I am here on the other side of the river that the elder said marks the border of his kingdom. He is not king here. This is neutral territory and I have the weapons and knowledge to start a kingdom of my own here if I choose to do so. The Vikings are another two months ride from here. I would be their king as ChOn is of the Arw'an. They are two worlds apart and we could live in peace if neither sets foot on the territory of the other."

"Arturo. The penalty for treason is death."

"And who is to carry out that sentence? You? You may be a Knight of the Arw'an but you have not the training we space commandos have. Leave well enough alone, Jez. I have no wish to kill you. Just get down and leave me your oruk, your helm and tablet, and your weapon belt and I will be on my way. Walk back to the village and have a life there with the girls from last night."

He had the stun pistol pointed at Jez now.

"Come on, boy. There is nothing to be gained by delaying."

Jez dismounted and removed his weapon belt, helm and armour.

"I would keep the multi-tool that ChOn gave me."

Gavan Connell

"OK. You may keep just that."

Jez took the precious tool from its pouch and stepped back from the small pile of things he had relinquished.

Ch0n left the turret and went downstairs to Guerra's command post for the nightly schedule with Jez and Arturo. He was somewhat surprised to see Arturo on the screen instead of Jez.

"Jez is feeling sick tonight. We think it was something he ate at the Matáng village. He is away purging himself. I hope he will be OK. He has bad pains in the gut and dysentery to go with it. I will watch him through the night when he returns."

"We have seen the images you sent us of the ground between the village and the crossing. Mark that crossing well for it is of strategic importance to us if we need to cross into the Viking land at any time. Tell Jez that Malek is well and I will talk to him tomorrow morning when he is feeling better."

"I hope he recovers quickly. I have nobody else to talk to. Send my love to Salina and tell her I hope to see her soon. Arturo out."

"Guerra. Switch to frequency three. Quickly man! Jez this is Ch0n….. OK. No answer. We'll have to wait until tomorrow to find out how he is."

"Why did you only call once?"

"Because in the year or more that I have known him, he has always answered after the first call. Either he is under water or he is away from the helm. He NEVER takes it off when he is away from the castle. Even to sleep. How far is it to their last known location? Direct line."

Guerra paused while he booted up the master tablet with the map of the known world and joined two points.

"One hundred and forty seven miles. They are north-west of us but have been west and north during their travels to touch base with Izaki and Mastelik."

"How long will it take to get the drone on line?"

"It has to be assembled but it is designed in such a way that it can be done by a team of two in three hours."

"Do it. I will be the other person. If something is wrong, I want to know about it. What range does it have?"

"You honestly don't know this stuff? I thought every commando would have to know it. It has four mini-mass drivers powered by a false fusion pack. It can stay in the air until it wears out the vortices."

"I am sure someone in the team knew but it wasn't me. And the payload?"

"It can carry up to ten pounds on the hook. Inside dimensions of the cargo container are twenty inches by ten inches by ten. Same weight restrictions."

Gavan Connell

"Get on it."

Guerra left. ChOn called Darel, went next door for his helm and measured it. It was less than ten inches in diameter. It weighed next to nothing. He told Darel to bring the metal storm kinetic pistol and a spare barrel-magazine. He knew before it arrived that it was sixteen inches long with the barrel-magazine attached and that it weighed six pounds loaded and two and a half empty. He drew a box on the desk, twenty inches by ten and waited for Darel. The unloaded pistol fitted into the helm and the two barrel-magazines beside it. ChOn guessed the weight of the helm at one and a half pounds. All together, the payload would be more than the permitted weight. He thought about partly unloading the second barrel and decided that if Jez needed more than one barrel he would not be able to fight his way out of whatever problem he was in anyway. He decided to put a hunting knife instead. It was exactly twenty inches long end to tip and weighed two pounds without the sheath. He did a quick calculation. Nine and a half pounds. He decided on three grenades to make up the difference.

"Darel. Wrap up the kinetic pistol, the knife and the grenades in a silk beanie, take them to the top of the tower and wait for me there. Send Buyo to find Karín and ask Karín to come to the top of the tower."

He bounded up the stairs and waited for Guerra and Carmodi to arrive with the drone kit.

Jez came-to with a throbbing head and a feeling like he had been beaten to within an inch of his life. He had no idea how long he had been unconscious, only that the sun still had not set. He stood up and staggered to the river, stripped off and flopped into it. The cold water cleared his head and soothed his aching joints. He assumed he had been shot with the stun pistol, not to kill him but to give Arturo the chance to pack up and leave without having to worry about him. He knew Arturo was going to cross through the pass and that he would not try it at night. While his head was still under water, a plan came into his head. He drank deeply and left the water, put his uniform back on, taking the remote control out of his boot. He pressed the test button and the light flashed once. Then he took off at a run at an angle north of the faint track to the pass. He kept to the low ground as much as he could, running until the sun touched the mountain to his left. He walked only to catch his breath and paused only to drink. As night began to fall, he turned towards the pass and started to jog until it was too dark to see the track easily. The moon finally came out and provided him with a view of the dark mountains and he could make out the pass. He walked as fast as the terrain would allow in the moonlight until he came to a short spur across his front. He felt the rocks at the top of the rise. They were slightly warm to the touch so he crawled forward and looked out into the darkness for anything that might give Arturo's position away.

Arturo considered his situation as he rode at the head of the caravan. The second oruk was on a lead behind him and then the two tlaque. He had not counted on the fact that the led oruk would not want to trot if it was being pulled along by the nose and so his progress was not what he would have liked. He had set the stun pistol to fifteen because he had not wanted to kill Jez, whom he had come to like but who didn't fit his plans. He knew Jez would safely find his way back to the village and that eventually Ch0n would send someone to pick him up. By then he, Arturo, would be king of the Vikings with a stable of Viking women to serve his needs. He rode towards the pass until it was almost dark and tethered the beasts. It took him quite a while to do it all alone and he decided he would have to stop a little earlier in future to give himself time to get his night routine finished before darkness overtook him. He spent time setting out the few motion detectors they had brought in case Jez tried to catch him on foot during the night, lit a small fire and then set up his bedroll well away from its glow. If Jez did follow him, the movement detectors would notify him via his helm and he could sit and wait for Jez to enter the circle of light and kill him. He had been given his one chance to live but next time, if there were a next time, there would be no quarter.

From his vantage point, Jez watched the fire below him. He had succeeded in overtaking Arturo and could now plan to ambush him on the track. He knew that the other Knight had a similar night routine to Ch0n and that to try and enter the camp would mean death. Instead, he turned his back on the campfire and waited for his night-vision to return. When he could make out the ground at his feet, he set off towards the pass, making sure he didn't use the path. Any overturned stone or broken off twig might alert Arturo to his presence. It took him most of the night to reach the highest point. Looking down he could make out the prick of light that was Arturo's camp. He found a place where water leaked from the rocks, drank until he was full and went to sleep on the ground.

Ch0n told Karín he would be needing her helm and why. She saw instantly the possibility of treason. She was fascinated by the drone that was taking shape in front of her. Ch0n explained its purpose as they assembled it. Finally it was done and he turned to Guerra.

"Can you fly this thing at night?"

"Yes, but what is the point? We can take off at first light and it will be there in two hours or less. I will fly it at eight hundreds of feet, which is the optimum air density here for the mass driver and when we are closer, I'll slow it down and go up to twelve hundreds and start looking for them. The best part of this is that it is completely silent except for the airflow over the fuselage so even at eight hundreds of feet unless they are looking for it, they won't hear it or see it."

"Darel, bring Marik to me. Tell him it is urgent."

"When we have spoken to Marik I will know what to do with the drone. I am tempted to launch it two hours before first light to get us there a little after dawn. They will be moving around in the camp by then and should be easy to find."

"I am going to test it while there is still enough light to see it in flight. The hand held remote is easy to use if you can watch the drone but for longer flights it has to be connected to a monitor, in this case the tablet so it can fly by instruments and we can monitor the camera. Are we ready for this?"

He pressed a button on the control and held it. There was a click from the drone as something booted. In a few seconds, the vortices started to whirr almost silently. Guerra did something and the four rotated so they were facing down. He did something else and the drone rose majestically into the sky above them and went into a hover. From below it looked like a large insect with four hollow circles evenly spaced and a box underneath. The cameras were like miniature guns pointing down and frontwards. Guerra rotated them one at a time. Two images appeared on a split screen on the face of the control.

"So far so good," he said to himself in English. Then he did something else and the two metre diameter annulus rose rapidly and hovered again.

"Five hundreds. Eight hundreds. Twelve hundreds." This time in Arw'an.

He rotated the cameras again and the castle appeared, one in colour and the other in pale green with four darker green, man-shaped blobs. He zoomed in until the four could be seen looking up. While they were watching, two more blobs appeared on one side of the screen and on the other, as Darel and Marik came into view. Guerra zoomed in some more and ChOn watched Karín's expression as she looked at the screen. The image grew bigger and bigger until Guerra could read the numbers on the screen, which he had changed to normal mode. Karín looked across at ChOn, her eyes wide with disbeLeif.

"Of all the things I have seen, this is the most wondrous."

"Then try to imagine something similar but as big as this entire castle and the village and you have the ship I was born on and lived on all my life until I came here."

Guerra flew the drone in a large circle and then brought it back to a hover a few feet above them before lowering it gently to the ground in the fading light. He pressed a button and held it down for several seconds before the vortices rotated to their default position and stopped spinning in their mounts. Carmodi looked at him with eyes of adoration, knowing that not even the ChOn could fly the drone. Only her man. Only her Guerra.

"I thought that went quite well for a first attempt."

"You mean you have never flown that thing before?"

"Never, My Lord. But my minitron showed me how and then I had to fly hundreds of flights on a simulator. Tomorrow when I take it off using the monitor, it will be exactly like the simulator on the ship, only this time I will have a real plane and not a computer-generated image."

"What is a computer-generated image?"

"This tablet is a computer, Carmodi. It is a machine with a brain that can remember everything you tell it. It uses that to tell you things when you ask it. It can make an image of anything so as to make it look real when you are practising."

"Oh..."

"Marik. Thank you for coming so quickly. Look at this screen. This is a village on the Matáng border with the Vikings. There is the ford used to cross the river. On the other side of the river is a track leading here to this pass over the mountains. This morning, Sir Jez and Sir Arturo were at the village and a few hours ago Arturo reported to us from the other side of the ford. They were going to the pass. I have a question for you. If you were Sir Jez and had been betrayed but were still alive with no weapons, what would you do?"

"Do? I'd hunt Sir Arturo down and kill 'im like a dog."

"OK, Marik, that's fine but could you be more specific?

The commander of ChOn's mounted Infantry scrubbed his chin and unbidden, took the tablet from his king and scrolled as he had seen ChOn do through the few images of the village, the track to the ford, the ford and the image showing the pass in the distance.

"The ground is stony 'ere on the flat. It is poor country for grass, which is surprising because there is water all around. I'm guessing the path up to the mountain pass is rocky so Arturo will have to negotiate it by day, both up and down the other side. 'E will camp close to the base of the climb tonight and at first light will start the climb so as to reach the pass by the middle of the day and be down the other side to whatever is there before dark tomorrow. I am going to use the time 'e is at rest to run past 'im without using the track and gain the 'igh ground. Somehow, I am going to surprise 'im and kill 'im."

"Thank you Marik. I agree completely. Guerra. Tomorrow at first light we are going to have the drone at the pass. We will approach it from the west side below the crest after locating Arturo. If Jez is with him and all is well, we will simply fly to the Viking harbour for a look and then fly back here with as many images as we can fit in one morning's flying. It will tell us a lot but I still want feet on the ground there for a close look. Images can tell you what something looks like but it can't feel the place like an Arw'an Knight. Now. Disable the micro satellite relay until further notice. Do it now. There may be no time to lose."

Guerra rushed below to the comms centre and put the satellite into sleep mode. He knew why Ch0n had ordered it and would have done it himself without Ch0n's direction. It was insurance against treachery by the three Knights and himself. If Arturo had killed or marooned Jez in the furthest village of the kingdom and could contact the remaining two Knights, a coup could be mounted here at the castle. He instinctively knew also that Ch0n had ordered him below so he could speak to Karín and Marik.

"Marik. Have the garrison stand-to and send a squad of men to the comms room. If you return here tomorrow at first light you will find out if your theory is correct. This is a secret mission, by the way. Tell nobody. Goodnight and thank you again."

Marik nodded and left. He was elated but refused to show it. The king himself, the same king who had single-handedly masterminded an entire defensive battle against the Matáng army, had sought his counsel. He shook his head as he descended the stairs to the village. And he had to keep it to himself. He rushed to the guard room and rang the big iron bell twice and after a pause, twice again and then again. Six bells. Stand to. It was something the garrison did at least once a moon cycle and so nobody was unduly surprised or alarmed. It took less than half an hour until every man was at his post and every Lancer and every Mounted Infantryman was on the square. Ivor and Harry took their places at the top of the turret with ChOn and Karín. ChOn turned to them and spoke quietly in English.

"If either of you has anything to tell me, now is a good time to do it."

"My Lord," began Harry. *"This is a general Stand-To. It can mean only two things. It's a drill or the castle is in danger of attack. What more is there to say?"*

"You are correct, Sir Harry. The castle is in danger of attack but not from without. I suspect there is treachery afoot. What do you think, Sir Ivor?"

"My Lord. If any were to betray you, we Knights are sworn to protect you."

"As a sign of faith, then, I want you both to return to your quarters and disarm yourselves on your own honour until further notice. If and when I have resolved the situation, I will send for you and we will have a frank and open discussion about the future. You may choose not to lay down your arms for they are yours to keep in my service but you should know that if you do not do so willingly, you will not live to see the morning."

"It is not much of a choice, My Lord," said Harry. *"But it is not a difficult one."*

"I regret feeling the need to do this. Please return now to your quarters and do not speak to anybody other than your squires, who need know nothing of this disarmament. It is between us three." And then in Arw'an. "The garrison will remain at fifty percent stand-to until mid-day tomorrow or until I order otherwise. Karín. Please have the Lancers return to the lines but at fifty percent stand-to."

Guerra sat at the main radio, the one salvaged from his own shuttle and waited. Ch0n knocked and entered.

"The micro-satellite is in sleep mode. No transmissions may be made using the retransmission facility. Line of sight comms between helms remains normal during this time. I see why you won your war with the Matáng. I watched it from afar but now I can see the depth of planning you have in place and why you were able to do what you did to them. You leave nothing to chance."

"No. And you know what that means as far as you are concerned. I have asked Marik to send a squad of troopers to keep a listening watch over the radios so you can sleep. Two hours before first light we will launch the drone to where Jez and Arturo should be. Nobody else can fly that drone so make sure you don't let yourself down. I need to be able to trust you and the others. If I can't, there is only one way out for me and that is to rid myself of all threats. I will have this conversation with Ivor and Harry in the morning after we have done what we need to do and if they can not satisfy me, I will have both their heads. Jez is like a brother to me. Or a son if I had one. If he is alive I want to know and if he is dead, I will track Arturo to the very gates of the Viking stronghold and bring him back alive for Malek to flay. Here are the soldiers. Leave them to their task and I will see you at the appointed time."

"You have nothing to fear from me. I have never been more at peace with myself or as satisfied with my lot. I have no desire to be more than this and I certainly have no desire for the death that would await me if I had further ambitions. The others I can not speak for but they will make their own cases on the morrow."

Arturo slept hard. Usually he would have the minitron send him to sleep but he had to monitor the motion detectors with the helm activated. The night passed slowly and before first light he was moving about the camp readying himself for the long climb to the pass. He had the four beasts saddled and ready as soon as he thought it was light enough to move. He mounted the giant oruk and urged it into a walk, towing the other three in his wake. Twelve hundred feet above him, the drone was in a hover. The thermal imagery was working without the other camera but to the onlookers in Guerra's office it was clear that Arturo was alone.

"Take it around to the dead ground behind the pass and see if Marik was right."

Exactly four minutes later, they found Jez asleep on his rock. Marik chuckled to himself. Ch0n patted him on the back and nodded his praise. Marik could not have been happier had he received a medal.

"It will take Arturo at least four hours to make the saddle. Let him sleep. Take me to the village by the river."

The drone tracked its way silently to the Matáng outpost. There was not much to see there apart from some new construction happening by the river. Guerra piloted the drone back to the saddle and waited in a hover where Jez would see it but Arturo would not. Jez finally woke, wet his tunic, placed it over his head and slithered to a place from where he could look down the path towards Arturo's camp."

"Ha!" said ChOn. "Always thinking that one. If Arturo is on thermal watching the horizon, he won't see him because the water is cool. Now Jez. Turn around and look behind you!"

Jez stared down the track. In the distance he could make out Arturo's caravan moving towards him. He estimated he had almost until the middle of the day to wait and decided to hunt around for a vantage point from which to detonate the grenade Arturo was sitting on. He worked backwards until he was behind the crest, stood up and turned around. There in front of him, not twenty feet away was the drone in a hover. Those present in the comms room could see the whites of Jez's eyes as he tried to make out what he was looking at. Guerra kept the hover until Jez grinned and then he landed the craft gently.

Jez rushed over to the strange looking thing. On examination he found a small latch in the top of the body of the drone. He opened it carefully to reveal the storage container as well as a host of wires and other things he had no intention of touching. He took out the Helm and the silk beanie with its contents. He put the helm on immediately and ChOn could see him talking.

Guerra was already booting the micro satellite and a few seconds later, Jez's voice came through on a preset frequency.

"Well come, My Lord. I had thought I might need to rid us of this traitor alone."

"Are you all right, boy?"

"I am, My Lord. He might have killed me but he chose not to. He has no desire to provoke a war with you. He just wants to be king of the Vikings as you are of the Arw'an. He says there is room for both if neither sets foot on the other's territory. I told him his words were treason and death but he bettered me, took my weapons and the oruk and here I am."

"Listen well, Jez. That which you were going to do to reclaim the oruk and your weapons you no longer need to do. Instead, use what I have sent you but show no mercy. There is no honour in treason and no dishonour in killing a traitor from ambush. Now close the box and make sure the latch is well fastened. We are going to visit the Vikings and take some images. Then we will return to you and you can repack the weapons exactly as you found them. Nothing more. We will bring them back. I suggest you return to the village and leave one oruk and one tlaque there for safekeeping and then travel alone to the Viking harbour. You will travel much faster alone anyway. I have set the pistol to fire without a thumbprint. Don't try to adjust it. Just use it and repack it when we return with the drone. Do you understand everything?"

"I do, My Lord. Pass my greetings to Malek and tell her I am well and looking forward to meeting my son."

"Be careful, Jez."

"Yes, My Lord."

Guerra lifted the drone soundlessly and dropped it down into the valley behind Jez. After a short while he circled it to the west and it climbed up into the pale purple sky.

Jez put the beanie in his pocket along with the three grenades. The knife he tucked in his belt. He assembled the kinetic pistol and ran the electronic test sequence. It was ready to fire. He applied the safety catch and tucked it next to the knife.

He had to make a plan of attack because he was at a disadvantage if he moved around. He did have the benefit of surprise with him, however. Arturo had no way of knowing he had re-armed himself and so might be a little lax if he saw Jez before the fight was joined. Jez, however, was determined that he should simply ambush the other Knight.

"Should I do it here or further down the hill on the other side?" He thought to himself. While he was thinking of the advantages and disadvantages of each, he went for a drink and saw his own footprints in the muddy shore of the small lake. That decided the place for him. He could not afford Arturo to know he was on the mountain if he wanted to maintain surprise and have Arturo a little relaxed. He began to look for likely places to hide. "Arturo is right-handed. So I should be on his right side. That way he will have to turn his body to fire anything at me with his right hand. I should be above him slightly so his line of sight has to be altered for him to notice me. I should be slightly forward of the rise so he is celebrating his arrival and looking towards the lake for water and not thinking about where an ambush might happen."

He selected a spot where two rocks had fallen over, creating a small triangular opening. It could not be seen from down the hill and if he lay flat, he would not be seen from the flank. He would wait until he could hear that Arturo had passed him, lift his head up and fire from the prone position.

"What else? What would Ch0n do?"

He looked around until he found the remains of an old fire, removed the helm and blacked his shaved head, face, neck and the backs of his hands. He put the black beanie over his head to make sure it wouldn't shine and then went away from the track and pulled up a small shrub. This he placed where it would not impede his vision or his movement but if Arturo were looking for an ambush, it might help hide the opening.

"A diversion? If I could make him look away for a second or two I could gain that time."

He grinned to himself, took a grenade out of his pocked, armed it and put it at the edge of the lake. He took the remote out of his pocket and checked the code for Arturo's saddle grenades for the eleventh time, had a drink, relieved himself where the wind wouldn't carry the smell of his urine to the track and went to his position to wait. He lay flat on his stomach with the inert helm by his side, his right arm outstretched and the pistol in his hand with the safety to 'auto'.

The drone flew like an arrow to the Viking harbour. Guerra saw it in the distance and summoned ChOn to look. The opening in the cliff grew larger until Guerra suggested they hover at two hundred feet, a thousand yards from the opening and try to see inside. ChOn was happy to try it so Guerra manoeuvred the craft into position and zoomed the cameras.

Ivor and Harry were in their respective quarters with their squires. Each had come up with a theory as to what was happening to make ChOn so cautious. They were unable to compare theories but Ivor wrote a note to Harry and told his squire to deliver it to Harry.

"Go, boy. The king said nothing about communicating by note."

The squire ran from Ivor's quarters to Darel.

"I need to see the king."

They went to the comms centre and the boy showed ChOn the note. It read:

"What is happening? Has Mastelik gone rogue?"

"Deliver it, boy and bring me the reply. Hurry now."

The squire raced to Harry's quarters and gave him the note. Harry started to write. He gave the squire the reply. ChOn unfolded it.

"I doubt it. More likely Jez is dead and Ch0n is covering the possibility that we are in on it."

"Deliver it as before."

The notes went back and forth for almost half an hour with Ch0n reading each one. Finally the squire stopped coming. Meanwhile, Guerra was taking images of the boats inside the cave and the town that was cleverly built along the banks of the cool river under the cliff structure that formed the cave entrance.

"We didn't see this town because of where we were orbiting. Had we been a little further to the north it would have been visible. As it stands it is hidden by the cliff."

"Show me the approaches to the cliff."

Guerra flew the drone away from the cave, gained altitude and swung around in a long arc until it was north and east of the cave. They could see the top of the cliffs, which turned out to be a flat tableland stretching away to the eastern tip of the same mountain range where Jez was lying in wait.

"Perfect country for waging war on tlaque and oruk. If we have to attack, we will do it over this open plain and if we control the cliffs, we control the town and the exit to the harbour. All we need is access to water."

"There is a spring here. But there is nowhere really from where the water can drain to give water to the approaches. We would have to supply it from further back. Here is a good

source. Let me see now. It is five miles from the spring. Not too far. I suspect the spring feeds this other one."

"We should have heard from Jez by now."

"We estimated up to four hours. It has been just three and a bit."

"Take the drone back there. By the time we arrive it will be over."

Jez had dozed off but was now wide awake. He had moved just once to stretch but had since adopted his firing position. He waited a long time in complete silence until he was jerked into instant concentration by the sound of one rock striking another. He tried to guess how far away it was but resisted the temptation to move. Then he heard it again and guessed it was less than a hundred yards distant. He started to breathe slowly, listening as intently as he could. The sounds were coming more frequently now as the caravan approached. They stopped for a minute or more and Jez guessed that Arturo was surveying the pass, perhaps looking for likely ambush sites, one of which was where Jez lay. He had deliberately avoided the best position in favour of where he was lying. The better position was a triangular rock a little further down from the saddle with a better view down the track.

"OK, Jez. I know you're here. I saw your tracks on the path. Come out and we will discuss our options."

Jez didn't move. He had avoided the track exactly for that reason. He knew then that Arturo was bluffing and whatever followed would also be a bluff. The silence grew deafening until suddenly the triangular rock exploded, forty feet in front of him, showering the area with fine, glassy stones. The oruk must have shied because Jez heard Arturo swearing at it and fighting it for control. Then Arturo laughed and while the dust was settling, the sound of hoof on stones started again and Arturo entered the killing ground. Jez waited until he was sure the first beast was past his position. He put his finger on the trigger and pressed the remote at the same time.

Arturo was looking at the track in front of his oruk, trying to guide it through the worst of the broken shards of shiny rock, cursing himself at the same time for making the beast nervous and causing this extra risk of injury. Suddenly the air was rent with a muffled explosion and he turned in time to see a plume of water shoot into the air on his left side. He was still reacting when the first of the .177 pellets struck the side of his helm and tore it away. He fell from the oruk almost to the ground, left hanging in the stirrup. His pistol fell from the holster and the oruk shied away from the noise and the unfamiliar weight against its side. Arturo's face was a mess down the right side. He could not see anything on that side but out of his left eye he saw Jez approaching, holding the kinetic pistol at the ready.

Jez rounded the oruk and blew gently into its nose. The creature recognized him and stood still. The other oruk and the two tlaque were already looking for pick in the rocky ground. He went to the helpless Arturo, took the stun pistol from the saddle boot and picked up the kinetic pistol.

"I'm going to set you loose and we can discuss out options."

He shot Arturo through both kneecaps, wrenched his left leg and it came out of the stirrup cup. Arturo was screaming in agony. Jez pulled the oruk away and tethered it.

"I fear I may have earned the wrath of the king," he said, smiling. *"I have ruined one of his precious helms. But never fear, I have another here."*

He put on the spare helm and booted it.

"Are you listening, My Lord?"

"I am."

"How long until the brone arrives?"

"'Drone'. Maybe another half-hour. Guerra? Make that twenty five minutes. That's the time it takes to run around the castle outer wall."

"I can keep him alive that long. He has quietened down a lot. He was screaming like a girl not long ago. Now he is just sort of pale and wondering how I came here and how I came to have a weapon and a helm. You would have been disappointed with him. He did not check the pass, tho' it was a perfect place for an ambush. He was sloppy and over-confident. He would have made a poor king for the Vikings, even had he arrived."

"I have some questions for him."

"I will relay them."

"Was he acting alone or in concert with another?"

Jez repeated the question.

"The other two were waiting for me to succeed in ridding myself of Jez. Then one of them was going to kill ChOn and become king. Guerra was tasked to co-ordinate it all using the micro-satellite," said Arturo.

"I heard that. Now ask him what the signal was to have been."

ChOn turned his tablet to 'record'.

"Two kings."

"How was it to be passed?"

"From me to Guerra and then from Guerra to the others."

"Jez, don't pass this on. I need a better recording. Tell him I didn't catch the signal code."

Arturo repeated the code, half shouting.

"OK, Jez. I have heard all I wish to hear. You may like to chat with him for a short while until we arrive."

"Yes, My Lord. I will….chat with him."

"ChOn out."

Jez turned to the stricken Arturo.

"Is this what you wanted? To die in the middle of nowhere? To have all we have given you taken away after such a short time? Ch0n will kill the others now. They may already be dead. He is an unforgiving man to those who would harm him or his people."

"It is not fair that he has it all and we have none of it."

"None of it? You had a house, a title, a squire, the pick of the village maidens, freedom to do as you pleased. All you had to do was be true to your oath and you would be returning to all that. Salina will miss you. She is a good woman and deserved better. But why did you not kill me back there? You must have known I would come after you."

"I had no desire to kill you when we parted but I thought you might follow me into the camp last night and I would have killed you then in my own defence. I underestimated you and overestimated my ability to protect myself. I did not think you would try anything but the obvious."

"I was the Ch0n's squire. I am his garrison commander and head of the army apart from the Lancers. He trained me day and night. Night and day. Together we fought the battle against the Matáng and during that battle he left me to command. He trained me and he trusted me. One who is trained by a king, a soldier of honour no less, does not forget easily. I did not forget a single lesson, the most important of which was, 'think of that which none other will think and then do it for they will never expect that which is beyond their imagination. That is why I wasn't behind the rock you destroyed. It was the best position. The obvious and the one you would be concentrating on."

"How will you kill me?"

"With the sword if I am permitted. Otherwise as the king commands. What does it matter to me? While I am waiting for him, take out your sai, your knife and remove your weapon belt. If you touch anything with two hands I will blow one hand off and leave you just the other to finish the task."

He watched as the other complied.

"Now, take off the remains of the helm and put it with the rest. Now your multi-tool. I know a girl in the village who will pleasure me all night long for that. Maybe all the way back to the castle. Yes. That sounds fair. What else do you have that you can give me to pass the while? I think ChOn will be here very soon. Then you will know your fate."

"I could use a drink. I have been on the trail since first light with nothing."

"You will not need a drink in a few minutes so I suggest you wait."

"The drone is approaching from the valley, Jez. I caught the sun flash off it just now."

"Then our …chat is over."

Jez did not take his eyes from Arturo even when the drone was hovering ten feet away.

"Jez. Tell A2 that Guerra had nothing to gain being the comms officer to Ivor or Harry when he can be mine. I will have him tell the other two to test their reaction as well. I doubt we will discover anything. I have seen an interchange of notes between them which tell me they know nothing."

Jez passed on the message. Arturo shrugged.

"Of course you are right, Ch0n," he said in English. "I was in this alone. Delusions of grandeur. Now I have lost everything. I don't even have my life in a tube to look forward to."

"Your real life lasted five months. Before that you had no life. Now you are going to take it yourself. Jez, give him back his short sword and tell him to cut his belly with it. It is the way the ancient Warrior-Knights of Japan killed themselves to try and recover their honour. Tell him."

"Arturo. My King has told me to return to you your short sword and that you are to cut your belly with it. It is the way the ancient Warrior-Knights of Japan killed themselves to try and recover their honour. Here."

"And if I do not?"

"My King has ordered it. You will do it or I will tie your ankles to the oruk and drag you to the Viking harbour."

Ch0n and Guerra watched Arturo open his shirt, take up the blade and place it against his belly. He plunged it into his body just as Jez shot him through the right eye.

"He spared me once when he might have killed me. I owed him a quick death, My Lord. And he did what you required. It is done. I will take everything from him and bury the body here. Then I will be on my way. I want to be down on the plains before nightfall."

"Jez, a more faithful friend no man could ever have."

"Thank you My Lord. Now I will pack the things you sent me and you can return the... drone to the castle. With this." He picked up a shard of the rock Arturo had destroyed. The broken face of it was fiery red, blue and green in turn. "I know all treasure is yours to keep and I will take you back a sack full of the best of this when I return but if My Lord sees fit, I would have this as a gift for Malek."

Ch0n laughed. Behind him, Karín let the sound wash over her.

"Fear not, Sir Jez, first Knight of the Arw'an. Your wife will have this trinket. I will keep it just long enough to analyze it."

Jez packed Karín's helm, the knife, the pistol and barrel and the opal shard into the beanie. He kept the two remaining grenades, removed the knife again and with the weight saved, put two more of the fiery stones into the box. He double checked the latch was fastened and stepped away.

"It is ready, My Lord."

"Thank you Jez. Go well. Guerra, bring it home."

Gavan Connell

Chapter Ten: Jez

Guerra went to Ivor's quarters and dismissed the squire. He looked at Ivor and said,

"Arturo sent me a message just now. 'Two kings.'"

Ivor looked at him blankly.

"Two kings? Is this a game of chess?"

Guerra smiled.

"Yes, Ivor, that's exactly what it is. The king wants you in the comms room. He is in a foul mood so don't keep him waiting. Take your weapons"

Harry was equally blank and went quickly to the comms room to find Ch0n, Karín and Ivor waiting.

Ch0n replayed the recording of Arturo telling of their part in the plot. Then he addressed them in English.

"Well? What do I do from here? The easiest thing for me to do is to kill you both. I have killed so many since I have been here that I no longer feel it is of any importance in my daily routine. If I were to do that, I would rid myself for certain of two threats to my reign and my kingdom. But I would also lose two of the most valuable people in the kingdom for you two have all the skills we need to teach and lead these sapients into a new era. They have had war among each other for at least three generations that I was able to work out and finally they have peace. They have a king who really just wants to be left alone with his women and his kingly duties. Commander Guerra and I have played out a scene over the last day that has left me a suspicious man. If I remain that way, I will never be happy and the kingdom will never be a safe and happy place. So! What is it to be? You swore your oath and I expect you to adhere to it under pain of death but I am going to give each of you one more chance to decide which direction you wish to take. If one of you would like to be king of the Vikings, leave now. You may take a single tlaque and your commando weapons and no more. I will allow you time to reach the Viking border and then you will lose your right of safe passage and any of my subjects may kill you on sight. If either of you would be king of the Arw'an, there is a ritual that enables you to have that. All you have to do, indeed all anybody has to do, is to challenge me to individual combat. You take my head, you get everything that goes with being king, including my bodyguard, my concubine, my weapons, my squire, even my wolf. If either of you would have that, speak now. No. Not now, right now."

He returned to the Arw'an tongue so Karín could understand.

"Sir Harry, would you be king of the Vikings or king of the Arw'an, Buq'ue and Matáng?"

"I would be king of all of those, My Lord but not if it meant having to leave this place or to kill you to have it. If one day you

were to appoint me king of the Vikings, well I wouldn't say 'no' to that."

"A fine answer. And what of you, Sir Ivor?"

"My Lord, I have seen what a king does, what he needs to do and what he suffers for being king. I have everything you have here. I have a house. I have a tlaque and an oruk waiting to grow. I have a woman who wants to please me and teach me. I have no need to watch my back because none here would harm me. And when I go to my bed at night I know that you are still being king because I see the light in the castle window. No, My Lord. I would not be king even if it were offered to me. I am a soldier and a Knight of the Arw'an. Five months ago I was a soldier of a different kind. I was created to be a soldier. That is enough for me to fulfil my life's purpose."

"Another fine answer, albeit so different from the first. Now I would have you watch the last minutes of the life of the one who coveted the throne of the Vikings."

Buyo moved into Ch0n and Karín's bed two days after the drone returned and Karín had not bled for two consecutive cycles. Ch0n forbade Karín to move into Buyo's room, which both she and Buyo wanted. Instead, he had said,

"We will be a family of three with Buyo having the right to lie with me at any time until the baby arrives and Karín being allowed the right to join in if she feels the need but not to break the taboo."

Jez returned to the Matáng village with the two beasts. He was met by Caron and her sister, Chenna, who knew immediately that Arturo was dead. Chenna shrugged it off and would have left Jez and Caron alone but he called her back.

"I have a task for the two of you. It is one that will make you favoured in the eyes of the king himself. I am going to leave here one of the great Oruks and one tlaque. You two are going to care for them on pain of death. In return, I will take you both from here, should you desire it and place you in the most elite part of the Matáng Army. Or if you prefer, I will take you to where the king resides and you can serve him there. Now, fetch me the head man so I can tell him of your task for it is on his head also that the creatures are safe on my return."

"What befell Arturo, My Lord? I had hoped he would return and take me away himself."

"He disobeyed my orders, Chenna and that is treason for I speak with the king's voice. I had to kill him."

No more was said until the head man arrived, his head recently shaved and his beard cut short. His clothes looked a lot cleaner than they had two days before. Jez explained about the beasts. He removed the saddles and showed them how to attach the lead rope to the spring clips. He was about to mount his oruk and leave but Caron called out to him.

"My Lord Knight! The villagers say we are favoured by the king but because we have lain with two of his elite, the menfolk have shunned us, even those who once looked at us with hunger in their eyes. We will go with you when you leave for

Matáng and Arw'an for to stay here is no longer an option. I would like to meet your king and his aget, Karín."

The three of them were outside the hut that Caron and Chenna now occupied and in which the saddles and tack were stored. The oruk and tlaque were tethered to the wall until their corral was built. Jez looked at the sun and decided he might as well stay the night and leave early. He went into the hut and the sisters followed him.

"I am going to show you the king and his aget if she is nearby. This is a secret thing and you must not speak of it but I wish to show you the powerful things that our king uses to rule us. Now sit behind me where you can see and be seen and speak only if you are spoken to." He booted the tablet, set it to video and pressed the call button. Guerra answered instantly and called over his shoulder to Ch0n next door.

The sisters watched as the giant man with his shaved head appeared and then just his face was visible as it filled the screen.

"What news from the corners of the kingdom, Jez?"

"Well, My Lord, Arturo is buried and I have returned to the Matáng village where I will leave his oruk and tlaque. They will be looked after by two of your fair subjects who are seated behind me. They wish to leave this village and go with me to the castle and join the Lancers. I have told them much about the kingdom. One of them is called Caron and I have said that if the lady Karín is available she may wish to address them."

"So you will leave the village tomorrow and go to the pass and beyond?"

"Yes, My Lord. I had thought of leaving this afternoon but there are some things I wish to…errr show the sisters before I go and I would not have time to reach even the ford before dark."

"So be it. The stones you sent me are called 'opals' and are highly prized as jewelry on Earth for their beauty. Malek has the one you showed me and I have given one to Salina. The other I will make into a necklace for Buyo. Bring back as much as you can carry because it will be much sought after. Aah. Here is my wife, who will provide a prince for your son to play with when he comes."

"Happiness to you both, My Lord and to you, Karín. Now I have two new Lancers for you to meet. They are Caron and Chenna."

Karín appeared on the screen and the two girls gasped immediately. Jez turned around.

"What is it?"

"She is one of the Eani. They are spirit people who once lived among the Eñame, those who sail the sea in large ekwo eaki. Their place is over the mountains where you are going. It is far away but they have been here once or twice over the years and left after they violated our women and stole all they could carry. They are a taller, light skinned race and their legend says that many generations ago, there came from the

skies, strange tall, red-haired teachers who mixed their seed with the Eñame and so they are as they are. It is also said that from time to time, one of the sky people is reborn among us and that he or she is here to make sure the blood lines continue. A woman of our village was born from the seed of the Eñame. She was the head-man's sister. She was taller and lighter skinned than the rest of us and once when the king, Sith, came here, he fancied her for his harem and so he took her. She was never seen again."

Karín listened to the story and analyzed its contents. She knew her mother was not from the Matáng capital. She had told Karín she was from a village far away. When she was with child and of no use to the king, Sith, she had escaped the harem and had followed a Matáng patrol to Buq'ue in disguise.

"Then I am the daughter of the head-man's sister for her story matches the one you have told me. And my blood goes back to the Eñame, whom we call the Vikings. And their blood goes back to the sky people. Jez, I will have our Lord make an image of me that he can send to your tablet. Perhaps when you arrive at the Eñame harbour it will be of some assistance to you if they believe in the legend of the sky people and their return in human form. Thank you girls. I would have you here in my service so you can tell me of my village. Jez will bring you back with him if you wish it for I would have nobody who is brought against her will."

"My Lady, we wish to leave this hole. There is nothing to do and nowhere to go. When the Lord, Jez returns we will go with him and keep him company on his journey to Arw'an."

"Then it is decided. Now I will go and think about my family history."

ChOn bade Jez a safe departure and the link was closed.

"What magic is this that you can see and speak with your king and the Eani, Karín?"

"The king, ChOn is one of the sky people as was Arturo. He brought with him these things many moon cycles ago. He uses them to rule his kingdom and to defeat any who would stand against him for he is a terrible but just king. He slew Sith in single combat not five moon cycles ago at the end of a great battle between the Arw'an and the Matáng and so he is your king as well as mine. You will meet him when we return. Karín was the bodyguard to the king of the Buq'ue, whom the ChOn also slew to become the king of the Buq'ue and she followed him and now she is his bodyguard and aget and is with child. Soon she will bear a son or daughter who has the blood of the sky people, the Matáng and the Vikings."

"And you, Jez? Do you have an aget?"

"I do and she is also with child and so I am forbidden to lie with her."

"But you are permitted to slake your needs with another during that time. You are fortunate to have come to this village and to have found such a one."

"I am and I would be even more fortunate if I had found two, would I not? Now I have to leave early on the morn and I would know how fortunate I have been before I go."

He rose at first light, dressed in his full battle order and went to prepare his beasts. He was saddling the oruk when two of the village men rounded the hut and stood one on each side of him with drawn swords.

"You come here in the name of a king we do not know and make demands in his name we do not want to fulfil. You lie with my woman and now she is forbidden to me for she is favoured by the king's man. You ride these beasts when we walk. There is no escape for us from here unless we change our circumstances. We are going to do that. We will take your life, your fancy weapons and your beasts and roam the plains seeking our fortunes. You will regret the day you mounted my woman for I would not have had the anger on me otherwise."

Jez walked backwards towards the hut and took up a position with his back to the wall.

"In the kingdom of the Lord Ch0n, women are not the chattels of men. They may choose what they wish and whom. To deny this right is not acceptable. As for the beasts, they are not mine but the king's. I can not give them to you for they are not mine to give and because they are the king's, they are not yours to take. Would you steal from your king? To do so is treason and would make you an outlaw and an outlaw is not free to roam the plains seeking his fortune. An outlaw deserves the punishment that a Knight of the Arw'an would deliver to him."

"You are but one. You can not prevail. We will have what we want and after we kill you we will have the women whether they wish it or not."

Jez took the stun gun from its holster, booted it and set the force to twelve.

"You who is doing all the talking, I sentence you to death."

He raised the pistol and the invisible cone hit the villager in the chest. He went down and didn't move. Jez replaced the pistol and drew the katana.

"Now we are one and one. You have your chance to take what you covet, which is my beasts and my weapons. And I have the chance to take what I covet, which is your life. Come now, you piece of goat shit who would violate one of your own village girls." He swung the katana in a half circle in front of his face and stood stock still, side on to his assailant, the katana pointed at the sky over his right shoulder. The villager advanced uneasily and then stopped, his sword still raised. He was about to speak when Jez moved his front foot forward a short pace, followed the move with his rear foot and slashed downwards and to his left. It cut the Matáng from the collarbone to under his opposite arm. Jez watched the body fall twitching to the ground, wiped the blade on his victim and walked to the unconscious second man. He lifted him to a sitting position and bound his ankles and wrists with cable ties. When he turned around, he saw the two girls standing at the door watching him with a mixture of fear and excitement in their eyes.

"We saw and heard everything," said Caron. *"It would be best if I went to fetch the elders before you move anything. We will bear witness to what happened."*

She ran from the hut calling the village to wake up. People started to emerge from doors and flaps. She told them to go to where Jez was standing and wait for the elders. In five minutes, the entire village was present, standing around the scene in a hush. The village head man was one of the last to arrive. He pushed through the crowd and surveyed the scene.

"These men tried to ambush me as I was tending the beasts before leaving. This one will be asleep for a short while but the other as you can see has suffered the punishment that all treasonous dogs will suffer. They were going to kill me, which is one thing but they were going to steal the king's property and then violate these two girls who are in the service of the king as the carers of the beasts until I return. To interfere with that service is to deny the king's wishes, which he has expressed through me. I have sentenced this man to death and when he wakes, he will be executed in front of all of you to show you I am serious."

The elder looked at Caron and Chenna, who both nodded.

"So be it," he said to his villagers. *"Even had this not been the king's emissary, any man has the right to defend himself. The fact he is the king's emissary and they tried to steal the king's beasts makes it treason. I concur with the sentence of death. Let it be carried out."*

A wail from the crowd was followed by a second. A woman rushed forward and cradled the top half of her son's corpse. The other ran to Jez and flung herself at his feet.

"*Mercy, Lord! Mercy! He is just a boy and meant nothing. Mercy, I beg you.*"

"*Mother, when I was his age I was already squire to the Lord Ch0n, the king of three kingdoms. I learned from him the virtues of hard work, loyalty and honour and now I am the first Knight of his kingdom and his most trusted servant. Your son might have trod that path of honour but chose otherwise. It is neither your fault nor mine that he chose his destiny unwisely. So be it. I will be merciful as you ask. I will kill him quickly but kill him I shall. He would have killed me like a coward with the assistance of the other. He would have stolen the king's oruk and tlaque and left you alone. Now he will leave with nothing and you will be no less alone for it but you will all know that to disobey me is to disobey the king and I will have none of it in is name.*"

It took another twenty minutes for the unconscious Matáng to come around and when he did, the first thing he saw was Jez standing over him with the naked katana. The second thing he saw was his companion sliced neatly in two.

"*What have you to say to your king's first Knight before you die, knave?*"

"*You can't do this! You have no right to do this here! We only meant to scare you. We were never going to steal the orok*

*or violate the girls. It was just in jest. I swear it. Please don't
kill me for that. You have no authority here anyway."*

*"You might have selected your last words a little more
carefully. Now, look at the faces of the women who listened to
your threats of violation even as you spake them. I will be the
last thing you see."* Without further ceremony, he took up a
balanced stance, drew back the blade and took the man's head
clean off his shoulders.

*"Such is the price of treason in the kingdom of Ch0n for he is
a hard but just king. He asks nothing of his subjects but loyalty.
No taxes, no tribute, not your goats and certainly not your
daughters. Just your loyalty. It is an easy price to pay for his
protection. Look at these men and know the alternative for I am
sent to the four corners of the kingdom to spread his laws.
Now! I am leaving the village and I will not return for four moon
cycles. When I return, everything will be as it should be. The
beasts will be cared for and these women will be left alone.
The baths will be built and everybody will remain clean and the
clothing and bedding will be cleaned or burned. The animals
that live on you suck your blood and then move to another and
suck their blood and if one of the village has a plague or a pox,
the bugs will spread it from one to the next and then the next.
Whole villages have been wiped out in the past and we knew
not the reason but the king, Ch0n has told us why and he would
prevent it. If all is not as it should be on my return, I will hold
this man accountable. He will tell me those who would not obey
him and those will be the first to die for to disobey him is to
disobey the king. He speaks from this moment with the king's
voice and to disobey is treason and an untimely end."* He
turned to the head man. *"Do you understand, you whose sister*

left here and bore a bastard daughter to the king Sith and whose sister's same daughter is now King Ch0n's aget? Do you understand?"

   "I do My Lord but how do you know about my sister, Gwyn?"

Jez walked to the oruk and untied the rein from the hut. He mounted it slowly for effect and turned it towards the ford.
   "I know it."

He looked at the two girls in the doorway, smiled at them, lowered the gold visor and left the village without a backward glance.

He pushed the oruk hard and crossed the ford well before mid-day. He also went hard at the early part of the slope to make up a little time. When he passed the cairn of rocks that marked the grave of A2 he barely glanced at it. He let the two beasts drink at the lake, camped for the night and then picked his way down the path into foreign territory. He was thinking of Ch0n's advice regarding solo exploration and never relaxed his vigilance. He was most concerned about dagononums and so he had the thermal imaging activated and scanned the plains as Ch0n had taught him; near to far, left to right. He did it every half a mile or so while the oruk ate up the plain with his easy lope. The tlaque had learned to stay close or suffer a painful pull on the lead-rope and so they made good time day after day, week after week without incident. By day he stopped only to register water sources near defendable features and then at night, if there was a cave handy from mid-afternoon onwards, he would clear it and occupy it with at least one of the motion sensors deployed. Each morning early he would clear his perimeter as Ch0n had taught him and spend an hour doing his katas with the edged weapons and then checking his electronics. He was a student of the master and his cast-iron self-discipline was what saved him when he finally came face to face with danger. He had been alone for a month when he rose pre-dawn as usual to check his perimeter. Before leaving the cave he checked the sensor log to find it registering the approach of something large less than a hundred feet from the cave. He quickly took both pistols, booted them, went to the cave entrance and searched his immediate surroundings. As soon as he saw the dragon he froze. It was walking towards the cave scouring the thick morning air with its orange tongue for the source of the scent. It was walking one steady pace at a time, pausing between each to maintain its disguise of invisibility. Jez slowly raised the stun pistol, put his thumb on the screen, checked it was at one hundred and waited. As soon as he moved, the great dragon turned its head and looked straight at him. It stood stock still, perhaps measuring the distance between them. Little did it know that Jez was doing the same thing. The creature took one slow step forward and paused again. Jez decided to shoot it as soon as it lifted its foot again so it would be knocked down with the first cone and then he would run in another twenty feet and immediately hit it with another pulse. For a while neither moved and Jez was wondering if the dragon would leave but he saw it shift balance and it started forward again. It was balanced on one leg when Jez sent the invisible pulse towards it. The cone struck the creature full in the chest and it bellowed as it fell. As soon as Jez had the red light he raced forward and fired another. The dragon's eyes popped from its face from the pressure and Jez immediately checked all around him.

"Always expect your enemy to counter attack, Jez and look for the reserve before you consolidate," Ch0n had insisted and Jez barely had time to react before the second dragon charged. He hit it in the face with the first cone fired instinctively and the creature's head rocked back and its eyes popped. It continued to run at him and the second pulse stopped it less than a metre from Jez's feet. He checked around him again and saw that the area was clear. Only then did he lift the visor to watch the dragons take shape as in death their bodies adopted the universal orange colour of the fauna of the planet. He had never killed a dagononum before and now he had had to kill two to save himself and his mounts. He decided to take the teeth from both as trophies and set to work at the grisly task with his hunting knife. By the time he was finished, the sun was well up and he was covered in gore. He had a wool bag with sixty four teeth in it, which he left on a nearby ant nest and he registered the location on his tablet. He took his own image with the timer and the tablet positioned so the two dagononums were both in the frame with him. He ate lizard for breakfast.

The meat was the first he had eaten for days. The rabbits that proliferated in Arw'an and Buq'ue were scarce here because the ground was damp and unsuitable for burrows. He had killed a few rat-like animals that were suitable to eat but had otherwise lived on the porridge and fruit he had chanced upon. He had to clean himself before he left his night location and it was almost mid-day before he was on the trail with his tablet suitably updated. In front of him on the line of march were the ragged hills that separated him from the Vikings and from a distance he tried to pick out the pass he would use to cross them. He estimated it would take him two more days to reach it.

That night he recounted his adventure to Ch0n and sent him images of the dead dagononums as well as the cave, the water and the hills in the distance. He also had the chance to talk to Malek, who was now visibly with child. She was wearing the opal he had sent her on a copper rope Karín had plaited using the precious wire from the shuttles. He felt a pang of loneliness when the link was disconnected.

As he approached the foothills of the mountains, he saw the herd of armoured beasts he had been told about and warned of; the bauda. They were grazing slightly off his line of march and he decided to give them a wide berth. He zoomed in as close as he could with the telescope in the helm and took images of what he assumed were the male and females and transmitted it back to Guerra.

"Don't mess with him, Sir Jez. Those horns are wicked and he looks like the stun pistol wouldn't even slow him down."

"I am going off the line of march to avoid the herd. I was warned they are very territorial and will attack most things on sight. I do not want to test your theory about the pulse gun but if I do, I will also go for his eyes with the kinetic pistol. Maybe then I will be able to get away if I blind him."

He passed the herd without incident and decided to start the climb to the pass he had selected. He didn't want to be camped where the bauda might wander in the night. He didn't really want to climb the faint path either but he could not see any other option.

That night he told Ch0n he was almost atop the mountains that descended to the sea. He slept hard with his beasts saddled and tethered, three sensors deployed and his helm tuned in to their signals. He was fully dressed and armed. When the dawn broke he was already checking his perimeter and bringing in the sensors. The orange sun warmed his back and burned away the haze, and for the first time, Jez looked upon the distant cliffs that hid the Viking harbour. He felt strangely relieved that he had made it thus far, even though he had several day's ride in front of him. Five nights later, he was camped close to the coast in a copse of trees near a spring when his helm cracked to life.

"Jez, we will send the drone to your position tomorrow. We are going to do another pass to see if there is anything more we can tell you. I want you to wait until dark to approach the actual town. Go on foot when you think the beasts are close enough. You can see as much with your night vision aids as you could by day. We have a lot of broad information on the site so we need you to do some close-in reconnaissance only. I don't want you to be seen. When you have seen as much as you can and have made images of everything important, return here. The drone should be in front of the entrance to the harbour shortly after daybreak. We will look inside the cave and then go around towards the town and then call in on your position on the way back. Start out when you are ready and we will find you. Keep your eyes out for a good place to leave your beasts and remember, do not engage them. I want this mission a secret."

"I will leave here after I have something to eat tomorrow afternoon. The beasts will be impatient to be off their tethers

but I can hobble them here near the water. I will look out for the drone."

Guerra flew the drone low across the sea to a place in front of the opening. The sun was low in the sky behind them and shining in to the harbour. They saw the same four ships as before, all the same in design. They each had a single mast and ports for oars and the dragon carved bow. They were built of wooden planks bonded together somehow and looked sturdy. They could not see further in because of the angle and the narrow entrance. A man was walking along the wharf towards the opening and Ch0n guessed from his size that the ships were no less than one hundred feet long. The man paused and stared long and hard out of the opening and then turned about and disappeared.

"I think he saw the drone," said Guerra. "He seemed to be looking down the lens of the camera."

"Hard to say. How far are you from the opening?"

"Nine hundred and sixty yards."

"Unlikely then. Go around to the village wharf and see if there is anything new. Then do another run down the tabletop at the rear."

Jez was half way down the stony slope when the drone banked and came to a hover in front of him.

"We can't see if there is a way down from the table mount behind the town, Jez. See if you can find one tonight. Spend

Gavan Connell

time trying to identify the purposes of the different buildings. I want to know where their leader lives and I want to know where the crew entrance to the harbour is at the back of the cave. If you can find those, your mission will have been successful and you may return to the castle at your leisure."

"I will see what I can find out, My Lord and then I will indeed return. I long for the company of others."

"Good luck and be careful."

"Yes, My Lord."

"I tell you, Jon, I saw a flying thing out there on the water. It was almost directly between me and the sun and it caught the light. It was made of metal I am sure of it. They have returned!"

"But it has been at least a hundred and fifty summers since they were last here, Erik. The last of them has been dead for generations. My grandfather's log claims he never saw them but his father did when he was a boy. How many summers is that? My grandfather has been dead these past fifty summers and he lived almost ninety summers. Then add another thirty or more summers for his father and we have a hundred and seventy. Why would they come now and why would they summon us again? Is it time for them to test the purity of our race? Will they show us more of the reading and writing skills? Will they at last reveal the secrets of their weapons and powers of silent communications? If you did see something, why didn't they come closer? They know us as we know them. The temple has been active all these years telling the story of how

244

they were sent from the sky and died for us to make sure this world was a better place. Are you sure?"

"I am as sure as I am of most things."

"Then we must go if they have summoned us. Have the crews ready three boats for a voyage of war as well as peace. We will have to be prepared for either. Tell the priests to be ready to set sail in three days. I will consult the navigation charts and the stars. Great-Grandfather sailed the last voyage to the sacred caverns in search of their flying vessel but he found only their tombs, which he left untouched. Perhaps we will know more if they choose to tell us."

Jez kept to the low ground until he was within an hour's walk of the river. He hobbled the two beasts and lay down to sleep. He was so tired from his previous night's hardships that he dozed off almost immediately and didn't wake until it was dark. He checked the beasts were safe and then, with his night vision array active, started to jog steadily towards the edge of the river where it entered the sea. It took him more than half an hour to reach the spot where it flowed noisily across the shallows. He manoeuvred around the point so he could partially see inside the opening on the other side of the river. The cave was lit with torches and there was a lot of activity and noise. Tall, light skinned, bearded men were carrying stores to the only boat he could see. He took out the tablet, made sure it would not flash and took an image of what he could see. He was sure something significant was happening. He waited some time but there was no lessening of the effort inside so he crawled away and made his way upriver until he was opposite the first of the buildings. It was an enormous stone structure with a sloping wooden and mud roof. A steady stream of men was coming and going and disappearing through a rectangular opening in the cliff.

"Back door," he thought as he took an image of it. He continued up river taking images of all the buildings, some large and some small. There was no real indication which of them was the king's dwelling until a man appeared in the street and went to a door and knocked on it. When the door opened, the visitor bowed low and went inside.

"King's dwelling."

At the very end of the village was a set of stairs cut into the side of the cliff, leading to the top. There were guards at the bottom but they were not alert. They were dressed in leather kilts and goatskin vests. The only weapons Jez could see were a long sword, perhaps longer than the katana but heavier and a battle ax with an iron double bladed head. Jez took more images.

"Those weapons are built to be used to chop and hack at an enemy which doesn't move a lot."

He turned back the way he had come. Suddenly his night vision lit up as a sentry turned a corner in the track not thirty feet in front of him. He froze. There was no way of avoiding contact. He drew the stun pistol from its holster as quietly and quickly as he could, booted it and fired point blank at the unfortunate sentry who was now less than ten feet away. The cone knocked him down, his eyes popped and blood spurted from his ears, mouth and nose. Jez had no idea how long he had to escape so he dragged the sentry to the edge of the river and slid him silently into the dark water. The weight of the sword in his belt dragged him under. Jez checked for a counter attack, then went silently down the path to the place he had entered it, jogged back to the beasts, mounted the oruk and trotted towards the mountain pass.

Gavan Connell

Chapter Eleven: The Gathering

Seven days before the appointed day for the Gathering, Kelda had set out for the cave overlooking the lake. She had with her Sir Ivor, whose job it was to make sure that the dagononum was not in the cave and to make sure it didn't appear after they arrived. Vana was on the back of Ivor's tlaque as his aget and as Kelda's chief assistant. The small army of logisticians was met by a similar group from Froncy's Buq'ue team and between the two groups, they established the eating facilities for the participants and spectators with a day to spare. The three teams and their supporters arrived the next day and went to their separate areas. Ch0n and Karín arrived last and went to the cave, which had been cleaned out and set up for them. Ch0n called in the three team captains and they went through the three day schedule, the rules and the points system. Ch0n had made a hundred medals from the aluminium parts of the shuttles for the individual winners and the overall team trophy was a sword that had been dipped in molten gold, mounted on a plinth made of polished wood and held in place with four crossbow bolts that had been dipped in silver. It was a thing of beauty.

"This prize will be held by the village that wins it until the next Gathering, which will be in three summers. It will be kept in a place where all may admire it for its beauty. The individual medals will be worn by the winners until the next gathering

Gavan Connell

when they will be returned to me. I will present them again to the new winners. These medals and the team prize will serve as a reminder that in this kingdom I will not allow any stealing to go unpunished. The medals can not be bought or sold or exchanged. They remain the property of the king on loan to the winners to show their skills. Any who would steal them will gain nothing but they will incur my wrath. The prize is a token. It has no value other than as a symbol of one village's temporary supremacy in military and athletic skills. Cheating in any form will not be tolerated and anybody caught cheating will be shunned by all until the next gathering. Now. Go back to your teams for tomorrow the games begin."

The following day, the opening ceremony was conducted. It was the first time the entire army of the three kingdoms had been assembled in one place. Karín had the three troop commanders maintain a tight control over their charges. Ch0n was just a little concerned that if one team were to be caught cheating it could flare up into an all-out three way skirmish right there so Izaki, Mastelik and Marik were seated immediately behind him where he could keep an eye on them. He was dressed as informally as he dared be, which basically meant he was in his black uniform with the weapon belt and no edged weapons in view. Darel, however was less than two metres away with his armour, weapons and helm, listening for any reports from the castle.

Guerra had been tasked to fly the drone over the site to make images of the gathering from the air. He was as usual sitting in the comms room with the command radio. He put the drone into a hover at 1000 feet with the sun just behind him and took several images and some video. Then he returned the drone to the turret, stored it in its new hangar and returned to the task of analyzing the strips of images he had taken on the last flight to the Vikings. It was then he noticed the faint parallel lines running along the tableland towards the tip. They were so straight they looked as though they had been drawn with a rule. He went back to the aerial images taken by ChOn's ship and joined them to the images he had taken from his own. It was painstaking work but it gave him the same satisfaction someone else might get from completing a complex puzzle. When it was done he drew an imaginary line from the castle to the Viking harbour and extended it along the tableland. It almost ran straight down between the parallel lines he had discovered earlier. And then he had an idea. He drew the same line from the lakeside caverns where the alien bodies had been found and extended it as before. It ran exactly down the centre of the two parallel lines. Exactly. His heart raced. He had found something significant but ChOn was otherwise occupied. He looked out the window. It would be dark in a few hours. He thought back to Jez's report following his recon of the Viking harbour.

"There is a lot happening. It looked as though they were provisioning a boat for a voyage in the next few days."

Guerra ran back up to the turret and he and Carmodi lifted the drone clear of its shelter. He ran back down and programmed the tablet to the drone flight control. Within ten minutes he lifted it off and flew it to the rock ruins on the shore of the lake. They had been almost totally restored apart from a roof section of the large hall. People were still working there at the site. The tower was complete and a sentry was pacing around the turret. Guerra programmed the flight path towards

Gavan Connell

where the lake overflowed into a river and sped it away from the ruins. The river took him to the sea and Guerra turned west and headed for the Vikings. An hour later he saw the three war ships directly ahead. They were almost certainly bound for the lake and the ruins. Or the caverns, more likely. He gained altitude and set the cameras to work as he circled above the three boats. Then he set a course directly for the castle. He called Carmodi.

"We are about to be attacked by the Vikings. Or at least the caverns are. We have to let Ch0n know right now. He will have to deploy a force to the ruins to prevent a mass landing. I am guessing there are about three hundred Viking warriors on those boats and if they land it will be a difficult battle. We have to keep them on the boats. Get Sir Harry while I land this thing and put it away."

Harry arrived before the drone had landed. Guerra was talking and flying it at the same time.

"Sir Harry. Get on the radio to Ch0n while I land this. He needs to know that the Vikings are on their way in numbers and we will have to deploy a force to stop them landing. We have no idea of their tactics but they may just swarm ashore and it's every man for himself until the enemy is destroyed. I am sure he has a plan."

Harry called Ch0n and Darel answered immediately.

"I need to speak to the king urgently. We are under impending attack by the Vikings."

Darel took the helm and ran to Ch0n who was watching the troops parade for the assembled multitude. The Lancers had passed and the mounted Infantry were in front of the dais, saluting him. The foot soldiers were last and there were hundreds of them all in their battalion groups. He took the helm and listened intently for a few minutes while Harry briefed him.

"That's all I know, My Lord. Guerra is on the roof putting the drone away and will be back as soon as he can get here. Here he comes, I can hear him running down the stairs."

"My Lord. There are three Viking longboats approaching under sail. I haven't had time to look at the images but I am guessing there are as many as three hundred of them aboard. They have no tlaque on the boats and as far as I could tell, they had no sophisticated weapons. I will look at the images immediately. I am assuming they will head straight for the channel in front of the tower but when they see the defences, they will probably rethink their strategy."

"You have done well, Commander. Sir Harry, can you hear me?"

"I can, My Lord."

"Go straight to the ruins," Ch0n said in English. "Take a rail gun with you and a standard issue of ammo. The guard there numbers twenty and they are equipped only with swords and spears." He turned around in his seat and reverted to Arw'an. "Marik! Are there any archers at the ruins? No? OK." And again in English to Harry. "Assume they have sent an advance party or will land one east of the ruins. That is the shortest land route from the lake's entrance. If they cross the mountains, they can try and rush the main gate of the castle. Have the garrison stand-to. The parade here is almost finished. I will dispatch the King's Own Lancers to the castle with a platoon plus of Infantry behind them to reinforce the guard. The other two troops will take a company behind and they and the Mounted Infantry will go straight to the ruins from here to re-enforce those already in place. Then we will have archers and electronic weapons at both places. Have Kelda's people load up the tlaque with rations and send them straight to the ruins. They will probably meet the Lancers en route. I will stop by at the castle and then go straight to the ruins from there. Do you understand me?"

"Yes, My Lord. I will leave here as soon as I have spoken to Kelda's people. My squire will prepare my things while I get the rail gun. I will take the one from our ship because it is unlocked and I can program it to my own thumbprint."

Ch0n turned to his three army commanders and Karín. He told them what he wanted them to do and they left to carry out his orders. He told Darel to prepare his tlaque and think about what he would have to do back at the castle to get the oruk ready to leave for a week or more. He called Ivor and told him to return to the castle and assume command of the defences until further notice. He had Kelda and Froncy come to him and told them they would have to run the games without him. Then he sat back and watched the rest of the parade as the athletes marched by in their coloured uniforms. When the parade was over, he stood and shouted to those assembled.

"People of the three kingdoms! We are under threat of attack from the sea on the other side of the mountains! I am dispatching the three armies to defend the settlement by the lake and the caverns that lie behind it. The games will continue. Team captains know the rules. I have appointed Kelda and Froncy to award the medals and the main prize. They speak with my voice. Compete fairly and well. I have to leave you. The aim of these games was to unite us and unite us they will because they provided us with a perfect opportunity to gather the united armies. To have them at hand when we need them is a blessing from the Gods themselves. Let the games and the war begin!"

There was a rush from the parade as military and civilians ran to where they were being called by voice and flags. In minutes the area was vacant. The Lancers were waiting for the Infantry commanders to allocate troops to mount behind them. The Mounted Infantry was the first to leave the area and they went at a canter towards the track leading to the castle and the pass over the mountains to the lake. Ch0n waited until he was satisfied that things were under control and he left with Darel behind him. He waved to Karín as he passed the assembled Lancers and gave her the signal to meet him on eleven.

"I am here, Ch0n."

"When the Lancers leave, I want you to go to the castle. Give your commanders the orders they need and then retire from the battle. I do not want you anywhere near the fighting. Do you understand me?"

"But Ch0n, I am their commander and your bodyguard!"

"You are also carrying our offspring. If making ijon can harm the unborn, a battle would be worse. Do not disobey me. I am giving this order to the commander of the Household Cavalry and not to my wife. Do you understand that?"

"I do My Lord but I am not happy."

"You can command the Lancers from the comms room if you need to. Plus there is a troop at the castle. See to Buyo as well. She has been not feeling well these past few days."

"She told me. I think she is with child. Two months of constant lying with a king who is not taking the milkyweed tea will do that to a female. You will soon be the father of two princes unless I am mistaken. I will have to find you a second concubine from among the Lancers unless you wish to abstain for the next eight moon cycles."

"Buyo too? Well she has wanted it ever since we brought her into the castle so I suppose it was just a question of time. I will see her briefly while I get ready to go to the lake. You should go as soon as the commanders are organized. I would see you before I go. Switch to channel one."

They pushed the tlaque hard back to the castle and arrived there mid-afternoon. Ivor had already arrived and was organizing the castle defences according to the rehearsed plans. The giant crossbows were restrung and the huge bolts stacked next to them, some already fitted with fragmentation grenades and others with white phosphorus. When the King's Own arrived, they went straight to their lines and prepared their tlaque for battle outside the walls. Doni's herders had already separated the herd and they were on the point of leaving for the grazing grounds near Ch0n's original fort. They were equipped with a hand held radio thanks to Guerra's mother ship and at the word from Doni, they pushed the several hundred tlaque, oruk and goats out the gate and up the track towards the knoll overlooking the castle.

Ch0n went from the corrals to the Lancer lines to the village to make sure the villagers were prepared to move into the castle but as usual Sonja was ahead of him. He passed through the kitchens to see Kelda's people already gathering up the stores and taking them to the great hall. He was satisfied. He returned to his quarters via his stable where Darel was busily preparing the oruk. Darel knew that he would be riding the tlaque so Ch0n would have the option once they arrived.

Karín and Buyo were both in their living quarters when Ch0n arrived. He went to Karín and patted her belly.

"This is why you are not going in to battle. I will not risk him." He turned to Buyo.

"Are you with child, Buyo?"

"I did not bleed this moon but I am almost certain. I need to confirm it and that will be when I do not bleed next moon. Karín will have to find you a new concubine, My Lord. But she has already told me she is going to give you the milkyweed tea because not even a king needs three women with child at once."

Ch0n laughed.

"I am happy you are with child, Buyo for I know you desired it. It seems I will have a prince from the Arw'an and one from the Buq'ue. Perhaps my new concubine should be from the Matáng Troop."

"I am sure Karín will choose well, My Lord."

"I'm sure she will as she did last time. Buyo. If you are needed to fire the crossbow as you were last time, do not take any risks because I do not want to risk your unborn either. Ivor will be directing the defence from the turret if it comes to that. Karín you should be with him and Buyo too if it is dark. I am going to speak to him now before I leave. He does not need to know of Buyo's skill. Karín, you might insert Buyo into the battle if she is needed." He kissed them both on the forehead. "Stay well. I will miss you." He strode out of the room and into the comms room where Guerra was as usual at his desk.

"Guerra, launch the drone but keep it well out of range of a pulse weapon," he said in English. "Do not deploy it at less than 1000 feet of altitude. I may have you orbiting over the battle or deployed to see what their rear and flanks are doing. The shore of the lake will restrict our capacity to outflank them if they attack in force and if they attack in a swarm, we may need to attack from the front. If they cross the mountains I want to know about it. Keep Ivor informed because he will be making the decisions here."

"Yes, My Lord. Go well."

"Stay well."

Ivor was in the stables, having ridden from the outer wall.

"We do not know how they fight. If they fight like a regular body of troops we will defeat them in a conventional manner with the Lancers sweeping them from the flank but if they swarm, it will be up to you to see where the danger lies and I think the risk of them breaching the walls at the baths will be higher. Do not be afraid to give them the outer village and fight them in the keep. They will have to bunch there whether they like it or not. Do not risk the Lancers in a close quarter fight. They will be slaughtered. Better they remain outside the walls and do not get involved at all than to get massacred. I do not think there will be more than a hundred of them here. One boat load. Two at most. The energy weapons will cut them down quickly. Guerra will have early warning. Or should. Keep me informed. This is your big test as Arturo's was the mission with Jez. Do not betray me or yourself. Justice will be swift if you do. Do you understand me Sir Ivor?"

"I do My Lord."

"I am leaving now. Tell the guard to open the gates." He mounted the oruk and Darel the tlaque. They trotted down the track to the gates and saluted the guard as they passed through. ChOn took the oruk into a canter and they ate up the ground to the knoll, turned right towards the river crossing where Karín, atop the turret lost sight of them.

"Erik. The watch on the second longboat has signalled that he saw the flying ship. I have a bad feeling about this. What if

the Eani have not returned and it is another race of sky people?"

"It is too much of a co-incidence is it not? They fly to us and leave. This time they did not use the landing ground above the cliffs but that means nothing. They may not have known. We ourselves have nothing but old logs to go by. There is a channel at the far end of the lake near where the meeting and mating place used to be. We will go there and meet them. If they are another race, they will not be there. It would be too much of a co-incidence but I will send a ground force down the shore to check the situation. They can signal us once they are in place. Have the second longboat hug the shore to the right once we enter the lake. But first we have to negotiate the river. If there is to be an ambush it will be there. Drop sails, raise the shields and row up the middle of the river. We should be there by morning. Wait until then before entering the river. The chart says it can be traversed in less than half a day and then there is another day under sail to the end of the lake if the winds are not favourable. If there is no wind, we will row. Send the signals."

Jon raced to the rear of the boat and took two flags from their holders and went through a complicated-looking set of signals that were orders to the other boats sailing line abreast behind the lead boat. As was custom, the senior captain rode the front boat and was always the first to jump ashore and wage war. Erik had never needed to go to war before and he was a little nervous about it. There was no doubting his courage. He had overcome all the pretenders in all forms of war games but he had never actually been blooded. They had always lived in times of peace since the Eani had arrived and then died out. Legend had it that before then they would always be at war within their tribal groups over rights to fishing, access to the port and the river as well as the usual raids on neighbouring villages to steal woman and booty. His grandfather had once led an extended land expedition into the exiled Matáng lands over the mountains but they were a shorter people since their exile and had not mated with the Eani. The orange-skinned, dark-haired women had been not to their liking as wives and there was nothing much to steal. They had raped the women and burned the village to the ground out of frustration and retreated to their harbour never to return. Now he was facing the prospect of a fight if the sky people that had been seen were hostile and he knew they possessed technology he could not defeat. If the Eani had returned, he knew the meeting would be peaceful because they were a peaceful race according to all the histories. They had brought reading and education in navigation and mathematics. They had interbred their females many times over to provide a new gene base and over time their leader had bred with all the females who were of age. More than a hundred and fifty years after the death of the last Eani, they, the Eñame were taller, fair haired and paler than before with a few darker 'throwbacks' born each year but never had a red-head been born. The Eani had apparently all been white skinned and red haired with pale green eyes. For some reason, the red hair never took and their sacred books had it that when one with red-hair were born, she would be the re-incarnation of the Eani queen.

Erik shook himself from his thoughts and looked at the charts again. They were too basic to glean any information of the hinterland but they showed clearly the way points from their harbour to the river entrance and the left and right shores of the lake to the channel. Behind was a range of rocky hills and in the foothills were shown the entrances to the three caves and a tunnel. The glyphs on the chart clearly explained that the Eani had lived in those caves and that they were buried there with all their secrets. He cursed himself for not ever having set up a permanent camp there to explore and if necessary excavate the caverns looking for whatever secrets might reveal themselves but the priests regarded the entire area as a sacred site and not to be visited without a good reason. They had agreed that on this occasion it could be permitted and had sent along the high-priest, Verge, to bless the voyage and to pave the way for an entry to the caverns.

It took Ch0n almost until nightfall to reach the ruins, which were no longer ruins but the name had somehow stuck. The two troops of Lancers had already arrived as had the Mounted Infantry. Harry had organized a defensive perimeter out to a hundred yards. The tlaque were in a temporary corral in a copse of trees closest to the path leading down from the mountain, where they would not be taken by surprise. The Lancers and their Infantry 'jockeys' were busy strengthening the walls of the corral and at the same time providing forage. A chute ran off one side to the lake so nobody would have to cart water. Harry himself was mounting the chain gun on the purpose-designed pintle-mount atop the tower. Alongside it stood the new giant crossbow that was even bigger than the two at the castle. It fired the same bolts but because of the extra velocity, they had managed to extend the range by almost a hundred feet but the degree of accuracy at middle ranges was much better as the bolt flew flatter for longer. Ch0n rode slowly around the perimeter checking to see if all was as he would like it. He moved some archers from their spot on the shore a little further inland so they would not waste half their arc on the lake.

He was trying to visualize the longboats moored offshore surveying the force on the shore. He realized that if their commander didn't like the odds he could simply go left and right and attack from one or both flanks. He touched the alien rod that was tucked into a special holster in his armour. He recalled the recorded message.

"There is a function which requires a secondary security measure to access it. Only one who has the intelligence to work out what it is will be able to access that function."

He retired to the small room in the ruins that had been allocated to him as accommodation and command centre. He pulled the screen across the entrance, took the minitron and placed it beside him, booted the translator and drew the rod from its holster in his armour. He turned it two clicks and waited. The light array flashed for a few seconds and stabilized. The recorded voice came on again as before. Ch0n already knew what he had to do. He had worked out that the first language would probably be the aliens' own tongue with some sort of message for the finder. He decided that the second would be the language the aliens had used to communicate with the Vikings and he knew that the last three Arw'an words in the instructions were 'yes or no'. This time, when the question was asked, he responded with the third last word 'da'.

"The staff recognizes the holder by identifying the bracelet. If the holder has no bracelet, it will not activate at all. The fact you are the wearer of the same bracelet as the One who once answered, means you have worked out the secret of the final function of the device. You do not realize it but the voice you are listening to is speaking to you in the language in which you just replied. The translation is being made by the bracelet and sent to your brain through your body's nerve mechanisms. You need not revisit this menu. If you need to translate into any of the six main galactic dialects, you will be able to do it with the staff activated. If you are in communication with any of the other wearers, they too will be able to speak any of the six tongues but they must be in communication with you for they can not do it alone unless they access the staff as you did with the code. This second position will now enable you to read the glyphs we have left you if you point the staff at them. They will reveal to you many secrets of our resting chamber. In the past short while, you have listened to and understood all of the six tongues. You are now ready to use this for peaceful purposes because dialogue is for peace. The weapon system is for use in war. Use the one before the other for we came to create in our own image and not to destroy."

Ch0n waited for more but there was nothing to follow. He turned the handle to the third position and pressed the fifth glyph.

"Karín, can you hear me?"

"Yes, My Lord. Well probably no. I don't really know. I can feel you in my brain more like it."

"Aah yes! I know what you mean. I feel it too. I have found the last function of the rod. It is a translator like the minitron's program but much more complicated. I can now speak six different languages and while we are communicating like this, so can you. I am not even sure if we are not rotating through all six while we speak."

"What a wondrous thing, My Lord."

"You need to know how to boot it and use it in case anything happens to me. It is too powerful for its secrets to die with me. There must always be two who know how it works. I will show you when I return. I must go now. It will be dark soon."

"Jon. It will be dark soon. Change the watch and navigate to the mouth of the river and drop anchor."

"Da Erik."

Ch0n left his quarters and wandered on foot around the perimeter. Harry was ahead of him some short distance doing the same. Ch0n chuckled to himself. They had been taught using the same subliminal lessons over and over by the minitron. They were two peas in a pod. Two warriors with no real free will when the heat of battle was near. They reverted to what they had been taught and Ch0n recalled it had saved him more than once already. He mounted the ladder to the tower's door, entered and climbed the internal steps to the turret. The uneven stairs as for the castle wound up and clockwise to give a defender the advantage. A right handed swordsman would be fighting at a natural angle outside his body from the high ground on familiar stairs while the attacker would be fighting at an awkward across his body, his defences opened by the angles and his eyes always trying to see the height of the next step. Nothing was left to chance.

Gavan Connell

The view from the tower over the outpost was spectacular in its simplicity. The lake dominated half and the other half was the shoreline dotted with small camp fires, the ruins dominated the foreground and then the slopes led up the hill with three dark blobs that were the cave entrances. He spoke briefly to the sentry and bade him a good night before descending and continuing the patrol of his perimeter. He caught up with Harry chatting to Salina among a knot of Lancers sitting about cleaning their tack and gossiping.

"You have done well, Sir Harry. If they come we will be ready for them. Even a shore patrol will not get through easily. Where is your bedding? Do you have a place to sleep?"

"Err. It is here with the Lancers, My Lord. I have the watch before dawn and my squire will wake me when my turn comes."

"Then you will sleep comfortably and warm. I bid you good night. And to you, sisters as well."

He walked out of the circle and went to check the tlaque corral. Behind him he heard a soft footfall and he turned quickly, on the defensive, his hand on the handle of his hunting knife. It was Maní.

"Be calm, Lord. It is I. Be not so ready to kill me, tho' my life is yours to take should you wish it. It is my turn to watch the beasts until the small hand on the…watch reaches here. Then I am to wake Batik for her turn but what am I to do then for I will still be alert and sleep will not come easily to me?"

266

"If you lie still and count the stars your brain will relax and your body will follow."

"How does a king sleep the nights leading up to a battle, My Lord? Do you not lie abed with your brain racing with plans and wonderings about the enemy? How does a king counter that?"

"Usually I plug my minitron into my ears and it plays a hypnotic rhythm I have been programmed to and I just fall asleep. It has always worked for me."

"My Lord. I am frightened like the others who have not tasted battle. Our troop leader, Robia, has told us we will not be in the thick of it but many of us are scared."

"It is normal and that is why we spend so much time training for battles than might never be fought. When the time comes and you are mounted, you will do what comes naturally."

"I believe you My Lord. And tho' it has been a long time for me, when the time comes and I am mounted I will indeed do what comes naturally."

ChOn caught the meaning in her answer and he knew then he would never be satisfied without knowing her body. She was standing within easy reach, her eyes never leaving his. He felt himself harden before he turned away.

"Try counting stars if your mind is racing, Maní."

"I saw it in your eyes, Ch0n," she thought. "One more word of encouragement from me and you would have had me right here on the ground."

Ch0n completed his rounds, ate what porridge Darel had prepared for him and retired for the night. The minitron stood like a sentinel beside his cot but he did not reach for the buds. His brain was racing with thoughts about the possibility of battle and the look in the eyes of Maní through the slit in the turban. They had been bold and inviting and her words left no doubt she wanted to lie with him. She had made it clear the first time he had spoken to her at the grave of her husband.

He tossed and turned for what seemed like an age before checking his tablet for the time. It was not long before the hour for the change of half the sentries in the camp. He pulled on his boots and left his quarters dressed in full battle order. He already knew where he was going and why. He reached the fire that marked the centre of the Lancer position. There was nobody outside but Ch0n could hear noise coming from more than one shelter. A figure loomed into the circle of firelight. It was Maní. She looked at Ch0n and went straight to the shelter where her sister was asleep. It took only a few seconds to wake her and return to her post. The sister Lancer emerged from the tent, acknowledged Ch0n and then disappeared to where Maní was waiting to hand over the sentry duty. Ch0n waited a few minutes and left the fire. He walked towards the sentry post and when he saw Maní coming towards him, he veered off towards his quarters, knowing she would follow. He led her to the side entrance, lifted the flap and held it for her.

"My Lord. I see no stars here to count."

He took off the helm.

"If you look hard enough you will see them. Or you may return to your shelter and count them there."

"I will stay or leave on your command. I will not stay unless you command it and I will not leave unless you command it. So, My Lord which will it be."

An image of Buyo flashed into Ch0n's brain telling him to wait.

"You will not stay, nor will you leave right away."

"What does that mean, My Lord? Did you lead me here to speak in riddles?" Her eyes were lauging behind the slit.

"No. You know why I led you here and I know why you followed for there is something between us that will not be denied. But you may not stay. Not yet. It would not be fitting."

"I know not for certain why you led me here but I do know why I followed. It is the right of a king to command his subjects. So command me. I have already told you I will not stay unless you command it so if you wish it, command it. If not, command me to leave otherwise I will stand here waiting and wondering."

"Then I command you to stay until I command you to leave."

"More riddles, My Lord, but I will obey your commands in turn. First I will stay."

She removed her fitted armour, then sat on a stool and removed her boots. She stood up, lifted the orange tunic over her head and then stepped out of the black pyjamis. She faced Ch0n her arms hanging by her sides, naked, only her honey-coloured eyes showing through the slit in the black turban which covered her head and face.

Ch0n was transfixed at the image of sensuality before him. The presence of the turban highlighted her nakedness and modesty at the same time. He wasn't sure what he should do next. Maní broke the silence for him.

"My Lord, I thank you for the admiring looks but I feel a little silly standing, waiting here like this. Is it your wish and my command that I serve you further or shall I leave now?"

Ch0n removed the katana and his armour. He too had to sit while he removed his boots and when he stood up, Maní moved closer to him. She removed the black shirt while Ch0n was working on the fastenings of his trousers and then she was kneeling in front of him, pulling them over his feet. She had seen his dewen at the overhang but she was surprised at what she now saw in front of her face. She stood up and pushed against him, her eyes ablaze through the slit. She pulled the running end free of the folds and took one of his hands. She put the cloth in his palm and reached down to grasp his manhood. She heard him suck air through his teeth when she touched him.

"I want to be naked now, My Lord. I want you to remove the turban so you can see my face."

Much later, she unjoined herself from him and rolled away, her body running with the sweat of exertion and the sensation that had wracked her.

"I have not lain with a man since Alangadale left for the Buq'ue war. Before that he used to pleasure me nightly but never like that. Never."

"I am sure that your prolonged abstinence has dimmed your memory of him but I thank you for the compliment."

"I remember well enough to know a normal man will never feel the same to me."

"Then I command you not to lie with another man."

"You command me and I obey, My Lord. Now, before you order me to leave, I am ready again."

"No. It is time for you to go. I command you to leave."

"Then I shall leave. Do you command me to return tomorrow?"

"No. We will be on the eve of contact tomorrow and I will have no distractions, however pleasurable but I do command you to be ready for my summons when it comes."

"You command and I obey as before."

She dressed while he watched her and then she left. ChOn was exhausted. She had drained him of everything. He dressed in his night tunic and fell asleep immediately.

Erik guided the first of the three longboats into the river shortly after dawn. The rowers' shields were mounted on the gunwales protecting them from spears and slings should they be ambushed from the banks. Bowmen stood in the prow. It was eerily silent, except for the dipping of the oars breaking the surface. Around mid-day, the river shoaled and ran faster but they were prepared. Erik's grandfather's log described the channel entrance and the rowers pulled the boat though. The three boats successfully navigated the entrance to the lake. Two continued straight ahead under sail but the third moored under some weeping trees and the crew disembarked in full battle order. Their commander, Biorn, wasted no time in forming them up and they started to run along the banks.

ChOn rose at dawn as usual and started his rounds as he had done the evening before in full battle order. The sentries were all alert. Harry was already ahead of him. Guerra had earlier radioed him and told him he would launch the drone at first light and would report back as soon as he saw anything. ChOn wandered through the Lancer lines where most of the sisters were already stirring. Maní was dressed and organized, despite her lack of sleep. She waited until ChOn was looking at her before wandering along the path to the tlaque corral. She knew he would follow. He found her waiting where they had left the track the night before, hidden from view in a copse of scrubby trees. She went straight to him.

"My Lord, you have put the hunger on me. Do not use me once and discard me. I slept little after returning to my shelter. The fire you quenched in me re-ignited while I re-lived what passed between us."

She pressed against him and her hand went to his groin. He stepped back from her.

"This is neither the time nor the place, Maní. When I am able to do so, I will request your presence. Trust me when I say this. You pleased me greatly and I would have you again."

Her eyes betrayed her smile behind the folds of the turban.

"Your request for my presence I will regard as a command, My Lord. I wish to serve you in every way possible."

"You had better see to your beast. You may need him before the day is done."

Guerra flew the drone along the lines he had drawn on the tablet. It was cruising at an altitude of two thousand feet when he saw the two ships sailing up the lake. He looked for the third and saw it moored under the trees and a few minutes later tracked the shore party. He went back to the boats and zoomed in to the leader of the first.

"There it is, Erik, higher than last time but the sun catches it occasionally. It looks too small to be piloted but what does that mean? Are we to confront a race of sky people the size of rabbits? One thing is for certain, it is watching us and so we will

Gavan Connell

not surprise them. When it left just now, it went to search for the third boat."

Guerra watched the two talking and then one of them pointed to the camera and he knew for certain he had been discovered. It didn't change anything other than the fact they knew they were being watched and would be more careful as they approached. He turned the craft for home and called Ch0n.

"Good work, Guerra. Launch again around mid-afternoon and give me a position report on the ground forces. I will warn Sir Harry."

"Thank you, My Lord. I will report back later. But for now, here is Karín."

"Good morrow, My Lord. I missed you last night as did Buyo. She is unable to tell you herself for she is too busy vomiting and feeling sorry for herself. There is no doubt she is with child. You are a man among men to have both your agets with child at the same time. But it will come at a price for us all for you are no longer permitted to lie with either of us for almost a full...year do you call it?"

"Yes. A year. Tell her I am happy for her and now you can see to her because your time of illness in the mornings seems to have passed. You and I both know I will want another concubine during that time even if she is a temporary one. Select one of the Matáng as Buyo suggested."

"Do you have a preference, My Lord? Has one already caught your eye?"

"In truth? The wife of Alangadale. I feel a bond with her and almost a guilt for killing her husband. I would elevate her in status to somewhere near to where she was before his death in the court of Sith as his son's wife. Consult with Buyo."

"I know her. Maní. She is taller than the rest and has lighter hair. If Buyo thinks she is a good choice, I will give her my blessing. Now I must go because I fear Buyo will throw up her toenails. She needs to eat and drink."

"Stay within earshot of Guerra so you know what is happening here. Or wear your helm. If I need your advice, I will call you. Meanwhile, I am going to send a troop of Lancers and the mounted Infantry out to form a screen and see how the enemy reacts to contact. Stay well."

"How are we going to approach the channel, Erik?"

"We will simply sail to it and see what is there, if anything. Then we will decide what to do. The small flying ship worries me a lot. It poses many questions and no answers."

"And what of Biorn?"

"He will get as close as he can, observe and then go to the shore where he can signal us. It should be a place close enough for him to see what is there while we are waiting offshore. I have told him to avoid contact unless he has no choice. My grandfather's log mentions the bolts of light that the *leader of the sky people could throw that were capable of wreaking slaughter on those who would fight them. So nobody ever did and the relationship was a peaceful one from the beginning and then the inter-mating and breeding made us one people with them. I am in no mood for war with the sky people or the Matáng for that matter."*

"If they are the size of rabbits, this time, Erik, I hope they don't want to mate with us. It would prove difficult eh?" They both laughed.

Ch0n called Harry, Marik and Reny to his quarters and gave them the full briefing. .

"Be prepared to move at short notice. Harry, I will go with the screen. I want you to co-ordinate the defence of this position. We will not venture more than an hour's ride from here so if you think you need us back here, let me know as soon as it becomes obvious. Don't wait too long. I would rather have the force concentrated here than divided as it will be to begin with. Do you understand?"

"I do My Lord."

"Marik and Reny, when we reach the place where we will set up the screen I will give further orders. Do you both understand?"

They answered in unison.

Biorn halted his men. They had been running for more than two hours. He sent them to the shore where they plunged in to the cool water and drank their fill. The boats were in sight but far too distant for a signal. He would have to negotiate the curved shoreline and close with them again before he could flag his report.

"How much further, Biorn?" asked his junior commander.

"Are you spent already, Mikel after a short jog before breakfast? We have probably another two hours at the run. We will rest before we get there. I need to be able to signal to Erik before we make any contact with the sky people."

"I am not spent, Biorn. I was hoping we might up the pace." He flashed a perfect set of white teeth as he grinned.

"Get the men back together. We will walk until the water stops running off our clothing and then we will run again."

Guerra reported that the Viking ground force of approximately one hundred men was jogging towards the ruins and was probably no more than two hours away.

"How are they running? Are they in one big group in files or are they just in a loose group."

"They are in four small groups running in loose formation. The bowmen are at the rear."

He added that they were armed to the teeth with shields; metal, conical helms of all types including some with horns; long swords and battle axes, and that they had at least ten archers. He sent an image of the force to Ch0n's tablet, where

Gavan Connell

ChOn assessed the quality of the men he would be facing as well as looking carefully at the bows. They were similar to his shorter horse bow and he guessed their longbows would outreach their Viking counterparts. The men were all tall, tanned and muscular from their seafaring life as sailors.

"They may be well drilled, then and the archers will be at the rear so they can be deployed to either flank without being directly involved in the initial contact."

ChOn led the fighting patrol out of the perimeter. He was mounted on the oruk, in full battle order. The Lancers came next and finally the Mounted Infantry, which numbered sixty tlaque and one hundred and twenty troops. The jockeys were all armed with the longbows. The Lancers had their shorter horse bows on this occasion. Harry bade a fond farewell to Reny who sat proudly at the head of the Lancers, just behind the king. ChOn led them at a brisk trot along the banks of the lake until he came to a short spur with a creek running alongside it on the far side. It was a perfect spot for an ambush. He sent half the archers to the spur where they stayed below the skyline. The Lancers were hidden from view and were tasked to sweep along the near bank of the creek on command, under cover from the Archers. The Infantry was assembled nearby to mop up and take prisoners.

ChOn wanted to speak with the Viking commander and so when they came into view some time after the Arw'an were deployed, he rode onto the track and positioned the oruk in their path under the protection of the archers on the hill. He booted the staff and set it to the language mark. Biorn was leading the group and like all ground forces running on uneven ground was looking five yards in front of him. When he looked up, ChOn was less than a hundred and fifty feet distant. He stopped his men and formed them into a loose defensive circle. ChOn saw from the manoeuvre that they were neither highly disciplined nor used to fighting on the ground as part of a larger force.

"If we attack them, they will probably rush at us instead of staying put," he thought. He walked the oruk forward to a place just outside the range of what he considered their archers could achieve and halted again. He sat in silence until the Viking commander spoke.

"Who are you and what are you doing here?"

"I am ChOn, king of the Arw'an, Buq'ue and Matáng and as to what I am doing here, I am merely riding inside my own frontiers. Now who are you and what brings you to our fine lands all armed for war?"

"Since when did the Arw'an own this land? We Ekwo Eñame have been coming here for hundreds of years. The channel further down and the stone building were built by our grandfathers' grandfathers' grandfathers. We reserve the right to enter the buildings and the channel and the caverns beyond where the sky people taught us and bred with us. One man will not stop us."

"I am one of the sky people and I forbid you to proceed further under pain of death to all of you."

"The sky people were tall and fair skinned with red hair. You are tall. I can not see your skin or your hair. I do not believe you are of them."

"Then proceed but you will all die in the process. That I can guarantee you. Are your wives as ready to become widows and your children, orphans as you are to make them so?"

Biorn shifted uneasily on his feet. He had been ordered by Erik to go to the channel and send him a report by flags. Now this black-clad warrior with the gold mask over his face was threatening to wipe out his entire group if he continued.

"What are your orders, man? Tell me your name for it is bad form to kill someone when you haven't even met him properly."

"I am Biorn of the Eñame. I am the commander of this crew that sailed on the third long boat from our harbour. I was ordered to go to the channel and report what I found there."

"And how do you do that?"

"We have a system of codes that we send by flag movements."

"Then you are between a rock and a hard place for you can not obey your orders or you will kill all your men. Or I will and it is the same thing. And if you are dead, you will not be able to send your report. So what is your plan?"

"You are one and we are a hundred. You can not possibly prevail."

"Do you think I would come alone to be killed so you can go and find the Arw'an Army at the channel? Let me strike a bargain. Send your men back to their boat and I will take you myself to the channel and from there you may send your report. Nobody has to die. Not even you. I will release you in good faith if there is no trickery afoot. We sky people do not come for war. We come for peace and the development of the worlds we visit. What say you? Send you men away and come with me."

Biorn considered his options. He could go to the channel and send whatever message he liked to Erik and this ChOn would be none the wiser.

"I will give the order." He turned and went back to where his men were waiting.

"I am going to the channel and from there I will send my report back to Erik. Go back to the boat and sail it to where the other two will be anchored. Erik will know what to do then. Go now for you have a lot of ground to cover and a lot of time to make up. Mikel. You are in command. Do what needs to be done."

The Eñame sailors turned towards where their boat was waiting, some three hours hard jogging away. ChOn spoke quietly to Reny and Marik via his helm.

"I will trust their leader because he will be with me and I will have control of him. The others have left but we don't know what he said to them. Stay here until I call you back to the ruins. Your orders remain the same. If they come back, let half cross the creek and then ride them down from the flank while the archers rain arrows on those behind and in front. After one pass, turn and come back but do not stop and fight them. Mobility and speed are the keys. When they are no longer in one group and half their people are dead or injured, Marik will set the infantry on to them under cover of the archers on the hill and from the Lancers, who will regroup where they are. Stay out of sight. Report to me if anything happens. Reny, you are in charge because you will be the first to commit and your timing must be right. Good luck. Now I must leave."

He waited for Biorn to approach him after his men were running in the opposite direction.

"Walk in front of me, Biorn. Or run. I would like to make sure we both arrive safely."

Biorn went into a ground covering trot and Ch0n set the oruk to stay with him. They arrived at the perimeter almost two hours later. Biorn was blowing but not beaten.

Ch0n called Darel to come for the oruk and then he invited Biorn to take a tour of the facility. He did not let him go into the tower so that the crossbow and rail guns remained hidden from him but it was obvious to Biorn that the channel was blocked and dominated by the tower. He noted the force on the ground and thought it might be stormed if the boats ran aground on the far side of the camp where he could see a number of women staring curiously at him.

Your boats will be here soon. My sentry atop the tower can see the sails already and those of us below will have a better look before too long.

Mikel ran at the head of his men but he was not happy with the direction things had taken. He was thinking that Biorn was weak to have given in so easily. He slowed to a walk after half an hour and finally stopped.

"Biorn told me to do as I see fit, did he not? Well I am up for a fight even if he is not. Turn around boys. We are going to storm the defences at the channel so Erik can land. There will be something for everyone I am sure. What say you?"

There was a growl of approval and they turned as one and ran back to where Biorn had left with ChOn. They eventually reached the place and Mikel didn't even pause. He climbed down into the creek and waded across. His men were strung out behind him and he turned to urge them on. What he saw turned his blood to water. The King's Own Lancers were leaving the assembly area at the trot, lances lowered and a cloud of arrows came from the low spur. He didn't even have time to shout a warning before an arrow caught him in the neck and amid the confusion, the Lancers swept through his men as though they were so many straw practice dummies. He watched even as his life ebbed away as they turned and went again. Not a man was standing on his side of the creek. A roar went up and the last thing he saw was the Infantry running in a tight formation to finish the task.

Marik ran at the head of his men. Arrows proceeded him all the way to the first of the Viking sailors who raised his enormous broadsword to strike but was instead pierced in the face by a metal-tipped arrow. Salina called out, 'one' for it was her arrow that had hit home.   The Eñame were almost exhausted from their long run and short rations and within minutes all had been killed or captured. Marik had lost three dead and six wounded. Reny had lost nobody, thanks to her following Ch0n's orders to stay away from the hand to hand fighting. Marik was in no mood for niceties. He had his man tie the seven prisoners together on a single rope, neck to neck. Marik himself took the end of the rope and jerked it hard to get the coffle moving. Behind him, his men were remounted and they had collected their dead and all the weapons of the Vikings and strapped them on to a travois. Reny led the way back at a fast walk and the prisoners had to jog along as best they could to keep from falling.

Ch0n was furious at the betrayal of the Vikings. He told Reny to take twenty Infantry to find the boat, capture it and to bring it to the ruins, towed by a tlaque in the shallows if necessary. He said nothing of the skirmish to Biorn who was preparing to send his report. He told Ch0n that he was going to tell Erik that the place was well defended but that he would be permitted to send a small shore party to talk to Ch0n and from there the details of who would be allowed ashore and who would be permitted to do what would be thrashed out. In reality he had another plan.

Kelda and Froncy were at that very moment presenting medals to the winners of the last individual event, the wrestling. It had been won by a bull of a man from Matáng and he held it proudly for all to see. The individual medal count had come out narrowly in favour of the Matáng, largely because they were slightly taller and stronger. Froncy called the team captains in for a briefing prior to the first team event, the obstacle course. It was a timed event and involved a team of men from the logistics areas of the three centres having to dismantle a travois and feed it through a hole the size of a man's head. Once through, they had to reassemble it, attach it to a tlaque and drive it a hundred yards. All the teams had been practising for weeks and Kelda was feeling confident. They adjourned the games for the day and most went swimming in the huge lake.

"What is that tower doing at the channel, I wonder?" It was Jon, and Erik was none the wiser.

"It is a defensive tower because I can see some soldiers on the top and there are no windows. Move close enough so we can see if Biorn has arrived. On my estimation, he should have been there for some time just to the right of the defences. Perhaps he is in those few trees hiding until we give him further orders."

The two ships dropped anchor a hundred yards from the shore and the gentle breeze soon had them lying parallel to the coast. Jon saw Biorn first.

"Erik! There he is on the position in front of the tower. He is ready to signal."

"Give him the sign you are ready to receive it."

Jon went to the prow and held two flags above his head with arms outstretched. From the channel, Biorn saw him and started his message.

"I am a hostage. King wants to talk. Lightly defended. Thirty soldiers sixty women. Weak point to my right. Land and rush easy."

Said Erik to Jon who was standing beside him, *"A hostage? What does that mean? Did he try and go in alone? Where are his men?"*

"Ask him," ordered Erik, who was feeling even less like a battle than before. Jon waved the flags and stood at the ready.

"Captured by the king. Sent men back to boat. Should arrive by nightfall," said Jon.

"That seems like the actions of a civilized king to me. We should send in a shore party to talk. Send in a dinghy. You go. Take the high priest. Look around and see what they have done but your priority is to see if there are sky people among them. Tell him to advise the king we are coming ashore."

Ch0n received the message and told Biorn he would receive a delegation. It was then that Karín's voice came to him through the entrance.

"I don't care if he is busy. I will see him."

Ch0n went under the flap and straight to her. He kissed her on the forehead and whispered in her ear,

"You are not supposed to be here. Say nothing at all about the skirmish. Nothing. I have a Viking commander in there and soon we will have a few more."

"I want to see my Lancers when they get back."

"They are holding outside the camp. I want the delegation here and talking when they arrive with the prisoners. Meanwhile, now you are here, go and change into something more in keeping with the queen of the sky people. I have a plan. You will have to go along with it as it plays out."

He went back into his quarters where Biorn was waiting under guard.

"So who is coming ashore?"

"Jon, the boatswain of the first boat on which our leader, Erik will stay and the high priest who is an expert on the sky people and their history. Four rowers. All unarmed."

They went to the channel to meet the delegation. The dinghy was able to negotiate the shallow entrance where the Arw'an had blocked access by a larger boat. ChOn picked out the high priest from his robes and Jon who was dressed for battle except for his lack of weapons.

ChOn shouted to the men atop the tower to kill all the rowers if they left the boat, something he told Jon he had ordered. Jon told the men to stay and then he and the priest accompanied ChOn and Biorn to ChOn's quarters. ChOn had the staff hidden

Gavan Connell

in his vest booted and still in 'translate' mode. He was also in contact with Karín via the bracelets.

After the introductions, Ch0n opened the dialogue by asking Biorn to confirm he had sent his men back to the boat. Biorn confirmed it.

"And the message you sent? The one you read out to me? Did you sent it just as you told me Biorn?"

"Yes."

Ch0n lowered his voice.

"Yes what?"

"Yes I sent it errr King Ch0n?"

Ch0n turned to Jon.

"Tell me, Jon, word for word what he sent. No treachery now. Just repeat what he sent."

Jon looked at Biorn uneasily."

"That he is a hostage and the garrison is poorly defended and that he had sent his men back to the boat."

"Aah Biorn, you are one for playing false are you not? That is nothing like what you told me you were going to report. As for you, Jon and the priest, here, what are we to do with you?"

"You gave your word we would be released unharmed if we came in peace and good faith. I expect a king would be true to his word."

"Well spake, Biorn. Well spake. But you were not true to yours."

He picked up his helm and put it on.

"Marik and Reny. Come to my quarters now with your friends."

The priest was first to speak.

"How is it you speak to us in one tongue and into the helm in another?"

"I told Biorn I am of the sky people and we brought language to this place and others like it."

The priest began to talk to ChOn in the first guttural language ChOn had encountered through the staff. Jon and Biorn looked smugly at each other for they knew the priest was talking to ChOn in the ancient, dead language of the sky people that none knew except the priests.

"So tell me. If you are of the sky people you will be able to understand these words in the long dead language of your people."

"I do understand them for I am of them. Now I have a surprise for you. In a few minutes, two of my commanders will arrive. Meanwhile I would show you something of which only you will see the significance. Come now."

He spoke to the guards in Arw'an and told them to kill any who tried to leave the room.

The shocked priest went with ChOn into the great room where Karín was waiting, dressed in a white silk tunic. Her turban was lying across a table at her side allowing her red hair to fall free. The priest took one look at her green eyes, prostrated himself at her feet and spoke to her in the same guttural tone he had used with ChOn.

"So it is true. He is of the sky people and you are the returned queen. Have mercy on me for doubting, My Lord."

Karín answered him in the same tongue and told him to leave her in peace until further notice, that his services would be further required and that when the others left he was to remain behind to serve as ChOn saw fit.

The unfortunate priest backed away from her, touching his breast, lips and forehead continuously until he was out of the hall. ChOn ordered him back to where the others were waiting. A short time passed during which time the priest told Jon and Biorn that he had seen and spoken to the returned queen and that he would be remaining behind to serve the sky people as he had always done but now more practically. He fawned over ChOn who was tempted to kick him out of the way but resisted the temptation to do so.

ChOn spoke again.

"I hear footsteps on the cobbles. Here comes our surprise. Come outside and we will look at it together."

They went out. Biorn gasped out loud when he saw his men roped together in front of a force of a hundred mounted soldiers and another forty or more mounted lance carriers with horsebows.

"What happened?" he asked his men.

"Mikel took us back but only part of the way. He said you were weak to surrender so easily and that we should come in and complete our mission."

"And you all followed like sheep to your deaths."

"Yes, Biorn we did and it was horrible and over in just a few moments. We are all that is left. Seven of us."

"Now," said Ch0n. "Whatever am I to do with you two?"

Erik stood on the prow of his boat and watched his men dragged into the camp behind Marik's tlaque. He recognized them all as being from Biorn's longboat and guessed from the number of mounted troops that there had been a massacre. He also knew that Biorn would not live to see the next day but thought his brother Jon should be freed because he had had nothing to do with the shore party.

Ch0n led the Vikings to the channel where their boat was waiting. Instead of telling his hostages they were free to return to the ship, Ch0n gave a message to the oarsmen.

"Hear this and repeat it to your Captain if that is what he is. I was prepared to allow a shore party to come and explore the caverns, provided they could keep their hands off their swords and axes. It is now obvious to me that you came to raid us and kill us, take our treasures and violate our women as is your way. Because of the treachery of Mikel, three of my men are dead. There is a price to pay for that. Tell him the high priest has left your people for service here at Arw'an and that he has until the shadow of the mountains touches the top of the tower to leave or we will destroy both ships and let the crews drown. Do I need to repeat that message?"

Four surly oarsmen shook their heads.

The dinghy pulled away from the shore and Ch0n talked to the Vikings again.

"It is fitting that we are standing here on this spot. I want to show you something we built to haul heavy things up to that landing just below the turret. It is called a winch. It has a stout rope woven from the stringy stalks of a bush that grows locally. You have no idea how much time it saved us. Marik, make a turn around Biorn's neck for me like a good fellow."

Erik watched the dinghy approach. The crew jumped aboard the longboat and ran to Erik. After they had passed the message, Erik looked back to the tower. He was just in time to watch Biorn being winched up the tower by the neck. A growling noise that could be heard clearly on the shore emanated from the crew of both ships. When Biorn's body stopped kicking, Marik lowered it to the ground. Ch0n turned to Jon.

"I offer you the same end or you may choose to die like a warrior. You were not a part of the treachery as far as I can see so I will give you that choice."

"I would rather die like an Eñame. Or prevail like one as it may be."

He selected an ax from the captured weapons. Ch0n was not surprised. The great broadswords were very cumbersome one on one and were better in a battle where speed and dexterity were less important. He watched Jon weigh the ax and make some forward and back cuts with it. It told Ch0n that Jon knew how to handle the weapon and that this was no time for heroics or silly games.

Erik watched Jon select the ax and knew there was to be a fight to the death. It was better than hanging but not much. Two hundred pairs of eyes watched as the two faced each other on the shoreline.

"Marik. Karín. Stand to the perimeter. Lancers mounted and Infantry dismounted but central. Jockeys to your bows. If they don't leave they may attack instead and I want to be waiting for them when and where they arrive."

Jon stood his ground with the ax doing figure eights in front of his body. Like a pendulum. Rhythmically. Ch0n drew the green katana and the sound reached those closest. Ch0n took up the note and began to sing to himself. Only Jon could hear it but he couldn't understand it.

"Forehand, backhand, backswing to forehand then backhand, backswing to forehand then backhand, backswing to forehand then backhand."

He took up a stance just outside the reach of the ax and continued his song.

"Forehand to backhand, backswing to forehand then backhand." As Jon started his bigger backswing Ch0n moved both feet and cut Jon's right arm clean off with a vertical sweep. Blood squirted from the stump. Jon started to scream with rage and pain. Ch0n looked out to the boats and looked Erik full in the eyes. He saw naked fury there and knew that battle would be joined. He calmly turned to Jon and severed his head. A roar went up from the boats. Ch0n sprinted to the ladder, shinnied up it and then ran to the turret of the tower.

"Karín. Get out of here. At least go to the pass. This is no place for you."

"Yes My Lord. I shall go." She mounted her tlaque and trotted away to the path that led to the mountain pass; when she was almost there she halted and took in the scene before her.

"Harry. Marik, Reny. Robia. Listen. Reny, take your troop to the left flank and form up in ranks. In case they assault from the left. Robia, you do the same on the right. Marik. Archers to the roof of the ruins and the rest centrally placed in two squads. Deploy one squad at a time against whatever side looks like getting breached. Keep the rest as a reserve to be deployed only on my order. Harry, you go where the energy weapons will do the most damage"

He directed the crossbow operator to test the breeze and range and to fire a single bolt at Erik.

"I'm guessing you will have to aim two body widths to the left and one body high. Are you ready? Wait for my order to fire and then give it to him. Load fast and learn from your fall of shot, son."

He checked that the rail gun was activated.

"Look at which side they are coming from and aim it at them while they are still in the shallows. I am guessing from the depth of the channel they will need at least half the height of a man depth of water under them before they can jump overboard and start rushing us. Aim but don't fire until I tell you."

Erik was talking to his crew and the captain of the second boat.

"We can leave now and sail home leaving our dead behind us. We know from the books and the priests that the sky people have terrible weapons but they are not used to fighting against the Eñame. I say we go ashore and avenge the hundred lost and the two executed and rescue the prisoners. I want not a creature alive. Not even the rats living in the latrines. I will go left, Eden go right. Disembark on the outside

Gavan Connell

of the ship so you are guarded by the hull. To your oars, men. On my order raise the anchor and if we do not prevail, I will see you in hell. Wait for it, wait for it."

He got the nod from Eden to say his boat was ready.

"NOW!" shouted Erik and the anchors came up even as the longboats jumped forward and headed for the shore.

The sentry atop the tower rang the bell for general stand to and everybody went to his or her position and waited. Ch0n already had the staff out, booted and on position three. He pressed the red button and a red bolt flew across the water to Erik's boat and exploded against the hull. A plank went spinning away and Ch0n could see that water would be getting in.

'Crossbow.... fire!" he shouted and the one bolt went straight for Erik. He didn't see it coming but it hit the prow not a foot from him. He looked at the tower and saw Ch0n firing at the other boat with the red thunderbolts. Then he was hit in the upper arm with a four foot bolt and he was knocked over the side by the impact. The boat continued towards the shore and Ch0n gave both boats a long stream of the orange flame thrower. The sails caught fire and rained flames down on the rowers but still they came. He heard the order to easy oars and they disappeared from sight. From his vantage point above the battle, Ch0n could see the oarsmen taking up their shields and weapons and getting ready to jump over. He took a grenade-loaded bolt and armed the crossbow.

"Aim it in among the crew! Concentrate on just that boat."

The bolt left and the crew had the cocking winch working before ChOn detonated the grenade over the heads of the crew of Erik's boat. The second bolt and the third exploded with similar results. ChOn ordered the rail gun to Eden's boat.

"Fire into the crowd. Give them a decent burst to think about."

The gunner fired a long burst and adjusted the stream into the middle of the packed crew. He kept hosing them until he had to change the barrel and reboot the activator, which his number two did in seconds.

"Marik. You will probably have to go to the right flank first. Get ready." The Lancers waited their turn and when the first of the Vikings reached the shore, they were cut down with arrows. Harry rode the oruk across the flank and fired both pistols into the crowded shallows. The water ran red but still they came. Forty or more reached the shore and started to run at the tower. Robia held her troop while ChOn watched helplessly. He was watching the Lancers and willing them to move at the right moment. He opened his mouth to give the order to go, but Robia put the Lancers into a gallop before he could shout. Thirty wide and two deep they hit the running Vikings head on and when the sisters turned to go again, there were none left to kill. Marik's men had cut them to pieces with arrows from the roof. The same scenario was taking place on the left flank and when ChOn ordered the bell to sound for consolidating the position, the only Vikings alive were Eden, some of his crew whom he had ordered to surrender, the seven original prisoners and the few left to guard the boats.

"Take all the weapons and trinkets you want but do not desecrate the bodies," yelled Ch0n. "Look for survivors and kill those who are badly wounded. The rest go in the great hall to be cared for."

A shout went up from the right flank.

"There is one swimming towards the shore but he looks wounded."

Erik stood up at last in the shallows. The bolt from the crossbow was through his arm and out the other side. He was bleeding profusely by the time he arrived at the aid post. By then Ch0n was waiting for him.

"Cure this one if you can. He is their leader. I have plans for him."

Karín rode back into the confusion with Jez and went to Ch0n's side.

"It was a good battle to watch from up there," she said.

"It was like all battles. It might have been avoided but now, three hundred of the Vikings are dead. Centuries of breeding from the aliens gone to waste. All because Mikel disobeyed an order. Now I want you to go home while we clean up. Tell your Lancers on the way that they did a good job and Robia's timing was perfect."

Karín went to Reny's troop first. She heaped praise on them all for the way they had conducted their two skirmishes. She walked through to the Matáng Lancers and told Robia what Ch0n had said.

"And now I would speak to Maní. Where is she?"

Robia pointed and Karín picked her out. She was taller than the rest. Not quite as tall as Karín herself but tall and like the others, she was splattered with blood. Karín went over to her and took her to one side. Maní's heart began to beat faster because she thought Karín was about to kill her for lying down with Ch0n.

"Maní, I am with child and so is the king's second aget, Buyo. You know then, that we are forbidden to lie with a man during this time of carrying and until we have our second bleeding after the birth. Ch0n told me he has a liking for you and I can see why. Buyo told me she thought you would make a good concubine and if you wish it so, I will tell Ch0n for I would have nobody who wasn't willing."

Maní's eyes showed nothing but she was smiling under the turban.

"Lady Karín, I am but another subject of the king and his merest wish is mine to obey. If he desires me as you say, then I would assume it to be a command and one I would willingly obey. Will I have to leave the Lancers?"

"Yes. At least while you are living in the loft where Darel, his squire lives. At the end of the year when we are allowed to lie

with him again, you may see fit to stay or not. That is for you to decide. Not me. Now. When you get back to the castle, collect your belongings from the Lancer lines and take them straight to the king's stables. For the time being that is all. Welcome to the family."

When night fell, everybody was both eshilarated and exhausted from the fighting, the cleaning up and general lack of sleep. The two longboats were a mess of burned sails and holed hulls. But they were afloat. Late in the evening, the third boat arrived, having been towed half way around the lake by two tlaque who walked in the shallow water with the boat further out, being steered by the Viking helmsman who had been caught sleeping on the job.

Erik was drifting in and out of consciousness. His upper arm was a mess with the arrow having to be cut off and pulled through. The bone was broken and it had taken all Ch0n's strength to pull the arm straight so the bone would re-enter the wound and sit against the broken end inside. They had washed it with boiled water, sewn the wound shut and finally put a splint made from three arrows in place. He had lost a lot of blood but now he needed to rest and let his body and will to live make him whole again.

Ch0n felt filthy so after the light failed, he wandered along the shore and went for a swim to rinse the blood and dust from his clothes. He was naked in the shallows when Maní appeared out of the gloom.

"Is it Lancers' Day at the lake, My Lord?"

"It is, Maní."

The Ever Queen

"Then I will swim too. I am excused sentry tonight. It has fallen to those from the second rank."

Ch0n could barely make her out in the darkness but he saw enough to know when she was naked and easing into the cool water. She waded out to him and pressed her full length against him, feeling his manhood against her belly.

"Lady Karín spoke to me today. It seems I am to be your lover for a year while your agets are carrying. During that time, I am going to make up for all that time without my Alangadale to pleasure me. Are you ready for that, My Lord? And tonight is a good night to start for my body is aflame with excitement after the rush of battle. Is that a normal thing?"

By way of an answer, Ch0n lifted her and carried her to the shore and lay her down on her own tunic.

Much later, Ch0n summoned the priest, Verge.

"I want you to go to the caverns above this place and find what you can find. It will yield many secrets to the one who can read their signs and who knows their history. Karín may be the queen re-incarnate but she has no idea what happened in this place. You who have studied their language and their way of life may see something nobody else sees. You will live here in the garrison and you will go daily to the caverns to work. Anything you find, anything, is to be brought to me personally. You will enjoy this work because it is the culmination of everything you have studied for. Learn the Arw'an language so others may converse with you. One final thing. You are not to

301

speak with the prisoners under pain of death. Do you understand me, Verge?"

"I do My Lord but I am puzzled as well. If you and the lady Karín are sky people, why are you so different from each other and the Eñame who were favoured by them?"

"The sky is full of stars, each one a sun capable of supporting a place like this one. I come from a different star system from the others but I am still a sky person. Karín does not know her origins other than that her grandmother was violated by a Viking, err Eñame during a raid. As a result she ran from the village and her child was born the daughter of a Matáng slave. King Sith of the Matáng later took the child as his slave and she bore him a daughter, Karín, The mother escaped from Sith to Buq'ue where Karín lived until I found her."

"The legend of rulers says a queen will return to us from the other side to rule us. We would know the one by her physical attributes in general but the hair above all. Red hair and green eyes like all the sky people had. I have already seen that the lady Karín is such a one. There has never been another recorded in the history of the Eñame."

"Verge, you will do well to keep that story to yourself for a time. Meanwhile, settle in to your new dwelling and on the morrow you will start in the caverns. Tell me what you need and I will provide it."

Jez left the pass early with nothing more than a cursory glance at the place Arturo was buried. He had a filled porridge sack of the finest-looking of the opals on the tlaque's saddle next to his bag of dragons' teeth, all cleaned by the ants. He eased the oruk down the slope, over the ford and turned for the village. Hours later, he rode unannounced to the hut where he had left the two girls to guard the beasts. A corral had been built against the wall of the hut and a roof covered half of it. Both the animals seemed in good health. He dismounted and removed the saddles and bridles from his mounts and led them into the corral, where they promptly ignored their former cousins. He knocked on the door of the hut and entered unbidden. It was empty but he wasn't surprised. It was well past mid-day and people would be eating. As he walked from the hut to the square, people started to appear from their dwellings and they stood and bowed to him as he passed. He continued to the eating area and ordered some food before asking where Caron and Chenna were to be found.

"They went to the baths just now, My Lord," said an old man with a shaved head and trimmed beard. *"They have their routine of bathing daily after lunch to show an example to those who are fearful of wetting their whole body at the same time."*

Jez wolfed down his food. He hadn't eaten this well for at least a month. He had pushed his oruk hard on the return journey because of the situation at the ruins and he wanted to get back to the castle as soon as possible. He washed down his goat and yam stew with a cup of fermented-grain beer and left for the baths. They were relatively small but adequate. Caron and Chenna saw him coming down the slope and waved to him. He waved back and without pausing, entered the walled off area and plunged in, uniform and all. The girls splashed over to him, oblivious of the other women present and hugged him. Jez looked around, apologized to the women present and left again. He was refreshed and fed and now he longed for a comfortable bed to sleep in. He went to the hut and fell into a deep sleep. It was dark when he woke. He had no idea how long he had slept but he cursed himself for a fool when he discovered he was naked and not alone. How could he have slept so deeply that the girls could have undressed him? In the darkness he reached for one of them and she accommodated him sleepily. He had no idea which it was and so to avoid any recriminations, he turned to the other and she drew him into her. Then he drifted off again to wake with the sun.

"Men's' Day at the baths," he said to the girls, who were sitting at a table watching him wake himself up. *"I need a shave and a proper bath. So tell me. Did everything go smoothly in my absence?"*

"It did, My Lord," answered Caron, *"but it is smoother still now you are back. We will accompany you to break fast and then we will take you to the baths and shave you in the hot room. It is something our forefathers learned from the Eñame when they were here. And it is mixed."*

Jez took his cleanest dirty tunic out of a duffel and pulled it over his head. He buckled his weapon belt and pulled on his wet boots. The duffel he slung over his shoulder.

"Let us go then."

The shaving area was a steam bath. It had been made from felled saplings and caulked with their sap, which was orange and sticky to the touch. Inside was a fire pit with a metal shovel, which Jez discovered was for taking rocks out of the fire and putting them into an artificial pool of water. The steam rose thick in the confined space. They were the only three in it and the girls quickly stripped off their tunics and Jez did the same. Jenna took some shaving implements from a shelf designed to hold them and bade Jez lie back and enjoy the experience. She produced her bar of soap, now barely a sliver and washed his face and beard and then started to shave him slowly and carefully. Meanwhile, Chenna went to work on is feet, massaging them with some pungent-smelling unction. He settled back into Caron's bosom and closed his eyes. He felt Chenna's hands creeping up his legs to his knees and then to his thighs. Caron had rid him of his beard and was now shaving his head. Despite his best intentions and attempts to control himself, he felt his manhood rising, followed by Chenna's hands on him. And then they were not, as they moved up his belly to his chest. Caron wiped the soapy film from his head and massaged his face and scalp while Chenna worked his arms. Then they rolled him over and worked his aching shoulders and lower back at the same time. He could feel the months of sitting in the saddle being stripped from him. A sudden hiss raised another cloud of steam and the sweat ran from them all. Jez had never felt so good, even if his manhood was rampant and remained unsatisfied.

"Now we leave this room. Outside you will find a container of cool water from the river. Pour it over yourself. It is most invigorating. Then we will go back to the hut and see if we can't do something with that dewen of yours. Chenna will wash your clothes. You will have to think of a way to thank her."

"I will do my best but before we leave this room, you need to decide if you are going with me because I want to leave today.

There has been a small war between the Arw'an and the Eñame and I want to be back at the castle. If you come, you will be permitted just enough clothing for the journey and one personal item each. The pack animal will be loaded with stores and there is not much room on it. Now. Who is going?"

They both answered him in the affirmative. Jez left the room and poured what seemed like freezing water on himself and felt his skin tingle all over. He watched the two girls do the same before they all dressed. Two hours later they were riding out of the village.

ChOn arrived at the lake in time to watch the final event, the men's tug-o-war, which was won in fine style by the Arw'an team, thanks to ChOn's inside information on how to actually pull in unison. The Buq'ue won the overall trophy for most points with the Matáng a close second and the Arw'an another close third. At the presentation, he made a long speech about the need for such events as well as praising various heroes of the battle of the lake. He presented Sir Harry, Marik, Robia and Reny with the Aluminium Star of Service and singled out the aid post people who had not lost a single wounded patient, although there were some few still in bad condition. He finished by calling them to return to the same place in three years and for all those with medals to wear them as often as they could as a sign of their success. He was pleased with the way things had turned out and the fact his forces had been divided and had been able to function without his immediate presence buoyed him. He didn't want to have to supervise everything all the time. As the crowd dispersed to the castle, to Buq'ue and the far away Matáng, he called Darel to bring his tlaque.

Chapter Twelve: The Homecomings

Ch0n called the council together at the castle and defined the priorities for the coming few months. The shock of having to deploy to the lake ruins at such short notice made him realize he needed a permanent force there as well as at the site where the ranch was to be built. He re-stated the plan to set up an outpost at the future ranch so that families could have their plots of land to grow and sell or trade to the castle dwellers. The system of money he had recently introduced had changed the dynamic of the castle inasmuch as people realized they could advance themselves by producing and selling or hiring themselves out as skilled or unskilled labourers to the council or indeed to an individual who had the means to pay. Little businesses had sprung up selling food, clothing, metalwork, woven goods and the like. Ch0n had fixed a wage of two gold and one silver bar per day to those who worked for the council, including the army and those working for Boro, Doni, Kelda and Sonja. A group of enterprising young men had set off the day after he had announced the value of the gold and silver pesos. They started a flurry of activity towards the places they knew the Lancers had found the shiny stones. Ch0n had put Guerra in charge of the 'minting' of the peso bars and had let it be known that the shiny stones were of value to the council at a rate less than half by weight of the actual minted pesos. He had also let it be known that to steal gold, silver or minted pesos would be a capital offence.

He sent Harry to oversee the building of the lake garrison. It would take the form of a walled garrison big enough to contain all those employed in its defence and maintenance as well as those working with the priest, Verge. The tower would remain the central defensive feature dominating the channel. Boro went with him as well as a crew of his best and fastest masons. Sonja and Kelda sent people to oversee the housekeeping aspects of the design. Erik, the Viking had been pressed into service along with the other prisoners and a gang of Arw'an labourers to repair the two damaged boats and to reopen the channel. ChOn ordered them to go one step further and build a wharf on the windward side of the channel where the boats could be moored and easily accessed. Erik was happy to assist having been promised by ChOn that as soon as the work was complete, he would be allowed to take his own ship and sail it back to the Eñame harbour with his seven men should they wish to return, and a crew of Arw'an volunteers. His arm seemed to be healing. There was no infection and he had it slung across his body where it would not get further injured. He and the other prisoners were free to roam the lakes area and were taking advantage of the hospitality of several of the Arw'an girls. ChOn was pleased because he planned to ask them to stay with the Arw'an and crew the vessels he had commandeered.

Izaki marched into Buq'ue at the head of his team. He held the trophy aloft and his men and women showed the medals they had won. There was cheering and hallooing on all sides, which only increased when Izaki announced two days of feasting and revelry to celebrate the dominance of the Buq'ue over the Matáng and Arw'an on the field of games. He also announced that his wife, Elaine, an Arw'an member of the Lancers, was with child. Izaki was a popular leader and the villagers went wild with delight at the news.

At the end of the second week following the battle, Karín and ChOn rode down the track from the pass to see what was happening at the ruins. From their vantage point it was obvious that Boro and Harry were well advanced with their plan. The rock-strewn foreshore made for easy building because the stones were already lying where they were needed and those taken from the channel were already being stacked on one side where they would be used to make the wharf. The two boats were high and dry and resting on their sides. Erik had never seen tar before but he knew as soon as he did that it could be used to caulk the joins in the planks and decking. ChOn and Karín went straight to the main building where they were greeted by Harry, Boro and the priest, Verge who immediately prostrated himself on the floor before Karín and spoke to her in the ancient tongue. She answered him in the same, told him that she preferred to speak in the Arw'an tongue and that he should learn it as fast as possible so those present would not feel excluded. Verge was more convinced by this display of generosity that Karín was the reincarnation of the sky people, the 'Eani' he had called them whilst talking to her.

"Priest. You know of those who came before through written records. Have you memorized those records?"

"I have, my queen. They make up the written history of your people going back to the time you first came to us in the flying ship and took us from the caves to the seas. The story of the Eñame and the story of the Eani is but one story and the

mixture of blood between us has brought us to where we now are. Is it your intention to interbreed with us again?"

"No. I am but one and do not plan to breed with any except the Ch0n. There are others from a different star. The Ch0n is one and there are three more, all males. He and the others will breed with the Arw'an as we once bred with the Eñame. Even now I am with child. My child will be a king born from the blood of two stars and the people of this place, including the Eñame for I am one of you as I am one of them."

"I see it, my queen. I see the Eñame in you and I see the Eani too. I see the Ch0n and know he is not of this place nor of yours. The child will be a formidable king, uniting all the people of this place as never before. I would speak to you of the bracelets and rings because they are mentioned in our records but were never found. I see one upon your wrist and the Ch0n bears another. There are four more are there not?"

"You may search for the others if you say they exist, Verge. These two came fortuitously into my possession when we first arrived at this place. I suspect it was by design of the Gods that we two found them and they fit. The king has given you the right to search everything and everywhere?"

"He has, my Lady. I read long ago of the rod of power and its rays of death and the Ch0n used it in the battle against us did he not?"

Ch0n butted in.

"I did. I came across it with the two bracelets and rings. The rod was in one of the stone caskets along with this bracelet and a ring. The other bracelet was found by Karín in another casket. We must assume they were destined to be found by us."

"Might I see it, Lord?"

"Yes, but not right now and only in the presence of both Karín and myself."

Verge bowed and withdrew into the crowd.

Ch0n and Karín walked to where the boats had been beached for repairs. Erik was overseeing the overall task and he approached them as they arrived. Karín's features were obscured by the black turban, only her intensely green eyes visible.

"So at last we are graced with a visit from the king and his lady," he said.

Karín was immediately upset with his tone.

"Thought you that we would rush from the castle to greet the one who has brought death and destruction to his own people as well as ours?"

"So you speak the tongue of the Eñame as well as that of the ancients and the Arw'an? I meant no disrespect of course. Forgive me for I am a prince of sorts of my own people."

"No more. The Lord, Ch0n is now king of the Eñame as he is of the Arw'an, Buq'ue and Matáng. You are at his pleasure, whether you like it or not and you would do well to act like it if you value your head. He may have given you free passage back to your people but I have made no such promises."

"Enough with the pleasantries for the moment," interrupted Ch0n. "How long before the boats are repaired? You said you would have some idea by today."

"I am guessing for I know not the capabilities of your labourers nor the time it will take to cut the planks for the hulls. If we are not finished by the next full moon I will be disappointed. That should give my arm time to heal somewhat as well, thanks to the skill of your people. As soon as my boat is fit to sail, I would leave."

"You will leave when I say you can leave and not before. And when you sail, you will be sailing with an Arw'an crew. It is my intention to keep the others here should they desire it and the three boats. You will be taken to your harbour in your boat as I promised and then it will return here and you will be left there. I will need three captains to sail them and three crews, which they will train."

"But you told me I could take the boat. Do you now put conditions on it?"

Karín drew her katana and took a step forward.

"Get on your knees, Viking, or die."

"You would kill a one armed, unarmed prisoner? Who will repair the boats once I am dead? Sire. I fear you have allowed this one too much power."

Ch0n sighed.

"It is she who gave me the power. I gave her nothing except the sword and now your loose tongue has brought your early demise."

Erik's eyed showed fear for the first time.

"My Lord. You promised me safe passage!"

"See how the cur cringes now, My Lord when before he mocked you? This one is not to be trusted. He will play you false at the first chance."

Karín removed the turban and for the first time, Erik saw the flaming hair and his blood turned to ice before her.

"So it is true. You have returned to rule us."

"That I have, Viking and there can be only one."

Erik opened his mouth to speak but it was far too late for that. For the smallest fraction of time, he realized he was looking up at his own headless body and then everything went black.

"My Lord. You are far too lenient with your prisoners. He would have healed his arm and surely tried to kill you. Have *you learned nothing from Palik and Mikares? I beg you. I am less able to defend your back as the days go by. In three moons I will be heavy and slow. Watch them all. Let nobody too close to you."*

"You are right of course. I trust easily. But now we have lost our boat builder. I hope one of the other seven knows how to do this."

Jez arrived at Matáng shortly after the throng that had attended the gathering had made their triumphant homecoming with the most number of individual medals. Mastelik received him and the two girls in good humour. Jez asked the two if they would like to remain in Matáng or continue to Arw'an. The comely Chenna gave Mastelik a sideways look and told Jez she would let him know on the morrow but if it pleased the great Lord, Mastelik, could she serve him in the meantime? Mastelik agreed instantly.

That night on their scheduled radio link, Jez reported to Ch0n that all was in order and that he would be leaving on the morrow. Malek was present and she showed Jez her bulbous stomach and told him to hurry home so he could feel the baby moving inside her. Caron was a little put out with the affection Jez showed Malek but at the same time, she knew Jez would take her as his concubine until at least he was able to lie with Malek again. Ch0n told Jez of the situation at the lake and how Karín had dispatched the Eñame leader.

"My Lord, she is right. You are far too trusting with your former enemies. They are not all as honourable as Izaki and Mastelik. I will be at the castle in another ten days and from

there I will go to the lakes to survey the situation. And, My Lord, the castle will soon be full of the laughter of children. It is a sound you have not heard in your time with us. Our sons will grow together. Is that not something to look forward to?"

"It is Jez and I do look forward to it. Now come home quickly for we have missed you and none more than I."

"Erik should have returned by now, Karl. I fear there is something wrong. I told him to take more boats. A full-scale sailing would have meant that any force which had established itself on the lake could have been vanquished."

"You are too nervous, Rej. He will come sailing around the spit any day now. And when he does, he will have treasure and slave women enough for everybody."

"I think not. We Eñame haven't raided anybody for treasure and slaves for six generations. I can't imagine he would start again now. Anyway, he should have returned at least five days ago. I will warn out the captains of another four ships that they should get ready to sail in three days. We will have to send out another patrol to find out what happened. And if there is something afoot, it will need to be able to defend itself."

Guerra was almost exhausted. He was running the comms room, the mint and overseeing the mapping of the planet in concert with all the active tablets and their data. He turned off the light in his office, leaving just the duty watch to listen for any unexpected communications in the night and retired to his cottage. He had never been more tired or more satisfied with his life. Astride him, a naked Carmodi nestled into him and the feel of her banished his tiredness. She was the culmination of everything to him. He loved his work and he loved his woman and now as she straddled his hips he let himself fade away into the bliss he had come to know with her. When they were done, she put her lips to his ear.

"My Lord, Guerra. There is a contagion in the castle and I have caught it. You have planted a child in my belly at last. I did not bleed last cycle and if I don't bleed again, it will be confirmed. We must enjoy the time we have together until then for it is forbidden for me to lie with you while I am with child."

Guerra's face split in two in the darkness.

"My heart flies at the news, Carmodi. Our child will be an important part of the next generation of kings and Knights. I will make him or her indispensable to the future king. I am sad that you are not permitted to lie with me during that time. I do not wish another while it is forbidden. I will sleep with you and we will do that thing you showed me that arouses us both without the ijon. Now, roll over. There is no time to lose."

"You may not be king of the Arw'an, Guerra but you are a king indeed when it comes to the ijon."

ChOn and Karín were also abed. The wolf growled to warn ChOn someone was approaching and Maní entered the room. She pulled her tunic over her head and lay beside ChOn. She reached over his body and touched Karín on the face. Karín rolled towards ChOn so she could reach Maní's body and when Maní raised herself to receive ChOn, it was Karín who guided ChOn into her. ChOn's hands sought Karín's centre and it was she who cried out first. In the darkness, Buyo watched. Tomorrow she would lie with Maní and Ch0n, and Karín would occupy the spare room. She faded away with the wolf paying her no heed at all.

Jez and Caron rose early in Mastelik's guest quarters. They washed in a bath made from polished stone glued together with the sap from some glue-trees that grew near the city. Chenna joined them in the bath and declared she was staying with Mastelik. She kissed her sister on the forehead and playfully grabbed Jez's dewen.

"I will miss you both but if things fare well for me here I will have a good man and a position above my station. Thank you, Jez for freeing us from our bonds back there. Now I feel I can live my life as it was meant to be. We will see each other from time to time. If things don't work for the better, I will join the Lancers. Go well, Caron. I hope Jez takes you for his second aget. He deserves you."

"My Lord, Ch0n," said one of the Viking prisoners, *"I am a sailor like the others and familiar with the boats but the manner of repairing we will have to learn on the job. Erik told us of the…tar and it's qualities as a caulking agent but the manner of shaping boards is something new. He told us they had to be cut and put in place while the sap was still in them and fastened with spikes made from hardwood but nothing else. We saw one being done yesterday and so we will try it."*

"Then do it. Make it from the outside so that the pressure of the water will be holding it in place and not pushing it away from the boat. If you look at this one, you will see it is not cut straight but at the angle so it fits tightly."

"Yes, My Lord."

"Guerra, are you there?"

"I am, My Lord."

"If you were the leader of the Vikings and set sail for a possible fight, would you not set a time by which you would return?"

"I would, My Lord."

"And if you hadn't returned, would you not expect a patrol to look for you?"

"I would."

"Send the drone to their harbour via the river and let me know what you find. Stay there for a while and observe. Can you have it circle around without having to fly it yourself?"

"Yes. I can program it to circle and I can program the camera to stay fixed on a point."

"Does it have a mechanism whereby it can drop a grenade to a target below?"

"No."

"OK. Get it airborne and report as soon as you know anything. Izaki, are you there?"

"I am My Lord and I was listening to your conversation with Commander Guerra."

"I am sorry to do this to you but I need your Lancers and Infantry at the lakes as soon as you can get them here. They will stay for no less than fourteen suns and no more than twenty."

"I will dispatch them immediately."

"Sir Ivor, are you there?"

"I am, My Lord and having heard your conversation with Izaki, I am one step ahead. We will leave almost immediately. I will take the extra rail gun."

"Good. Tell Karín to stay at the castle. Tell Doni to be ready to send the herds to the grazing grounds. I want you to stay at the castle and prepare for a battle in case we need to withdraw. Tell Sonja to prepare the villagers."

"Yes My Lord."

"Sir Harry. Stop everything. Tell all the civilians to prepare for another possible battle. Now. Leave the two ships under repair and get the prisoners aboard their own boat with twenty of the garrison soldiers. I want them to be able to sail that boat within two days. Do not tell the Vikings why but we may be going to battle against their counter attack. I will need to be able to sail with the wind. No fancy stuff. In two days or less, depending on what Guerra sees, we will sail that boat to the mouth of the river." He took out the tablet and brought up the map. "Here". We will sink the first of their boats in the shallow channel that they told us is the key to entering the lake. As soon as the King's Own troop arrives, I want you to take them at speed to this place with a tube and a chain gun. Have the Lancers here, mounted against a land attack from the river but firing arrows into the second boat. We know their bows do not have the range of ours so we should be able to cause a lot of casualties. If they try and swim ashore they will drown because the river runs fast just there in the shallows. I am going to take this boat to the lake side of the channel and stand off with the other tube and the crossbow with grenades. Try and stop the first boat getting through but if it succeeds, I will meet it on the lake side while you concentrate on the second boat and the Lancers on the third. If a force gets ashore, sweep through it immediately and before they consolidate. Do not allow the Lancers to get involved in any hand to hand fighting. Once they have swept through, withdraw them and yourselves to the next suitable place for an ambush. I am thinking we should be able to destroy them on the water but we have to pre-empt their landing. If they have as large a force as they did last time we will not be able to defend the ruins without the Buq'ue and Matáng. The Buq'ue will be here in three days but it is possible the battle will be joined at the river before then. Do you understand all that?"

Harry grinned.

"Yes, My Lord. This is much better a life than living in a tube and waking up every few years to explore a barren wasteland is it not? I was born to do this. Yes. I understand."

"Ivor. Are you there?"

"I am, My Lord."

"When you come, bring the three tubes, all the ammunition, the crossbow and bolts from the corner tower and all the white phosphorus WP grenades as well as a box of fragmentation grenades."

"Aye My Lord. I am already a step ahead of your orders. We will be leaving within the hour. The mounted Infantry left minutes ago."

"What is it Harry?"

"My Lord, the prisoners are asking about the heightened activity levels in the camp. They are asking if their countrymen are going to attack."

"Tell them we do not know just yet. Do not let any out of your sight. Kill any who disobeys you. Use the stun pistol. They are hard men and I do not want you engaging in any close combat with them."

"They say they will help us sail the boat but will not engage in any battles against their countrymen."

"That is OK. They have never sworn an oath of allegiance to me and so I have nothing against them. But my previous order stands. Kill any who try to escape or sabotage the mission. This is an all or nothing battle for this place. If we lose control of it, they will have access to what lies hidden in the caverns. The priest, I trust. He is living a fantasy he has had for decades. Do you have the volunteers?"

"I do. Some were volunteers and some were 'volunteered'."

"Get them on to the boat right away and have them sail a circle to the left and a circle to the right. That will have them sailing with the wind, across it and against it."

"As you wish My Lord."

"My Lord. This is Ivor. The Lancers are riding out the main gate."

"Good. Izaki, are you there?"

"I am, My Lord."

"Pass by the castle and leave there a platoon of infantry and the Lancers. The rest of the Infantry will come here as my tactical reserve. You should come with them. You need to get out more."

"We have already left Buq'ue, My Lord as befits the king's champions."

Ch0n laughed. Somewhere in the distance, Karín sensed it and let the sensation wash over her.

"Good. Make haste. I know not how much time we have available. Commander Guerra should know soon. The drone is flying the line the Viking boats have to sail. He will be able to tell me what is happening soon."

Ch0n watched the longboat push out into the lake. The oarsmen were obviously not trained because what had been a thing of beauty when crewed by the Viking crew looked awkward and the oars were not dipping in time. Then the sound of shouting drifted across the water followed by the rhythm of a single drum beating time. Within minutes, the oars moved as one.

"Sir Harry. My compliments to the Vikings. They must be good teachers. It looks quite good from here."

"Karl. Some fishermen have just caught the body of the missing sentry. He was in the river opposite the entrance to the harbour. There is not much left of it. I sent some of the men a little upstream and found some strange footprints in the dried mud. They bear a pattern that is strange to me. As if carved. We have been spied upon by land as well as by air."

"All right Rej. When can the boats leave?"

"They are scheduled to leave on the morrow but they could leave by nightfall."

"Then they shall leave at nightfall. Have the Captains meet me in the chart room."

Jez and Caron were making good time from Matáng. They passed the first spring and stopped at the stream for the night. Jez checked the surrounding landscape for dragons before tethering the beasts fully saddled. He put out the three sensors and soon the helm picked up their signal as they paired to it.

"I need a shave and a bath, Caron. I am going to put this helm on your head. While you are shaving me, look about this place. The helm gives you the ability to see the dagononum. If you see one, tell me immediately for we need to protect the beasts."

He booted the stun pistol and stripped naked. Caron did the same but donned the helm while Jez sat down on a rock. Caron shaved him expertly with the multi-tool's main blade. Jez nestled into her bosom.

"Are you looking around for the dagononum?"

"Yes, My Lord. Now I have finished your beard I will shave your scalp. Be still."

Caron finished her task and Jez took the helm from her head and put it on his own, looking around as he did so.

"Wash yourself and our clothing. I will stand guard." He took Caron by the hand and led her to the water's edge. She washed the clothes and her body while Jez watched her, occasionally looking around for a dragon. When she had finished, he went in and pressed against her. She washed him and then led him to the flat rock where he had sat earlier.

"What will happen to me when we get to the castle, My Lord?" she asked afterwards.

"I will present you to Malek and if she is agreeable, I will take you as my official concubine. If she is not, it will be for you to decide your immediate fate. You may remain with me until Malek is not forbidden or you may opt for the Lancers and take a husband. Either way, I may not choose for you. What would you like?"

"I would like to be your second aget with the rights and responsibilities of it. I would be happy in the beginning to be your concubine but not forever. I want more than that and I deserve it. I could have stayed with Mastelik or even back in the village and been someone's lover. I trust you to protect me and to look after my interests. If you wish me as your official concubine at first, your wife will see to it that it comes to pass. Wives like to have their men under observation. If she sends me away, she will always wonder where you are,what you are doing and with whom you are doing it. It is a satisfactory outcome for all three of us if she knows you are lying with none other than me."

Ch0n received the Arw'an forces at the ruins as they arrived. He had Harry supervise the unloading of the special weapons and he had one of Boro's men mount the giant crossbow on the stern platform of the boat near the tiller where it could be spun around to fire in any direction. Ch0n checked out the mount and nodded his approval to the carpenter. The two operators also checked it out and in turn nodded at Ch0n. One of them had come up with the idea of painting the grenade and WP bolts so as not to confuse one from the other in the heat of battle and they set to work to do it before they started to fix the WP grenades to a dozen white bolts. These they stowed separately. They then fixed the fragmentation grenades, twenty in all, to blue bolts and stowed them. The remainder of the standard bolts they stored to one side in a dry well. Ch0n handed them the tube and a box of rockets which they put with the grenades.

"Will you be accompanying us on this boat, My Lord?" asked one of them.

"I will. I would not miss this sea battle alongside my best crossbow crew. I have been studying a man called Nelson, who was a sailor of note in his time, and a man called Lafitte. I will use their tactics if the crew can manage the sails."

Guerra had the drone outside the Viking harbour. He lowered it so the camera could look deep inside. He could see seven boats and a hive of activity. He did not care if the drone was seen. They could do nothing about it and it would add to the mystique of their voyage.

"There is the flying ship that Erik told us about. It is looking at us from beyond the cave entrance and well out of range of the best archer. But why is it doing that? How small are the beings that fly it? What do they want from us? What have they done with the others? I think it is fair to say they aren't coming back now. Perhaps these tiny creatures have enslaved them or reduced them to the size of rabbits. What say the priests?"

"They have had little to say, Rej. Bring them here and ask them again."

Harry rode out of the camp and led the Lancers along the banks of the lake. He would make good time until just before dark, set up camp for the night and make an early start the following morning.

The Eñame priests could offer no solution to Karl and Rej.

"We have studied all our records since this was sighted first and there is no mention of anything that gives us a clue. All we can find is a reference to a queen being re-incarnated and ruling us."

"There shall be one of us who will return in the body of another but you will know her because she will be one of us. Look upon us now and know us. The red-fire hair and green eyes will be the sign and she will speak to the priests in the tongue we shared with them alone and no other. She will be in the company of others but you will know her and obey her as you have known us and obeyed us," chanted the priests in unison. *"To deny her will be to bring the wrath of all of us upon you, whom we have taught and with whom we have mixed our seed."*

"That is all we have to go by, Karl. There is no mention of a flying ship or miniature beings, although we know not if they can make themselves smaller and larger at will."

"So be it. We will have to find out for ourselves what it is and why it hangs there watching. Rej. Fetch the other captains. I want to know how much longer they need to prepare for sailing. You. Priest. You will come with me and there will be another on each of the boats. You will pray to the Gods and the Sky People alike to see us through this voyage unscathed and wiser for the taking of it."

Harry and the King's Own Lancers came to the place of the Viking massacre and pushed through the smell and rotting bodies until they came to a suitable clearing where another stream entered the lake. He checked in with Ch0n before putting the Lancers on fifty percent stand to, sleeping with their tlaque tethered and saddled.

Guerra switched the camera to thermal. He stayed over the cave entrance until the sun was gone and then lifted the drone up to two thousand feet and stabilized the cameras on the entrance to the harbour. The drone made lazy circles on autopilot waiting for another command from the computer. Guerra had Carmodi get him something to eat while he monitored the screen and balanced the books from the mint. He was having trouble this night. There was either a mistake in the amount of raw gold entering the melting area or the number of gold pieces that left. He had allowed a five percent difference because of the tendency of the metals to spill over the edges or to stick to the sides of the mould. But today there was a difference of fifteen percent. He massaged the raw data and could find nothing wrong from the storage to the mint to the melting room so that meant there was a miscalculation or some error in the count of the rods. It might also mean that someone were trying to see if they could escape detection by putting a fistful of the small rods in their clothing. He decided to do nothing but to monitor who was working that day and follow up the next time he or she was present. He looked up from his ledgers in time to see the third and fourth longboats slide greenly into view and take up their positions in line astern behind the others.

"Lord, Ch0n. Are you there? This is Guerra."

"I have been waiting for you, Commander. What news of the Vikings?"

"You were right. They have just sailed from their harbour with four longboats. I am looking at them through the thermal lens and it appears they are full of sailors. We can guess there is a force of four hundred heading to the ruins. Based on last time, they will be three days sailing. They will enter the river the morning after tomorrow and be at the ruins late the same day."

"Good work, Commander. Put the drone into a flight pattern over the entrance to the river. I want to know when they enter it so that Harry has time to prepare. Harry, are you listening?"

"I am, My Lord. We will make the river by early afternoon tomorrow and set up as you ordered. I don't think they will enter the river by night so I am guessing we will see them early the day after tomorrow."

"Keep me informed."

"I will, My Lord." He sought out Reny and shared her tent until it was dawn. They ate their porridge and were on the move again with the sun still low in the sky.

Ch0n had the Arw'an longboat half way down the lake by mid-morning. It was sailing across a gentle breeze and Ch0n could visualize the concept of tacking he had been reading about. He had the line on his tablet, defined weeks earlier by the drone's cartographic function and he knew that he would soon have to tack to maintain his overall direction to the mouth of the river. The Viking, Eden told his trainee captain to come about onto a port tack.

"Crew! Stand by to come about left! Tiller man! Stand by to come about left!" He waited until the tiller man repeated the order and then gave the command. *"Come abooooout!"*

The tiller man swung the tiller to the right and the boat started to turn left. Twenty men were ready at the rectangular sail. When it started to flap, they slackened off the ropes on the starboard side of the boat and pulled them tight through wooden pulleys on the port side and tied them off. It was a little clumsy but effective. The breeze re-filled the sail and the boat heeled to the left and started to make headway. The 'captain' looked towards Ch0n, expecting some critical comment but Ch0n just grinned widely and nodded. They tacked twice more before the two banks almost joined and through the scope, Ch0n spotted the rapids at the lake's exit.

"Down sails," he said to Eden, who relayed them to his 'captain'. *"I don't want to be under sail this close to those rocks.*

330

He looked at the thread on the masthead. "Take me to the edge of the lake over there near those trees."

"Aye, milord," offered the Arw'an 'captain'," *that is where we found this very boat moored. Tiller man! Tiller left! Hold! Tiller amidships. Down sail!*"

The sail began to flap uselessly and twenty men pulled it down and sat on it to flatten it out.

"All hands to the oars! Standby! Oars down! Steady boys and row!" Twenty oars hit the water as one. The tiller man held the tiller so the boat made a gentle arc until it was pointed at the bank. He held it amidships until they were a hundred feet from the bank and swung it gently right.

"Up oars! Stow oars!" The boat steered gently towards the bank until the trees were close enough to grasp. The sailors brought the boat to a halt and pulled it to shore with the same branches.

"What is your name, Admiral?" Ch0n asked the Arw'an 'captain'.

"*Admiral, My Lord. I used to be 'Remo' but I like 'Admiral' more because it were you who gave it me.*"

"Then Admiral it will remain." He looked at Eden as he shouted. "Well done to all of you. I am surprised at how easy you made it look and yet I know it is a thing new to you all. Now we will stay here until morning. Then we will take this vessel and anchor it near the channel. Eat and rest. Admiral, six-man watches. Two at the bow, two at the stern and two in the middle. The Lancers are nearby somewhere I hope, so there may be noise. Do not fire unless you have identified the target absolutely as a Viking. I am not anticipating any contact before dawn. Are you there Harry?"

"I am, My Lord. I can hear your shouted commands from our position. We have been here about two hours watching your sailors at work. We have taken up a position with the chain gun overlooking the narrows. I have four sisters with me. Reny has the remainder along the banks ready to move forward and engage the second boat. We are lucky the wind is behind us. Our arrows will almost carry the far bank."

"I don't believe in luck, Sir Harry. Guerra told me the prevailing winds were from the south-west before the previous raid. Otherwise I would be on the other bank, as would you. Now there is one unknown. We have to know if the Vikings are willing to paddle the river by night. I think not because the narrows are shallow and they will want to manoeuvre them by daylight. That is not to say they won't anchor or even attempt to moor the boats on the banks and get closer to the narrows for an early start. Be prepared for any of those things. I suggest the tlaque remain tethered and saddled. If the Vikings come ashore after dark, get out of here fast. We will do the same. I don't want the Lancers skirmishing in the dark."

"You leave nothing to chance, do you My Lord?"

"I try not to be caught by surprise."

"Perhaps I should take the rail gun to the left flank in case it is needed there while we withdraw. It will be easier to make a break if the Vikings are all hiding behind trees."

"Good thinking. But it needs to be back when the lead boat attempts the narrows, Harry. Allow it to negotiate the narrows and then open fire on it. That way it should drift back into the channel and block it, perhaps even sink. Aim for the portholes. The pellets will not penetrate the hull. If you can see sails, aim for them. If they are holed, they will tear when the wind fills them. Reny. Are you listening?"

"I am, My Lord."

"Close your eyes, Reny. Go back to the day we lost half of Eloik's troop. Visualize it. Do NOT allow your troop to engage the enemy. As soon as it appears they are going to come ashore, get out. Harry, you too. I will deal with the front boat. They will be forced back on to the other boats or I will sink it in the narrows. But I am hoping the other boats will be in disarray by then from our archers. Reny. The initial order to withdraw will be yours to give because neither I nor Harry will be able to see what is happening down river. Give the order and give it over the radio so Harry can get out with the rail gun. Do you understand?"

"I do, My Lord."

"Sir Harry?"

"I do, My Lord."

"Move the rail gun. Now. Everybody on this frequency listen up. From this moment there is to be NO talking or shouting unless it is to warn of a Viking landing. If the boats paddle up the river we will let them anchor in silence. We need discipline here. No talking and no radio transmissions until I break silence or someone has to signal the withdrawal."

"We will not reach the entrance of the river before dark, Karl and we have no experience of it. I suggest we anchor this side of it and paddle it by day. The wind will not help us at all in there. If we are vulnerable by day, we will be more so at night to an ambush. It is too far for a shore party. The safest way is to wait and negotiate it by day using half the oars and the bowmen behind the shields."

"I agree, Rej, although a part of me wants to go quietly up at night. The problem with that is if we were to be attacked, we would not be able to come about. We would just have to drift backwards with the current and that is not something I would like to do in the dark for we would surely crash into each other. The logs all say to navigate the river using oars, staying in the middle until the narrows where the water runs faster. Then we need all hands to the oars for that short stretch through the canal and we are safe in open waters again. It will be dark soon. Make a little more way, drop anchor and raft up. I wish to speak to the other captains."

The lead boat dropped the anchor a short while later. Rej gave a flag signal to the second boat to come alongside. The two boats were lashed together on the two anchors. Soon the third and fourth boats were rafted. Karl called the three other captains to him.

"I would love to be able to tell you what we will find at the top of the lake. The priests know from their records that there is a building where teaching and mating took place. Behind the building is a series of caves which were forbidden to our fathers to enter on pain of death. It seems that Erik has blundered into some problems with the Sky People and may have been taken prisoner or simply the Sky People asked him so stay for some reason. We know Erik didn't leave harbour with violence on his mind. I am guessing we will have no problems once we get out on to the lake. Stay away from the banks. If we are to be tricked, it will be from the shore. At first break of day we will leave here and row up the middle of the river. No more than two boats lengths apart in the river. When I am clear of the shallows I will signal to the second boat and he will signal to the third to enter them in turn. That way we will not all be vulnerable at the same time."

"This track leads us to the castle in that direction and to Buq'ue in that direction," said Jez to Caron. *"We are getting close now. In a day and a half we will be inside the walls."*

"I am going to miss our adventures together, My Lord. This whole trip from the day you and Arturo came into our lives has been new and exciting. I can not imagine a dull moment now. If this is to be our last night out here together, let us not waste it with idle chit-chat." They paused to listen. Off to the right they heard the sound of many hooves on the track. Soon the Buq'ue Infantry came into view. With no more than a cursory wave to Jez from Izaki, they thundered past. Jez put his heels to the oruk and it lumbered off after them with the remaining three beasts in tow.

"I am sorry, Caron but last night was our last night on the trail it seems. Those soldiers were in a hurry to get to the castle and now, so are we. Welcome to the life of a Knight of the Arw'an."

They rode all through the night behind the Buq'ue Company. It was dawning when they topped the rise overlooking the castle and thundered towards the gatehouse. Ivor had the gates opened as they descended and the entire company raced into the castle and stopped at the square. Jez and Caron rode straight to Jez's dwelling where they were met by Beny, Jez's squire, and Malek. Jez jumped down and ran to Malek. He took her in his arms and held her close while Beny helped Caron down. The two of them led the beasts to the stables where they were unsaddled and washed. Jez wasted no time rushing up to Guerra's comms room where he was given a full briefing on the situation and the deployment of the force at the lake. Soon after, Izaki and Ivor entered the room and they exchanged greetings.

"Jez, I am to leave a platoon here and send the rest to the ruins so the king has a tactical reserve. The Buq'ue Lancers will be here shortly and they are to also go to the ruins. Harry is waiting to deploy them along the bank. The king has forbidden radio transmissions until he breaks silence. It will be full light soon. I have ordered the Infantry to rest and eat and then be ready to move again at first light. The Lancers will do the same but will leave later."

"No," said Jez. *"They can rest when they get there. It is only a few more hours but it might make a difference if they are here and not there. Send the Infantry now to the knoll and they can pick up the Lancers when they arrive and all go together. Izaki. Where will you be?"*

"I am to command the reserve so I will be at the ruins awaiting orders from the king."

"Ivor?"

"I am to remain here and defend the castle against attack. I have only enough here to defend the actual castle and keep. The king says that if we can deny the tower, a force from the lake will come and relieve us by attacking the Vikings from outside. He is not expecting any attack but as always he is prepared. As are we."

"Then I will go to the lake where I may be needed. I will ride out now with the Infantry and keep going. Remember the radio silence. Once our Lord allows radio transmissions, we will be able to report to him. Beny! My tlaque!"

"Jez!" It was Malek. *"Are you leaving again? You haven't even had time to clean yourself up."*

"I must go to where My Lord needs me. I will return in a few days. Meanwhile, you should get to know Caron. She comes from a far flung Matáng village and came with me to know the Lady Karín whose name is so close to her own. It is my desire that Caron take up residence with us if it pleases you. Beny!"

Jez led the Infantry out of the gates and up to the knoll with Malek waving, her other arm around Caron's waist. The

Infantry waited for the Lancers while Jez continued towards the ruins at the lake. When he reached the top of the pass some time after dawn, he looked back and saw the dust and colour of the Buq'ue troops not far behind.

The black started to turn to grey and silver in the East. Soon, slivers of pale orange and purple appeared through the trees. Harry had long since returned to his position of ambush with the rail gun. Ch0n's crew had untied the boat and turned it to face the direction he wanted to take. All were at their stations apart from two who were holding ropes that rounded the trees.

Reny and the sisters waited patiently until they heard the sound of voices and oars dipping the water. They were dismounted. Half of them were waiting to move forward to the edge of the river and fire at the boats. The other half was occupied holding the tlaque to make for a quick withdrawal if necessary.

Karl's longboat eased against the current. A light mist hung over the water. Rej was the first to see the narrows.

"Karl. A little to the right and full ahead or we will make no way against the current." He pointed at the narrow channel and Karl's helmsman followed Rej's arm to the centre of the still water that ran between the rapids. Suddenly the oars went faster on a signal from Karl and the longboat jumped forward. They went smoothly through the channel and Karl gave the signal for the second boat to advance.

Harry looked down the optic of the rail gun. He centred it on the tall figure giving instructions to the helmsman. The rear of the longboat cleared the channel and the tiller came left to head the boat into the open water. At that precise moment, Karl heard the chain gun open fire. He had no idea what it was and when he turned to the sound, he was hit in the face by the opening burst. The helmsman took the next and he slumped over the off-centre tiller. The oarsmen stopped in shock when they saw Karl's face turned to a frothy pulp. The boat kept heeling to the right but with no oarsmen to make way, it stalled and went sideways onto the rocks. The current held it there for a short time until the sheer force of the water tipped the hull onto its side and broke it on the rapids.

Marik's archers were pounding the second ship as it made its way to the channel and soon the third came into view and Reny opened fire with her own archers. The river was too narrow for the boats to turn and so they had to sail the gauntlet of arrows and rail gun pellets. The crew of the second boat stayed below the railings behind their shields and the boat hit the channel at full speed. Harry raked it with the rail gun but he could not stop its progress. He watched it gain the open water and turn for the shore.

"They're going to mount a counter attack from the right!" he shouted into the radio. *"Reny! Get out now."*

Reny gave the order and the Lancers left immediately. Harry gathered up the rail gun and mounted his tlaque. He and his detachment of Lancers bolted for the clearing they had nominated as the rendezvous. Through the trees he could see Ch0n's vessel at anchor, the stern being pulled by the current and the crossbow towards the second Eñame vessel, which was still making for the shore.

"That's one of our ships ahead. What is it doing there at anchor? Go to the shore, offload the skirmishers and then pull alongside it. There has to be something wrong."

Ch0n waited until he had the boat broadside to him and he told the crew of the crossbow to get to work. The first bolt went long but the second flew true. The third had a white phosphorus grenade attached and Ch0n detonated it just as it reached the half raised sail. Smoke turned to flames as the globules of sticky stuff burned everything they touched. The second grenade started more fires. Ch0n indicated they should launch some fragmentation grenades and the next three bolts exploded among the disoriented crew. Meanwhile, the boat had lost way and was drifting back to the channel. It almost entered the channel in reverse but at the last moment, swivelled and capsized. The hull was sent down the channel where it hit the prow of the third boat. Ch0n guessed the range of the third boat at three hundred feet. He took up a tube, loaded it with a high explosive rocket and let it fly. It hit the large target amidships and holed it. A second rocket also found the target. The river was full of debris and men struggling to stay afloat in their heavy clothing. The fourth boat came into view and then disappeared again, going backwards with the current.

Ch0n ordered Admiral to raise the anchor and make for the shore further down the lake. He did not want to get caught up in a sea battle with an inexperienced crew. They put him ashore and he told them to return to the ruins. He ran to the rendezvous and mounted a tlaque that was being held for him.

"Commander Guerra, are you there?"

"I am, My Lord and I have been watching the battle. It seems that you have decimated the Viking forces. The fourth boat has found its way out of the river and has moored against the bank. They are all disembarking and are making their way along the near bank of the river, perhaps to help the survivors, perhaps to launch an attack. If you were to withdraw another fifty yards to the rear of the clearing, you should be able to engage them in the open. Otherwise it is mostly light bush."

"Good. Infantry form two ranks, archers front. Lancers, form up over there out of sight and await further orders. One sweep and withdraw. Just one. Do you understand me Reny?"

"Just one sweep, My Lord and stay away from the hand to hand ...stuff."

"Infantry. Take them with arrows. When they get half way across, I will put the Lancers through them. When they are out of the way and not before, we will mop up." He took the rod from its sheath, turned it to the second click and doubled the handle to form the pistol. He pressed and held the orange button and the orange light shot forward into the scrubby trees. Suddenly one caught fire and Ch0n held the button until the entire other side of the clearing was burning. Shouting and screaming could be heard from where the fire was thickest. He released the orange shaft of light and waited. Through the charred sticks he could see the Vikings forming up. He pressed the red button and a bolt of red shot forth and exploded among the first group of the enemy. He repeated it several times until he realized there were no more left to fire at.

"Reny. Get back to me now. Right now. I don't know where they are. Get out!"

He heard her give the order and then they were racing across the clearing towards Ch0n and the Infantry.

"Commander Guerra. Where are they?"

"They have formed a knot of maybe fifty and are running for the foothills. They will either use them for cover, go to the ruins or they will cross the mountains and find the castle. Either way they will not last long."

"Am I clear to ride back to the ruins?"

"Yes. I can see nothing between you and the ruins but that may change if that group of fifty wants to drop down and surprise you."

"Ivor, Izaki, can you hear me?"

They could.

"The castle may be at risk. You heard Guerra. Prepare to move the villagers into the keep. Man the tower and the guard house. Robia. Take your troop back to the castle and unite it. Form up on the knoll overlooking the castle and wait for them. If they appear, wait until they are in the open and ride them down from the flank just like we trained for. Izaki. Stand-to the troops at the ruin. Get the civilians into the caverns now. We are coming back at all speed. Guerra, where are they?"

"I have lost them. They simply disappeared from view. My guess is they are in a cave or under an overhang. Wait. Wait. Yes! There is an opening in the cliff face; it looks to have been man-made because it is perfectly square. Could there be a tunnel leading to the caverns?"

Ch0n weighed up his options.

"Izaki. Cancel my last orders about the caverns. Get the civilians up the track and onto the pass. I will send Reny back to the ruins. Use her only if there is fighting to be done in the open. I am going to take the infantry and see if we can clear the rats from their hole."

The Eñame priest urged his people onwards. He had discovered the reference to a tunnel many years ago but had not needed to revisit that script until three days ago when he had been told he would accompany the force to the lake. He had hunted for it and found it. It told of a tunnel, an escape route for the Sky People if their caverns were compromised. Now he was leading the remains of the disastrous mission towards those same caverns in reverse to find out what had befallen Erik and his men. They lit torches and ran like men possessed for they were men of the sea and not accustomed to small spaces. It took them a full six hours before a faint light appeared and they slowed down. In front of them the tunnel opened out into the huge cavern with a table in the middle and alcoves around the wall, each containing a stone box, decorated with glyphs. The priest Verge was leaning over the table with a brush, cleaning off the dust of many centuries. He looked up when his understudy appeared at the mouth of the tunnel.

"*Ternen? Is that you?*" he called out in the ancient language the priests used among themselves.

"*It is, Verge and I have almost sixty skirmishers behind me in the tunnel.*"

"*So the tunnel was real? I remember your telling me of it years ago but I had forgotten. I had explored only a little way down through that opening, thinking it led to another cavern*"

"*Where is Erik? Where are his men?*"

"*The fool, Mikel, disobeyed an order and attacked the Arw'an defence and they were massacred almost to a man. Erik came close to the channel not knowing what had happened. He sent me ashore with Jon to talk with the local king. Mikel was already here a prisoner but we knew nothing of what had happened. The king hanged Mikel for his attack. He was going to hang Jon but Jon prevailed upon him to die a soldier's death. It was brutal to watch. The king cut off his hand and then his head and at that point, Erik attacked with the two ships. They never made it to the shore. Erik was badly wounded and they healed him but just a few days ago, he was slain by the Ever Queen with her own sword for treason or something akin to it. I have been placed here by the king and the reincarnate to investigate all I can find about the Sky People.*"

"*The Ever Queen? Can it be true?*"

"The one in the prophecy is here. 'There shall be one of us who will return in the body of another but you will know her because she will be one of us. Look upon us now and know us." Teṁen joined in as Verge continued. *"The red-fire hair and green eyes will be the sign and she will speak to the priests in the tongue we shared with them alone and no other. She will be in the company of others but you will know her and obey her as you have known us and obeyed us. To deny her will be to bring the wrath of all of us upon you, whom we have taught and with whom we have shared our seed.' I have seen her and spoken with her. She spake to me in this, the tongue of the ancient Sky People. Only they and we priests know this language but she spake it as readily as I, if not more fluidly. And the king spake it as well. He is also a Sky Person from another star."*

Teṁen looked worried. *'To deny her will be to bring the wrath of all of us upon you, whom we have taught and with whom we have shared our seed.'* Could the prophecy be the cause of all the deaths of the Eñame? He knew the prophecy to be true just as he had known the tunnel would be there.

"I want to see her with my own eyes. Not that I disbelieve you, Verge but it is such a thing that I need to see it. To see her and speak the ancient tongue with her. Then I will believe. Meanwhile, these men are hungry for revenge and for battle."

"Call them off, Teṁen. There has been enough killing for today. And tomorrow. There are seven here from Mikel's crew and others from Erik's disaster. They have been living as have I among the Arw'an. It is not so bad. I have my life's work here.

You too. The king Ch0n is ruthless but fair. The reincarnate is his queen and she is harsher even than the king. How she will react knowing that we have killed hundreds of her children for no purpose, I can not imagine."

The sound of men running echoed down the tunnel.

"Decide, Teṁen. Those footsteps can mean no good for you."

Ch0n saw the light at the end of the tunnel and slowed down. He could see the Vikings silhouetted in the distance and the faint echo of voices reached out to him.

"Harry. Are you there?"

"No. But I am here My Lord."

"Jez! Well come and not too soon. I am in the back of the main cavern with fifty Infantry. Ahead of me there are some fifty Eñame skirmishers. I need you to bring all the soldiers from the ruins to the cavern. Draw the Vikings out so we can ourselves get into the light. We will see what unfolds from there. Move quickly, now."

Ch0n had his force in three files facing the cavern. It was as wide as he could deploy and he knew the Eñame would be restricted to the same width if they attacked. He could hold them off indefinitely with the stun pistol or even the katana but the stun pistol would be better. He drew it and booted it. He turned the helm to thermal and assessed the risk. The Vikings were bunched together in no real semblance of order. Beyond, he could see the priest Verge, who was talking to someone at the front of the Viking group. He removed the rod and selected the translate option. He was sick of the stalemate so he walked quietly towards the Vikings, hoping he would have Jez's support before things went bad.

He spoke to them in their own language.

"Eñame. Lay down your arms. There has been enough fighting for one day. You do not want to die when living is an option to you." He changed to the ancient language of the Sky People.

"Verge. Tell them they must surrender to us or die."

Temen looked stunned as Verge did his best.

"My Lord. There is another priest here. He is Temen, one of my understudies and an honest man. I can vouch for him but he is hard to convince and would see the lady Karín and speak with her."

"That will be arranged but not before we resolve this situation. In a few minutes, another fifty of my soldiers will enter the cavern from that entrance."

"How do you know that?" asked Temen.

Ch0n turned on his mike.

"I know it, priest just as I know that the first person who enters the cavern will do so only when I say the word, and that he will be carrying living fire in his hand and will have fifty men behind him."

"That was close, My Lord. I almost went in before you had a chance to set this up. I have the fire maker in my pocket. Wait a moment. Here it is."

"How do I know, priest? I know because I am one of the Sky People."

Jez strolled into the cavern with the fire lighter in his hand and half the garrison company behind him. Temen gasped.

"Tell your men to lay down their arms, Temen. I have no wish for more killing but if it needs to be done, we will do it and you will be the last to die and it will be at the hands of the village widows. None will be harmed. That I promise."

"I am a priest, not a soldier and I do not command these men. I will come forth and surrender to Verge in the hope he and you will allow me to study this place with him." He walked into the cavern to Verge's side."

"Jez. We have to break this impasse somehow. I do not want to fight inside the tunnel where visibility is poor, even though I could do this with the helm and the stun pistol. I will give them an ultimatum and you will carry it out. Move towards the entrance of the tunnel. Do you understand?"

"Yes, My Lord."

"Men of the Eñame. Listen to me. I want you to move one at a time into the cavern and lay down your arms. Failure to comply will result in my Knight, Sir Jez taking action to convince you. The first of you should move now."

Nobody moved. Jez raised the stun pistol and focused it on the doorway. He waited long enough for someone to emerge and when none did, he fired a pulse into the tunnel. Three of the Eñame went down, stunned and those behind them were almost pushed over.

"Move now and surrender or we will be forced to kill you all. You are trapped. There can be no escape for you, only death or surrender."

"We Eñame do not surrender. We fight to the death," came a voice from the crowd.

"I am going to try and force them out, Jez. Do what you need to do." Ch0n raised the stun pistol and sent a pulse down the tunnel. He felt some of the force in the confined space but in front of him, the Vikings took the brunt of it and those closest were felled. He fired another and another until the throng burst out of the tunnel, axes waving and into the waiting Arw'an infantry and Jez. Jez fired the stun pistol repeatedly into the rushing Vikings until they got too close so he switched hands and the kinetic pistol rattled its hail of pellets to accompany the arrows from the infantry. Blood and spume clouded the air in front of the Vikings until Ch0n left the tunnel behind them, still firing the stun gun. Bodies lay everywhere between the two priests and the tunnel. None had reached the front rank of the Arw'an force, which was waiting with swords still at the ready.

"Jez. One man each while they are still stunned. Secure their weapons and the prisoners. Leave the dead for now. I want these men bound before they regain consciousness."

"Guerra, are you there?"

"I am, My Lord."

"Take the drone to the bottom of the lake and tell me what is happening with the boats. Then bring the drone back. Ask Karín to come here as quickly as she can."

"Yes, My Lord."

"Jez. Put the prisoners in the corner against the wall and stand guard over them yourself. Stun any who would fight or try to rally the others. I am going to ask Karín to speak to them. Then have the men take the dead out and dispose of the bodies."

"Verge. Explain to these men what you have seen here and why it is not wrong for them to surrender as have the others. Tell them they have the option of surrender and fealty or death. There will be no other choices. The Sky People spent many years here sowing their seed and bearing your young to better the sapients of this place. In one moon cycle I have killed five hundred of their children. That was not my intention and is a waste of hundreds of years of breeding. Enough is enough."

Twenty minutes later, the first of the Eñame started to regain consciousness. Verge shouted at them for a full minute before they settled down to listen. For another minute he harangued them with the story of the reincarnated Sky Queen and the prophecy of her coming.

"Those who would surrender peacefully to the Arw'an Knight and serve the Queen Karín and the king, Ch0n, lift your heads and look at the Knight Jez. Hold his eye until he signals his men to release you."

Jez watched as ten of the twenty or more heads were raised. He pointed them out to his men and one by one they were taken to the front of the group where they were formed into a squad in a single rank facing their comrades.

"Jez, watch these ten. Have your pistol out and armed. If any moves to help those still bowed, kill him. I am about to test their word." He looked at the remaining eleven men. They were hard men, he could tell. They were rudely dressed in skin vests and chap-like trousers. He chose the best-dressed of them and pushed him over with his foot. The man looked up at him with pure hate in his eyes. Ch0n pushed him again and the man made to rise but a kick from Ch0n sent him sprawling again. Ch0n went to the pile of captured weapons and selected a sword. He slid it across the flagstone floor to where the man lay still but not cowered. Ch0n motioned with his eyes towards the sword and took a step backwards. The Viking looked around him as though he were unsure of his next option. After a moment, he ran his bonds along the blade until they separated, took the handle and heaved himself to his feet.

Ch0n addressed him in the Eñame language.

"You have your chance, you who scorn the reincarnate Queen, Karín. You came here to kill those who serve her and I as her champion and a king in my own right will not stand for that. This is the fate that will befall all those who will not bow to her. You will be the first. The lucky or unlucky first." He looked around the room and shouted for all to hear the insult that followed.

"This man is typical of those I have seen of the Eñame leaders. They come here in charge of ships of war and then lead their men to their deaths. Well those ten standing before you have shown true courage for they have decided to serve the Ever Queen Karín tho' they know not where she will take them or send them. Now this coward will face the future he selected when he refused to serve her by his silent insolence."

The angry Viking took up the sword and held it two handed in front of him, pointed at ChOn. It was five and a half feet long, of which the blade measured four feet. At the cross, it was four inches wide and when ChOn had picked it up, he guessed its weight at ten pounds, most of which was forward of the handle. It was designed only to chop down two handed on a man holding a shield. The force of the blow would either break the shield or drive the opponent to one knee or knock him to the ground. In order to strike such a blow, the sword had to be lifted over the swordsman's right shoulder in a circular movement and then the strike would be almost vertical. The mere action of the backswing rendered the swordsman vulnerable to attack from his left. ChOn reached behind his right shoulder and the pale green blade slid into view. When the tip cleared the koiguchi, the blade began to hum. The sound was somewhat amplified in the confines of the cavern and caused all those present to look up at the blade, including ChOn's adversary. With no more than a quick downward arc, ChOn slashed the Viking across the lower abdomen. The blade cut the man's vest and opened up a long, clean cut that immediately started to bleed. The Viking looked down at his belly and, while his eyes were averted, ChOn slashed again, the tip of the katana passing through the bridge of the Viking's nose. Blood squirted into his eyes and ran down his lower face and when the Viking sought to wipe his eyes, the green blade cut the air and took the last two fingers of his left hand. The Viking was nothing if not brave and he took a two handed grip on the broadsword and went into a long backswing. When the sword was almost at its highest point and the Viking's left side was exposed, ChOn's left foot moved and the terrible blade cut off his opponent's left arm above the elbow. The sword clattered to the flags only to be picked up by another of the Vikings who raised it and charged at ChOn. ChOn took a half step to his left, raised and cocked his right hand and the broadsword slid down the length of the katana, which was now covering ChOn's entire right side. Without even looking, he went to his left knee and sliced a wide horizontal arc to his right, taking the Vikings two hamstrings. He stood and in three fluid strokes severed the heads of the two men and a third who had risen to his feet. The blood lust was on him now. He positioned himself to strike at the next prisoner when his bracelet thrummed and he heard Karín's voice in his brain.

"Enough! The others offer no fight. They choose not to serve me. So be it. Try them as prisoners of war and then have them executed if you must but I forbid you to do it here."

Ch0n stood up and looked around him. The faces told him he had done as much and as little as he needed to do to make his point.

"Take them away, Sir Jez. Try them as prisoners of war and carry out whatever sentence is deemed fit. The other ten may join their brothers at the jetty after they swear fealty to me and their Queen. Verge. If you think you can trust this priest, Temen, take him on your staff under the same conditions as you are here. He is not to speak to any of the other Eñame except in my presence under pain of death. Now when this lot is cleaned up, you can both get back to the study of this place and the glyphs on the main table."

Karín was waiting for him in the cavern entrance.

"There has been too much killing of late. The king does not need to engage in it unless it is on the field of battle. If you wanted to make a point, Jez could have just as easily done it. I want you to promise me you will never kill for sport again for it is not like you and I do not like it."

"It was not for sport. I wanted to test the ten to see if any would flinch and betray themselves."

"You toyed with the first. You made a brave man look like a helpless novice. Yes, he was armed but against your skill that sword of his might as well have been a stick. The second was quick and the third probably not necessary but who can tell what he might have done had he reached you. I will grant you the second and third but the first was cruel. Cruel is not you. Just is you. Hard is you. The people call you ruthless but fair.

They respect you for that. They will not like the story of what happened today."

"That from the one who killed a line of Matáng one after the other?"

"I was not their queen. At the time I was your bodyguard and would-be lover. I had to make sure treason was seen as a death penalty. I did not toy with them. It was quick and clean, brutal tho' it also was."

"And the one you had flayed?"

"That was also necessary to show you that women could be Lancers. I do not deny I whispered sweet nothings into his ear reminding him of our youth and yes, I took some satisfaction from it. Look at me now! Tell me you will not make sport of executions as you did today. If you have to do it, do it as you have always done. Look at me now and tell me."

"So be it. But I reserve the right to make sport of any who would challenge my right to rule. I want all challengers or would-be challengers to know that to lose a challenge is to die a slow death."

"My Lord. None will rule but you while I still live. If any should better you, I will mount a challenge myself against them for if you are not the king, I would want to be queen in my own right or dead at your side. Now, I want you to know I luv you even when I am angry with you. As I have to wear these teeth to remind me, you will wear something to remind you."

She looked around the flagstone floor until she found what she was looking for.

"Here it is." She picked up the severed finger of the first Viking, removed an ornate gold ring from it and held it out to Ch0n.

"Put this on and when you look at it, remember your promise to me and that I luv you even when I am angry with you."

They emerged to the afternoon sun. Below them a crowd had gathered. Jez was sentencing the prisoners. Behind them in the cavern, Teṁen was awestruck at the sight of Karín but he had no time to stare because the priest Verge was already showing him the caskets of stone and the glyphs chiseled into the walls.

"It feels good to have Jez home again. I missed him in the mornings at training and I missed him at council."

"I will speak to him and tell him to work you harder now he is back to take some of the raw energy from you. You need to calm yourself and relax more. With Jez back you can do that and let the council have more responsibility. Now. Take me home. I am weary. Your prince in waiting is draining my energy and I need to rest."

Chapter Thirteen: The Queen of the Eñame

Ch0n rose early as usual and checked the grounds of the castle, starting with the communications room across the hall from his apartments. The operator was sitting alert at his post waiting for Guerra to relieve him in a few hours. He made a complete circuit of the castle walls, returned and surveyed his chambers where Maní lay sprawled naked across the bed. She was alone now. After Ch0n's rising Buyo had retired to her quarters where she and Karín shared a room during their pregnancies. Karín was now noticeably with child and Buyo's bump was more obvious. Ch0n rarely had time to himself with Maní. Both his wives wanted to be present during the ijon and afterwards to enjoy the many permitted ways to satisfy their needs with either of the lovers. Ch0n looked at the sun rising through the window and calculated he had enough time to wake Maní before the obligatory training sessions for all the Knights and squires. He lifted the tunic over his head and climbed onto the bed beside her. She woke at the movement, saw his aroused state and sleepily held out her arms to him.

"My Lord, Ch0n! Are you always thus in the mornings? You are a king in every way. I have long awaited a moment when we were alone and I could know the ijon with you as I did that first night at the ancient ruins. It is not the same with your wives present tho' you satisfy my burning. I would have you satisfy

my yearning as well. Let your mind think only of me for once and let me revel in the ijon and thus touch your inner self as well as your body. Look at my face. I want you to see the pleasure you take from me instead of it being hidden in the darkness. Yes, My Lord. Watch me and know I am your slave. Now I will speak no more for I wish to concentrate on nothing but your swordplay before you have to depart for your morning training session."

When Ch0n arrived at the training square he was invigorated and relaxed. He used his standard katana at these sessions and not Shiew because he would have broken the precious blades of his training partners with it and he did not want Harry or Ivor to know its power against a conventional composite blade. At the end of the main session, he stayed behind with Jez as usual and they sparred furiously for another twenty minutes in private. They and Karín had a specially choreographed routine that started out exactly as the others but the sixth move had been changed. Instead of a short pace forward with the katana almost vertical to deliver a forehand upstroke to the head, it involved the same short pace forward with the left foot and a strike to the opponent's left knee. They practised for ten minutes as the first player and ten as the second. There were no further moves because the routine was designed to end there and then with only a killing strike to follow. The normally choreographed kata, which they practised with the other Knights and squires, went for a full minute at breakneck speed.

"You are well relaxed, this morning, My Lord. I found it hard to keep with you."

"That I am, Jez and it is because we are going sailing. I decided last evening that we are going to present the Vikings to their reincarnated Queen. They must be frantic by now, wondering what has happened to their fleet and their sailors. You and Karín and I will talk after breakfast as to the when of it and then I will take it to the council. It will be a peaceful mission with just the two boats. One will dock at the harbour and the other will stand off with the heavy weapons just in case. "

The two started back to their quarters, walking in step as always.

"Karín may not want to go."

"She will go because I will ask her to go. It will be uncomplicated. We will take the priest, Verge and split the Viking crew, half in each boat with no weapons. All we need them for is to make sure our crews can handle the boats for the two and a half days at sea. We should be there and back in a week."

"No Lancers and no tlaque?"

"No. It will give Marik a chance to command the Infantry and archers. I don't think we will have room for beasts."

"My Lord. I beg to differ with you but I think we should look at other options as well before we decide this. If we could take just one tlaque and land a Knight in the shallows west of the main harbour, we would have the advantage we have had since you arrived."

"I have thought about that. If we can adapt one boat to take a tlaque, we will do it. I have not made a plan for it. It is just an idea. I will include the priest, Verge in the planning. He remains loyal to Karín and his life's work depends on his remaining loyal to us. He will prove valuable at all stages of the planning. I will send for him immediately and he should be here by afternoon."

"I will think about it over breakfast and go to your quarters afterwards. Will there be anybody else apart from us three?"

"I will ask Guerra to do a map reconnaissance and look for a landing point west of the main harbour. If we can manage to offload one tlaque, we may be able to offload some archers as well."

Jez nodded to his king and turned into his entrance. Through the open flap, ChOn could make out a heavy Malek and a lithe Caron in the main room.

ChOn mounted the stairs two at a time. The three women were waiting to accompany him to breakfast. Karín had the shaving tool in her hand as well. ChOn changed into his tunic and they descended and headed for the communal eating area, greeting as many people by name as they could along the way.

They sat at the same table as Jez, and Guerra, and their women. ChOn told Guerra he would be needed for a meeting after ChOn had bathed but Guerra motioned him to one side.

"My Lord. I have a problem at the mint," he started, inserting the English word into the Arw'an tongue. *"For three weeks I have been watching a certain shift because there has been a*

shortfall in pesos compared to the weight of gold being melted. I first noticed it when you and the others were fighting the Vikings. I didn't say anything because I thought I had made a mistake but it has happened twice since. Same shift. Three workers in all."

"OK. We will deal with it separately. For the moment, I want to concentrate on a trip to the Viking city. If you like, take the camera we took from Arturo's broken helm and rig it up in the melting room where it can view the raw gold being transferred from the bags to the melting pot. It is unlikely that pesos are being stolen. Tell nobody but when the suspect shift is working, record everything to be used in evidence. Get someone here to mind the radio when you go back, I need you to copy the images of the coast immediately west of the harbour for a few miles and take them to the meeting room. Now, let's eat."

They returned to the long table and took their places. Ch0n wolfed down a huge plate of porridge and stewed goat while the others looked on in awe.

"What are you all looking at? For some reason I am extra hungry this morning. Nothing more to it."

Across the table, Maní was inwardly smiling.

"Yes, My Lord. You were extra hungry this morning and not just for porridge," she thought. "And now I know you feel the need strongly in the mornings you will be hungry every breakfast." She looked demurely up at Ch0n, caught his eye and held it fast. She parted her lips just sufficiently for the tip of her tongue to show and slipped it back out of sight. She was seated between Karín and Buyo and neither of them saw her flirtation but ChOn's heart thumped twice hard in his chest and he felt himself stir under the tunic. He noted she had finished eating whereas Karín had called for more porridge.

"I have a lot to do this morning so if you will excuse me I will take my leave and go to the baths. Karín, I note you have not finished eating so if you don't mind, I will have Maní shave me this morning."

Karín gave Maní the precious soap and the blade and started eating her porridge. She was eating more and more now she was well into her time. Beside her, Buyo felt her gorge rising again at the smell of the food but managed not to throw up. Maní patted them both on the cheek as she rose and followed ChOn to the baths.

They entered the public shaving booth. At a signal from Maní, the attendant drew the curtain and left them alone and ChOn lay back in Maní's lap on the flat stone.

"My Lord, you have forgotten to remove your tunic. It will get soaking wet." She took a woollen towel from a pile and held it out to him. He pulled the tunic over his head, dropped his undergarment and reached for the towel but did not wrap it around his waist. Instead he sat on the flat stone and waited for Maní to adopt her position behind his head to shave him. She lifted her own tunic over her head and stood in front of him.

"My Lord. This will be a shave the likes of which neither of us has ever had. I will shave you as you desire but first I would have you shave me. Shave my head first and then my iduw.

But do not delay for you have much to do this morning and time is of the essence."

Ch0n shaved her already short hair back to the scalp and then carefully went to work on the light wisps below her hard belly. By the time he had finished he was hot for her but she would have none of it.

"Lie back and let me do my work, My Lord. I will leave time for play."

She shaved him expertly and quickly, first his head, then his beard and finally his groin. She took the wool-oil from the shelf, oiled her hands and ran them over his scalp and his face. The fire between her thighs was raging and when she told Ch0n to stand up, her mouth was so dry that her voice cracked. They stood face to face for just a moment before she lowered herself down onto the same flat stone and held out her arms to receive him.

"My Lord, I know not what has come over you this morning but whatever it is, I will reap the benefits willingly." Later as he stood up from her she was wifely towards him. *"Now go and bathe before you attend to matters of state. Unless you would have me again for I see that it would take little for me to ready you once more for battle."*

Without waiting for a response she bent over him and he growled deep in his throat before hefting her bodily and turning her about. He mounted her from behind without ceremony as he had seen the buck tlaque mount his does. Below him, Maní was revelling in the sheer brute force of the act. Ch0n sated himself with no regard for her. It was a first for him to mate like an animal and when he was spent he separated himself from her and reached for the towel, his eyes wide, his chest heaving.

"Did you like that, my rutting bull who once killed a bull? Did you feel the strength of your staff in me as I did? Know well that I am at your beck at any time for I much like to be taken as a bull orok would mount his cow unbidden. Now go. You have learned something this day. I see it in you. And so have I and now I have learned it, your days will be full of surprises."

"You pleased me and pleasured me both and you know it. Now I must go for if I do not, I will forget I am a king with kingly duties."

"I will not let you forget, my king, for only a king may know me as you know me and especially only a king may take me like a beast at his whim. Know that as my king you have that right and you will come to take advantage of it as does the bull orok for I am in constant heat for you. That is my promise to you and in return I seek only your protection and your favour."

Ch0n dragged himself to the baths and when he arrived back at his quarters, he had to rush to get ready for the meeting with Karín, Jez and Guerra.

"Greetings again to you all. You know why we are here, to plan a voyage to the capital of the Eñame. I would have them know the situation here because if we do not go and tell them, they will send another force and another. We do not want all-out war with them nor their decimation, for the blood of the ancient sky people is in them as it is in Karín and probably

Maní. Their priest, Verge will accompany us to pave the way for Karín's grand entrance. It will need to be soon or it will need to wait until after she bears her child for there will soon come a time when she will not want to travel."

"My Lord, I am already at that point. I do not want to travel so far at my stage. In another month, for it will surely take that long to organize the voyage, I will be beyond it. I have no desire to appear before the Vikings as their queen whilst I can barely walk. I wish to appear regal and not like a goat stuck on its back in a wadi and unable to right itself. Allow me that if you would."

"So be it but I will send a ship or two first to let them know their people have been defeated here and that their queen will soon visit them. That much can not wait. How much longer before you give light to our offspring?"

"Before the fourth full moon it will happen. Kelda's woman, the midwife has told me. And Buyo will follow two moons later. You may go to the Vikings but I wish you to be here when the new prince is born. I will speak also for Malek for Jez will not. He is far too loyal to you to suggest otherwise but he should not be leaving Malek until after her time which will be before the next full moon." She looked at Jez, who smiled at her by way of thanks.

"Then I will go. Ivor and Harry will accompany me. Commander Guerra, please pass my compliments to the admiral and inform him we will be travelling tomorrow to the ruins to discuss the logistics of the plan for we will need to remodel a boat to take tlaque or an oruk. Or perhaps two.

Now. I propose we send three boats with two companies of Infantry and two platoons of archers. That will allow for two hundred troops in all. The third boat we will modify to take at least one oruk and one tlaque plus the two Knights and their squires. It will need a bamboo cage, Boro, perhaps two, and the back or side will need to open and lower so the beast can walk on or off without tipping the boat. It will need to maintain the mast and perhaps ten or twenty crew to sail and row. Commander Guerra should have some images to show us in a short while of a landing place for the Knights. Jez can brief them on the approaches from the land side. When they are within view of the town, I will take the lead boat with the crossbow, the rocket launchers and one hundred troops to the dock. The second boat will sit offshore and watch what happens. Marik will be in command of that boat with the second company. He will only come ashore when I give the order.   Once ashore, I will have Verge make his announcements and we will march to the town and have a meeting with the elders or chiefs. I am not anticipating a lot of resistance because we have killed and captured more than five hundred of their men. The town will be full of women and children waiting for their fathers and husbands to return. Harry. Is there one among the prisoners we can trust to take with us?"

"There is, My Lord. And more than one. Eden is one. He called his crew to surrender when the killing became too much for him. He is a man of peace and honour. I have had a lot to do with him in the repairing of the boats and the allocation of manpower."

"Then Eden will go with us in the first boat. Now, Commander Guerra, show us what you have found."

Guerra projected a series of images onto the wall. They were of the coast south-east of the Eñame town.

"I think this spot will do nicely. It has a bank that the beasts can dismount onto and these few trees will serve to stabilize the boat and to use as moorings. Just to the north is what seems to be a small track leading straight to the town."

"I know this place," cut in Jez. *"If you look at the next image you will see a small copse of fruit trees by a water hole and an overhanging stone. I camped there the night before I went into the town. We could do the same. There is water there for all and the oruk will need a day to rest and eat before they continue."* Then followed the next image and Guerra expanded it so they could see it more closely. *"From here,"* continued Jez, *"it is an easy ride to the town but the troops will need to leave during the night if they are to arrive by daylight. On foot it will be at least four....hours to the river mouth. If you go now to the edge of the village you will see where the oruk may cross. The river itself rushes across some shallows and then falls the height of three men to sea level. There it is! The cliff face continues around and forms a break water to protect the cave entrance from the waves. Any sea attack also has to be from the side for the same reason."*

"Well seen, Jez. Commander Guerra. Do you have the images from the initial reconnaissance flight?"

By way of answer, Guerra went to the menu and pulled out some thumbnails. He flashed them across the screen until Ch0n told him to stop.

"Look there! A boat can pull in and hide behind the raised bank but still fire into the cave. The Vikings can't assault for the same reason a boat can't attack. The curve in the cliff means they would have to attack across water. The Infantry could dismount and cross the shallows back here under crossbow support and the firing tubes. This is how I see things happening. First the two Knights ride to the shallows. The second boat will deploy to this place behind the bank. I will approach the dock with the priest in the front of the boat. If there is resistance, the Knights will attack the dock and we will make an opposed landing with the second boat providing cover. As soon as the battle is joined, Marik will deploy the second wave across the shallows. The two boats are to be prepared to leave without notice. During the battle, they will come about to face the open water."

"My Lord," interjected Guerra, *"Verge might save us a lot of trouble if he and Eden were to deploy on the boat with the Knights. The Knights could take them to the river and they could cross and announce your arrival. I could have the drone watching the activity levels with Sir Jez. We would know well ahead of time if the reception would be hostile. In a sense this is similar to our approach to a new planet and the more we can do in advance the easier it will be. I am not much of a soldier but this strategic stuff is what I used to do after all. I could keep you briefed all the way in."*

ChOn looked at Jez and the other two Knights. They all nodded.

"Well, then, Commander Guerra, we'll do it that way. You know the general plan. Tomorrow we will all ride for the ruins and you will give the orders on my behalf for the commencement of the operation. No surprises, please. Any more questions or suggestions from anybody? Good. I'm hungry. That training session must have been more physical than I thought."

The group broke up. Only Karín and Jez stayed behind.

"My Lord, I hope you are not angry with my position on this."

"Of course not, wife. I am going to have to start thinking on a completely new level soon. What with you and Malek and Buyo and Carmodi all waiting to produce offspring, we soon won't have time to fight. We'll be too busy playing with the children."

"My Lord." It was Jez, this time. *"Malek and I would like you to name our child. We would have called it for you out of love but we know Ch0n is not a real name and so we would prefer you to give him a name. It will surely be a boy. Your own son will be needing a squire and friend to play with and to practice with the wooden katanas."*

"I will look into my history books and find a suitable name, my friend. I will miss you at the Eñame town. I am used to you at my side and Karín at my other. Somehow this mission will not seem the same."

"Will you be taking Maní?" Karín asked Ch0n after Jez had left. *"She has proven to be a concubine much to your liking."*

"Put your concerns behind you, Karín. She is but a concubine to me and when you and Buyo are permitted to return to me, I will give you the choice as to what becomes of her. I would keep her if the choice were mine alone for she pleases me in her way but I feel not the ebon for her. And, no. I will not be taking her. There will be no women on this trip for it will be cramped quarters. If I could take even one, I would take a Lancer for she would be of more use to me."

"I am not jealous of Maní but I know your desires and your capacity for the ijon and it grows stronger. She is but one woman and I do not want you to get too used to her ways. That is all. After I am cleansed, we will have some time together alone. I would go to the overhang so we can renew ourselves. I will be needing some serious weapon training as well to recover my fighting skills and my body will need to harden. It will be a time such as we have never had together. When that time is complete, we will return here and then go to the Viking stronghold together so they can know their queen as she wishes to be known to them."

"So it shall be for I have missed you. It will be the first thing we will do after you are permitted. Buyo will want something similar. I hope you are ready for that too. Talking of offspring, I am pleased Jez wishes me to name his child. I will find a warrior name for him. Or her. But I already have a name for ours. Dorak. It is for one of the names of the greatest of all the ancient Samaurai Knights, Miyamoto Musashi, or Dorak-u. I would call our son for him. It is a name like no other. He will be a child of three planets. He will grow up to be a king. Perhaps he will lead the people against the invasion that is surely coming for the people of the Earth know no bounds to their greed and capacity for war. That is why we were sent forth to explore and that is why I can not allow any mission to land here without a battle. I have to unite all the peoples of this world in order to protect its future. I fear I may never have time to sit back and enjoy what has passed and I am tired of fighting. I was tired before the Eñame battles and I am more tired of it now but it is not over until they have agreed to a peace."

Karín laughed and then was serious again.

"I did not mean to start a conversation so full of melancholy, My Lord. You are tense now. It is still a short while until we eat. Come with me and I will relax you in a manner that is not forbidden and perhaps you can show me and tell me again how much you miss me."

Ch0n spent the evening informing Izaki and Mastelik of his plans to send an expedition to the Eñame harbour. Mastelik was all for sending his Lancers overland for support, a plan that Ch0n found appealing but he decided not to run with it because there was not enough time for the initial expedition. He did, however tell Mastelik that for a subsequent expedition, it would be appropriate and that with enough warning, he would be deployed. He left the comms room satisfied that he had briefed everybody who needed to know. He decided to visit Doni and check the progress of the oruk females impregnated by the tlaque buck. It was something he had not done for some days. He arrived at the corrals and Doni was at his post as usual. Together they went to the breeding oruk females.

"They are growing nicely, My Lord. I would say they are more than half way to birth. Not one has lost the calf so I think

Gavan Connell

we can assume that if we want to proceed with this program we can just do it. Ten or fewer heavy tlaque will be nowhere near enough. What we need is for the whole oruk herd to be crossed one year to give us eighty or a hundred mounts. After that we can put the oruk bull back with the wild herds. Your beast will be busy if we do that. You will be without him for a month after the next calf drop as it is."

ChOn wondered how he might manage being without his tlaque for a month after so long but it wouldn't be for another four months anyway so he knew a solution could easily be found before then. He imagined the beast wandering from cow to cow, smelling each one and mounting those who were ready. Maní's face flashed into view and he felt himself stirring even at the merest thought of her and what she had said this morning. He reminded Doni he was doing well and turned for the castle, knowing he would call at the stables on the way to see to his tlaque and its needs. He called in as always to visit Mori. The old man was as usual sitting outside his house with the kwidada on its perch and they were chatting together like an old married couple. The dáguia were asleep in their cages. ChOn liked to maintain a level of breeding stock in case the satellite went unserviceable and so Mori's work was not as frenetic as before. Just so, he maintained his birds in first class order and knew which bird was mated with which and which chicks were ready to fly free for the first time with the tiny tubes attached to their legs.

"Good evenin', King," he smiled as ChOn approached. The bird looked around at ChOn.

"Good evenin', King," it said in Mori's voice.

372

Ch0n laughed. A trip to Mori's gate was as good a way to have one's ego smashed as any Ch0n knew.

"Good evening, Mori, Royal Keeper of the Birds. What gossip have you for me today?"

"Not too much, King. I did hear that Berik found gold down yonder by the crack in the 'ills. Funny that. I used to go there when I were a boy collectin' me eggs and young whistlers and all the time I spent there I never saw nothin' so much as looked like a shiny stone. Not as it would ha' mattered. In them days, your gold wasn't worth pickin' up off the ground unless you was going tae throw it at something. Not like now."

"Some people have all the luck, my old friend. And I am lucky to have you looking after the security of the kingdom's communications system." He looked at the old man's chest where the aluminium medal always rested comfortably as a reminder to all of his service. "Goodnight, now. I'll call by again, soon."

Ch0n turned and took a step down the path.

"Goodnight, King," said a voice behind him. It might have been Mori but it might have been the bird.

Ch0n arrived at the stables where he found Darel and Maní.

"Darel, I need you to go to Commander Guerra's office. Tell him old Mori mentioned that Berik has found gold in the hills. Wait there for me with my pistol."

Darel raced off on his errand. ChOn looked at Maní and without a word, climbed the ladder to the loft and ducked through the curtain into her quarters. He could hear her on the ladder and when she lifted the curtain she saw him lifting the tunic over his head and her heart raced. He took her by the arm and pulled her closer to him. She moved quickly to her cot and knelt there, feeling his hands lifting the hem of her own tunic. ChOn was on her in an instant, the vision of his tlaque before his eyes. Beneath him, Maní braced herself as best she could and let him have his way until he slumped, spent over her.

"I have wakened the beast in you, My Lord," she said softly. *"As you have in me. My centre itches for you every moment of the day. Know that. And now you have whet my appetite for more. Tonight I will come to you and I beg you to be gentle and slow with me and your reward will be the greater for it."*

ChOn dressed and started down the ladder. He paused before his head disappeared. Maní was sitting on the cot arranging her tunic.

"Don't be late. I am already eager for more. Tonight Buyo will join us. She likes to pleasure you almost as much as I do."

"I will not tarry, My Lord. And yes, Buyo knows how to quell my fire but there is no substitute in battle for the sword of a king."

By the time ChOn arrived, Guerra had all the details on Berik's shift. Darel gave ChOn the pistol and ChOn Guerra what oldMori had passed to him about Berik's find.

"He is the leader of the shift I told you about," Guerra announced. *"They are due to work again tonight. In two hours they arrive and we will watch them for their eight hours of work. He has found gold all right but it isn't in the hills. All we have to do is catch him and his crew and find out how they are doing it."*

"It has to be something simple. A complicated plan is beyond him and would be hard to implement. We'll know soon enough."

ChOn woke early and went straight to the comms room. Guerra was there waiting for his arrival.

"My Lord, I am reviewing the images for the night shift. I have just arrived so there is nothing as yet. I will call you as soon as I have seen something."

ChOn returned to the royal apartments and surveyed the wreckage of his bed. Maní was sprawled naked next to Buyo's tiny body. ChOn felt a pang of something in his chest when he looked at Buyo. She may have been forbidden to him because of her pregnancy but her capacity for innovation, her desire to please him, and Maní's sheer wantonness had made for a wild night for them all. He put thoughts of returning to them out of his head and instead donned his uniform and strode purposefully to the training field. It was early and only Darel was there. ChOn put him through a vigorous session and was as usual impressed with the young man's capacity for weapons handling. He was adept now with the katana and the short sword, better than both Ivor and Harry with the double swords and lighter on his feet. He had grown taller in his few months with Ch0n but was still a head shorter than the earth Knights and would probably grow no more. Ch0n told him to select the sais and they went through the fluid sai katas slowly as they always did. Darel was like a dancer with them and Ch0n decided to increase the tempo of the sparring katas. By the time they had finished, they were going at full pace with no thought for injuring each other for their skill levels were on a par. They ended the routine and bowed to each other, Ch0n nodding his approval. Sporadic clapping reached their ears. Jez, Ivor and Harry had arrived with their respective squires, who were all agog at the skill of their brother. As a group they continued their session with Darel looking composed but smiling inwardly at the recognition Ch0n had bestowed upon him with the nod.

Guerra was waiting for him when he returned to his quarters. He was grim faced and Ch0n knew he had found out how the gold was being stolen.

"Come in, My Lord. You were right. It is simple." They went to the monitor and Guerra pressed the 'play' icon on the screen. Together they watched Berik look around him and draw his sword. He worked the bellows to fan the furnace then plunged the blade into the puddle of boiling gold and withdrew it again, holding it point-down until the last drip had formed and fallen. Then he leaned it against the stone in a shadow, took a second sword from a niche and sheathed it. It was over in seconds. Guerra hit a bookmark icon and the image jumped to where Berik took his sword and hid it, replacing it in the sheath with

the gilded version. He called to the other two to finish up and they left together.

"It was Berik who made the gilt sword for the Gathering, My Lord."

"Well it is my fault for giving him the idea I suppose, so I should be the one who officially catches him out. We don't want people to know we have the capacity to put cameras anywhere we like. Well done. Next time he is rostered on, let me know and I will prepare a welcoming party for him at the end of his shift in the main square."

They rode to the ruins later in the day. Verge was his usual fawning self with Temen one pace to his rear equally as obsequious. Verge was almost beside himself with humility and excitement at seeing Karín. He spoke to her in the ancient tongue as always before she stopped him as always. He had something to tell the Lord Ch0n, he told her. Something very important.

Guerra gave the orders for the voyage to the Eñame Town, including the time frame for the modifications to the third longboat to support the carriage of two oruk and supplies. Eden was placed in charge of the modifications and his command of Ch0n's boat was restored. Admiral was officially appointed captain of the second boat and Ch0n appointed one of Kelda's most experienced logisticians to be captain of the modified boat after consultation with Eden and Kelda herself. The appointment provoked some murmurs of surprise for it was a woman, Mathilde, who had never been on a boat in her life.

"Neither had you, Admiral a month or two ago. We have Eden to train her over the next month. The boat is not a boat of war and will not be required to manoeuvre swiftly to avoid battle. It will be manned by a volunteer crew from Doni and Kelda's teams and a squad of soldiers to defend it when it is moored. All must be able to row and trim sails as well as look after the animals and ration the supplies. None of us has the ability to do that which they make look easy. There are no men's or women's positions in this kingdom. Mathilde will be afforded the respect and position to which a captain of the Arw'an Navy is entitled, with land and a dwelling. She will be permitted a first mate from the Eñame to assist her as she needs. In my kingdom, ability, hard work and loyalty will be rewarded on merit. She will arrive here in two days with her husband, who will probably not want to be a member of her crew."

The last comment drew laughter and the matter was closed. Verge was bursting to speak to Ch0n and rushed to his side as soon as he could.

"My Lord!" he said in the ancient tongue of the sky people so nobody else could understand, "I have found out some important things. Firstly, we now know the head man among the sky people was called Toltemic. But more important still, Temen and I have been cleaning the top of the table and it reveals some glyphs which we can read and others which we can not. There is also a hole here in the middle which with difficulty we have cleaned. Sir Harry gave us a piece of…. hose, which is a thing of miracles, and using it we blew air from our mouths into the bottom of the hole and dust was forced to the top and out onto the surface. We think it is important but

know not what might fit inside. We measured the depth to be three cibits and two mibits." He took a rule from his robes that was graduated and showed ChOn the length he was talking about. ChOn's heart skipped a beat because just by looking he could see it was about the same length of the rod in his armour. ChOn did a quick appraisal of the time he had remaining in the day and decided he and Karín would go to the cavern. He told the priest to lead the way and they followed him up the now, well-trod path to the entrance. Karín was struggling a little in her advanced stage of pregnancy and ChOn took her hand to assist her.

"I hope your son realizes how much I suffer to give him life, ChOn. I am embarrassed to need help to walk up a slope as gentle as this."

"He will know because I will tell him how much we desired his presence and how much it is appreciated. Now try and hurry because Verge is going to burst if we are late."

They entered the main cavern. It was as clean as the inside of a dwelling, brushed and swept by the few assistants Verge would allow in a place so holy to him. The table top was almost shiny and ChOn could tell instantly that the glyphs had been cut by a machine of some sort. In the middle of one glyph that looked like a flying machine of some sort was a round hole with a groove running towards the edge. ChOn knew that the rod, folded into its pistol shape, would fit. He was tempted to try it but decided he would let Verge tell him everything he had learned and then he would send everybody away except Karín and they would try and work out the secret to the keyhole.

"My Lady. My Lord. We have decided that this line of glyphs here are instructions. Like those on a map, telling us how to find something but we know not what. The hole seems to be the secret because it is placed in this glyph which seems to be a flying machine, and the glyph before says 'hide, or store' and this one after it says 'nearby or not far away'. We are confused by this series which says, 'read' and this glyph we do not know but it looks like the glyph for 'sun' or sunlight' and then 'find the manner' or perhaps, discover or learn'. There are others telling of the purpose of their visit and the population of the stars by them. It is the ones I have shown you that are confusing to us."

ChOn sent a thought message to Karín through the bracelet and the rings.

"Yes, My Lord. I, too am curious." She replied in the same way. "Shall I send them away so we can try to find out what is written?"

ChOn nodded.

"I would be alone here with the king. Return to your dwelling and we will summon you when we are ready."

Verge looked as though he had been slapped but he nodded to Teṁen and they backed away touching their breasts, lips and foreheads.

ChOn waited a few moments after they had departed and took the rod from his armour. He doubled it into the pistol shape.

"If this is a trap, you should not be here. There is no point in us all dying here at once."

"If you die, what is there for me, My Lord? I would die with you or in your place."

"And our offspring? I would that he live a full life and not die before he sees the light of day. Now go outside. I will call you when I know it is safe. Go now."

"Of course you are right," said Karín as she withdrew. "You are always right."

Ch0n put the tip of the rod into the hole. Nothing happened. He eased it all the way into the hole and clicked the 'handle' into the slot. The table started to hum slightly and then some of the glyphs were lit from below. Ch0n called Karín to come.

"Look at this. It must be a code. If we circle those lit, we can ask the priest to read them out to us. He withdrew the rod only to find that the glyphs remained lit and that the energy source lighting them made them hot to the touch. He had an idea and pointed the rod at one of the first glyphs in 'translate' mode and the thought flashed into his head, 'Craft'.

"I can read them with the rod,"

"What say they?"

"They say, 'To find our craft, which has been stored nearby, look for a mark in the plinth on the far side of the lake that looks like this'." He pointed to the symbol 'Ŧ' and then pointed the rod at it. "It has no specific meaning according to the translator so it is just a signal. If you use your imagination a little, it might be an arrow pointing at something. We will have to find it. It will have metal and glass and wire and goodness knows what else we can use. Maybe even a mass translator. No. That would be here. Tools! Something cut these letters. Look! The lit up glyphs have gone dull again."

A thought went into his head and he pressed a button on the rod. The three lights lit. Blue, Orange and Red. He knew the blue was a pulse gun, the orange a flame thrower and the red would throw an explosion but he had never tried any combinations. He went to the cavern entrance and looked for a place he could fire the rod without endangering anybody. He pressed blue and orange and watched an ice crystal the size and shape of a teardrop form and grow to the size of his head. He released the buttons and the crystal dropped to the ground. Karín touched it and pulled back her hand in surprise.

"My Lord! It is impossibly cold to the touch! What harm could this do to any living thing?"

"It is not a weapon. It is called 'ice' and it must have been needed for something in their lives. It can be used to make water cold to drink. I have tasted cold water and it is very refreshing. Much more so than tepid water." He thought for a moment and then added,

"I will see if it will break rock. Expanding water might be used to break something without violence and bits flying everywhere."

He kicked the ice out of the entrance and pushed the blue and red buttons together but nothing seemed to happen. The tip of the rod glowed red, though and Ch0n pointed it at the roof of the cavern. He was rewarded with a point of intense red light the diameter of one of Karín's intensely brown pupils. He walked to the entrance of the tunnel and scuffed his boot in the dirt which stirred up the dust. He pressed the blue and red again and the thin beam became visible as it passed through the dust cloud in a glittering red display.

"This will be their cutting tool. It is called a laser and the light can be used for many things but watch this." He held it close to the edge of the table and wrote a glyph with the sound, 'Ch0n' in the very stone in a precise hand. He went to the other side and wrote the sound, 'Karín.' He went to the tunnel and took a handful of the loose dirt and returned to the table. He filled the letters with dust, making sure not to spill any on the clean floor and smiled at her. "That will confuse them no end."

"What did you draw, My Lord?"

"I drew our names in the ancient script. This rod allowed me to do it as it allowed me to read them. Now let us see what the other combinations will do."

He went to the cavern entrance and pressed the orange and red buttons. A white light filled the room as though the sun had broken through the cavern roof. Ch0n was delighted and Karín was enthralled.

"This is magic, My Lord, is it not?"

Gavan Connell

"No. It is called physics or science where I come from but it may well be magic for I know not how it works. It will make a big difference to our lives, though, for the power source in the rod will never run out and we can light the entire castle if we need to. Now there is but one combination to try." He pressed the three buttons and nothing happened. He could see no result near or far.

"It must have a specific purpose. We will know what it is if we are confronted with the problem."

He walked outside the cavern and looked around for something and when he found it, he called Karín. He placed the tip of the rod in a narrow crevice in a large rock and pressed the blue and orange buttons. Nothing happened until the rock suddenly split in two and a wedge of ice fell between the two pieces.

"This will come in handy some day when we have no explosives to split stones." He went back towards the cavern opening to where he could see down into the area of the ruins. He saw Verge looking up at him and waved for him to return. The poor man almost ran up the hill. ChOn put the rod back into his armour and waited for the priest.

"We found nothing other than that we think the glyphs may be a sort of code if they are read in isolation. For example, what does this Glyph say? It feels warmer than the others and some are warm and some are cold."

"It says, 'find', My Lord." He ran the palm of his hand over the glyphs to the next warm one. It was the one that looked like the flying vessel. 'Craft'. *"Find craft, My Lord. You are right."* In minutes he had worked out the secret.

"Find our craft hidden nearby. Find the mark on the other side of the lake in cut stone that looks thus." He pointed out the symbol 'Ŧ' proudly to Ch0n.

"If we find this, we will find the craft. I think this is an arrow pointing us at the craft."

"Well done, Verge but why did you not find this before? It was Karín who told me the secret of the warm glyphs but she knew not why they would be warm. Perhaps it is her presence that warms them. Now. Search the entire table top to bottom in case there are other clues. I will organize a search party for the missing plinth."

The sun was sinking and when it was low enough, the first rays of it snaked into the cavern and touched the table. Or touched half the table where the sun symbol had been cut, the shadow of the edge of the entrance running down a straight line carved the width of the table. Ch0n ran to it looked along the line where the sun and shade met. He laughed and saw Karín smile at the sound.

"Verge. The edges of this table will hold a secret. The sun has just told me where to look for the symbol. There will be other secrets on the edge. Find them and report to me what you find." He took his helm from on top of a sarcophagus and put it on.

"Guerra, are you there?"

"He is here, My Lord," came Carmodi's voice.

"Look at the aerial images of the lake and find me the point exactly west of the main cavern entrance. Then send the drone and take strip images of that point east-west for a hundred and fifty yards and for fifty yards north and south. I want a grid to search. I will know what I am looking for when I see it."

"I will send it first thing tomorrow, My Lord. I know you want the information right now but I can not hold back the sun, though my own curiosity would make me do it if I could."

"Good enough. I will come back tomorrow."

"Berik is scheduled to work tomorrow night's shift so you can plan your surprise for him the following morning at breakfast."

"Good."

They were half way down the hill when they heard Verge shouting at them.

"He's found our names. We'd better go back up and see."

They pushed back up the slope with Karín grumbling about her inability to run there. Verge was beside himself with excitement as usual.

"My Lady. My Lord. I have found a prophecy. I know not how I missed it before but perhaps I might have looked harder. Look here." He pointed at a glyph. *"It says 'Choon' in the*

ancient tongue. And here is one that says 'Carán.' 'Choon' as you know means 'powerful one' in the old language and 'Carán' means 'to obey'. In between the two we found another less pronounced glyph which says, Eñame, which you know is the name the sky people gave us. If we read them in order starting with 'Eñame', they say, 'Eñame obey the powerful one.' If we do not translate the final glyph but leave it as 'Choon', it says, 'Eñame obey Choon'. Choon sounds like Ch0n. It is you, My Lord. Carán sounds like Karín so the prophecy is fulfilled. We have our queen and we have a king to accompany her. This is a most amazing discovery indeed. Temen will curse himself for not being here with me at the time of finding it."

Ch0n looked at Karín and said to her in Arw'an,

"I knew nothing about the middle glyph. I promise you."

"Then a prophecy it must be, My Lord. You have but filled in the blank spaces."

Ch0n turned to Verge.

"Verge. It is fitting that the highest of high priests found this alone. Temen will but confirm it and when we go to the Eñame town you will tell those there what you have found without embellishment."

Verge was almost weeping with pride and humility at the same time. Ch0n had used the exact words from the holy books. *'When the queen returns, the priest will be called the highest of priests and will be called into her service by one of power.'* He prostrated himself before them.

"I am but your humble servant, My Lady. My life's work has not been in vain, nor has that of those who served the holy scripts these many years."

"Keep searching, Verge. There are still clues to be found, I am sure of it."

"As you command it, My Lord, so shall it be done."

Chapter Fourteen: Like an Eagle

"This is becoming stranger all the time," said Ch0n when they arrived at his quarters.

Karín, who was quite superstitious, was not fazed.

"I knew you were a God that night in Buq'ue when I saw you standing over the old king's body and five of his bodyguard. My heart knew it and my instinct told me to stay close to you and I would be free and our people would be one. The Eñame prophecy is but another piece in the puzzle."

"Umm. Don't get too carried away, Karín. Remember I wrote those glyphs there not two hours ago."

"Yes, My Lord but you did not write the one between them and that is the link."

"The glyphs mentioned a prophecy but say nothing about a God. Let's just leave it at King, shall we?"

"And what is the name of the Buq'ue god of the clouds? Chon'i!"

Ch0n laughed and Karín allowed the sound to wash over her.

"Just leave it, Karín. Just leave it. I am happy to be your God but I do not want to be the God of the Eñame and Buq'ue at all. I just want to be King and sometimes I'm not even sure I want that."

"Very well, My Lord. You can be my God."

"And you are already my Goddess so we make a fine couple."

"Yes, Ch0n. We do and soon we will make a fine family. Very soon."

The following day at the castle they were informed that Malek was near her time and Karín rushed to her side. Ch0n went to Guerra's office and told him that the following day at the end of the shift he would have a public meeting. It would be announced on short notice and only after Guerra could confirm that Berik had gilded his sword again. From the previous images, they knew it would happen when the gold was melted and deep enough to receive the full thickness of the blade. Guerra decided he would take the night watch in the comms room and Darel was warned out to wake the town silently with the remaining squires and have the people converge on the main square at first light.

Jez was in no mood to socialize but Ch0n didn't care. He wanted to get the poor Knight away from his dwelling where he had been pacing the floor for hours.

"There is nothing a man can do while his child is coming. Kelda herself told me so. She has her best midwife, Caron and Karín all attending to Malek so just try not to worry. Perhaps you could look on my minitron at the images of Earth to take your mind from it.'

"My Lord, I need to be at my quarters and not here. My impatience does you no honour for I find no solace in your words, true tho' they be. Forgive me and grant my leave."

"You have it, Jez. By the way, his name will be Fidel. Or hers. It means, 'faithful' in our language and fits the offspring of one as faithful as you have been to me. It is fitting that the friend of my own offspring should have a name like that."

"Fidel," repeated, Jez. *"Fidel. It is a strong name. It is a man's name. It will be a son."* He took Ch0n's proffered hand. *"Thank you My Lord. Thank you from the heart of a shepherd boy who is now the first Knight of the Arw'an. Our families are destined to be forever intertwined. Fidel. So be it."* He left and Ch0n felt strangely alone without his presence.

Some time later, Guerra called to him from the door of Ch0n's quarters.

"My Lord. It is done. Berik has gilded his blade."

"Darel. You know what to do. Wait until just before sunrise and do it."

Berik left the gold foundry with his two assistants. They had no idea he was wearing a sword that was worth more than they

Gavan Connell

could earn in a month of shifts. They had spent their night breaking open the moulds to release the still-hot gold pesos and they were eager for their beds. They had not progressed far when Darel informed them there was to be a public meeting in the square and they were already late. He shooed them towards the milling crowd and then into the square proper. There, Berik could see the two other crews assembled in front of the dais where ChOn was waiting to address the crowd. As soon as they were in position, he started to speak.

"People of Arw'an. There is much happening at the moment and I have been a poor king for not having gathered you more often. You see before you, the three teams who work day and night to produce the gold and silver pesos we are using to provide independence to you all who wish it and who wish to earn more in your enterprises. Because they work all day and all night, it is hard to get them all together but before the day turn commences, I wish to honour them all before you. It is hard for a man or woman with not much property to work with gold and silver and not to be tempted by its glitter. These men have all done it and will now be rewarded accordingly. Step forward the three team leaders and receive your rewards."

The three stepped forward and ChOn descended the stairs carrying three bags. He went to the first team.

"Ali. Draw your sword and salute your king for I am about to reward you and your team with gold pesos for your honesty and good faith."

Berik's blood went cold as Ali drew the blade and held it to one side of his body in a military salute. ChOn handed Ali a bag and told him to share it three ways with his team. He moved to the second team and the process was repeated. Then he moved to Berik.

"Berik of the Arw'an. Look at this bag. It is but two thirds full. Do you know why?"

Berik nodded his head because he did not trust himself to speak.

"Berik. Mount the dais and stand before your people."

He followed Berik up the stairs.

"Berik! Draw your sword and salute your king for I am about to give you and your team your just rewards, tho' they will not be the same. Do it man! Do it now!"

Berik put his hand on the handle of his sword and with a sigh of resignation, drew it and saluted his king. The crowd was hushed at first and then a noise something like a collective intake of breath filled the air.

"Berik of the Arw'an. Your people see your treachery. You purport to have found gold where none other has found it and you were right, tho' the place is not where you said it was. You have stolen from your king and your people by melting their gold and coating your blade with it. You have benefited from it by selling to people things ill gained. Many of them fought two wars for the freedom you enjoy. You belittle their trust and mine and for that you will be punished. Give me your sword, Berik."

Berik handed the sword to Ch0n who made much of looking at the blade and shaking his head in disappointment. Suddenly he raised his left hand and Berik followed the motion with his eyes. While his chin was lifted, Ch0n swept the gilt blade across his throat and the blood gushed forth. The body was still twitching when Ch0n spoke to the two remaining men who were quaking with fear.

"Fear not my hand any man who is loyal," he said to them in a low voice. "We know Berik acted alone for he knew you to be honest men and true and would have shared no part in his deceit." He handed them the bag of gold and silver, nodded to them both and walked off the square.

Guerra took Ch0n's place on the dais as Ch0n left.

"People of the Arw'an. You have seen the wrath of a king betray'd. You have yourselves been betray'd. See the penalty for stealing from your King and your own people. You knew it. He knew it. Now I would seek another who is honest enough to work in the foundry. One of these two will be promoted to shift leader and the new person will be an assistant. Only those honest among you need apply. Go to Kelda and she will decide."

The whispered questions and rumours started immediately Guerra left the dais. How had the king found out? How did he know who it was? It is because he has powers beyond those of mortal men. Remember the early days when a Buq'ue Infantry soldier sunk his sword into Ch0n's back and he rode back to camp with the blood coursing from the wound only to emerge from his shelter unscathed?

Jez was getting worried. Malek's screams had become fewer and then started again but now she was cursing him and wishing his death. Caron, his concubine left the delivery room and went to him.

"My Lord, Jez. These things are not meant to hurt your feelings. She is in much pain and soon she will be herself again and we will have a new baby in the family. Be not sad at her words. The midwife says Malek is being very well behaved compared to most. Aah! Listen! I think something is happening."

Jez stopped his pacing and listened at the curtain.

"Come on, now, Malek. I can see some black hair. Next time you feel the urge, push the baby out. Here it is. I can see your stomach muscles tensing. Now push!"

Malek gave a shriek and the midwife cried out in delight as the slippery thing slithered from its rubbery tube into her waiting hands and started to wail. She looked between the baby's legs and declared it to be a boy before placing it on Malek's naked breast. The little creature started to wriggle and nuzzle at the warm flesh underneath its belly until it found the ripe nipple its instincts had driven it to seek. It grasped the object of its search and started to suckle immediately.

"Just like his father," laughed Malek, not realizing that every mother on every planet probably made the same joke at the first

suckle of every baby ever born. They all laughed except the midwife who had heard the joke before but was also engaged in chewing the cord from the baby's belly and removing the bloody mess that had followed the infant's arrival into the light.

"No problems with your iduw, Malek," she declared. *"The Knight Sir Jez will find it in good working order after your second bleeding and not before."*

Karín had been horrified at the obvious pain Malek had suffered during the delivery and was not looking forward to the experience that she knew would come before long. But when she looked at Malek's pale face gazing in adoration at the orange wrinkly thing attached to her breast she knew it didn't matter how much pain came with it, it would soon be forgotten. The midwife finished her grisly task and announced that Jez might enter. He burst into the room and flung himself at Malek and the baby, tears on his cheeks.

"Thank goodness you're all right and so is the baby. I heard Luci say it is a boy. I knew it would be. Ch0n has named him Fidel, a name meaning 'faithful' in his tongue."

"Calm yourself, Jez. Don't make a spectacle of yourself. Everything is all right. Look at your son, Fidel. Now go away and leave me to rest. I need to sleep."

Jez raced to the castle and bounded up the stairs to Ch0n's quarters.

"My Lord! I have a son! Your son will have a squire and a friend. Your daughter will have a mate!"

Ch0n laughed and far away, Karín sensed it and smiled.

"Slow down Jez. Your son hasn't even seen his first moonrise and he's already married off to my non-existent daughter. That's great news, boy. Now you should go to bed and sleep. You are excused further duties for seven days so you can spend them with Malek. Of course if there is a battle you will have to take your place."

"Yes, My Lord. I will," answered Jez, missing the joke. He turned and left Ch0n and Buyo alone.

"Will you be so excited when your offspring see the light, My Lord?"

"I suppose so. I have no idea. This is the first birth I can remember in my life. I have never seen a new father or a new mother but all that will change soon enough. He patted her bump. Twice."

"Is it time to eat yet? I am hungry. For some reason I want to eat something green and leafy. Kelda will know what to give me. And perhaps something sweet with it. Yes. On top of it."

Ch0n was about to go down to see Fidel when Guerra called to him from the doorway.

"My Lord. The drone has returned. The ground crew will put it away. Would you like to see what images it recorded?"

"Yes. I would. Call them up on the big screen so I can look from my seat."

Guerra connected the tablet to the projector and threw the image on to the wall of the comms room. ChOn studied it for a few minutes before he called,

"Stop there. Back it up. More. More. There!"

There could be no doubt. The rock they were looking at was at least three metres tall and a metre square at the base. And square it was. The rock had been chiselled or otherwise worked into a geometric object that nature could never have produced. The top was shaped into a four-sided pyramid. ChOn looked for the symbol but saw nothing.

"That has to be the plinth on the glyph but the symbol must be on one of the other faces. Do you have another angle?"

"No My Lord. I wanted a quick result so the runs were only up and back. This rock is right in the middle of the frame so there will be no overlapping images from the return runs either side of it."

"OK. Show me exactly where it is on the small scale image."

Guerra fiddled about with his tablet for a minute or so to combine the co-ordinates of the two scales and triumphantly pointed a spot to ChOn.

"Right here. It's about eighty yards from the edge of the lake. There is no track but there is a strange flat spot just west

of the plinth and behind it......" he paused and fiddled with the tablet again to bring up the large image, *'Yes! There! If that rectangular space behind the trees isn't man-made or alien made...,"* he laughed at his own joke but ChOn didn't. *"Hmph! Well all right then, I'll be very surprised."*

"Show me a close up of the shore below the plinth, if you would."

Guerra backed up the image to show ChOn what he wanted.

"Is that a man-made mooring point there? Those rocks look like they've been put there."

Guerra was going to make his 'alien-made' joke again but thought better of it.

"Hard to tell but it would be easy to find out. Take a boat there and test the depth with a chain. How much water do you need? Three feet? Four?"

"Four. Thank you. I will go straight to the ruins. Please tell Harry to have a boat ready to leave at first light tomorrow. I will arrive during the night."

"Yes, My Lord."

"You had better go with me. Just in case we find it."

"Find what, My Lord? A spacecraft?" He laughed again but the grin on ChOn's face silenced him. *"No! A spacecraft? Oh My!"*

"Be ready in two hours and tell nobody what we are looking for. Nobody."

Guerra raced to the console and spoke to Harry. Then he called up his main operator and told him he would have to reorganize the shifts to cater for Guerra's absence for at least one day, maybe two. Or three. Then he went to Carmodi and told her he would be absent for at least one night, perhaps two or three. She helped him throw his equipment into a pack and held him to her.

"I can see how excited you are, My Lord. I hope your trip is everything you want. Go well."

"Stay well, aget. I will miss you."

He hurried down the stairs to where Darel was busily preparing the tlaque and ChOn's battle order. He sat and waited for ChOn to arrive, images of all manner of craft flashing in front of his eyes.

ChOn was with Karín and Caron. Fidel was asleep on a cot Mori had made for him. To ChOn, the baby looked like a wrinkled up old orange rag but Karín hushed him.

"ChOn! Don't you dare say that! Malek will never forgive you!"

"Well it's true! Look! But I have to go right away to the lake. Guerra found the plinth and we're going to look at it. If you want to go, you will have to leave within the hour. You remember an hour, don't you? Good. Can you go tonight or will you follow me tomorrow or just keep track of events using the bracelets."

"I am in no fit state to travel. Nor am I inclined to rush away. I will follow the news here." She held up her hand unconsciously giving the signal they shared to signal private communications. *"OK? Now get along."*

When Ch0n arrived at his stables, the two tlaque were saddled and waiting, his equipment laid out. Maní was standing by dressed in her black pyjamis.

"I would go with you, My Lord."

"All right. You ride behind me. Guerra behind Darel. How soon can you leave, Maní?"

"You know me, My Lord. I am always ready." She held out a small woollen bag. *"Well, almost. I just need to finish dressing."* She unwound a long black cloth from around her waist, and re-wound it around her head and neck so only her eyes were showing. *"Now I am ready."*

They rode out of the gates at a canter, pushed for the small knoll and turned towards the pass through the hills across the river. Maní held Ch0n a little tighter than was necessary for a former Lancer but he only smiled to himself in anticipation of what would follow when they arrived. Guerra on the other hand was hanging on to Darel as though he were about to slide off the beast at any time, which was a distinct possibility. Finally they reached the foothills and slowed down. Guerra felt more secure in his seat and the tlaque kept a steady walk up the slope to the gap in the hills. Below them in the middle distance they could see the glow of the settlement where only ruins had been a few months earlier. They paused for a minute and then Ch0n eased his mount down the slope on the now well-worn track to the ruins. The tlaque followed the track with no guidance from their riders and they were soon entering the site through the main gate where the sentries waited, expecting them. Ch0n dismounted at his quarters and Maní slid down the beast's rump to the ground and followed Ch0n to where Harry was waiting. Guerra was only a few steps behind and Darel took the two tlaque to the corrals to tend to them.

"Well come, My Lord. Commander. Maní. My Lord, the boat is crewed and ready to sail at first light. Might I ask where we are going?"

Ch0n nodded to Guerra, who took out his tablet. He opened the image of the small jetty and put his finger on it. The coordinates showed on the screen and Harry's tablet received the transfer within a second of his booting it. He touched another icon and an arrow pointed across the screen. Harry aligned the tablet and nodded.

"Due West. I'll tell Eden it is a short trip. I think he was expecting to go to his former home."

"Tell the priest Verge to accompany us as well. If you would."

"Yes, My Lord. If that is all, I will retire. Safe journey."

Ch0n waved him out and told Guerra there were guest quarters in the next room, ushering him out as well. After the ride and a night with almost no sleep, Ch0n was exhausted but he allowed Maní to strip off his uniform and put him to bed. He craved sleep but Maní would have none of it.

"My Lord. I have not been with you for two nights now. Have you tired of me so soon? This is the very bed where you first lay with me. Remember?" Without waiting for an answer, she removed the turban and pulled the tunic over her shaved head. Even in his tired state, Ch0n managed to rise to the occasion while Maní used his body until finally she collapsed, heaving upon him. Ch0n closed his eyes and slept like a dead man with her lying on his chest and felt no more, even when she rode him again. *"Well, Ch0n, that is a first for me,"* she said to him as he slept. *"But even unconscious you make ijon like a king."*

Ch0n came awake in the gloom, roused by the wolf who growled at the movement outside his door. Darel called softly to both the beast and to Ch0n. Before long, Ch0n was dressed in his full battle order, striding to the dock. Darel provided him with milk and porridge for the journey and they joined the remainder of the mixed crew aboard the former Eñame longboat. Ch0n put the tablet where Eden could see it and they rowed backwards out of the channel, turned a lazy half circle and then raised the sail. There was barely a breeze but it was enough for the boat to make way and they eased across the glassy surface following the general line on the tablet's display. After an hour they tacked gently and the arrow changed until they were sailing on the other side of its path. The sun brought the breeze and the boat picked up speed and before long was skimming across the chop. The other side of the lake, formerly a grey line of hills with darker shadows indicating bush became a variety of colours as they approached. Finally Eden told Ch0n they would have to tack once more and then for the final few hundred yards, row along the path shown to the small jetty, testing the depth. He ordered a sailor to the prow with a length of chain marked in several places with wool and they went about across the breeze in fine fashion, Ch0n thought. He watched Eden looking at the sail, the helm and the tablet in turns and knew the man was a good sailor. He was using all the tools available until he shouted to down sails, and the boat slowed its pace and entered the lee of the hills.

"Out oars! Easy oars! Stand by to row. Walking speed! Row!" The drum beat out a slow rhythm and the boat crawled towards the shore. Eden nodded to the prow and the chain dropped to the bottom. Three fingers went up indicating that it was deeper than the height of two men. The process continued until two fingers were shown and then one.

"Half easy!" Every second man raised his oar out of the water and waited. Eden raised his left arm and made a chopping motion towards the small jetty. The tiller man pushed the tiller to the right and the boat eased around. *"All easy. In oars!"* The boat glided and the tiller man followed Eden's arm. There was a moment when the boat rocked a little from the wash it made against the pier and two men were suddenly overboard and the boat was made fast with three woven baskets protecting the side from the stony pier.

Ch0n looked at Eden who was in turn looking at him. He nodded to his captain and added,

"Well done, Captain Eden. We'll make a sailor out of you yet."

The crew laughed at the joke and Eden nodded with a smile.

"Just wait until these land crabs know how to use their oars, My Lord. Then you'll see what the boat is capable of."

Ch0n donned his helm and surveyed the slopes with the thermal and telescope activated. He knew where the plinth should be and he spotted it after just a few seconds and cleared the area for dagononum at the same time. He reached into his armour for the fifth time and felt the rod still in its place.

"Verge. Commander Guerra. Come with me. The rest of you may stand down with just one sentry to each flank."

They walked up the steep slope with Ch0n leading and Verge scurrying to maintain the pace. After a few minutes, they arrived at the plinth. It was partially obscured at the base by low scrub but it was an imposing structure, some three men tall and perfectly square at the base. Ch0n looked for the symbol and found it on the southern face. It was pointing upwards and to the left and Ch0n followed the direction with his eye. Some fifty yards away on the far side of a small raised clearing was the rectangular opening they had seen from the drone. He pointed to it.

"We are going to find something in that cave. I know not what it will be but I swear you both to secrecy until I give other instructions. Do you understand me?"

They both did. Karín was 'listening' via her bracelet and answered him.

"What are you waiting for? I am dying of curiosity."

ChOn led the two across the clearing and paused at the cave entrance. It was some thirty feet wide and fifteen or sixteen feet high. His helm told him the cavern behind was unoccupied. He took out the rod and pressed the orange and red buttons. The cavern was lit with a dazzling cone of light that surprised Guerra and frightened Verge. The cavern was at least thirty feet deep and was almost circular in shape.

"This is man-made," offered Guerra resisting the temptation to make his joke again. *"Or perhaps enlarged but the fact it is exactly due west of the ruins makes me think it was made specifically for something."*

"I agree, Commander. The spoil was probably used to make that raised platform that we crossed just before the entrance."

They surveyed the walls and roof. The walls were smooth but covered with drawings of the Eñame and what ChOn imagined were the Eani sky people. There was a map on one wall of the lake, showing the buildings which had fallen into ruins, the caverns above the buildings, the tunnel and also the site where they found themselves. On another side was a map of the known world, ChOn supposed. It showed the lake, the sea, the land that was now Arw'an, Buq'ue and Matáng with drawings of humanoids at various locations, including the site of the Buq'ue fort and further on where Matáng Town would be.

The Eñame harbour was in greater detail as was the table above it, including the lines that marked what Ch0n and Guerra both assumed was a landing site.

The roof was strangely relieved. The shallow grooves and smooth ridges on it had been carefully manufactured or carved in the living stone. Three large circles were equally spaced to form an equilateral triangle. In the very centre of the roof was a rectangle barely visible but there nonetheless, and it was when Ch0n saw it, that he realized what they were looking at. Had he not been the crewman in the bubble at the bottom of his landing craft he would perhaps have missed it. But he had been. He laughed. Miles away, Karín let the sound wash over her as it always did.

"The ship is attached to the roof." He was pointing as he spoke to Guerra in English so Verge could not understand. "Those circles are the three legs and the rectangle is the access hatch."

"It's too small to be a galactic cruiser."

"I agree. It's a landing craft and if it once flew, maybe it will fly again."

Verge knew when he wasn't wanted. He wandered off until he came to another rectangular stone at the back of the cavern. He took out his dagger and ran the point around the edge of it. It was not attached at all to the wall.

"My Lord. I have found a door. It has to be a door!"

407

ChOn and Guerra rushed to where the priest was trying to clear the space around the block. His blade finally went all the way in and he worked it down one side until there was a small gap. He did it to the other side and then to the top and as he cleared the top he heard a click as the blade released something and he had to jump back to avoid being struck. The slab fell cleanly out of the gap on hinges of some sort, showing a small space behind. ChOn's light revealed a narrow staircase leading upwards and around in a circle and he allowed Verge to take the lead as it had been his discovery. At the top of the stair was a narrow tunnel which in turn led them to another small room which ChOn guessed was directly above the cavern. It seemed to be empty but Verge was running his hands and eyes over every dusty surface. It was Guerra who found it, though. He almost tripped over a small hole in the floor containing a recessed lever. He looked at ChOn who nodded. Guerra pulled it and nothing happened. He tried to turn it and nothing happened. He tried to turn it in the other direction and was rewarded when it turned through a quarter revolution. Nothing happened so he tried to pull it again. After hundreds of years, it came smoothly upwards a few inches and stopped. They heard a hissing noise in the walls and a crunching noise and then just the hissing again.

"I think that is the sound of air rushing in to a vacuum. Some mechanism in the roof is lowering the craft to the ground."

They rushed back down with Verge following in confusion. When they burst out of the small doorway, they were confronted with the sight of a flattish, egg-shaped craft about twice the size of ChOn's landing craft, hanging from the roof on three thin strands of something that looked like the nylon fishing line in Ch0n's survival kit. It was still five and a half feet from the floor.

"Well, then, Commander. What do you make of that?"

Verge was almost in tears. Before Guerra could answer, he raced forward, stood facing the nose of the craft and ran his hands over it.

"We came to you in a craft that shone in the sun to be your teachers and to give you our genes. Long after we have gone will our blood course through your veins and when the new queen comes, so will a new dawn of discovery. My Lord this is their craft. It is the prophecy again. Look! It is dusty but shines in the light from your staff."

Guerra looked at Ch0n.

"It looks like an areo spider hanging there on its web. Give me a minute to look it over and I will tell you what I think of it." He walked around it and touched it in various places before returning to Ch0n. *"It is an aircraft designed to be flown where gravity prevails. There are retractable stabilizer fins on two sides and two retractable vertical ones under the tail. I have no idea what sort of propulsion system it uses because there is no outlet for a jet stream and nowhere where a vortex could be. If you forced me to guess, I would say it might use some sort of magnetic motor drive, which could be activated by the same sort of false fusion battery that we ourselves use. If it could somehow tame or harness the local magnetic forces it might be able to surf the planet's magnetic field. I know the technology exists on earth because the next generation of experimental*

Gavan Connell

magnetic drive craft were already in production when our ship left. I saw them on the minitron. They have no moving parts, which makes them indestructible by normal use. If it isn't that, I couldn't even hazard a guess. This one has retractable fins, which may be the weak link here but they are sealed off so tight I could feel them but not even insert my figer nail into the seam. I am hopeful."

"How do I get in?"

"With the key, of course." He laughed again at his own joke but this time Ch0n smiled at him and pressed the three coloured buttons on his staff at the same time.

It took a few seconds before they realized something was happening. The craft started to hum and lights appeared in the front 'window'. A small cap flipped out right next to them and made them all jump. Guerra turned to it and pressed an icon on the small screen. With a whirring sound, the three legs started to telescope downwards to the floor and when they had the weight of the craft, the filament lines went slack and were suddenly retrieved into three holes in the roof. Guerra pressed another icon that had appeared when the legs were locked and was rewarded with the opening of the rectangular hinged hatch in the floor as a set of retractable steps descended. He started forward before turning to Ch0n.

"If you would like to enter first, My Lord, please do but as we have no idea of the layout, it might be best if I do."

Ch0n jerked his head to let Guerra know he should enter first. His own heart was racing. What if this thing still flew? It

410

was almost too much for him to imagine. He ducked down and followed Guerra under the belly of the craft and stood on the bottom step with his head inside.

It was purpose designed for six people, which was why there were six caskets in the other cavern. At the front were two seats, side by side and an inclined panel like a desk with dozens of lights and icons. There was no obvious physical steering control. Guerra was poring over it as though he knew what each meant.

"I'm guessing this was flown in here at the hover because there is no way it could have been man-handled. There are no handles on it for a start, just the three legs. Then again, if it is a magnetic field drive it could hover and one person could just push it around like a weightless balloon."

Behind the two front seats were two more, separated by a narrow aisle and then two more to the rear of the hole in the floor where the steps were attached. Ch0n turned around and his face lit up. There was a hatch in the rear wall which could only be access to the drive system and storage. Storage on a vehicle meant tools, metals, maybe weapons, computers or perhaps something he had never dreamed of. He mounted the seven steps and found he could almost stand without bending. He now knew the Eani were taller than the Arw'an by some margin but perhaps shorter than Ch0n himself. He opened the door to find a space big enough to house three lockers on each side. A small hatch occupied the back wall and when Ch0n opened it, he saw the drive. It meant nothing to him. He closed it and looked in each narrow locker. They were empty apart from two fixed hangers   He called to Guerra to come back.

Gavan Connell

Guerra managed to drag himself away from the console and took ChOn's place in the back of the craft.

"There has to be something there in the way of tools or weapons. Something. It looks as though they knew they would never come back and cleaned it out."

Guerra looked around, opened and closed the drive access hatch and scratched his head.

"If this flies, it has to be balanced. Weight of passengers up front, weight of the drive down back. For stability, the weight has to be low down." He lifted a thin sheet from the aisle to reveal three hatches in the floor.

"One of these will house the computer to drive the thing and maybe the false fusion batteries. One should have tools. The other may be food or water storage."

He opened the closest hatch and found it empty apart from a series of what looked like electrodes on the four sides.

"Nothing in here. They really did clean the place out. This one has the computers by the look of it and this one has the tools." There was an array of what were obviously tools but nothing ChOn could see an immediate use for. All in all he was disappointed.

"They must have a storage space back there. Now we know they like to use blocks as doors, we can look for them."

"I would like to explore the console more. There are icons and glyphs all over it and it is too risky to just push a button. One of the icons must be a maintenance and operating guide but I would hate to start this up and have it hit the wall before I could get it under control."

Ch0n told Verge to return to the boat and tell Eden they would be staying the night. When he left, Ch0n joined Guerra at the controls. He pointed the rod at each glyph and told Guerra what they were for. When he reached, 'flight instructions' Guerra pressed it immediately. A heads-up display appeared on the 'window'. Ch0n read aloud to Guerra, who was furiously writing on the panel with a permanent marker pen beside the various icons and glyphs.

"Well that sounds easy if you know what it all means."

Guerra did. He pressed an icon and lights on the outside of the craft illuminated the cavern. He pressed another and the fins extended. They could both see them on the display, two long fins along the side and two short ones under the tail. Another one they had not known about rose from the tail. Guerra placed his hands on a floating transparent plate that moved under his touch as though it had a series of springs holding it in place. A hologram appeared in the space around his hand. It was almost as if he were wearing a pale blue glove made of laser circuits in the form of the craft. When he moved his hand, the sprung section of the panel moved with it and the display showed the fins moving relative to the body of the craft.

"This is amazing. I am quite sure that when the drive is activated, I can drive this craft by driving the hologram. Watch."

He moved his hand up and down and the plate and hologram followed it. On the display, they could see the fins changing their degree of extension or angles slightly. He pressed his fingers against the plate and the hologram tilted slightly as if it were moving forward. He pressed the heel of his hand and it tilted backwards. Finally he tilted his whole hand and the hologram went into a turn aspect. He pulled his hand away and the hologram remained in place for a full minute before it disappeared.

"That's so it won't crash if you take your hand away to wipe your nose."

"How much time do you need to play with this before you can start it? If it will start at all, that is."

"Give me a few more hours, My Lord, but first read me the next bit of the manual if you would."

The next section turned out to be about weapons and ChOn was keen to find out what armaments the craft had at its disposal. The manual revealed a similar array as the rod with twin pulsers, the flame thrower and the explosive bolts of lightning. There was a rear facing pulser as well. All the weapons were operated from the second seat. The co-pilot had a separate heads-up display and icons for weapons selection and control.

"This vessel isn't made for light speed and it doesn't look as though she could take much of a strike so those weapons are only for local defence. Here, though, they will be devastating because nobody has anything that can shoot back. Yet. This will come in handy against the landing craft from roving patrol ships like yours and mine and especially when my rescue mission arrives in force to exploit everything they know is here. We will need to move it to the castle and build a hangar that looks like a stable and we will have to keep the doors permanently closed when we aren't using it. We must never mention it on the radio either. We will need a nickname for that. I'll let you think of it. By the way, if you get this started and off the ground, you will need to train up a second pilot. Think about that. You have an idea of what is needed already. I'll have to promote you to Squadron Commander. You have two aircraft under your command."

"Don't you worry My Lord. If this thing can be flown, I will fly it. Now. What is the next bit of the manual?"

ChOn read it with the aid of the rod. Using ChOn's instructions, Guerra identified more icons and wrote their functions with the marker. One lit up a numeric sequence that ChOn thought was a frequency display with up and down arrows. He pressed the auto-transmit button on his helm and started to count. He touched the up arrow and watched it blur into motion and then there was a squeal of feedback in ChOn's ear as it locked on to his frequency. He turned off his helm and tried to work out how the radio worked. He had to resort to the manual and found the transmit button in the arm of his seat and a matching one on the pilot's. He pressed it.

"Are you there, Harry?"

Gavan Connell

"I am, My Lord, but my ears are ringing. What happened to the frequency?"

"Two radios too close to each other. This is really just a radio check."

"Loud and clear this end, My Lord."

"Loud and clear here. We will have a surprise for you tomorrow I hope. I need the flat space between the corrals and the water clear of everybody and everything by then. Can you do it?"

"I can."

"Good. That is all. Ch0n out."

"Aah! They have left that till last," said Guerra when Ch0n *started to read the final section of the manual. "It is the pre-flight sequence. It seems our alien friends are no different from us in that they would have just read them and nothing else if they were at the front of the book."* He pressed another icon when Ch0n read the appropriate section and the panel went blank. He pressed it again and lights started to come on one by one. *"It's self-checking. Ours used to do the same thing when it was in orbit and the main drive was switched off. If it gets through the entire sequence, it will fly. If not, we will have to find a mechanic."* This time they both laughed.

They waited a minute while the craft booted itself again.

"You know, My Lord, using your rod to open the flap at the side enables this to boot itself from outside the craft. That's why it was all lit up when we arrived inside. There is an icon on the small screen outside the same as this one I just touched."

"That is handy to know in case we have to make a run for it some day. Now I am impatient to see you fly this but it is dark outside and I am hungry. Tomorrow you can come back and play as much as you like but we will secure this from prying priestly fingers overnight. Shut it down."

Guerra reluctantly touched a red icon and the craft started to shut down completely. It had not been booted for hundreds of years and was still in perfect working order, it seemed. Guerra decided it had a system of automatically programmed self-maintenance, even when it was in sleep mode.

Once outside the craft, ChOn pressed the three buttons on the staff and the little armoured hatch snapped shut. Using the beam from a flashlight they made their way back to the boat where Darel was waiting with the wolf. Verge was bursting as usual and wanted to know if they had made any progress but ChOn told him only that they were still working on the control panel and that perhaps tomorrow he could help Commander Guerra translate the operating manual. Guerra smiled at ChOn's concession to the old priest and realized just what a great leader ChOn was. Everybody was allowed to feel important in their role, regardless of what it might be. He was a true king.

They slept under a tarpaulin with just the two sentries and the wolf. By morning they were all stiff from the hard ground but Ch0n summoned Darel to training as usual and the two of them went at each other for an hour with different weapons and the session included a repeat of their sai battles of the previous days and the two-sword katas. While the crew watched on in amazement, a glimmer of an idea was forming in Ch0n's brain and he almost lost concentration at one stage and had to fight for his life because Darel was going at full speed and had no idea Ch0n was distracted. After the session, Ch0n ate his breakfast and talked to Karín using the bracelets. He told her every detail of the craft and in her woman's analytical way she asked him an unrelated question he had never considered.

"My Lord. If they were here for so long with no support, how did they manage to clothe themselves for decades? Their lockers were tiny, you said, but we know from the caskets they wore flowing garments like…silk but not silk, which would not have been what they wore on their mother ship. They must have been able to make cloth somehow. And slippers. Would they not?"

"Yes. It is a puzzle I had not considered. Now I must go and make sure Guerra does not try and enter the ship by breaking something. I had forgotten he needs the rod to get in. He will be getting impatient."

Guerra and Verge were pacing the cavern when he finally arrived.

"I am sorry. I forgot about the key," he said pressing the three buttons. He noted a look of annoyance on Guerra's face and called him over.

"Commander Guerra. I have a lot of things to try and do and if I occasionally forget something it is not the end of your world. I would give you a gentle reminder that even though you are the most important player in this little game of flying ships, it does not give you the right to question our relative positions. If I think you are getting ideas above your station, I will not hesitate to change it. Do I make myself clear?"

"Yes, My Lord. For just a moment there I thought I was commanding the ship again. It won't happen again."

"Good. Now go and find out how to fly this thing. I'm guessing that you will let me be present when you try and fly it out of that cavern?"

"If I can make it hover without smashing it into the roof or walls, I can either try to fly it out or just hover and have you or someone else turn it and push it out. There is not much clearance with the legs deployed but I don't want to try and hover inside without them. There is too much at risk."

"How much clothing and shoes would six people or aliens need for a century?"

"What? What has that got to do with the ship? A lot, I suppose. But their lockers are only a few inches wide. Enough for two or three garments and no more."

"Exactly. And each has only two hangers. But when Karín and I found the bodies, they had been buried in new robes. Interesting." He left his seat and returned to the rear compartment. He opened a locker and noticed the 'electrodes' on the three sides and the door. They were the same as those in the locker under his feet. He looked around but could find nothing else.

"My Lord," said Verge as he opened the rear door, *"I have translated the eerrr..manual for Commander Guerra as best as I could given the technical nature of it and I believe he now has enough knowledge with which to try and fly this ship. It would give me much pleasure if you would allow me to be present when he tries it."*

"Verge. You are the link between the past and the future. I can not manage without your knowledge of the sky people. I will ask Commander Guerra and if he is confident he will not kill you both, you may stay with him."

Verge wasn't sure whether he was pleased that Ch0n thought so highly of him or frightened at the prospect of dying before lunch but he managed a smile as he backed away.

"That's it, My Lord," announced Guerra. *"I am as ready as I will ever be. I would like to try and fly this. First I will try and start it and then hover and then I will tell you if I need help getting it out of the cavern. If I get it out, I will try and hover it a bit higher before I take it for a quick trip around the hills. By the time I get back, you will know if it is safe for you to come with me."*

"OK. Do it and good luck. Verge would like to go with you. I'll wait outside and if I don't hear you wrecking it, I'll come in. Before you do, though, I will change the frequency to 5. You know how to lock on to it?"

"I do. Verge can wait outside and I will pick him up from the clearing"

ChOn left the cavern and watched through the entrance. Guerra tuned in to frequency 5, the Knights' frequency, and they established comms. For a minute, ChOn saw nothing. He took off his helm but he heard nothing. He was trying to deal with his disappointment when he saw the legs lengthen as the weight started to ease off them. Then they were free of the ground as Guerra held the craft in an unsteady hover. Over the next minute, the hover became steady and then the ship rose slightly and held the hover again. The legs shortened at this but when the vehicle lost height, the legs lengthened again.

"I think the legs are proximity operated. The higher I go, the more the panel shows they retract. Can you confirm it?"

"I can confirm it."

"I am going to try and turn it at the hover." ChOn watched as the craft slewed unsteadily and then turned on its axis. *"Not bad for the first try if I do say so myself. I'm coming out. Please confirm I have clearance from the ground and the roof before I attempt the entrance."*

"I confirm ground clearance of one foot and roof clearance of two feet including the upper tail fin. Bring it out. Maintain that line... Maintain that line... You are half way out.... Maintain that line.... Steady as you go.... You are almost clear.... One metre more.... Maintain your line.... You are clear of the entrance."

He watched as Guerra flew the craft to the middle of the clearing and hovered low. He gradually did a vertical climb until the legs were completely retracted. ChOn estimated that the craft was some fifteen feet above ground level by then.

Guerra looked down at ChOn and Verge. He lowered the craft and ChOn watched the legs deploy. Verge entered the craft and there was a delay before the vessel left the ground silently. Guerra told ChOn he was going to try a few manoeuvres and lifted his hand rapidly in the hologram. The vessel shot into the air so fast that Verge cried out in terror but Guerra was shrieking with the sheer joy of it. He continued the ascent before levelling off and doing a fast circle around the hills. He stopped mid-flight and reversed, turned, and finally flew straight up at breakneck speed while Verge howled and screeched beside him. The entire flight only lasted five minutes before he landed safely in the clearing beside ChOn.

"Verge, you may leave now. The Lord ChOn might wish you to tell the captain of the boat that he may return to the settlement."

Verge left the craft and struggled across to ChOn.

"My Lord. Do you wish me to tell the captain to return without you?"

"Good idea, Verge. Did you enjoy your first flight?"

"My Lord. Commander Guerra is like a child with a new toy. When he has recovered his demeanour, I would like to fly again."

Half an hour later Guerra did a flypast of the settlement and eased the craft down next to Ch0n's quarters. The entire populace was out to see the amazing flying ship that flew soundlessly and landed without making any dust. Ch0n told Guerra not to shut down the drive. He told Harry he would be back in an hour and he would take Maní plus three worthy passengers who wished to return to the castle. Harry selected a soldier, a cook and a nurse. By the time they arrived at the castle, the townspeople had gathered in the square. Karín, Jez, Doni, Sonja and Boro took a turn around the castle, across to the lake and back before being replaced by Buyo, Mori, Marik, Carmodi and Kelda for the same circuit. Finally Ch0n took Maní and the three original passengers back to the lake where they were hailed as heroes and quizzed about the experience.

The following day, Ch0n sent Maní back with Guerra to the castle while he rode back with Darel on the tlaque. They rode side by side where the track allowed it and when they reached the plains leading to the knoll in front of the castle, Ch0n told Darel of his plans to create an elite group of fighting men trained in weapons and stealth. They would wear all black pyjamis and a black turban similar to that worn by the Lancers.

"I have seen them in the minitron. They were assassins in ancient Japan but that is not the purpose I would have you trained for. Rather you would be an elite force that I will insert behind enemy lines now I have the means to do it. You will wage hit-and-run warfare against small targets using every trick

I can teach you and some you will invent for yourself. Your main weapons will be the katanas but I will also make you some iron throwing weapons and you will carry grenades and the like. Only certain men will be suitable. They must all be agile and quick. All must be adept in the use of weapons and hand to hand fighting as are you. You will be called 'ninjas'. You will remain my squire until further notice for the identities of the ninjas must remain something of a secret. Are you happy to command such a group?"

"I am My Lord as I am happy to remain your squire. I am sure you will tell me all I need to know to be a ninja and how to train my men."

"Good. We will start tomorrow."

Over the next month, Ch0n visited all his outposts in 'the areo' as Guerra had named it after the spider. He took Karín when she felt up to it and Maní the rest of the time. Guerra was living out a dream and every night he blessed Jez for shooting the hole in his landing craft. Ch0n had been tempted to fly to the Eñame port but Karín had asked him not to go without her and certainly not until she considered herself in a fit state to travel and to be received royally. Just so, Ch0n and Jez went to the Western outpost with Maní and Caron. They renewed acquaintances with the village elder who remained clean and well-groomed as Jez had ordered. He and Maní confirmed the identity of her mother and thus the fact that she and Karín were full sisters. Ch0n and Maní were sleeping in the hut where Caron and Chenna had lived when Guerra received the call from Carmodi. Karín was with the midwife. She had started her labour.

"Can you fly this thing at night?"

"Yes, My Lord but are you sure you want to leave right now? It will be hours before anything meaningful happens if Malek is any indication."

"This is not Malek. If it is safe, I would leave as soon as practical."

"We can leave in half an hour, My Lord. I will tell the others and we will meet at the areo as soon as we are ready. When all are present we can go."

Guerra followed the inboard positioning system and his artificial horizon for the two hours it took them to return to the castle over the black water of the gulf below. He landed in the spot outside its new hangar and ChOn dragged Maní to the delivery room. Maní raced inside where she was greeted by Buyo and the midwife. Karín was lying back, naked except for a woollen blanket over her belly. Maní went to her and kissed her on the cheek.

"I am here if you need me, sister, for I have just confirmed that sisters of the blood we are, having the same mother."

"Thank you, Maní. I always knew deep down we were sisters. And I knew you would come to me. Now I just need to concentrate on what is happening here so please don't get offended if I ignore you for a while."

ChOn was pacing backwards and forwards outside the delivery room. Jez laughed at the reversal of circumstances as did ChOn when Jez finally dragged him away. ChOn sat with him and told him of his plan to create a small force of five ninjas under the command of Darel. Jez managed to keep him talking for a couple of hours before ChOn declared he had to return to the delivery room. There he waited and listened to Karin's grunts and groans but as she was to point out to him later on, she never cried out once, even when the head appeared and passed through her opening. The first sign that the baby had been born was the pathetic wailing as it took its first breath of air. As she had done with Malek and hundreds of others, the midwife placed the naked yellow-skinned baby boy on his mother's breast and let instinct take over as she cleaned it and chewed through the cord. Buyo being the second wife was the one who left the room and told the waiting ChOn that he had a son. ChOn raced into the room and looked at the creature suckling furiously at Karin's breast. He kissed the back of the baby's head and kissed Karín and held her as close as he could.

"My Lord ChOn. Look at him at work there. He is just like his father," she laughed weakly. *"We have a princeling. What would you call him?"*

"I told you once. I will call him Dorak and he will be everything he wishes to be. Now I will leave you to rest. I have to tell Jez."

Chapter Fifteen: Ninjas

Dorak was just a week old when Karín started her training again. Her milk had dried up and they had found a wet nurse to feed him. Karín was put out at her failure as a mother in her own eyes but the midwife, who was a wise old woman had seen it all before and took Karín aside to explain to her it was quite a normal thing. By way of reply, Karín threw herself into a punishing diet and fitness regime that started before first light in their quarters with stretching and flexibility exercises and continued at the training session. Her light breakfast was followed by a run to the knoll and back and then several trips up and down the stairs from the ground to the top of the turret. Maní went with her at first but as Karín's fitness improved and the weight fell off her, Karín was able to outstrip even Maní, the fastest of the Matáng Lancers.

Meanwhile, Ch0n could be found staring in wonder at Dorak and his nurse. The woman was Nelik, the buxom wife of one of Doni's masons, who looked as though she could lay stones herself. She managed her child, Tomis and Dorak, one on each hip while Karín was at her exercise. Dorak was now smooth-skinned and Ch0n had decided he looked like his father. His eyes, were bright green like Karín's, but had Ch0n's vertical pupils and were slanted like Ch0n's. His skin was notably a lighter orange than that of Tomis, and he was three inches longer, even though he was two weeks younger. The pale hair he had had at birth had fallen out and he was completely bald. The midwife had never seen that happen before and was not sure it was a good omen for the future but said nothing. He punished Nelik at feeding time and she commented how much stronger he was than Tomis at the breast and that he drank as much or more than him. ChOn was well pleased with the boy and with himself.

After a month, Karín looked as though she had never been pregnant. She divided her time now among Dorak, ChOn and her fitness schedule. Naked, she was as hard and flat as before and perhaps even leaner through the belly but thanks to her weights regime, was more muscled in the thighs and upper arms. She told ChOn she would be starting the training sessions with the Knights again as soon as she bled and that she would be riding every afternoon for a week. ChOn was amazed at her recovery compared to Malek who had tried to lose the weight she had gained during her pregnancy but was struggling with it. Nelik was another story completely. She had probably never been a hard-bodied woman and she viewed Karín's work rate as something like unnecessarily self-imposed torture. The first morning back at the training square, ChOn had had to force Karín to use the wooden training sword and to slow her down to make sure she had her routines right. To go too fast and make a mistake was to kill or die with the composite katanas and he knew too well that after a layoff of half a year she would be rusty.

Meanwhile, Darel's private sessions as a trainee Ninja had become more intense and involved. He had already selected ten potential Ninjas without telling them what their final role would be. They all joined the Knights and squires in the mornings under the tutelage of Ch0n until one morning, Ch0n told Darel it was time to reduce their numbers to five. Ch0n devised a series of exams that involved hand and foot co-ordination, climbing of trees and the castle walls, hand to hand combat, endurance, weapons handling, katas, teamwork and then a mock task to infiltrate the Lancer barracks and place a throwing star with ten sisters without being discovered. For this last task, the sisters had been warned that someone was planning to pretend to assassinate ten of them and that if they caught the perpetrators, they would be rewarded with a ride in the areo to the overhang and back. The test was to be conducted over three days and four nights to give the trainees time to plan their 'assassinations'.

Buyo was almost immobile now. Her tiny body struggled with the task of carrying her baby through to her due day. She was constantly attended by the midwife who thought she might deliver at any moment, even though she was still a month short of her time. Maní helped her by spending time with her and Karín looked in at every opportunity. Ch0n was getting nervous about the co-incidence of Buyo's time and the proposed voyage to the Eñame, although the existence of the 'areo' made it possible for him to return if he had to. Protocol demanded that he be with Karín as his senior wife for official duties such as the Eñame trip but Buyo had made him promise to be with her when it happened. The midwife put her on a range of potions and rubbed her belly and loins and poked and probed her every morning and night trying to get a clue as to when the baby would come.

The Ninjas started their three day ordeal with an endurance test that included weapons testing. After just a month, they had developed a fair skill with various weapons and the testing was more to select those who could show the most aptitude for further learning. ChOn had guessed that once the final five were selected, that it would take at least another six months to train them to an acceptable standard where they might be deployed as a group. The ten were relayed at last light in the areo to a point part way to where ChOn's original cave was. They were anonymous, dressed alike in their black pyjamis and turbans with all their wooden training weapons and 'magic' tricks. ChOn confirmed their mission. They were to return to the chain-gun turret of the castle, overcoming any resistance they might encounter along the way. They were to travel as individuals and when they arrived at the turret, to pick up the top disk from a pile, return to their quarters and wait. As soon as ChOn stopped speaking, the fastest of them shot away, followed by the remainder who had been waiting for some sort of release from their king. ChOn smiled to himself. It was what he had wanted. The Ninjas would be operating in a special-forces role and there would be precious little time for additional or supplementary orders. He and Darel mounted the areo and flew a leisurely circle at altitude. ChOn selected the heat imaging display on the 'window' from the gunner's seat and saw the ten green men running in almost single file towards the castle. As the areo tracked towards the castle, small knots of green men could be seen lying in ambush at various way points. It was not going to be just a footrace. There would be skirmishing and fighting to be done. Any Ninja captured would be held for a slow count of five hundred and then released. They landed in front of the 'hangar' and ChOn went to bed. It was going to be a long night and a long few days for the trainee Ninjas and also for the Knights and ChOn himself, as they all had a role to play.

It was the wolf that woke him. It growled a warning as the midwife's girl ran up the steps. Buyo's time had come. Maní and Karín sprang out of the bed and pulled their tunics over their heads. Ch0n told Maní to keep him posted on events so he could be there at the end. He tried to go back to sleep but was unable to do so. He went to the comms room and checked that all was well, dressed in his uniform and wandered to the guard room. The guard commander called the guard to order and Ch0n reminded them that the Ninjas would be trying to enter the castle some time during the night or just after dawn. He wandered from the guardhouse to the corrals where Doni's man was tending the creatures. The half oruks were now almost due to drop by his reckoning. Another year had passed since their oruk dams had been rounded up, pregnant and they had been served by Ch0n's tlaque after they calved. It would soon be time to try and separate the entire oruk herd from its mature bulls so that the tlaque could cover all the females and create a generation of super tlaques for the mounted infantry. That would be a difficult exercise as the oruk bulls were not as easily driven as their tlaque counterparts. Ch0n knew deep down he would have to kill all the mature bulls from the herd or to stun them and geld them, which would not guarantee their docility in the weeks that followed. His tlaque would be in possible danger from them if their testosterone levels weren't under control. It was that thought process that led him to decide to go to the overhang as soon as the Ninja selection test was complete and to geld all the bulls in advance.

He made his way towards the castle past Mori's house where the old man was awake as always.

Gavan Connell

"Evenin' king. I see the midwife has been called to yur second aget. Ye'll have another hatchling befur the night's out."

"Yes, Mori, I will. I must go and see how things are going there. Good evening to you."

Jez met Ch0n at the foot of the stairs.

"Well, My Lord, we are soon to be a big family here in the castle. Do you have a name for another boy?"

"Buyo says she had a dream it will be a girl. She is sure of that. So I have had to think of a girl's name. There was one on Earth many centuries ago who was a warrior queen, burned at the stake but later vindicated. Her name is the female version of John, which sounds like my own name, such as it is. Joan. She was Joan of Arc. My daughter will be Joan of Arw'an."

"It is a good name, My Lord. But if it is a boy?"

"Then I will have to revisit my minitron."

"When do you expect the first of the Ninjas to return to the walls?"

"There is one who is more of a thinker than the rest. He will arrive well before dawn, even though he should be the last. I will tell you why. He is leading the footrace but he is cunning and will allow one other to overtake him and thus when they are ambushed by Marik's men, he will run past and allow another to pass him until another ambush is joined. They know there are five ambushes somewhere out there in their path. If he remains

432

in second place until the fifth of them is captured, he will run free to the walls. If he allows more than five to pass him, he will not arrive first and I will be wrong."

"*You are never wrong, My Lord. Well almost never. And then what?*"

"They have to go to the chain gun turret and pick the top disk to show the order they arrived. Each disk is worth points. Tomorrow Marik will report on their part of the test and we will do the skills tests with the weapons."

"*If I were first to the turret I would win the battle but lose the war. Only five will be culled so winning is not the order of the day. Coming fifth or better is the aim. First would not necessarily be better than fifth overall. I would not go to the turret, tho' I were first to the wall. I would scale the wall, go to the Lancer lines and assassinate my Lancer and then go to the turret. The sisters are all saying they will not be in danger until tomorrow night. They are sleeping soundly tonight and so they are vulnerable.*"

"Aah my first Knight, your father chose you well as my squire and you have learned well the lessons I have taught you and more. I would do the same thing. It will be interesting to see if our leader thinks as we do."

A scream filled the night and they both looked up at the lighted slit on the wall where Buyo was in labour. It was followed by another and another. ChOn turned and ran through the door and mounted the steps three at a time. The curtain was drawn and when Ch0n made to look past it, Maní blocked his path.

"This is women's business, My Lord. Tho' you be a king, you should not enter. She is having a hard time of it. The baby's head is big and she has torn the flesh of her iduw quite badly. The midwife says the baby will come out next time Buyo pushes for the opening will tear to fit the head. Now go and wait until I call you."

A few minutes later Buyo screamed again and soon afterwards the sound of a baby wailing reached Ch0n. He turned to the curtain where Maní waited, her eyes looking back into the delivery room. Then she turned and nodded to him.

He almost ran to the entrance and pushed inside. Buyo was lying with the baby on her breast. It was searching for the nipple its instinct told it was there somewhere. The midwife was chewing the cord and Karín was putting a bloody mess into a container between Buyo's feet.

"My Lord," said Buyo weakly, *"I have given you the daughter I promised you. Look at her. She is a fighter. Already she has found my milk. What will you call her?"*

"She is to be Joan of Arw'an. She will grow to be a clever and loving woman like her mother and a warrior like her stepmother."

"Look, My Lord. She has my eyes."

Ch0n looked at the great red orbs that half-opened and closed in the dim light.

"Yes. She does. You will have to teach her how to use them as you have used them in the service of our people."

"Ch0n, I have wanted this from the first time I saw you at the overhang. This is my most precious gift to you who never felt the ebon for me as you do for Karín but I feel it for you. Know that."

"I know it. I always knew it and Karín knew it. And she knows I feel it for you, tho' I have never said it to you nor to her."

Ch0n bent over her and kissed her forehead.

"Sleep now and I will see you when you are rested," he said to her as he turned and left the room.

Buyo smiled sleepily and closed her eyes. A short while later, a fat nipple flipped out of baby Joan's mouth as she fell asleep on her dead mother's breast.

It was the midwife who noticed it. Karín and Maní both thought Buyo had dropped off to sleep but there had been too much loss of blood and so the midwife looked for the tell-tale rise and fall of Buyo's chest. She had seen much in her life of service to the village and was not given to outbursts of emotion at what was an unusual but not altogether rare occurrence when the mother was as small as Buyo. She turned to Karín who was busy picking up bloody woollen swabs and sheets.

"Karín, you should tell your lord and mine that Buyo is dead and we will need another wet nurse by morning."

Karín and Maní both looked at Buyo's pale, smiling face in disbeLeif. Karín felt tears fill her eyes and wiped them away.

"Try and clean her up and then go and find Nelik. Ask her if she can manage three babies if we give her someone to help manage the other things she has to do with them. ChOn will want to see Buyo before she is moved. Maní. Take the baby and look after it until I return."

Karín ran to find ChOn. She knew he would be with Jez, celebrating. As soon as he saw her, he knew something was wrong. Karín motioned for Jez to leave them and sat down, her head in her hands. ChOn sat next to her. She leaned over and held him to her.

"My Lord. I bear terrible news. Buyo lost too much blood and died. She was smiling in death and it was you who put that smile on her face with your words of the ebon you feel for her."

ChOn's heart thumped twice in his chest and the anger rose in his gorge and just as quickly went away. He was used to death and even though he felt like he had never felt before, he knew from past experience that there was nothing he or anyone else could do to bring her back. He lay down, his head in Karín's lap.

"And the baby?"

"The baby is going to be fine and I will raise her as my own daughter as befits the senior wife of a king."

ChOn looked up at Karín. Tears were running from her face.

"This is my second dream. I told you about it. Do you remember it?"

"I do, ChOn. We knew not its meaning at the time but now it has been revealed. I wish it were otherwise."

ChOn closed his eyes and cast his mind back to the first day he had met Buyo at the overhang and had discovered her secret. She had followed him in the blackness and he had known she could see in the dark. Over the ensuing years she had served him as a spy and lover and he would never know her again as either.

"Take me to her. I would see her once more before we take her to where she called our special place upriver from the castle. There we will bury her with full state honours for she was a true servant of the Arw'an and saved us twice from possible annihilation."

They went to the delivery room. The midwife had done her best to clean up. She had put Buyo's tunic over her nakedness but otherwise had not moved her. The smile was fixed to her face, which looked so relaxed, ChOn half expected her to open her eyes and speak. Without saying another word, he left the room.

"Leave her now," ordered Karín, *"Have Kelda send up someone to prepare her. The king has ordered a state burial. Tell Kelda to leave the details of that to me."* She went to their quarters where Maní was waiting with Nelik and the baby.

"What say you, Nelik?"

"My Lady. Look at these. Do you not think there is enough for three if there is enough for two? Everybody knows that if more is needed, more will be produced. I will have my sister come to help me with the bathing and other tasks. We will need more space if you can provide it."

"It will be done. Maní, I will speak to ChOn about the arrangements with you. I will bleed again in the next few days and after that I am not forbidden to him except for those days each moon cycle. I would have you remain as the official concubine but given what is happening here, we will need this room and you may have to go back to the stables where you were before. At least temporarily. I am sorry but I am sure you understand the protocol we must observe."

"I do, Karín. I will wait for word from my lord and yours before I move what possessions I have here."

"Thank, you, Maní. It will not be for long. You will be the second aget after the period of mourning has passed. I will see to it. Now. Nelik. It has been but a short time since Joan was born so there is time for you to get your sister or would you prefer to wait until morning?"

"I can wait, My Lady. If I need help before then, I will ask you or the lady Maní."

Ch0n strode out of the main gate in full battle order. He made his way up to the rise that overlooked the castle. There was no moon and so he selected the thermal imaging option on his helm and peered out into the green-ness. There was nothing to be seen. He sat down with his back to a tree and patted the ground beside him. The wolf padded over to him and lay down by his side. Together they waited through the passing hours until the wolf stirred and Ch0n realized he had been asleep. He looked out into the eerie green light and saw the unmistakable shape of a man running towards him. He stood and flexed his muscles. He was not going to ambush the Ninja but he knew that if he were not ready and the Ninja ran into him, he would have to fight to prevent being bettered. As it turned out, the man turned away early and approached the castle more from the Eastern side and Ch0n watched him all the way to the wall, which he scaled like a spider and disappeared. Ch0n looked back the way the Ninja had come and in the distance saw two other green dots. He smiled under his visor and started for the gate. When he reached it, he went directly to his stables.

"You'd better come, Darel. Go to the top of the castle where you can see the chain gun turret. They're arriving already. Rai, you may stay until morning under the circumstances."

Darel secured Ch0n's equipment, ran lightly to the top of the tower and looked over the edge. He could see nothing at first but soon a shadowy figure appeared over the wall and entered the turret. He emerged soon afterwards with a disk and disappeared as swiftly and silently as he had appeared. A second figure appeared and claimed his disk. It was several minutes before the third man reached the turret and he approached from inside the castle keep and ran up the stairs to secure his disk. Over the course of the next hour, the other seven arrived and left.

"My Lord, how did you know Rai was in my quarters?"

"I didn't. But now I do. I suspected it, nothing more. I bluffed you into telling me that which you thought was a secret. I have seen the looks that pass between you. Clues. She is a fine girl and a fit lover for you. If you wish to have her as your aget, I release you from service as my squire. You are ready to leave me and melt into the village as a ninja might do. You would remain on the public payroll. I would find you a position that would afford you your cottage in the village near the castle as befits your role as the head of the ninja."

"Thank you, Lord but I do not wish to leave your service. It gives me the perfect foil for my status as a ninja and a single man. I am not ready to take Rai as my aget and she does not wish it. She is too involved in her role as teacher and Commander Guerra has told her he wishes her to be his assistant pilot. She is not a woman like others. She is independent and wishes to make her own name and her own way. She uses me when she needs to make ijon as I use her. It is a good arrangement is it not?"

Robia woke at first light. As the Troop Leader of the King's Own Cavalry Troop, she was always first up and around her charges to make sure they were on time for their first appointment of the day. Today it was to go riding with Karín for the first time in six months. She threw back the light woollen blanket and was surprised when a heavy object fell from her cot to the floor. She looked down and picked it up. It was a six-pointed iron star with a hole in the middle of it and some scratchings. She knew it was a weapon and she knew who had put it there. She was 'dead'.

Karín didn't go on her morning run. She went to the Lancer lines to warn the King's Own that they would be needed for a state burial later in the day. When she arrived at the lines, she was greeted by Freda, the adjutant and Robia who told her that the first Ninja had struck. The other sisters were chattering excitedly about their good luck.

"Let this be a lesson to you all. You all knew the king is forming a new, elite fighting force and we don't even know who they are. Robia might well be dead. The guard commander is already feeling ChOn's gaze because he allowed ten, TEN people into the castle unchallenged. Now. These men have three full days and nights to 'assassinate' nine more of you. Be on your guard for they are trained to be like shadows in the darkness and they move on slippers that make no sound. Remember the reward for catching them out. The overhang with no all morning's ride to get there. Robia. I am not happy you were the first. It shows an arrogance. These men are good!"

The guard commander was squirming. First Jez and then ChOn himself had weighed into him about the intruders. The cabot was convinced ChOn would kill him for dereliction of duty or even worse, demote him in public but suddenly the king softened his tone.

"These men are being trained in a way that will enable them to slip past even the most alert of sentries, Cabot. You just happened to be pulling duty on the night they came in but let it be a lesson to you all. You might have been killed by them had they been an enemy force. I will talk to Colonel Marik and ask him to come up with a warning system for people climbing the walls."

They all arrived at the training area together. Darel had told the Ninjas to report for training as usual. They were in their pyjamis but had their faces uncovered. ChOn lined them up and walked in front of them all. Their faces were impassive as he spoke.

"I am told by my Lancer Commander that she lost her troop Leader last night. That means one of you has already struck. That was extremely clever. Darel has the first shuriken and is waiting for the remaining nine. Now we have some practical weapons testing to do. Ninjas against the Knights and squires. Wooden swords to begin with."

They put woven, reed baskets over their heads to protect themselves. The Ninjas had nowhere near the experience of the Knights or squires and were soon defeated but not without showing their wares. The swords were followed by short swords and then sai, some ball and chain weapons and finally fans. ChOn graded every Ninja by name and performance with each weapon until he was happy they had all had a fair time to prove themselves.

"It is organized for this afternoon, Ch0n. Doni has sent men to dig the grave where you told me. The Lancers and Infantry are ready to go as are the rest of the council members. We will leave here when Kelda informs me that Buyo is ready to travel. I will let you know in time."

"Good work. Thank you. I will lead on the oruk. You will follow behind me. Then Buyo. Then the Knights. Then the Lancers. Then the infantry. Then the council."

"As you wish, Ch0n. I had Guerra print two copies of an image I made of Buyo and Joan together before Kelda's people came to take her. One we will keep for Joan and I thought the other could be buried with her. Look. Do you like it?"

Ch0n took the print from her and studied it. Buyo was smiling, her eyes open for the image. Lying in the crook of her arm was her baby, awake and seemingly looking at Buyo's face. A lump formed in his throat at the sight of her.

"She will like that."

"I think so. Now come and have breakfast. My sister and I need to talk to you about her station and living arrangements while Nelik and her sister are living in the castle."

Ch0n halted the procession at the bend in the river where he and Buyo had swum before the battle with the Matáng. There they left her in the cold earth before turning for home. Doni's men filled in the hole and a team of masons immediately started to make a plinth to guard her forever. During the morning,

ChOn had used the laser function of the rod to carve out her epitaph.

Buyo, twice saviour of the Arw'an, sleeps beneath this stone

The mood was heavy when they arrived back at the castle and the Lancers were not prepared for the ambush. Six more of their number were 'assassinated' in broad daylight in their lines as they reached the top of their ladders, the three on each end of the row of stables. Not one of their sisters was outside to see the black-clad figures as they disappeared in plain view.

"It isn't fair that they should do it now. The girls were mourning one of their own," complained Karín to ChOn.

"There is no such thing as fair in war and these men are being trained to know their moment. I would have done it too. In fact I would have taken out someone on the trip back from the burial. They will be Ninjas. They will come and go unseen and do their business. Now we have lost Buyo with her capacity to see in the dark they are more important than ever. They now have two days and three nights to get three more targets."

The Ninjas were in a group celebrating their success so far. Only three had not attempted to 'assassinate' a Lancer and all those who had tried had succeeded.

"It will be hard now. They are going to be prepared," said one.

"I have a plan," said a second. "I am going to earn a big bonus for mine."

The others also had their plans and talk went to the following day's test of hand to hand contact before the group broke up.

That night after dinner, the next of the sisters was 'assassinated' as she walked from the central dining area to the baths. As she rounded a curve in the track, a noose was passed around her neck from beside her and she was pulled out of sight. Once in the shadows, the Ninja removed the noose and presented her with his shuriken. He bowed to her and disappeared into the darkness in two steps.

Nelik's first days as the provider of milk for three babies had been busy ones. Dorak was his usual greedy self, Tomis demanded his share and Joan was almost drowning in the flow that greeted her when Nelik let down. Nelik's sister was washing out dirty diapers and making sure the two boys were asleep when they were supposed to be. She bathed them all in a beaten aluminium tub. Karín and Maní were chipping in to help between tasks. Finally Karín decided to take Dorak for a walk around the castle. She had had little time with him over the past few days and this was a routine they had become used to. It was a cool night and Dorak was well wrapped as they passed Mori's hut. He was awake as usual and tugged his missing forelock to Karín as she passed by. He did not see the shadow that passed behind his hut. He said later he did not see Karín move when she did but the result of the Ninja trying to 'assassinate' Karín as she walked was a wounded Ninja. Mori may not have seen it but Karín had sensed something and her dagger was already moving when the Ninja darted from the shadows. It found its mark in his shoulder even as Karín was pulling a sai from somewhere and backing away from her attacker.

"You fool! I almost killed you! You are supposed to be after the Lancers."

"But you are the commander of the Lancers Brigadier General Karín so I thought to gain more points by selecting you."

"Well you have one point you didn't want to get for your troubles. You had better report to Kelda's people for attention and next time, pick a more sensible target if you are using pretend weapons. Make sure I get that back when they remove it."

Ch0n laughed at the story.

"Silly man. Still, one has to admire his courage if not his planning. That leaves just one and two more days and nights to do it. On the bright side, we only have to cut four now instead of five. You have already done our work with the other one. I owe you a trip to the overhang in the areo."

Despite the best efforts of the Lancers, the final 'assassination' was successfully completed and Karín was angry. She could not see the point Ch0n was trying to make that one man fighting with no rules and no structure to his plans or his methods could sneak around unseen and unheard. The final attack had occurred as the troop returned to the castle after a day of manoeuvres and the last rider had been picked off in the half light of evening by an unseen assailant dropping from the roof below the guard house between the two sets of gates. By the time her sister had realized what was happening, the Ninja was gone, leaving an empty tlaque and an embarrassed Lancer sitting on the ground with a noose loosely around her neck. The shuriken was attached to it. Karín wanted to punish Robia for her lack of vigilance but Ch0n would not permit it.

"Yes, you are angry. Yes, there is a lesson to be learned. But the skills we have taught these especially selected men are designed so they can be invisible in plain sight. They are all in black working at night and the Lancers were in a safe haven. The Guard Commander was almost within touching distance of him and didn't know he had arrived or that he was sitting on the gatepost on the corner of the wall and the roof. Imagine an enemy who has no idea these assassins exist. They will just disappear one by one in silence and panic will follow. They can infiltrate a space and lie listening and leave again without a trace. Or they can kill or kidnap and then leave. We may never need them but we will always have them. In the open against your Lancers they would not stand a chance but in the dark the tables are turned."

So the final five were selected and none of the sisters was able to win a flight in the areo. The five who had been cut from the squad were sworn to secrecy on pain of death and allowed to return to their former lives. Darel and the five remaining stepped up their training under Ch0n and the other Knights, never knowing what would be next but always ready for the unexpected. After training, they melted back into the castle routine with their families and neighbours knowing only that the king was training them for something but never knowing what and no longer asking for they had been told the same thing time and again, that it was part of the kings overall plan for the protection of all. In his workshop behind the stable, ChOn kept busy with the laser, cutting and making the shurikens and exotic blades designed to be hidden in the secret pockets Kelda herself was sewing into the black uniforms and gloves.

Jez, who had designed and built the giant crossbows, had set himself to the design of a miniature version that would fire an eight inch, aluminium-tipped bolt over a distance of ten paces One morning at training, he presented his prototype to ChOn and Darel. The stock was made from a narrow tube of scorched bamboo that doubled as a quiver for three bolts and the demountable arc. When needed, the laminated bamboo arc could be mounted in a slot at the end of the stock and the string attached to a cocking lever. ChOn was surprised at the force needed to draw the eighteen-inch bow to the trigger mechanism. He put a bolt into the groove in the stock, sighted along the bolt and used his thumb to let it fly. It was made from a reed and had fletches made from dáguia feathers and flew truly, seven paces to its target, the hind leg of a goat. The aluminium tip was sharp enough to penetrate half the length of the bolt and ChOn knew it would kill a man at that range. He looked at Darel who was smiling and at Jez who was grinning. Jez dismantled the bow and stored it in the stock with a beanie to stop any rattling of the contents. Then he slung it over his shoulder. It looked innocuous enough to be carried in public.

"How long have you been working on that, Jez?"

"Since the day after you told me of the plan to train silent assassins, My Lord. This is a perfect weapon. It can be carried in a crowd and assembled quickly behind a tree or the back of an accomplice and makes almost no sound. After firing, the assassin merely removes the arc and wanders away in the confusion with the weapon under his tunic. It has three bolts only because of the size of the tube. One would be enough but then it would rattle too much. With three there are enough to do the job and maybe fire one or two more to assist the escape but I originally planned it for one bolt only. I couldn't make the tube any thinner because it wasn't wide enough to hold the arc."

"It is a thing of beauty and function. Karín will want one and the boys will need them when they are old enough to draw them. Of course that won't be for a few summers yet. Darel, what do you think?"

"My Lord, they are wonderful for a specific purpose but I do not see them as being an integral part of the uniform of a Ninja, any more than, say a longbow would be. The tube needs to be carried outside the pyjamis and would impede movement. But as I say, it is a wonderful addition to the arsenal of a Ninja for a specific task."

Jez was a little put out at this suggestion at first but as Darel explained, he saw the reasoning behind it and nodded.

"I will make enough for all to be used when needed. I will also make some bolts with pads instead of tips for training purposes against live targets."

Ch0n called in all the attendees, including Karín.

"This Ninja project has to remain a secret as much as possible. Obviously people know something is happening with their family and neighbours but the true purpose and the nature of it must remain as closely guarded as possible. Because Darel has taken a different direction from the other squires, he will not become a Knight in the form that others have done. Not for him will be the armour and the visibility. He has, however, earned a promotion and a title to go with it and people may know him by it and call him by it. Those who bore it were given it by their teachers as a sign they had reached a certain level of skill. It is a name from the same culture from which the ancient Knights of Japan, a nation of my world, once served their kings. The Knights were called Samurai and Dorak, for whom my son is named, was the greatest of them. The assassins were called Ninja. Darel and the rest will be Ninja and he as their commander will be known henceforth as 'Shodan' and will be equal in status to the Knights. Come forward, Darel. Kneel there, boy. For services to the people of the Arw'an, I name you, Shodan of the Arw'an. You can stand up now."

Darel stood proudly to the congratulations of those present.

"My Lord. If we don't get on with training, we will be late for breakfast," he announced.

Chapter Sixteen: Return of a Queen

Harry's preparations for the trip to the Eñame city were completed before the second moon cycle. The modifications to the longboat had been trialed and tweaked. The discovery of the areo had changed the execution of the plan but Ch0n still wanted a show of force. The new plan called for Guerra, Verge and Karín to arrive in the areo while Ch0n would stay with his original plan to sail in the lead boat. Temen, who had not originally been in the party, would accompany Ch0n and be in the first group to land and pave the way for a spectacular entrance by Karín and Verge.

Karín planned the departure day to coincide with the end of her bleeding. She told Ch0n she wanted to spend a night alone with him before they departed and that it was more important to her than a day or two as queen of the Eñame. Maní would remain behind with Dorak and Joan in her role as official concubine and babysitter.

Two days before the scheduled departure for Eñame, Karín announced to Ch0n that the time had arrived where she could make íjon with him for the first time in almost a year. They passed the night rekindling their fires and Ch0n realized he had missed her body, despite the presence of Maní who had been more than a match physically for both Karín and Buyo during their simultaneous pregnancies. By morning, they were both

451

spent and had to drag themselves out of the bed to attend training. Karín was back to full strength and agility and nobody who looked at her would guess she had borne a child less than three moons prior. She was again using steel weapons and only Ch0n and Darel could match her for speed with the katana. She had become adept at the short crossbow, or the 'toy' as Jez had named it and only Darel could best her with the shuriken. She had tried to teach the Ninjas to use the sling but only one of them was even reasonable with it but they were all equipped with and deadly accurate with slingshots. Darel had adapted one so it would fire a short arrow, which he managed to hide on his person and the others had followed suit. Each morning became a circuit of katana and sai with short swords and daggers, shuriken and slingshots all combined. A short session of willing hand to hand sparring ended the sessions with the occasional cut or bruise.   This morning was no different but Karín was even faster and more concentrated. She felt whole again in mind and body and afterwards Ch0n commented.

"My Lord, remember we were going to go to the overhang and renew ourselves before the Eñame voyage? Buyo's death has changed a lot of things but when we return from Eñame, I would go there alone with you. We have not been alone together for months. I would ride with you on the one tlaque and you can sing the songs to me you used to sing. Up until this morning I was fit of body but my mind was wandering a little, counting the days until we could make ijon. I have missed it. In fact, before I take my bath I want to try it again. You have learned well from Maní. I feel a difference in your power and it pleases me."

Afterwards in the common eating area, Karín was all business again as they sat with Maní and the children at one table with Nelik and her sister.

"Tomorrow you will be going to the lake village and the following day you will be sailing for Eñame. Tell me again how you want me to make my entrance. I will have the bracelets so I have the option of speaking the ancient tongue to impress their priests or to speak Eñame to impress their king. Or I can do both but in which order? I personally think the king should be addressed first before I make any claims to be their returned queen."

"Eñame first. Let Verge talk about queens. You can address the priests when he gives you the opening. He will be telling them you can do it so that is the time. If we need to put on some sort of show, we can do a telepathy display using the bracelets."

"What if the king does not accept me as queen?"

"Then I will kill him and it will be obvious."

"No. I will kill him and THEN it will be obvious."

They all laughed at her little joke before Dorak interrupted their merriment by vomiting his morning milk all over Karín's tunic. This time, only Nelik laughed.

"Welcome to breakfast, My Lady."

The following morning, Ch0n and Darel rode out of the gates with the other Knights and their equipment for the voyage. Ch0n chose the Oruk and Darel rode behind on Karín's tlaque. Ch0n's tlaque would be spending the time they were away with Doni at the corrals and the herd of pregnant tlaque and oruk. Karín was busy with the children and Guerra studying the layout of Eñame and confirming the landing site for the areo, which would be on the wharf to one side of the second longboat.

Maní took the opportunity to clean out her lodgings above Ch0n's stables where she would be spending most of her time except for a few days each month. Patience was not something she was good at but she knew she would have to master it before Ch0n would be ready for Karín to invite her to become his second aget. She pondered her future as she watched Ch0n leave astride the massive oruk with Darel following. Ch0n had smiled and waved a farewell to her from the bottom of the ladder but they both knew that even had he wanted to climb the ladder and take her, it was forbidden to them now that her sister, Karín was not forbidden to him. That was the worst part for her, the waiting while she yearned for him and burned for him.

Ch0n and his entourage reached the saddle overlooking the lake and eased down the slope towards the small village as it had become. Below them, Harry was fussing about the boats before Ch0n's inevitable inspection. The three Captains had their crews stowing their equipment in their sparse spaces while the forage for the two Oruks they had managed to provide for was being packed in two of Ch0n's waterproof bins at the front of their stalls. Eden had managed to design a rear-loading ramp that could be lowered to the ground or to a wharf without the boat tipping over, which it almost certainly would have done under the weight of an oruk disembarking from one side without a counterbalance. It was hinged using two long iron pins passed through a tubed section salvaged from the landing gear of ChOn's doomed craft. Liberal quantities of animal fat made for a smooth operation of the ramp and two lengths of precious chain enabled the ramp to be lowered and fixed at the necessary angle.

ChOn rode his oruk straight to the modified craft and dismounted. Darel led the beast by the nose ring up the slope without problems and then turned it and led it back to ground level. ChOn nodded his approval to Eden and turned to Harry.

"Well, Sir Harry, if everything goes as well as that did, we shall have a trouble free departure on the morrow."

"My Lord, all is in readiness. Even Verge is looking forward to his next flight. We will leave at your convenience tomorrow after breakfast. There is no need to leave earlier as we will be clear of the river before last light and we can anchor in open water or sail on if the weather and winds permit. So says Captain Eden."

"Very well, Sir Harry. You and Ivor will take your oruk to the landing with Marik and a platoon. There is no change to that part of the original plan. I will go with Temen and Eden in the first boat. Verge as you mentioned will go with Karín and Commander Guerra. If you would send two of your best soldiers to accompany them, I would feel better. Admiral and his boat will stand off at the far bank and provide cover for the areo when it lands. By then we should have a force on the ground inside the entrance to their harbour. I will be in constant touch with Guerra and if it looks tricky I will have him land on the plateau above or even with Ivor and Jez. I will not risk the areo being rushed. Your soldiers' role is to protect it and Karín. Do you understand your orders?"

"I do, My Lord. Fear not. They will protect that which needs protection although I doubt it will be Karín."

At first light, ChOn was doing his rounds. As he expected, he encountered Harry doing the same thing. Harry wasn't quite as tall as ChOn. He, Ivor and Arturo were all alike but had been cloned from a different gene pool. Their habits, though were all from the same school, long ago programmed into their minitrons before their missions had ever left Earth. Around the camp, the activity had begun. The cooks were hard at work as usual at this hour. The sailors were usually not up and about but today was different. The three captains were already aboard their boats even though they would not be sailing for some few hours. They were all equipped with hand-held radios and Eden had cleverly mounted his ear pods and remote microphone inside his Eñame helm. He looked a little comical with the goat horns sticking up from the sides of it but he had informed Harry that he regarded it as part of his captain's uniform, along with the long handled ax that was never far away from his right hand.

ChOn and Harry continued past the boats to the Infantry compound where Marik was pacing about impatiently, though there was no hurry. Even Verge and Teṁen were seen about outside, which was unusual. They were famous for their late rising, which they justified by reminding everybody that they often spent most of the night poring over the glyphs or even exploring the maze of tunnels and caves that kept opening up under their explorations. Because they worked in the dark, they had no sense of time. Someone had made a joke about their never being late for dinner despite their never knowing the hour. The general mirth had wounded their haughty opinions of themselves but they managed a weak grin.

"Sometimes I miss the esteem in which we were held at home," complained Temen in a whisper.

"The ChOn and the queen hold us in high opinion, Temen," Verge assured him. *"Here we have everything we ever wanted thanks to them and tho' the people might tease us they do not mock us. In three days we will be back with our people and we will be revered as never before for our discoveries for it was I who discovered the way to the control room where the flying vessel was hidden. It was I who found the names of the ChOn and the queen in the table yonder. And there is more. I have a plan to ask the ChOn to allow the entire order of priests to relocate here to the holy site. Our work will be magnified a hundredfold. I know there is something we have missed somewhere here. Something big. There is a piece missing of the puzzle and when we find it, our life's work will be complete. You see, I know now as do you that the sky people were not Gods as we have always thought. It suited their purposes to have us think they were but look at the ChOn and his... Knights. Mortals every one. I know not how they do their magic with the many tongues they speak but to me, only Karín is the product of our original sky people. The prophecies are too accurate not to be true but she, too is mortal as were the originals. They may have lived far longer than our fathers but in their turn they all*

died and left us here to grow in their image. It was just a matter of time before their appearance was duplicated. Look at the number of people we have among the Eñame who look like each other. It has something to do with the seed a man plants in the woman. If it is weak, the woman's seed makes the offspring in her image. If the man's is stronger, the offspring is made in his image and sometimes we can see the eyes of the one or the mouth of another. It is no coincidence. I will ask the ChOn. He seems to know about most things but in my opinion, sooner or later one would be born in the image of the sky people. Karín may not be the first or the only one. She is but the only one we know of. It matters not. It has made my life's work all the more important and yours. Now, soon you will sail with the ChOn to the harbour. Go well and wait for the welcome we will receive."

ChOn left his quarters after they had eaten their morning meal. It was the signal they had all been waiting for and as he appeared, various groups were seen getting to their feet and making their ways to their respective boats. Darel stayed with ChOn. Harry and Ivor watched as their squires led the two oruk to the logistics boat. ChOn bade them a good voyage and they nodded to him and turned towards their boat. ChOn and Darel went to theirs where Eden was waiting, dressed in his Arw'an uniform, his horned helm and his ax. The Admiral was barking orders to his crew and extolling Marik to make haste with the infantry. In short order, they were all aboard and looking towards Eden as the senior Captain. He raised his arm and pointed to the open lake. As one the various ropes were loosened and the boats poled in sequence out of the small harbour. When they were clear of the wharf, the orders rang out to 'out oars' and the voyage was under way. Before long, they were all under sail tacking towards the end of the lake and the river. Overhead, the drone followed their progress. Guerra, Jez and Karín watched as the formation took shape with Ch0n standing in the stern of the lead boat approving in his mind. The others followed in echelon behind and to his right so nobody took the wind of another boat.

"You have done well in a short time, Eden. They are almost sailors."

"Thank you, My Lord, but sailing is not difficult nor is being a sailor. Once a captain and his bosun have the crew trained in the simple things, the rest is merely practice. There are enough of us Eñame sailors to maintain the competition going between crewmen. But yes, they do look good and are holding their positions well, even the logistic boat with Mathilde. She has done well. She even swears like a sailor."

Ch0n laughed and left Eden to his work. He went below to his tiny corner below the helm, the only concession to a king being a square of cloth to keep the sun at bay.

They reached the end of the lake well before last light and Ch0n listened to Eden giving instructions for the passage under oars. They were simple and brief. Sails were lowered and the vessels rowed to a point short of the rocks where the current would slowly take them to the channel. The helmsman would control the boat once they were in the current and the oars would be out but not in the water unless there was a need for extra steering. Eden was watching the two sides of the channel and suddenly barked the order for the port side to make one stroke. This they did. The boat slewed to the right and they were through to the river. Ch0n was watching anxiously as the second boat passed through and then the logistic boat was in the current and slightly off centre. Just as Eden was about to send an order by radio to Mathilde, the port rowers gave two strokes and the boat straightened and passed without problems through to the river.

"Well managed, Mathilde," Ch0n heard Eden in his own helm and he nodded and patted him on the back. He had another good leader in his team.

They rowed down the river with the bowmen at stand-to but without incident. When the last vessel was clear, Eden gave the order to raft up at anchor. It took a little while for the three boats to co-ordinate this more difficult manoeuvre but by the time the sun fell behind the horizon in a blaze of red and purple, they were already passing the rations from the logistic boat, and the three captains and the two Knights were with Ch0n.

"Well done to you all for this day's work. We left on time and arrived here without incident. Captain Eden tells me that sailing is not difficult but that comes from the mouth of one who has been a sailor all his life. I know it is not easy. Marik here could tell you that to be a soldier is not difficult but we know that for many it is. Each of us has his or her own skills and abilities but the one I admire more than any is to be able to lead. I have seen it today in all of you. In Mathilde who as a female has more to prove than you, Admiral but she has done it and the way she took the boat through the canal when it might have turned and been swamped was a sign of good teamwork between her, her Eñame bosun and her crew and I commend her for it. I also commend Captain Eden for his praise of her when she did it because to notice good work and to not give praise is worse than to see fault and not to correct it. Learn from it all of you. Now I have a gift for you, Captain Eden. It is a small thing but it is something you must guard with your life."

ChOn passed a small rolled up green cloth to Eden and the others stretched to see what it was. Eden nodded to ChOn and unrolled it. It was a long triangle of green with ChOn's coat of arms, a stylized Knight with the twin katanas over his shoulders.

"Do you know what it is, Eden?"

"I have not seen this design before, My Lord but I know what it is. It is a pennant. I assume it is your pennant to be flown at the mast of your vessel. It is something we Eñame do when our king is sailing with us. He has not been to sea for a long time now."

"You say, 'we' Eden. You are now one of the Arw'an and tho' your blood be Eñame, you are an Arw'an and so the Eñame are 'they'. I will forgive you your error this once but yes, that is my pennant. It flies over Arw'an Castle on a flag. You will be commander of the Arw'an Fleet and Captain of my Flagship. From this moment it will be known as 'The Buyo'. I would have you paint two red eyes on the bow."

"Thank you, My Lord. Yes, it will be done as you wish. Now if you will permit me to leave, I will have the pennant flying shortly."

He left and was heard giving orders to a crewman. The sailor ran to the mast and freed a thin line. He connected the strange metal clips on the pennant to the line, making sure it was not upside down and raised it to the masthead in the failing light. Cheering broke out among the crew and spread to the two other vessels. Ch0n was already confirming the orders for the arrival.

Sleeping on a longboat wasn't easy as many of the men discovered that night. Some were sick over the side to the cheers of their companions and with all the noise and merriment not many managed to sleep well. One exception was Ch0n who had his little corner of the boat and the minitron plugged in to his ears. The familiar sound of the default program soothed his senses. Just the same, he was awake before first light because of the movement of the crew who had not passed such a blissful night. It wasn't long before the porridge and water was being passed around with strips of dried goat meat and when the sun peeped over the horizon, Eden shouted to his fellow captains to cast away. The two outside boats used their oars to push themselves off and soon they were sailing on a starboard tack towards the Eñame shoreline. They were in the same echelon formation as the day before but this time the two rear boats were on the port side of Ch0n's flagship because of the direction of the breeze. Eden explained to Ch0n that they usually sailed around the coast because they had no means of open water navigation by day apart from the sun's angle. It had too big a margin for error when looking for a small spot like the entrance to a river, which had no landmarks. For the trip to Eñame it was more reliable because even if they were quite amiss with their bearings, the cliffs in front of the table could be seen for miles and the boat could be steered towards it. Ch0n in turn showed him the inbuilt navigation system on the tablet. He explained that everywhere he went, the tablet marked it on the map so that when the map were opened, the line would appear with way points that had been registered. He also explained that the drone could fly a course and then download the track to the tablet and that the line on the screen was made as a result of the first drone flight. They were tracking right of the line on the map but ChOn knew as did Eden that when they came onto a port tack that they would be tracking right of it until they were close enough to the harbour to row the rest of the way. Eden was naturally curious and picked up the concept quickly. He asked ChOn if they had boats where he came from and ChOn decided to show him some images of boats on earth. He booted the minitron and searched for Vikings and was rewarded with some painted images of their boats and the people. Eden was shocked to discover that there were Eñame on Earth but then ChOn explained the time factor and showed him images of some of the Spanish galleons and the sleek clippers of the eighteenth century followed by some racing yachts and steam vessels. He showed some images of the giant American Battleships and aircraft carriers of the mid twentieth century and the cruise ships and oil tankers of the same period. Finally he showed Eden the biggest ship ever built, the giant Chinese catamaran aircraft carrier and battleship of the mid twenty-second century, big enough to carry the entire air force of a medium-sized country as well as deploy regiments of marines on giant hovercraft and squadrons of armoured fast attack catamarans from an internal protected harbour in each hull. He showed him vessels that skimmed half a metre above the surface using air pressure to stay airborne and which could also race along the surface as conventional boats with their wings retracted. Eden was shocked at what he saw but having seen the areo and ChOn's terrible weapons of fire, he knew that everything he saw was true.

"My Lord, those boats are almost beyond my comprehension but why are most of them built for war? Has your planet always been at war?"

ChOn pondered the question for a short while.

"Yes. It has. I never really thought about it but yes. And that is probably why I want to unite all the peoples of this place so we will have no more wars. It is but a dream for everybody has something that somebody else wants. I will do my best to make a lasting peace and have always given my conquered enemies the chance to serve me in peace instead of dying at my hand in a needless war."

ChOn's helm came to life.

"Lord, ChOn, this is Guerra. Are you there?"

"Yes, Commander, I am here. What news of the castle?"

"The areo is ready to leave with Karín and two of Marik's soldiers. We will call by the lake and pick up Verge. We will stay there until after midnight and then leave for Eñame. About five hours from then, at dawn, we will be at the Eñame landing place. Are you on schedule?"

"Yes. The logistic ship left the formation about an hour ago and Sir Harry will advise us when he and the rest are on land and heading for the Eñame. If you arrive before we do, just stay away until everybody is in place. We have no idea of the reception we will receive."

"Guerra, understood. Out."

Karín mounted the areo in her tunic and placed her white, parachute-silk gown on a hanger in one of the lockers. Guerra was already at the controls doing his pre-flight sequence. Or rather, the areo was self-checking. The two soldiers followed Karín nervously but both were proud to have been selected to be her personal bodyguard. They both knew she could outfight either of them but today they would stand behind her to watch her back because she would be unarmed during the visit. They placed their equipment on the floor beneath their seats and waited.

The Eñame lookout saw the drone as it approached the entrance to the cave. It sat off some five hundred metres but made no attempt to get closer. Guerra put it into a hover and placed his tablet on a flat, vacant section of the console of the areo. A light appeared underneath the tablet and the screen of the tablet was reproduced on the heads up display of the areo. Guerra looked at Karín.

"Every time I fly this thing I learn something new. That can only mean the sky people had portable digital computer equipment. Verge and Temen have missed something somewhere."

Karín nodded. She was wondering what treasure trove of information was hidden in some secret place above the ruins and whether the rod under ChOn's armour had the means to reveal it.

Guerra touched the button on his seat.

"Lord ChOn, this is Guerra. We are leaving the castle bound for the Lake within the next half hour. I will notify you when we depart that location later in the night."

"This is ChOn. We have the cliffs visual. We will go closer to the shore and anchor until midnight. Eden says we are three hours from the harbour. We will arrive shortly after dawn. You should land after the support boat has secured a beach head. I will keep you informed. Out to you. Sir Harry, what is your progress report?"

"This is Harry. We have landed safely and are readying the oruk. The Infantry patrol has already left and Jez told us it will take them four hours to arrive. We will be there well before dawn with the shallows secured."

"Good. ChOn out."

He told Eden to find a place to raft the two boats for the night and went to his personal corner of the boat. He booted the rod and waited until the bracelet signalled it was connected.

"Karín are you there?"

"I am always here My Lord."

"I have found the flaw in my plan. I had assumed until now that the Eñame would be on land when we arrived but I had not considered that they might send the remainder of their fleet to meet us if they thought we were going to attack. They must know by now that the force they sent months ago has been defeated or they would have returned long ago. I know not how many ships they have nor how many men but in their shoes I would not let the castle be overtaken without fighting to the last soldier to spare the women and children. We are going to land a ship in a position of fire support and I will sail into their harbour under cover of the tubes and the crossbows but they don't know I will be coming in peace. That is not the flaw. The flaw is if I have to engage them in a sea battle with just two boats and inexperienced crews. My rod is formidable but if we are against say, four or more boats, we will probably be overpowered by sheer weight of numbers. The areo has an arsenal of weapons that can be activated from the co-pilot seat. I will tell Guerra to show you how to use them while you are in transit. You may have to destroy their fleet as it leaves their safe haven under the cliffs to prevent our own boats being destroyed."

"I will learn and I will do what I have to do to keep you safe. I am after all, still your personal bodyguard. I will tell Guerra. You worry about your end of the plan and let me deal with this. The fact you have thought of it means it is not a flaw. We are about to take off. I will speak to him as soon as he can relax a bit."

The Eñame lookout told his partner to fetch the on-duty captain.

"There it is, Link. It has been sitting there ever since I saw it and sent for you. What is it?"

"It is the same craft that visited us before we sent our ships to investigate the holy place of the Eani. It puzzles me, though because it seems too small to carry an intelligent being yet it flies and watches us. It can mean nothing good. We have lost six ships with all hands as far as we know because of it. It will be dark soon. Keep watching it. I will speak with the Commander."

Eden called for the anchor to be dropped and the second vessel pulled alongside and was lashed to the rail. Admiral jumped aboard and went to Ch0n and Eden.

"Captain Eden. How many ships remain in the Eñame harbour?"

"There were twelve in all. Two were in the initial voyage with Erik and four with us. So six remain. They had full crews so there would be the six boats and about five hundred crew and skirmishers."

"Will they come out to meet us or will they defend the town?"

"My Lord, in truth I know not. I was a boat captain for certain but those decisions were never mine to know. The truth is, we... that is they, have never been threatened before. Perhaps the king will decide."

"Do they have drills for sea battles against other boats?"

"Yes. But they do not have the weapons that you have or even the support boat has with the crossbow. The plan *involves attacking from the front or rear in a single line of boats, never from the side. That way, only the lead boat can be threatened. Then the lead boat moves to the left of the enemy boat and the second to the right of it. The third and fourth do likewise with the second enemy boat and the fifth and sixth with the third and so on. The aim is to arrive on two sides and with grapples secure the boat and the skirmishers board and overpower the enemy crew. It is practised constantly as is the land skirmishing, which you have seen. It works well but Eric attacked with two boats when at least four would have been needed to overpower that fortified position. Biorn had no idea when he told Erik the fort could be overpowered. He did not realize the women were fighting troops. That was the undoing of the attack."*

"I am going to assume we will meet the other six boats. I truly hope their commander is a sensible man for he will learn early that to attack as you have said will mean the destruction of almost everything the Sky People have planted on this world. A thousand breeding age males will have died. All of them have their roots in the seed of the Sky People. We can not allow that to happen if it can be avoided. I am going to change boats with Temen and go with Admiral. We will sail immediately. We will track the shore under cover of darkness. You will leave at the appointed hour and arrive at first light. If they are ready, they will deploy their fleet when they see your sails. We will wait just west of the entrance and hope to go un-noticed and sail in behind their fleet. Your role is to draw them to you but not to get involved in a fight. When I tell you I am behind them, you are to run with the wind until they give up the chase or are otherwise distracted. Then you are to sail into the harbour behind them. By then I will have occupied the harbour and there should be no need for bloodshed because Karín and Verge will have landed. Do you understand?"

"I do, My Lord."

"OK, Admiral. Are you ready to leave?"

"Aye My Lord. By the time you and Teṁen have transferred we will be at our stations."

"Good luck, Captain Eden. I know this is not easy for you against the people of your blood but if the plan works, there will be no killing. If it does not, well I do not want to think of the futility of hundreds of years of lost breeding and the effect on the future of the Eñame as a race."

"Teṁen! Get your belongings and go to the other boat!"

The Eñame commander called his six captains to the entrance of the huge cavern that protected their fleet from the outside world. The sun had set and the sky was bright crimson splashed with horizontal lines of orange and blue shadows under the clouds. Five hundred metres away, the drone hovered, its camera focused on the cave, its external lights twinkling in the fading light.

"It is a passive vessel. It has no means of attacking us. It is far too small to be a carrier of weapons," declared their Commander. "It is watching and somehow sending messages to a larger force. I see no other answer. Those flying it are obviously the size of rabbits, perhaps another race, not the Eani at all. The Eani would not have destroyed our other patrols."

"But Gert, creatures so small could not defeat two and then four of our ships. Surely."

"What say the priests? Norwhal, you were Verge's assistant. What do you priests make of it?"

"My Lord, Gert, we know the Eani had powerful weapons. The books tell of a fire and ice breathing staff borne by the leader of the Eani. There is one mention of the sighting of a flying vessel with the same weapons but on a bigger scale. That there is no further mention of it suggests it was a false sighting but perhaps this vessel is it. Perhaps it has the power to destroy us tho' it is so small."

"Bah! Legends and half-truths! Have you nothing more certain that that?"

"No My Lord. Even Verge, the high priest had no more knowledge than that contained in the books. He left us with his library and no more."

"This small flying ship can mean no good but it poses no threat in itself in my mind. Nonetheless, we will place half the crews on level one readiness and the others on level two. Every day we will alternate. You know the plans. We have practised them oft enough. Wake me if there are any changes but before you wake me, all hands to level one. Understood?"

They all nodded. Link gave some brief orders relating to the lookouts and the other captains nodded and went their own ways. Only the priest and the sentry remained at the cave entrance.

Norwhal spoke first.

"Legends and half-truths they may be, Link, but we would do well not to mock them. The Eani were real. The books are a log of a hundred summers of their presence and four hundred more of their absence. We are part of them. There is not one of us remaining here that has not their blood in our veins. All the others were taken to the lake and left there to form their own tribes and some were banished to the morning sun. Perhaps they are angry we banished those not of the fair skin and hair and to whom we did not teach the new languages. Perhaps those we exiled have raised an Army, an alliance with the tiny creatures in yonder vessel. It can mean no good sitting there watching us."

"Fear not, Norwhal. None can defeat us on the sea. Even if the Arw'an outcasts have an army and an alliance they will not have the ships to defeat us." Something dawned on him and he looked automatically to the east where the land had been swallowed up in the darkness. *"Oh no! We are so blind. They can come by land!"*

He ran towards the town calling to one of the captains whose crew was about to go to level one readiness. "Get your skirmishers to the far side of the shallows and send a small patrol out to check for any enemy that might be out there. And double the lookout at the top of the cliff while you're at it." He ran to Gert's house.

"Gert! What if they have come by land?" he asked his commander when the door flew open at his pounding.

"It is possible but improbable. It is two month's walk to the outcasts' village beyond the mountains. There is nothing in between to supply an army. A small force perhaps but nothing of concern. Put a patrol out there and tell the lookout above the city to look for anything to that side. Put a crew of skirmishers on level one readiness. I will tell the king in the morning. He will not want to be disturbed tonight. His new concubine will occupy him well into the night. Such a shame. She is far too young for him." Without further comment he shut the door in Link's face.

Link returned to his own boat and made sure the crew was in the process of moving to level two preparedness. They were always at level three and level two was really only placing rations and water in the vessel for a three day voyage and making sure their weapons were at hand next to their beds at home. If the bell rang, the level one crews, who were sleeping in their boats, could be deployed almost immediately and the level two crews would follow them out of the harbour as soon as they had run from their houses and manned the boats.

Harry and Ivor walked their oruk past the Infantry and took the lead. They were both on high alert so close to the Eñame city and so it was no surprise that three hours after they started, Harry spotted the Eñame patrol in the distance with his thermal scope. Igor was watching his own arc when Harry called the halt. In the two boats and the areo, everybody listened to the transmission.

"I have ten Eñame skirmishers ahead. Maybe a thousand paces. They are moving towards us but not in a patrol formation, just a loose group."

Marik ran forward to where Harry was waiting. Harry pointed with his whole arm.

"They will be part of a bigger patrol somewhere behind them," said Marik into the mike.

Guerra interrupted.

"At last light they had a meeting of sorts outside their cave. They were pointing at the drone so it is likely they are on heightened alert. I can fly the drone to look at their layout."

"Do that," ordered ChOn. "No lights on the drone until it is back in place outside the cave."

Link was standing at the cave entrance when the drone disappeared. One second it was there and the next, it wasn't. Guerra had turned out all the navigation lights and was in the process of moving it east of the city to check the ground forces and their dispositions. To do that, he had to put the areo to auto pilot and operate the drone from his tablet. He was feeling pretty pleased with himself for flying two aircraft at the same time when he reported back to ChOn and Harry.

"There is a large force of some sixty occupying the Eastern side of the shallows. The smaller force to your front has ten in it and is about a mile out from their main force. In between the two forces is another group of ten in a static position."

Ch0n looked at the images Guerra was transmitting to the tablets.

"That second force is a delaying screen to protect the outer patrol if it has to withdraw in contact. It will allow the first patrol to run through it and redeploy behind while the main force either defends or attacks. Sir Harry, bypass the first group with Igor and attack the second. They will not have time to get back to the main force to warn them. Pulse guns only. On 12 percent. It has to be silent. Marik, follow them in and take prisoners while they are still groggy. Then do the same for the first group. I want to arrive not having just killed twenty of their number. It will be hard to sue for peace."

Guerra held the drone in place so Ch0n could watch the two Knights overrun the holding position, which they did in a matter of a few minutes. After Marik's men had consolidated, they overpowered the forward group in the same manner.

"OK, now hold there until I give the order to move forward to the shallows. Guerra, send the drone back to the original position and light it up."

"There it is again, Link," said the sentry.

"I see it. But what happened in the last while? Why did it disappear and return? I am not happy. I am going to tell the remaining two captains to go to silent level one." He ran into the cave and told the sentries to run and get their captains and crews to level one. Then he went back to the cave entrance to wait for the morning.

Marik's men had the twenty Eñame prisoners bound and gagged. His soldiers were sleeping in their advance formation with two sentries out as far as the synthetic cord would reach. Two tugs would signal that an enemy force was approaching and they would immediately wake everybody in sufficient time to repel any attack. The two Knights were awake but resting beside their oruk and would be back in the saddle within seconds of any alert.

Ch0n's boat was edging towards the Eñame harbour. He stopped short of the protective spit, knowing that the force at the shallows would see him or hear him before he was ready. His plan needed the fleet to sail out of the harbour before his own boat was spotted.

Eden sailed towards the lightening sky until the land started to take form. When it was light enough to see, he told the tiller man to head straight for the highest point of land, the table above the city.

The sun peeped over the horizon and lit the sails of Eden's boat like a beacon. Above the city, the lookout rang the bell in a pattern of continuous double rings to warn of the approach of an enemy boat. It was the first time in four hundred years that the bell had been rung in such a way. For a drill it was always rung in threes and then it would stop and after a time it would be repeated. The city stopped moving for a second and then people started running to their posts. The boats were all crewed but one, and that crew was securing the shallow ford east of the city. Their captain sent them back and waited for his patrols. He suddenly realized he had split his force and was now alone with no way to recover the position if the patrols had been overcome. He turned to the shore only to see the mast of a boat passing behind the bank but before he could shout a warning, a noose passed around his neck and he was pulled to the ground. A shadowy black figure with only the eyes showing was holding his finger to his lips in a gesture that could only mean one thing. In the other hand was the leather handle of the short noose. Darel gradually loosened the pressure until he was sure the Eñame would make no sound before removing it altogether. He put a gag on the hapless captain and rolled him over, binding his hands and feet. Then he disappeared at a run towards the still moving mast.

Five of the six Eñame boats left the cave and made for the single sail still some distance away. They did not notice the egg-shaped craft that watched their every move from altitude. Guerra waited until the boats had put a mile behind them before signalling to Ch0n that he could enter the harbour. Harry used the same signal to burst out of the low scrub to where he and Igor could secure the shallows. Behind them ran Marik's men less those leading the prisoners slowly behind. Harry's oruk almost trod on Darel's bound and gagged Eñame captain. He looked around to see who had captured the Eñame but saw nobody.

Eden held his course until he was sure Ch0n had had enough time to manoeuvre behind the Eñame fleet before turning tail and running with the wind. The Eñame cheers died quickly when the alarm was raised by one of the lookouts and they all turned to see Ch0n's boat entering the channel to the harbour. At the same time, they saw the areo landing and they knew they had been tricked.

ChOn stopped his boat short of the wharf because he was faced with some fifty skirmishers who would board him as he drew alongside. Karín saw the opening and told Guerra to land and also told Harry to ride across the shallows with the infantry covering to secure the far bank.

Link ordered the boats about and they made for their city. He knew his men outnumbered the enemy by at least five to one and he could easily blockade the entrance while the skirmishers landed to the east and made a land attack.

ChOn called out across the narrow channel to the assembled Eñame,

"Where is your leader? We come in peace but we have the manner to destroy the city if you choose war."

"I am Gert and this is King Svenn."

"Tell your men to lay down their arms. I bring one who would speak with you."

Verge looked at the scene outside the areo and told Karín who the major players were. She went to the rear of the vessel to change and when she opened the locker, there hanging beside her silk dress was one identical in a soft, white material. She didn't have time to try and work out how it had appeared but pulled it over her head quickly and arranged her hair as best she could. She heard a hiss as the hatch release activated and she returned to the main cabin.

Guerra opened the hatch and Verge made his grand entrance. There was a hubbub of noise before he silenced them with one hand.

"Look upon me and know me for who I am. I am Verge, the high priest of the Eani, Eñame and now servant of Ch0n, the king of the Arw'an, and whom you see before you. I have come to tell you, King Svenn that the Ch0n has amassed an army of thousands across all the known lands, uniting all the exiled tribes. He is of the Sky People, not the Eani but from another place. His queen is Karín who is the 'Ever Queen' from the holy texts, the 'One' of the Eani foretold to us therein. Norwhal, I see you. You know what I say to be the truth from your own knowledge of the holy books. Now. Look upon the queen of the Eñame."

Karín made a theatrical descent to the foot of the stairs and when she stood up straight, a gasp could be heard even across the channel. She was wearing a pure white garment that Ch0n had not seen before. It was the same as the silk gown she had made from the parachute. Her red hair caught the morning sun for all to see.

"People of the Eñame, I am here to claim my throne. Svenn, do you accept me as your queen?"

Ch0n looked back out to sea. The five boats were closing. Three of them started to veer towards the east and Ch0n knew they would try to land and assault through the shallows if ordered to do so.

Norwhal took Svenn's elbow before the king could answer.

"Tell me, you who would be queen," he shouted in the old language of the Eani, *"by what right do you claim the throne of the Eñame?"*

He looked at Svenn.

"Only the priests and the Eani know that tongue. She will not answer, My Lord."

"I claim it in accordance with the holy prophesies left to you by my people before your great grandfather's great grandfather was born, Norwhal," shouted back Karín in the same tongue, and then in the Eñame tongue, *"Decide, Svenn for if you do not accept me as the queen of the Eñame, I will take the throne by force."*

"I will need more evidence than a flying ship and a strange tongue to give up what has been my family's throne for four hundred years, woman."

"So be it!" shouted Karín. She turned and quickly entered the areo. It took off seconds later.

"Ch0n. I am going to sink one of their ships with these weapons. I will try not to kill anybody but if I do nothing, the harbour will be blocked. Trust me."

The areo rose vertically as Guerra followed Karín's instructions. He pointed the nose at the two ships, now almost at the entrance to the harbour and Karín took the weapon controls.

"Take me low and to the side so I can fire at the sails. Yes that's the line. Hold it there."

She unleashed a bolt of orange flame that touched the sail and it instantly caught. The crew reacted as expected. Some started to jump overboard and others stood still while a few took to action stations and tried to beat out the flames. Karín pointed to the other boat and Guerra spun the areo until the nose was in line with the sails. This time Karín sent a blue pulse through the air and the sail took most of it and ripped from top to bottom. Many of the crew were hit and knocked down. Link was thrown from the bow down the three steps onto his back into the lap of two oarsmen. Finally, Karín told Guerra she was going to make a big finale and to point at the cliff. She let loose a bolt of red that hit the rock face and exploded a section of it into shards that flew around like a swarm of wasps.

"Do you concede your throne, Svenn? Do I have to cross this gap and take it?"

Sven looked at Ch0n and the two Knights with their company of Infantry securing the near side of the shallows. He had no idea that Ch0n had an array of personal and mounted weapons at his disposal that could have killed half the onlookers in mere seconds. He estimated correctly that there were less than a hundred Infantry with the two black riders on their elgr. He knew that shortly, three hundred skirmishers would land on the other side of the shallows and storm the port. But the presence of the areo and its weapons worried him. If he were to survive on the throne, he would have to allow it to land where it was vulnerable to his skirmishers. Then he would have to overpower the ground forces in one assault without allowing them to regroup. Ch0n saw him looking about and knew he was assessing the options.

"Guerra. Do not land the areo until I tell you to. If I am dead, do not land it at all. You will have to destroy this place and every boat in it except what is needed for the return to the lakes. Return Karín to the castle and then when things are resolved in the kingdom, a calm decision can be made on the future. I am going over to reason with the king. Take up a position west of the shallows. We know that their skirmishers will be coming and they will be in no mood to be chatting about their new queen unless their king has abdicated. Do not engage them unless they attack the shallows and then do only what is necessary."

He spoke to Admiral about his role as support, called to Darel, Verge and Temen to join him and then the three of them and the wolf rounded the small spit of land to the shallows and crossed. Above him, Karín and Guerra were watching the skirmishers.

"If they come at a run, let the areo do the damage." Ch0n ordered as he walked. "Hold here on this side and only deal with the ones that make it past the Infantry. Let them hold the ground. That is what they do best. Keep the oruk away from the axes. Use the kinetic pistols. They make a lot of blood and will distract their king."

He walked confidently to where the king and his entourage were standing. People allowed him a clear passage.

"Svenn. I am ChOn of the planet Earth," he said in the Eñame tongue. "I have been on your world for three summers, during which time I have joined the three main tribes of the other side of the sea. Instead of fighting and killing each other for petty reasons, now they are united under one king and have a much better existence. I can muster an army of three or four thousand men and women that would come here and take over this city, killing everybody in it but I do not want to do that."

He spent a few minutes allowing Verge to explain the reasons they had killed or captured every member of their two sea patrols, including the account of Biorn, Mikel's disobedience and Erik's failed attack and how Eden and others now served ChOn in the Arw'an fleet. Svenn listened without interrupting and at the end of it all, he finally spoke.

"So you would have me abdicate and allow the Eani queen to take my place? And what of my family's rights? What happens to me and to them?"

"You would remain here as the ruler of the city but operating under the laws of the Arw'an. I do not seek war. I seek unity and peace. Had Mikel listened to Biorn, you would have been standing on the dock at the lake ruins as the king of the Eñame, talking about a lasting peace with your fleet intact and five hundred of your men spared. Instead, because you have invaded our lands twice and been defeated, we have been forced to come here and sue for peace through your surrender. That is your option. To do otherwise will oversee your own death and the deaths of hundreds more. Is that what you wish?"

Gavan Connell

"You speak calmly for one who is in the midst of many. I could have you killed where you stand in an instant and then where would we be?"

"Well I would be dead. But I have already given orders to the flying vessel that if I am killed, they are to destroy every living thing they can see, plus all the ships and then to return to Arw'an and decide if they will send the armies of the Arw'an, Buq'ue and Matáng to raze the city. Those who follow us through time will think that the Eñame never even existed except for the stories of the old priests who will continue doing their research into the ending of the Eani. Tell me again if that is what you wish. Is it what the commander of your fleet wishes for his men? Annihilation?"

"Gert wishes what I will order him to wish for he is but one of my subjects as are the remainder of the Eñame. I will not abdicate. I will take you prisoner and with a hostage such as yourself, I will have a bargaining lever. Guards!"

Many years later, when Teṁen was an old, old man living in Mori's stone cottage on Knights' row in Arw'an Castle, Ch0n's, Jez's, Darel, Harry and Ivor's, Marik's and Guerra's throng of great grandchildren would often gather around him to listen to his wonderful stories in the ancient tongue. Behind him on a well-worn perch, Mori's ancient parrot would sit chatting away in the voice of his long-gone master. Teṁen would tell them what happened next, even though the years between had not made his own memory of it any clearer.

"The evil king of the Eñame," he would say each time they demanded to hear the story, *"called for the guards to arrest the Lord Ch0n."*

"And where were you when it happened, Teṁen?" one of them would always ask when he paused.

"You all know I was right beside him. Closer than I am to you now, boy. Next to me was the high priest, Verge, who later went on to discover the secrets of the caverns and to write down the first of the Arw'an chronicles but that's another story. On the other side of the king stood his squire, Darel. Your own grandfather, young Darelik. Well, the guards made to move but suddenly the king's head fell off just like that. Fell off I tell you and rolled away to where people had to jump out of the way to avoid it."

"But how did it fall off, Teṁen? Heads don't just fall off," would come the next inevitable question and here Teṁen would shake his head for in truth, he had no idea what had happened. *"I think Verge magicked it off,"* was his stock answer.

Darel's matte black short sword left his pyjamis and swept upwards in a single heartbeat. It was already back in the folds of his garment when the king looked around for his guard and in doing so, lost his head. Darel had struck at the precise moment the guard moved and everybody's head had turned at the noise, including Teṁen's. Nobody saw anything for it had happened so quickly and nobody heard anything for there had been no sound. The head just fell off and rolled towards some of the king's household. Ch0n deliberately drew his katana and the crowd pulled back at the humming sound it made as it cleared the koiguchi. He looked at the commander.

"You're next," he said. "Call off the guard or you die first and then I will start on those around me. By the time they get to me there will be a hundred dead." He raised the dull green blade and the commander held up his hand.

"*Enough! Stand back. There will be no more killing.*" He looked at his aid. "*Run to the river and tell the skirmishers to lay down their arms. Quickly man before it is too late.*"

Karín watched and 'heard' the proceedings at the wharf and then turned her attention to the west. Three loose groups of skirmishers were heading towards the shallows at the trot.

"*There is not enough time to stop them. Guerra. Take me down to their left flank so I can slow them.*"

Guerra took the areo down and Karín let loose a long burst of orange light that lit the grass between the skirmishers and the Arw'an Infantry. She set the pulse to the lowest setting and a blue wave knocked down a group of the Eñame who had tried to get through the flames. She ran the orange light a second time next to the first to make the obstacle thicker and then Guerra pointed to a lone man who had run past the Knights and was heading for the skirmishers. They watched as he reached the first group and animatedly passed his message to them. They lay down their weapons and allowed the Arw'an to round them up and push them towards the dock.

"*We can land now, I think. ChOn, may we land?*"

Guerra waited for ChOn's reply and glided the areo to where Marik's men had secured a landing site. He eased it to the ground but kept it booted while Karín dismounted. Then he took off again and hovered nearby. Eden's boat berthed inside the cave but Admiral stayed put with the crossbows and tubes ready for action. The Knights approached the crowd, which parted in the face of the enormous oruk.

Karín allowed Gert to bow low to her. He was instantly smitten by her looks and bearing. She recognized the reaction and was pleased to know she had a loyal subject in him.

Eden went to where ChOn was standing.

"My Lord," he whispered, *"you should know that the king's son, Eluf is the captain of one of the boats and he will not be so easily swayed. He has always been a difficult man to deal with. Be wary of him. I will point him out to you when I see him."*

It took some time but finally the crowd was gathered at the main square of the city. ChOn and Karín were mounted on the dais with the widowed queen, Ylva. Gert and his wife and children stood beside them. Eden was beside ChOn. Verge started proceedings by reciting several verses of their holy books, concentrating on those which foretold of the coming of a tall, pale skinned woman with flame red hair and bright green eyes who would rule them as the reincarnation of the Eani queen. Gert had overseen the re-arming of the Eñame skirmishers, who had sworn they would not take advantage of the situation. They were loosely gathered at the back of the square with the Arw'an Infantry and the Knights in a block at the bottom of the dais. Guerra was hovering overhead.

In accordance with Eñame tradition, Ylva, the wife of the dead king was the first to swear fealty. Normally this would involve swearing to her son and the heir of the dead king but in this instance it was to Karín. Gert was second because Eluf chose to remain with his crew of skirmishers. Eden pointed him out to Ch0n, who did not like what he was watching. The young Eñame prince was talking animatedly with another of his crew.

"That's Leif, his bosun," explained Eden. *"Something is afoot."*

"Eluf of the Eñame! I call upon you to come forward and swear fealty to the queen of the Eñame or face her champion."

Eluf looked up at the shout of his name. He spoke a few more words to Leif and strode forward.

"I will meet the false queen's champion if he has the courage to face me!"

Ch0n stood and adjusted his armour. He looked at Ylva, who was standing with a look of horror on her face and walked calmly down the steps to face off against Eluf. Eluf had a battle ax in one hand and a shield in the other. On his head was a metal helm with a long nose guard. Ch0n drew the katana and even over the crowd noise, the humming of the blade could be heard by those closest. Eluf circled around to Ch0n's left, with an ease Ch0n recognized as the movement of a skilled fighter. Ch0n was forced to move so as not to expose his left side to a strike. He took a step back and drew the short sword. Eluf's movements to the left stopped as he saw the danger of exposing his own right side. ChOn started a kata which had the two blades moving in intricate circles and figure eights. Eluf's eyes left ChOn's for an instant to follow the short sword, which had almost touched his sword hand. It was the moment ChOn had been waiting for and he cut a backhand downwards arc that Eluf narrowly avoided, but which sliced through the top of his flat shield as though it were made of paper. It now protected nothing of his upper body and ChOn tossed the short sword to Darel so he could use the katana two-handed.

Eluf felt naked without the shield covering his shoulder and neck. He was shocked at the ease with which ChOn's sword had sliced through the wood, which could withstand the blow from a broadsword and stop an ax. He made a lunge at his adversary and swung the ax at ChOn's shoulder but was rewarded with a swish of air as ChOn easily evaded the stroke. His next attempt resulted in another piece of the shield being sliced away. He decided it was of no use in its depleted state and allowed it to slip from his forearm. In return, he saw ChOn squat side on to him with his sword pointed skywards. He moved closer and backed away but ChOn did not move. Only when Eluf circled to ChOn's left again did he force an adjustment to ChOn's stance. ChOn's left foot was following Eluf's progress and his right foot was merely turning as if on an axle.

ChOn knew the stroke would have to come from his left, either high or low. When Eluf dropped his wrist, ChOn waited for the upstroke and when Eluf raised the ax, ChOn prepared himself for the downward stroke. Eluf was a better match than any he had faced so far. The others had been clumsy or impatient but Eluf was neither. He was waiting for Ch0n to lose concentration before trying his killing stroke. Ch0n decided to make Eluf attack with a downwards stroke. That way, his wrist would be forward of the ax-head and facing upwards. Ch0n waited until Eluf was ready to strike and let his eyes dance away from the battle to a point over Eluf's shoulder.

Eluf was waiting. He knew that Ch0n's light sword was easier to wield than the ax and that he would perhaps get only one opportunity and he was prepared to wait. He was planning to attack Ch0n's left side with either an upwards or downwards strike. A flat strike was too cumbersome and too obvious because of the backswing. He feinted and feinted but Ch0n never moved, except to make sure he was always at the same strange angle, half side on with the sword up. Ch0n's stroke would have to be downwards or downwards and across. Downwards would attack his left side and across would attack his head, which was protected by the iron helm. Suddenly, Ch0n's eyes darted away and Eluf swung the ax downwards at Ch0n's shoulder and upper arm. He realized he had made a mistake half way through the strike when Ch0n's muscles twitched and Eluf couldn't get his arm out of the way before he lost it just above the hand. He screamed in rage and pain as Ch0n went out of the crouch and stood in front of him, the sword still raised.

"Fealty or death Eluf?"

Harry, Darel and Karín all saw the movement in their peripheral vision and then watched as Leif's ax arched twenty feet across the square and the six-inch spike above the double blades caught Ch0n squarely in the back. He was felled instantly but by the time his body touched the ground, the Arw'an were on the move. Two Knights set their oruk at the edges of the crowd and started scything through Eluf's crew with their kinetic pistols. Sixty Infantry raced to Ch0n and formed a square around him. Karín picked up the green katana and stripped the gown from herself so she was not impeded in her movements. She stood over Ch0n in her petticoat before hacking the head from a grinning Eluf. She told Darel to find Leif and bring him back to her alive if possible but to bring him back. The Infantry widened their square and Guerra landed the areo in their midst. Willing hands put Ch0n's body in the vessel and he took off with Karín still not strapped in to her seat. Below them the square was in turmoil. The Knights had cut a swathe through the Eñame skirmishers and the Infantry, now their king's body was safely out of the battle, formed a phalanx and joined the fray. On the dais, Gert was screaming for his captains to get control of their men. Ylva was screaming at her dead son for a fool and Verge was weeping with sadness and rage at the treachery of his people. Karín watched the blood pooling on the floor of the areo. In all the confusion, she had not removed the ax. She saw a place near the square where no Arw'an troops could be seen fighting the skirmishers, who were bunched into a tight knot, and told Guerra to point the areo at them. He looked back at Ch0n and took the areo into a tight turn facing the melee. Karín let fly a barrage of orange and red bolts that both burned the skirmishers and exploded in their midst. Time and again the red bolts flew until Karín realized that people had stopped fighting and were looking up at her in sheer terror.

"Take me up to the table."

Gert took advantage in the lull to shout for calm. Harry and Igor saw that he was trying to establish order and Igor called Marik to form a square and wait. He and Harry rode their oruk back to the dais over dozens of dead Eñame and climbed the steps, still mounted.

"Verge!" It was Harry. *"Tell this traitor that if Ch0n is dead, we will burn every house and kill every living creature, including the rats and fleas. He will be last. His wife will be second last after her children die. I will personally kill his wife after I have given her to Marik's men to play with. Say it man!"*

"Marik," he shouted into the mike, *"Send someone up here to guard Gert's wife and children. Let no harm come to them under pain of death. But do not let them escape either."*

"Verge, tell Gert to have the surviving captains or the senior member of each crew standing in front of this dais now."

Gert was pale.

"This was not planned," he said to Verge, who translated for Harry, who was now dismounted. *"I swear by the Eani queen that this was not supposed to happen. It was that fool Eluf and his equally foolish bosun. Because of them, hundreds are dead. Hundreds on top of the hundreds we had already lost. This time women and children as well as our men. This has set back the Eñame a hundred years."*

"What do I care about that? Just get those captains here."

Igor was trying to make sense of Karín's garbled transmissions. She was calm one moment and almost hysterical the next. Guerra had watched as she took the heavy ax from Ch0n's armour and the blood flowed freely from the gape in the sprayform. Karín raced to the closet to get her dress to make a bandage and was surprised to find another white garment next to it. She managed to get the armour off Ch0n with Guerra's help and together they tried to staunch the flow of blood. Guerra went to the first aid kit and produced a needle and thread.

"I have to sew up the wound as fast as possible, Karín. If the edges are together, his reptile genes will heal it quickly. The inside will be more difficult but at least the sprayform took the brunt of it."

"Will he live?"

"If he doesn't bleed to death overnight, he might live. There is nothing we can do but patch him up and bandage him to put pressure on the wound and fly him home where Kelda can see to him."

"Ivor, has Darel found Leif?"

"Not yet, Karín. He may already be dead but Darel won't stop until he knows one way or the other. Harry has taken charge down here. Take Ch0n back to the castle. We will manage here. We have control of the square and the administration buildings. They won't get us out and we won't leave on their terms. Gert is not up for the fight. He swears it was just Eluf and not a coup. Eden and Admiral will take the

boats offshore. Before you go, if you can sink the other boats it will make our withdrawal easier when the time comes."

Guerra and Karín sewed and bandaged their king. He was breathing easily, which Guerra said was a good thing as it meant any broken ribs hadn't punctured a lung. She had no idea what he was talking about but was comforted by the news anyway. They took off and turned to the West. When the three ships came into view at their moorings by the shore, Karín sent three red bolts into them so they wouldn't be able to float without major repairs. Then she told Guerra to see how fast the areo would fly.

One by one the six captains or their replacements reached the square and reported to their commander. Of Eluf's crew, only eleven still lived. Harry and Ivor had hit that crew hardest after seeing Leif's ax launched from within its ranks but Leif himself was nowhere to be seen. Link had survived with most of his crew, which he had ordered not to get involved in the fight but to run from the square and defend their women. He was ashamed at what had taken place. So were the others, none of whom had much time for their dead comrade, Eluf. The fight had been so spontaneous that most of them had been fighting solely for dear life against the Arw'an Knights and Infantry who had reason to attack. Harry learned from them that about two hundred skirmishers had been killed, mostly by the kinetic pistols and Caron's bolts from the sky, as well as thirty seven women and three children trampled with the count still not completed. Of the Arw'an, three of Marik's men had been killed and sixteen wounded.

Harry turned to Verge.

"Tell them I want Leif and I want him now. Tell them to send out their crews and their families and to bring me Leif. I want him alive but if he is dead I want to see his dead body lying right there. If they don't find him by dark I will kill her." He pointed at Ylva, who stood proudly, not realizing what had been said until Verge translated. She waited until Verge had finished and said to them,

"If you do not find him by nightfall I will kill myself. Find him for the honour of our people and my family."

Verge translated her words and Harry managed a smile and a nod of approval.

"Tough old biddy," he said to Verge, who cackled and translated it for Ylva despite Harry's protests.

The areo could fly quite quickly as it turned out. When Guerra had been at full throttle for almost a minute, a small section of the nose extended and immediately the noise of the air rushing past went silent and Guerra's tablet showed an increase in ground speed. They reached the castle four hours later. Jez, Kelda and Maní met them at the landing zone and they carried Ch0n to his quarters and put him to bed. Kelda herself sat with him and bathed the wound and forced a potion down his neck to stop the tremens.

It was late afternoon when Harry's voice sounded in the comms room speakers.

"Guerra this is Harry, are you there?"

"Yes I am here. What news of Eñame, Harry? Karín is listening."

"Things have settled down now. Eden has pulled out into the shallows and rafted with Admiral, and Mathilde has arrived. They are still in crossbow range of the shore and the tubes are deployed but not armed. Leif has not been found despite every man woman and child looking for him. Darel has not been seen since the fighting. How is Ch0n?"

"Kelda says that if he lives until morning, he will live. Karín will wait until he seems a little better and then she will return to claim the throne. We are going to take Maní back with us as well as Marelik's mother, Izaki and someone called Eloi whom we will collect from Buq'ue on the way."

"I am sure she has her reasons for those people. Izaki is probably to tell the Eñame what it is like to be a trusted person in Ch0n's kingdom even after having been his enemy. Wait. There is a commotion happening outside."

Harry went outside to find Darel with Leif in tow, a noose around his neck and his hands bound behind his back. He called Darel over, took off his helm and gave it to him.

"Karín, this is Darel. I have Leif. What shall I do with him?"

"Search him thoroughly. Have someone check inside his body cavities for anything he might use to escape or to harm himself. Take his clothes and give him one cup of water and no food. Lock him in a room with his hands bound and a guard *present in the room with him. He is not to be harmed or to harm himself in any way, even if he has to be restrained. Give him my regards and tell him I will see him on the morrow around mid-day. He had better hope that the king lives for I would hate to be him otherwise. Well done, Darel. You can tell me about it tomorrow. Now see to the wolf. He will be worried and frightened without his master as will we all be."*

Ylva presented herself to Harry as the sun was going down. Verge was at hand and translated for them.

"I am here, Sir Harry. Have they found Leif?"

"They have, my Lady. Fear not, your life is safe."

"Fear not? Do you think I fear death now? I have lost my son and my husband in one day, both to the sword, although my husband's death remains a mystery to me as to how it actually came about. I fear not death. I fear for the future of my people. The Eani reincarnate was terrible in her wrath at the treachery to her king. I fear she will be a cruel queen. We have always been a peaceful people. Well since the Eani came. Before that we had cast out all those who were too dark of skin or too short of stature. The Western tribes were all Eñame back then. Verge. Is it not so?"

"It is, Ylva."

"The Eani picked us out to breed with and to improve us, and look where we have come," she continued. *"After four hundred summers we have lost as many in a few full moons as we*

gained in all that time. And the last ones because of my silly boy. Well it is done now. I would see Leif before I go."

"No, Ylva. None may see him or go near him until Karín gets here. Not even the former queen but when Karín arrives, she may allow you to have a word with him. And you may rest assured that she will not be a cruel queen. She will be hard but fair as was the ChOn for she was his mate and they were as one mind."

"Yes. If she wishes to oversee the punishment, that is fair. She wants to mete out justice as befits a queen in these circumstances. I would have done the same."

Guerra retired with Carmodi on the pretext of needing sleep before flying the next morning. Maní and Karín were both sitting with ChOn when the stillness was punctuated with Carmodi's muffled cries of ecstasy through the slit window.

"She is due shortly but it hasn't slowed her down in bed," observed Maní.

"He must have become an expert in the game of slippery finger," agreed Karín.

They left ChOn in the good hands of Kelda, who shooed them away as being of no help whatsoever.

Izaki and Eloi were waiting for them when the areo touched down in Buq'ue.

"Do you have it?" asked Karín of Eloi."

"I do."

"Have what?" asked Guerra and Izaki in unison.

"Women's business," replied Karín and that was the end of the discussion.

Karín left her seat and went to her locker. She took a white cashmere tunic from her tote and hung it on the hanger. In the next locker, she hung a pair of black pyjamis. She took the camera Guerra had provided from the mint and putting it on image intensifying mode, positioned it in the bottom corner of the second locker. She tuned the tablet to receive the camera signal and returned to her seat. What she saw on the screen astounded her. She showed it to Guerra who explained that the locker must have been some sort of 3D printer-scanner crossed with a knitting machine. They watched fascinated as the threads snaked from out of the hundreds of holes until they formed a duplicate of the garment hanging in the locker. Karín waited until there was no more movement on the screen before returning to the lockers to retrieve the contents, one pair of new black pyjamis and one new white tunic, both made from the same thin threads Karín's dress had been made from the previous day.

"Another secret revealed," she said, *"but there are many more inside the cavern that we know nothing about. When this is over, I will move the priests from Eñame to the Lakeside where they can study everything. Eloi, Marel, would you like new tunics?"*

They had been able to shorten the distance to Eñame having left from Buq'ue instead of Arw'an and three hours later, Karín went back to change out of her tunic and into her queen-dress.

"This is the last time they will see me in it except for state occasions," she said as she re-emerged. *"I failed Ch0n because I was too busy being the pretty queen for them all. Otherwise I would have fought Eluf myself. My death had he killed me would have had no consequences for the Arw'an. Maní would become Ch0n's aget and life would have gone on as before but if we lose Ch0n....."* Her voice trailed away and she wiped a tear from her cheek. *"There is the cliff. We will soon be there."*

Chapter Seventeen: Long live the king:

Ch0n saw the light in the distance. It became progressively closer and brighter as he watched it. Then he realized it was not the light getting closer to him, but that he was floating towards it. He was flying. He looked down and there was nothing but blackness. He could hear the voices of someone calling him. Then he saw the six. There was one tall redheaded male accompanied by five tall red-headed females. They were beckoning him in the ancient tongue. Behind them was a host of those he had known, among them, Buyo, her red eyes pleading to him. The first among the females held out her hand to him and he reached for it...

Karín felt the bracelet vibrate. She heard the Eani calling Ch0n with their sweet voices.

"No Ch0n!" she shouted. *"Don't you dare leave me without taking me back to the overhang! You promised me! You promised Dorak you would teach him everything. You promised Buyo! Ch0n! Ch0n!"*

Gavan Connell

Chapter Eighteen: Death of a Bastard

The bracelet stopped vibrating and Karín started to keen softly to herself. Her time with ChOn flashed before her eyes in a whir of motions and emotions. Beside her, Maní joined in the eerie death song of the recently widowed.

The areo landed and Karín was the first to exit in her pure white gown and the diamond necklace ChOn had given her the day he betrothed her. She carried the thin rod like a sceptre. Darel was waiting for her and when he saw the look of grief and determination on her face he didn't dare ask about ChOn. Nobody did. Guerra shook his head at them all, motioning them to silence. They went to the Administration buildings where Ylva, Gert and his family and the five senior crewmen, including Link were gathered. Norwhal and the other priests were huddled in the back of the hall with Temen.

"I am waiting for confirmation that the king is dead," began Karín, *"killed by treachery right here in this city. Harry has told me of his plan to kill every living thing in the city down to the rats and fleas and as I have not been crowned queen of the Eñame, I have no official place in this meeting other than as ChOn's first aget. Therefore, I can not countermand that order. He has told me that you, Gert will be the last to die and that your family will be the last family to die. So be it. But the first*

will be the traitor, Leif, who's ax struck down from behind a man who never in his life killed anybody without first giving them the chance to surrender or die like a true soldier. A hard man was Ch0n but fair to all. He deserved better than this. Leif will be tried before me and the Arw'an council members present with Gert and Ylva as Eñame witnesses to the proceedings. Where is Leif?"

"He is locked in a room behind this hall, Karín," answered Darel.

"Karin, I would speak with him if I may before the trial," interjected Ylva. *"I need only a few moments to say what I wish to say."*

"Maní, take her first and search her. Strip her and search her naked body. She can visit him dressed in a blanket and no more. Darel and Verge, you will accompany her. Verge, you will translate every word to Darel. Darel, if she says one word of comfort or tries to save him or kill him, kill her first. Leif is to face trial and punishment by the Arw'an and not be freed by his former queen. Do you understand me? Maní? Verge? Darel? Ylva?" They all nodded.

Leif sat on the floor, naked, his hands bound behind him. He had not been able to even try and escape. He had been so sure he was safe, hidden away in his barn under the floor with the goats above him. How the black-clad Arw'an and the wolf had tracked him to the trapdoor was a mystery but now it mattered little. An Arw'an soldier sat on a stool impassively watching him. Leif had spoken to him once but the ignorant soldier didn't even speak Eñame so it was a wasted effort.

Suddenly he heard the wooden board being lifted from its place and he knew the door would open. He propped himself up against the wall and waited the few seconds until Ylva entered with the priest, Verge and the one who had found him. At the sight of his former queen, he tried to hide his nakedness but she scoffed at him.

"I bathed you when you were born to my maidservant, Svenn's lover. You have nothing to hide from me but now I will tell you that you were a half brother to Eluf. The blood of kings and gods flows in your veins but it runs cold. You have murdered a king. I saw you throw the ax and I will bear witness to it when I am asked. Your actions have brought dishonour and death to the Eñame for we are to be eradicated from this place like so much vermin. No punishment will suffice." She took a step forward and spat in his face. *"That is all I wanted to say, Verge. You can take me out now."*

They dragged Leif to the square and knelt him before the empty throne. The five crewmen had passed the word and the square was full. The proceedings were brief. Ylva announced that she had seen Leif throw the ax that had felled Ch0n from behind. There was no more to be said. Karín stood to pronounce sentence. She spoke to them in their own tongue. Verge translated for the Arw'an council members.

"People of the Eñame! Six full moons ago, we of the Arw'an knew not of your existence. Then we were made aware of it when the traitor Mikel tried to capture the Eani settlement. That resulted in Erik storming the fort and your people losing three hundred men and three ships. Then we were invaded by Karl and Rej with four boats but that resulted in the loss of more

Gavan Connell

than three hundred men and all the boats. All we wanted to do was to live peacefully in our lands but you wanted to take what you had not visited for a hundred years. We came here wanting to sue for peace but we have been ambushed by this man and the Eñame prince Eluf. Our entire contact with the Eñame has been warlike because of your treachery. So now we find ourselves in control of a city we never wanted to control other than in name. We have at our whim, thousands of people whom we never wished to dominate. The spoils of war go to the victors and the vanquished must take their chances. But first to the sentencing of Leif. He has been found guilty of cowardly treachery. The punishment is death. I sentence him to be flayed."

Even Ylva was shocked but she said nothing. Leif started to sob. The crowd noise grew from a hum to a roar. Nobody had been flayed in Eñame for centuries. The Knights drew their pistols and with a wave of his hand, Marik had the Infantry adopt the phalanx. Karín raised the rod and pointed it at the crowd where the noise was loudest. The crowd settled, knowing that to riot would cause a repeat of the previous day's proceedings and today the Eñame skirmishers were unarmed by order of the one known as 'Sir Harry'.

Maní, Marel and Eloi stepped forward. Maní opened Buyo's matte black clasp knife. Marel revealed a piece of flint, razor sharp on one edge, shaped to fit the hand and with a hammer on the back. Eloi had a rasping tool used to scrape the fat from a goat hide. Marik's guard drove four pegs into the earth in front of Leif and spread-eagled him between them, bound face up. Maní's first cuts made a small square on Leif's scalp and the scream that issued from his lips when she pulled his hair and skin from the living bone rent the air. Karín carefully removed her precious stone necklace and pulled the white gown over her head. She stood proudly in her petticoat, otherwise naked for all to see. She took out of her tote a necklace made from carved dragon's teeth, a tiny green vessel and a small knife made of what looked to Ylva like a piece of water but was in fact a shaped, polished and sharpened white diamond, ground down relentlessly by Karín over several months to be used as a shaving and cutting tool that Ch0n had told her would hold its edge forever. She threaded the necklace over her head and it settled between her naked breasts. Opening Ch0n's green container of camouflage paint, she drew two green parallel lines from her left temple to her right earlobe. She looked down at the grisly scene being played out before her and nodded towards the white gown.

"Look after that until tomorrow, Ylva," she ordered impassively. *"I don't want to get blood on it."*

So ends the second book of the Arw'an chronicles

Gavan Connell

'Dorak of the Six Rings', the transcription of the eighth and final instalment of the Arw'an Chronicles follows soon.

"Pasha Kaur negotiated the various security screening points, logged in and sipped her tea while the portal decided what files she could look at and took her to where she had been the day previous. She was reading, watching and listening to Ch0n's chronicles. She was in thrall.

All that day and the next and the next she studied everything Ch0n had sent back via that second ship.

She closed the file, opened the next one, 1337-44-191-4 and started at folio one.

Ch0n's ship had come home and the crew had been debriefed. It was an enormous file but most of the information had been either blocked from her or had been deemed unimportant enough for her to see so there were hundreds of missing images and folios about the voyage, the various live planets, the deaths of clones, breakdowns, electrical issues, rations boring, boring. She had already read the electronic reports of the live planets in the earlier file. She told the computer to search for a few key words and then pressed 'NEXT'. She arrived at the debriefing interview of the commander who had been forced to leave Ch0n marooned and how he had sent as many stores as he was able to the surface before closing down the vessel for the journey back to earth. The final entry was a plea to return as soon as possible or to dispatch a rescue to the planet as soon as practical and informing the reader that the clone would have a radio permanently monitoring Frequency 1. There were marginal notes and a coded recommendation which Pasha didn't recognize."

Gavan Connell